BELVIDERE.

II

X

Sans Nom

To this special group, the spelling and grammar police, please put your pencil down; I will save you the suspense.

This novel may be a grammar and sentence structure nightmare to people who obsess about such things. The pages that follow are vaguely, or not so, reminiscent of Beat literature, which can be described, by some, as a rejection of standard narrative and linguistic values, including, but not necessarily limited to, syntax, punctuation, sentence structure and morphology. The writing style is idiosyncratic; it is how the author thinks, and how the author believes this fictional account should be told. And just as important, it's how real people speak and communicate in the real world, which is rarely textbook or correct. It is real, or at least how this author perceives reality, which is all that matters between these end-papers.

In any event, there **will** be mistakes. And all the mistakes in this book were purposeful, and will be defended as such, even if they weren't. After two long years of editing, this writer simply got tired of re-reading and proofing. So what you see is what you get, whether it's right or not.

My suggestion is to take the broader view: simply enjoy the characters and enjoy the ride they take you on. Along the way, if you feel the need to get enraged, do so at the abject violence, the graphic sex, the racism, the bigotry, the coarse language, the heathenism....but for God's sake, don't get enraged at punctuation....leave the poor periods alone.

WARNING:

This novel installment contains adult-directed narrative and dialogue not suitable for children, including, but not necessarily limited to:

racism, bigotry, heathenism, vulgarity, graphic violence and raw erotica.

Proceed at your own peril....

CHAPTER 29 – THAT LITTLE MUFFIN WAS SPORTING A SHIT-BURGER GRIN

April 22nd; Saturday morning, day number three.

Cord heard a light rap on the door; it was 9 am on the button – right on time.

"Come on in."

He yelled down the hall, in the rasp of a just-woke voice.

The door slowly swung open.

"Ready?"

"Not yet….almost; I'm just doing a little stretching."

Earl couldn't see Cord, but the voice came from the front room. Earl walked down the long hall, it was a carbon copy of the hall in his apartment, except Cord had a cool arched nook halfway down the hall. It was empty, but could hold a small desk, or a chair and lamp. It was framed by two cedar-lined closets; the second one, closer to the road, and further from the front door, held the aluminum foil packs, and the *box*.

Earl turned the corner into the big front room facing the road to see Ay, stocky and thick, grimacing as he tried to stretch muscles that were not cooperating.

Cord couldn't get the picture out of his mind, that huge stone-carved stick figure, the *fat* stick figure of a man, in pain, trying for eternity to stretch and touch its toes. Public art set along Coal Harbour, amongst the endless comings and goings of float planes in the shadow of Stanley Park. If public art was meant to inspire, it worked; Cord felt the fat man's pain.

"Whose idea was this?"

Cord said aloud, primarily to himself.

C looked up and was taken aback. Earl sported wild-looking, striped bicycle shorts, black and bright yellow spandex, like the obnoxious abdomen of a bumble bee.

That was one, big bumble bee, standing in his living room.

If anyone else donned those shorts, he would get laughed off the street; somehow he didn't think that happened much to Earl – people who knew him, punks aside, would never snicker at Earl; people who didn't know him would be so afraid of the massive man, they would never dare utter a word.

But the attire was not what caught Cord's attention; it was the size of Earl's thighs – his legs were sculpted like the trunk of an ironwood and just as large, larger even. Cord had muscular thighs, bigger than most men, partly genetics, partly from heavy squatting for twenty-plus years – but he looked downright puny next to Earl. Even at two-hundred fifteen pounds, thick and muscular, C felt scrawny.

Earl had on a ribbed white tank top, tucked into his black and yellow shorts. If Earl carried ten percent body fat, it would be a lot; his chest and arms were utterly enormous – if he wasn't Earl, he would be very scary indeed.

"Here, I used to watch the cats for Mr. Boeman, he lived here, and I still have your key."

Earl extended his hand, with a door key attached.

Cord looked at it, and kept stretching.

"Keep it, I never lock my door. There's nothing in here worth stealing anyway."

"Did your sister ask where you were going?"

"Nah, she's still asleep; she doesn't even know I'm gone. She's a sleepy-head in the morning."

"Did you leave her a note?"

"Yep, or she would get nervous wondering where I was and if I was okay."

"Did you tell her you were going with me? Is that going to get her mad?"

"She won't be mad; she invited you to dinner."

"I thought you and me were doing the ethnic thing up here tonight?"

"No, tomorrow night, she's making my *favorite*, homemade ravioli, they're the best! Even better than best, whatever that is! My mom used to make them, now Lilly does. I usually only get them on my birthday, and she complains for a week before, saying how hard they are to make, and how good she is too me to make them. But Lilly is making them for me, for us, tomorrow. I can't wait!"

"She's making them special for you, and not on your birthday, and she invited me? Why? Somethings up; what's the catch?"

"I don't know; she just wanted to invite you."

"I doubt it Earl; she's got something up her sleeve."

Earl didn't respond.

"Did you invite her to dinner up here tonight?"

"No, was I supposed to?"

Earl said as he started to stretch too, to mimic Cord. Earl easily touched *his* toes.

"You can if you want; I'm not inviting her, she'll just say something rude before she says no."

"She really likes you."

C chuckled.

"Hardly, Earl, but thanks for saying so."

"I know it, she does, I can tell."

Cord looked at him and smiled. It would be nice if Earl was right, Cord thought, but he wasn't putting any stock in that pipe dream. If she liked him, and treated him the way she did, heaven help the poor sap she *doesn't* like.

"Okay, enough of this nonsense; let's go, so I can embarrass myself."

Cord couldn't know how prophetic that statement was.

And with that, Cord cracked the knuckles on each hand, all at once, and out the door they went.

Another sunny day greeted the two, a beautiful Saturday morning, April 22nd; the air was a bit crisp, but it had the feel of a warm day approaching.

The plan was to run up to the Park, then do at least four laps; that was the plan. C figured it would be tough, since he hadn't run in awhile, but doable. Well, he was hearing himself breath heavy just beyond the Pequest River bridge, a half-block from the apartment, and that was before the slight incline, which felt like a mountain, up Mill Street. Earl was jabbering away, smiling like he was thoroughly enjoying the whole process.

Cord was already in trouble.

Thank goodness Earl was talking in a manner which didn't require Cord to answer, because he couldn't – too busy gasping air. A series of grunts and head nods Earl's way would have to do. His face was beet red and his breathing labored. Less than a half-mile; this was really pathetic, he thought to himself.

They finally made it up to the Park; thank God, level ground. They hopped onto the sidewalk and began the first slow lap, jogging counter-clockwise, side-by-side.

Cars were starting to line the Park on three sides, churchgoers all, the Methodists, Episcopalians and Protestants. Earl said they did it every year in April; some sort of a joint Saturday morning bake-off and all-day cook-in by the three Park-side congregations. It was a *dinner-in-a-basket* charity event; each church would sell the meals to their own parishioners, or anyone else for that matter, to take home and eat, raising money to send to the poor, in some far off, unnamed place that no one ever visited and half had never heard of. The faithful would cook all day, and sell the meals that night; it was a big deal in Town, talked of incessantly for weeks, with the old ladies sharing recipes, supplies and gossip. Mainly gossip. Each church group tried to outshine the others, and raise the most cash, but in a most polite way, because God apparently keeps track of this sort of thing.

Therefore, even at this early hour, the sidewalks were full of the diehard regulars, the parishioners who attended every church event, without fail. They were roughly divided into two camps; the elderly, trying to cinch that ticket to heaven as they neared the end of the race, and couples with young children, introducing the next generation of donors to the Almighty, as good parents are supposed to do. A couple heathen dog-walkers weaved through the sidewalk crowd; no room in heaven for them, that's for sure.

C was pleasantly surprised; most of the parishioners were dressed in what would be considered pleasant Sunday garb, like people once dressed when attending church, even though this wasn't church, per se. No sweatpants, saggy jeans or slogan tee-shirts, like *I'm With Stupid.*

The little-girl outfits were the best, lots of frilly dresses, some with bonnets, dressed by proud parents just to sling spaghetti and meatballs for the unfortunate. Cord's thoughts on religion aside, it seemed a sweet throwback. But here, it wasn't throwback, it was just a sunny, Saturday morning in Belvidere. That made him smile, even though his legs ached.

He wondered where the Catholics were, or the Jews. Were there even Jews in this place? Belvidere had a definite look and feel, and that feel certainly wasn't Jewish.

They were the only two runners in view; he used that term loosely to describe himself. He was gulping air, like a fish out of water. Earl looked as if he was standing still, that was the level of effort he was expending. Finally, he asked Cord a question which required more than a nod of the head.

"Earl....I can't....talk....when....I'm running....need to breathe."

That was all he could get out as they rounded the corner in front of Carol's house, a mere half-lap in. Oh great, that was all he needed, please let her be out of Town. He was afraid to look, but he did.

Yes!

No one on the porch; he already passed where the driveway was, so he couldn't tell if her car was there. Only three more passes; hopefully she's gone or still sleeping. Her, he *definitely* didn't need to deal with this morning; he had to focus on finishing the laps. Only three and a half to go; he already had a stitch in his left side.

Right about now, yesterday's cigar seemed like a very bad idea. He thought about the fat white trash he made fun of waddling around the Park yesterday; oh, the irony.

Earl was prattling away about some of the songs he watched on the internet last night; he loved 1980's music videos – most of the ones he mentioned Cord liked as well, but Earl talked about a lot Ay didn't know or remember. How did he miss all these videos Earl talked about? Cord used to sit for hours and watch music television, *MTV*, back then; they were white-bread videos, mostly; did white bands even make videos anymore?

He wanted to ask Earl about *Los Lobos*; whether he remembered *Will The Wolf Survive* or not - he was sure he did – Earl seemed to remember everything. He had to get the question out quickly, between breaths.

Of course Earl knew the song; he liked it too. Earl then went on past C's earworm and finished the verses of *Will The Wolf Survive* for Cord that he couldn't remember; he knew every damn word to the entire song. Ay smiled; he replayed the video in his head while Earl sang the words, and the big man didn't sing *a cappella* half-bad; in fact, he was pretty damn good.

Who knew in less than forty-eight hours in Belvidere, Cord would be shoulder-to-shoulder with a three-hundred sixty-five pound high-yaller, who was singing to him *a cappella* his favorite *Los Lobos* tune, while C mingled amongst God-fearing church folk milling around the Town Square, all while jogging. He thought some interesting things might happen here, but no one could dream that one up.

Neither of them noticed the police cruiser crawling along the Hardwick Street curb, till it became apparent it was keeping pace with them, which was a *very* slow crawl. Cord looked right to see Martin, with the window down, trucker-elbow out, his mirrored shades reflecting Earl and Cord. He sported a big cheeser grin.

Marty pointed at Ay, his hand configured like a gun and gave a clicking sound as he tipped his hand.

"Hey Cord, how's it going buddy? How's Lilly? You know, Saturday's just a week away!"

Cord wondered just how many times Marty had jerked off since yesterday, thinking about how to best use those handcuffs on Lilly.

Cord and Earl stopped to talk to Martin; there was no talking and running at the same time, it just wasn't happening.

"She's getting all excited about the Officer's Ball, Marty; she was showing off that little black dress last night - I saw it go on, and then I saw it come off. It was a beautiful thing."

"Really?"

Martin was so shaken by the thought of that little black dress, the *coming off* part, that he either didn't hear nor care about Cord calling him the dreaded *Marty*. Ay was apparently added to the list of approved users.

Cord elbowed Earl in the gut preemptive, since the big man was about to correct the record.

Cord couldn't see Marty's eyes behind the shades, but he knew they were all whites, savoring the vision of that little piece of black fabric falling to the floor around her ankles. He pictured a calendar hanging beside Martin's bed, with each day marked with a big red *X,* like a little kid counting down to his very own Christmas day, next Saturday night.

"Yep; but be sure you act like a gentleman; *don't disappoint* Earl and me, and *especially* Lilly. She said she was happy to *finally* go on a date with a man who would be chivalrous. This could be your only shot, if you blow it...."

Ay shook his head in the negative as he let the sentence sit undone.

"Don't worry, don't worry, she isn't used to going out with a guy with a real job; you know, a guy with class."

Cord just looked at Martin, waiting for him to pull the foot out of his mouth; he'd give him, say, a full five seconds?

Okay, how about ten seconds?

It still didn't register with Marty. C had a real swift one here. Bingo, it took a full fifteen-count.

"Oh, Cord, sorry, I didn't mean you, I meant all the *other* guys, you know, before you came along."

"Uh huh, yeah."

C said, sarcastic.

Martin figured he better get back to work, before Cord changed his mind about the date.

Did this mean he couldn't bring the handcuffs? Martin was conflicted; this was gonna take some serious thinking; there **must** be a dignified, chivalrous way to use the handcuffs on her.

"See you guys later; hey, looking good Earl."

"How about *looking good* Cord?"

Ay yelled to the taillights as Marty pulled away.

Dickhead Ay whispered under his breath.

They sped up to a slow jog.

"Why'd you say all those things about Lilly that weren't true?"

"I was just teasing Marty is all."

By this time, they had finished a full lap and a quarter, and were directly across from Carol's house, but on the far side of the Park.

Then he saw what he dreaded. One of the big black doors creaked open; he couldn't see her, but he was sure she was sporting a wide smile.

Oh, how right he was; it was none other than Little Miss Muffin, and that little muffin was sporting a shit-burger grin.

CHAPTER 30 – HAVING A BALL WITH TWO FAT-BOTTOMED GIRLS

He knew she saw them; how many people look like Earl, especially running in bumble-bee shorts alongside a short, bald guy with a too-big belly. She must have been in the house, looked out the window and reveled in her good fortune.

She leaned against the railing on the front porch and waited impatient for the procession to pass.

He hated to admit it, but she was a stunner; she might be a peg below Lilly, but only half-a-peg. In the sarcasm department, however, they were a dead heat.

Earl hadn't seen her yet; he was jawing excitedly about *The Secret of Skeleton Island*, and how the two teenage best friends-cum-junior sleuths, Ken Holt and Sandy Allen, were stuck in the underbelly of a ferry, hiding from car smugglers, plying down the Hudson River, by the Westside piers, circa-1949 in New York City. Earl kept rereading the same scenes because he loved them so much, getting ever-more-excited. He would pretend to be Sandy – the big tall redhead; and from now on, when he read it, he pictured Ken was Cord. The two were on the adventure together, trying to solve the mystery and catch the bad guys. He asked Cord if the Hudson River was really black and oily, like it said in the book.

Earl wanted to go see Skeleton Island, for real, but Lilly said no, he couldn't, because Skeleton Island didn't really exist, it was just a stupid made-up place in a stupid kid's book. But Earl didn't believe her, he figured she was just afraid of the big City, the oily water and the smugglers. But he wasn't afraid; he wanted to take off his shoes and socks and stick his feet in the stinky River; he didn't care a lick about all that oil, although he did feel bad for the fish.

Talk of discovering Skeleton Island was quickly shelved, however, when Earl's ears perked, like a dog honing a familiar sound. Earl was hypnotized, hearing a beautiful siren singing sweet nothings.

To Cord, however, that beautiful voice sounded something a little more like this:

"Does your belly always jiggle like that when you run?"

Here we go.

"I would imagine that would be annoying, running like that. Do you actually call that running, or is that trotting? I must say, Lilly's standards are slipping, badly."

Even if he could think of a quick, witty retort, he wouldn't be able to spit it out with any conviction. For Cord, running equaled scarce oxygen, so no talking. Yet he did glance Carol's way and threw an annoyed stare, which was the reaction she expected, and wanted.

Earl was in his glory; C figured if Earl didn't see Carol for another whole month, that smile would still be tattooed on his mug.

"Hi Earl, now *you* look fantastic. Hey, I bet you can run faster than that."

"I can!"

And with that, Earl lurched ahead and started to run at what Cord would call an Olympic sprint; anything faster than an old-man trot looked that way to C.

"Well, aren't you going to keep up with your friend? We wouldn't want to disappoint Lillian with your lack of wind, now would we? I'm sure male stamina is an important and integral part of that deep relationship."

He only heard the tail end of the last remark; Earl was already half way down the block, past the Methodist Church, where parishioners were still milling the sidewalk, pre-cook-off. Unknowingly, Cord had picked up his pace trying to keep up with Earl, or at least keep the distance respectable. He was breathing heavy, his mind was wandering, trying to remember the early warning signs of a heart attack.

Should he worry about that throbbing pain in his upper arm?

A couple of people recognized Cord, and said hi; he just raised his hand in acknowledgment. *Everyone* said hi to Earl, who summarily ignored them all, that big smile still plastered on his face. Cord figured that wouldn't wash off for a week.

The good thing about Carol and her snide remarks were it made him mad enough to run through his stitch and labored breathing. He got a good three-quarters of the way around the Park simply steaming about her. Earl realized after about a hundred yards that Cord was a speck in the distance; he felt bad and ran in place, waiting for his friend to catch up.

"I'm sorry."

Earl said sheepish.

"Don't be, no problem. I'll get better at it if we keep….practicing."

C almost got the whole sentence out in one breath.

They past a throng of Presbyterians milling about the front steps of the church, by far the best dressed lot on the Park, and made their way to the Episcopalian Church, on the south side. It looked cozy compared to the imposing edifice of the Presbyterian Church, with its mix of masonry and clapboard, and soaring spire. Once again, a smattering recognized Cord from Sam's; everyone knew Earl. Most looked on with puzzled expressions, never having seen Earl actually socialize with anyone, outside of Lillian and, occasionally, Martin.

Round three coming up; he girded himself for the next verbal assault from *L'antre du Lion*. He would have to get in shape just so he could casually jab something clever at her while running and not pass out from lack of air.

Unbeknownst to Cord and Earl, Carol had run into the house and quickly rummaged during their last loop; beside her was a portable CD player, already plugged into an outlet on the porch. She stood there with a wry smile, waiting like a spider.

She knew she had to get them to stop, to hatch her goofy little plan.

There's in excess of a million words in the English language, and many times that number can be strung together into little phrases; it would take more than a lifetime to sort them all. But Carol, on her very first try, picked the phrase that stopped Earl dead in his tracks.

"Earl, can you do me a *really big* favor?"

She purred.

Earl hit a brick wall. Cord ran into the back of him; his head smacking Earl's back, well below the shoulder blades.

Earl stood and waited for further instructions.

"I want to make a bet with Cord, but I need your help, *will you help me?*"

 A bobblehead yes was Earl's response.

"Wow, that's great, thanks so much, Earl, you are *so* nice."

Earl was already in heaven.

She redirected her attention to Cord, who stood hunched over, hands on his knees, thankful for the break, but dreading what surely was to follow.

He sucked in a deep breath through his nose, rattling snot, and exhausted a stringy goober into the grass along the sidewalk. *There*, he said to himself, that made nostril breathing a bit easier.

"Eww, that was a nice touch."

Carol scrunched her face, curling her lip.

"Really? Do you think so? I think so."

Cord didn't bother looking up to gauge her reaction; his hands were still on his knees.

"How many laps you planning to do; you know it's four to a mile [*it was really only 3 and a third per mile, but she rounded up, just to be annoying.*]"

"We've done two and half; were doing four!"

Earl yelled to her across the street, before Cord could even process the question; he was still waiting for her punch line – God only knew what she cooked up to embarrass him now. Whatever it was, it seemed that it was going to be accompanied by music....nice.

"Good, that's what I figured. I'll bet you, Mr. Brin, that Earl is being much too kind to his little friend. I'm sure if he tried, even mildly, Earl could lap you in the next two laps. Are you up for such a bet? Or do you concede defeat at the onset."

Now Cord figured Earl could probably lap him in one lap, let alone two. Two would be cake. He stood upright, placed his hands on his hips and exhaled long.

"Why should I care if Earl can lap me? I know he can; that's no mystery to Earl or anyone else watching us. So I concede; there, you win the *stupid statement* award; congratulations."

"Well, so much for stating the obvious; I suspected you'd give up without much of a fight, but I figured I would give you the benefit of the doubt and pose the question. Thanks for being predictable."

"You're welcome."

He snapped right back, and proceeded to spit a healthy gob of saliva and snot on the ground.

And as Cord stood there, gulping air, exhausted, out of shape and looking down at a too-big belly, his demeanor quickly changed, mercurial, as it often did. He was getting tired being the butt of her and Lilly's constant sarcasm and worn jokes; suddenly, he wasn't in the mood to be playful, or polite."

"What are the fucking stakes?"

He snapped at her, loudly, and in a decidedly rude tone.

She could hear the instant annoyance in his voice. She wasn't sure how to respond, she was a bit taken by his tone.

She took too long to answer.

"Well? You make this big-ass production getting us to stop; you stand there, smug, with the CD player on the railing, and you don't even have a proposition to make? So I'll ask a second time, since it seems you're a bit slow on the uptake. *What* are the fucking stakes?"

Truth be told, she really didn't think it through that far; she thought for sure he would just pass on the bet, they would continue their little jog, and she would play her tune to mock him.

She still didn't answer. C stood, hands on hips, and shook his head in the negative, saying *obtuse* loud enough for her to hear as he did. Then he continued.

"Well, here's **my** stake; I want a chit."

Cord spat again, this time in her direction.

"Excuse me? Did you say *obtuse*?"

"Excuse me what? You heard me; that's the bet."

"I'm *not* obtuse; and that's a bit open-ended, don't you think? I don't know what your intentions are, and that could be problematic."

"Please, don't flatter yourself. It's a moot point anyway, isn't it? We all know Earl could lap me in one lap, let alone two, so your end has no risk."

"Whenever there's a bet, there's risk at play, Mr. Brin; of that, I'm all too familiar. The risk is lessened in this case, admittedly, but Earl could turn an ankle, for instance."

"Well, you're the one who opened the dialogue; you offered a race, and I gave you the opportunity to name your stakes – you failed. I named mine, which are non-negotiable, and apparently you're the one without the stomach for it. I'll remember that distinct *female* character flaw – it might come in handy some day."

"Come on, Earl, let's finish up."

Cord got ready to resume his run. Right before he started, he looked up at her one last time and mouthed, in a disgusted tone.

"Pathetic."

That did the trick; she took the bait.

"*My* stake is a chit, just like you."

"Nope."

Was all Cord said.

"Why not, fair is fair; have something to hide?"

"I have too much to risk; the odds are stacked heavily in your favor. Look, I'll give you a chit for one lap, not two. We both know Earl could probably lap me in a half-lap. Oh, and I get a second chit, and I don't sign your nutty lease; month-to-month verbal is all you get."

"Forget it!"

"Fine; so predictable and timid, like most women. Word was you were this tough, hot-shot who didn't get intimidated. Guess not; just another pretender, wishing she had a dick."

Now she was the one getting steamed.

"Intimidation is the wrong term; how about taken? And I don't get taken. Forget the second chit and lease."

"Give me the lease, and I'll drop the second chit *[Now Cord never expected to get the second chit – that was a red herring all along; the lease issue was key, as was the original chit. She was easier than C thought she'd be; all it took was to get her a bit hot, and she was easy to rile....too easy]*."

She stood and studied him hard, hands on her hip.

She knew he had something up his sleeve; she was getting sucked in, but couldn't figure out how. She had a bad feeling about this; worse because she was the instigator in this stupid little exchange. She stood there, trying to convince herself there was no way he wouldn't get lapped, there was no way....right? He's way out-of-shape, wasn't that right?

She debated herself.

"Fine, but **no** take-backs on the chit; all is fair game – **all** topics, issues and acts."

Christ, he had better not lose, Cord thought to himself.

"*Acts*? Maybe I should be the one wondering about bad intentions. Well, as long as it's reciprocal, and you don't ask me to do anything illegal, you have yourself a deal."

"Something tells me *illegal* isn't a worry of yours."

Carol said in snark.

"Fine, deal; now get over *here* and shake my hand."

He barked, in a mock order.

"Yeah, right; you come over *here*."

"I'll meet you half-way, on the sidewalk."

He said.

"Oh, brother, whatever."

Carol snorted as she slowly descended off the porch; Ay plied the street to greet her midway. As he crossed, he glanced up to see a jet-black cat, actually two, in repose on the front porch roof, looking down at him with utter indifference. They got on the roof through a second floor open window. The one had its paws hanging over the roof edge, lazily studying him as he approached. They both had airs about them; how appropriate, he thought.

Cord gripped her soft, delicate hand harder than she expected. She shook back hard herself, to stake her position, but she had started out with a somewhat weak handshake, and it's hard to make a weak one strong mid-shake. She was pissed at herself for letting him get the better of her in the handshake; she felt weak, and didn't like it. He eked a small smirk, acknowledging her misstep, which riled her all the more.

He looked into her hazel eyes and broadly smiled. She was beautiful, for sure; he knew *exactly* what he was going to use that chit for.

"You'd better enjoy your little CD gag, because you're going to regret this bet."

He whispered at her.

She didn't answer; she had a pit in her stomach, the result of the bad feeling of being had.

Cord crossed back over Hardwick and onto the Park sidewalk to rejoin Earl; as he did, he called back to her.

"You might want to put the cats inside; this could get ugly, for *you*."

Carol looked skyward at the two relaxed cats above her head, above the dual *Medusa* and Griffin, and called out.

"Maguro, Tobiko, pay attention, watch the short, fat man over there get embarrassed."

She resumed her position on her porch.

"Ok, Earl, you ready?"

This whole time, during the banter between Cord and Carol, Earl had stood and watched, not really sure what to make of the exchange. He wasn't sure what to do next.

"What am I supposed to do?"

Earl asked quietly, in a confused tone.

"We're both going to run as fast as we can, okay, which means you're going to be way ahead of me. But that's okay, keep running fast, because what you're going to do is try to run **so** fast you catch me from behind. But you have to try and do it, to catch me from behind, before I get back to this spot, which means I'm only running one lap, but you are going to have to run almost two laps. Okay Earl? Do you get it?"

"Hey, what are you two whispering about? Bet's off, **no fair!**"

Carol yelled frantic across the street, figuring the fix was in.

"Jesus, would you keep your pants on! I'm just explaining what we're doing to Earl; do you want to come over and let him tell you exactly what I said?"

Earl shook his head vigorously in the negative; there was no way he was repeating all that to Carol out loud....no way.

"Why is Earl shaking his head like that - **the bet's off!**"

"He's shaking his head because he's shy about talking to you, that's all. I just told him he has to run as fast as he can and try to catch me from behind before I finish one lap; isn't that right Earl."

A second bobblehead in the affirmative from Earl.

"Hey, you should have to run a lap together first, since your dropping it to one lap."

Carol was trying to throw in new conditions, after the shake.

"No dice; you should have thought of that *before* you shook, Missy, and by the way, that was a pretty weak girly handshake, you know."

Cord said as he wagged his finger in the air at her for emphasis.

"You grabbed my hand before I was ready! I'm not a girly-girl!"

"Uh huh."

Was all C said, smiling.

"You just worry about losing the bet chit-boy!"

She yelled across the street.

Now, as this exchange continued, Methodists were walking past, on their way to the Cook-Off.

"Hey, what's going on, Earl? What bet?"

A fit-looking, fifty-something man asked, walking arm-in-arm with his wife.

Cord answered, because Earl certainly wouldn't have.

"Money's on Earl to catch me in a lap around the Park; the current ante is ten bucks, straight up....pretty good odds."

The man looked at Cord's midsection and immediately grabbed for his wallet.

"I'll say; I got ten on Earl."

"Henry!"

His wife shrieked.

"We are on our way to church!"

"Well, we're not there yet, are we? It'll be fine; just think of it as a bet for God, like church bingo you play every Thursday. I'll put the winnings in the collection plate tomorrow."

Cord cut in.

"Hold the bill, we'll settle later; I remember you from Sam's."

During the exchange, another two couples came into earshot; they both jumped in – the Methodists knew a sure thing when they saw one.

As the bets were laid, an unseen carillon in the Methodist belltower began to toll, calling the faithful in. And it was a real peal; someone in the tower yanked on the rope and down-swung that bell for a full eighteen chimes. There's nothing quite like hearing a resounding church bell in the early morning sun, standing in a Park in front of a true country Courthouse; the whole scene felt surreal….19th Century.

The only bad part of the idyllic equation was the foolish bet he just made; he was going to get creamed, he just knew it.

Cord and Earl lined up on the sidewalk across from Carol's front steps; the two gargantuan bronze lions stood guard, gnashing their teeth at them.

"We'll start only after I drop my arm, okay, Earl?"

He nodded yes.

Cord called out to Carol.

"Go ahead, start your stupid CD; I know your dying to."

She smiled and gently pushed the *play* button, Freddy Mercury geared up, and the boys were off.

"Are you gonna take me home tonight?
Ah, down beside that red firelight;
Are you gonna let it all hang out?
Fat-bottomed girls,
You make the rocking world go round."

As the fifth stanza ended, Carol's hand cut the air in a hard, downward swoop; she smiled as she saw the two boys dash off, weaving through the throng of Methodists in front of the church.

Earl carefully threaded his way amongst the parishioners, a circuitous zig-zag on and off the sidewalk, never making contact, always the gentleman.

Cord showed no similar restraint, bulling down the sidewalk center, arms flailing, shouting warnings to clear the way, shoving aside young and old alike, garnering stares, sneers and worse. When it came to running, and preserving precious oxygen, Cord took no prisoners; he ran a straight line, expletives be damned.

Carol smiled wide at the spectacle, especially at C mowing down the faithful.

They both actually had good-looking bottoms, she thought.

And Carol didn't really care who won, she really didn't.

As the two grown men dashed around the Park, she realized for the first time, in a very long time, that she was actually having fun; having a ball with two fat-bottomed girls.

CHAPTER 31 – THE FRAME FADED TO BLACK

Cord ran with his head down, scanning the sidewalk cracks; he didn't want to see how far Earl was ahead of him, but by the cheers in the crowd, he figured it was quite a distance. Word of the bet spread quickly through the throng circling the Square.

"I want in!"

Came a chorus of voices along the sidewalk.

"Ten bucks to anyone who wants a piece of me!"

Cord shouted as he fanned frenzy the crowd with his hand, a professional wrestler in the ring. Out of the corner of his eye, he swore he saw the minister keeping tabs, like a trader in the pit. This was quickly getting expensive.

All joking aside, he cleared his mind and focused on the run, nothing but the run.

Clear, clear, get mad! *Cheops, Cheops, Cheops, Cheops!'*

Since he was a kid, if he had to focus, C would recite that word in his head – *Cheops* of Giza - the pharaoh from the Egyptian pyramids. He didn't remember the first time he started reciting it, or why if first came to him – it really made no sense to say it, but for some reason, it would always focus and motivate him to do whatever he had to do. It would help him regulate his breathing, channel his anger, his adrenaline. It worked; it always did – the power of the pyramids.

He could feel his pace getting faster, and his breathing was starting to get in a rhythm; he was passing the Courthouse; a quarter of the way home. He could hear a roar of the late-comers in front of the Presbyterian Church; Earl was already a full quarter lap ahead of him.

"Holy shit!"

He said to himself aloud.

At that pace, Earl would catch him at the finish; his two laps to Ay's one.

He kept his head down; he couldn't look up – he couldn't worry about Earl, he had to just dig in and run.

Cheops....Cheops!

He could feel the stitch come back in his side as he approached the Presbyterian entryway; people were shouting past him to yell to Earl on the other side of the Park, telling him that Cord was winding, petering out....that he was toast.

Nice, real Christian of them; weren't these people late for charity work? Fucking Presbyterians.

C still hadn't come across the rooting section for the *visiting* team, that's for sure. No one was calling his name, well maybe in vain. At least this group hadn't got wind of the bet; as it stood now, based on the show of Methodist hands he saw, he was surely down over a hundred if he lost.

He was starting to tire, when he heard a lone voice – the entire *Cord Cheering Section* – it was Linda, from the *Palace*.

"Come on, come on! You can do it!"

That was it, that sweet little voice was the roborant he needed. But, unfortunately, his legs weren't buying it; he was at full throttle and still slowing down, quickly gassing out.

Maybe he *was* toast.

He turned the corner off Mansfield Street, onto Third, the last quarter-leg. But just as he did, he inadvertently glanced down Mansfield, behind him, down the long length of sidewalk he just ran and saw Earl had turned onto the same stretch, at the far end, about four hundred feet away, a runaway freight train, bearing down on him, fast.

Fuck! he said aloud.

Earl had picked up his pace and made up ground. Cord had another four hundred fifty feet to go; that last fifty feet was going to be his undoing, the spot just before the finish line, where Earl would pass him.

Panic set in; he felt the rush of adrenaline numb his extremities.

Cord could sense his field of vision shrinking, it was getting dark around the edges, like the old picture tube television screen did when you turned off the set – it would blacken on the edges, and fade toward the middle, till only a small white dot was left, until that too, slowly faded to black.

He'd been down this road many times before.

He could feel himself getting lightheaded as the screen continued to shrink; he had to make it down Third and onto Hardwick before he blacked out.

Please make it he thought to himself.

Cheops, Cheops, Cheops....as the frame faded to black.

As he began to slowly focus, Cord realized he was prone on the grass beside the sidewalk, across from Carol's house, staring blankly at the gnarling lions, the cool grass pressing against his cheek. He was at the finish line. Earl was sitting next to him, cross-legged, Indian-style, smiling.

"What happened?"

C said, still in a bit of a fog.

"You know what happened, smart-ass. How long are you going to rub it in?"

Carol said, as she stood next to the two of them, hands on her oh-so-pretty hips.

"Boy, you sure ran *fast* at the end!"

Earl said, as he pushed Cord gently on the shoulder, still smiling.

"Thanks Earl, I guess I won, the bet that is. Obviously you won the race."

"I'll tell you this, I never saw so many people gawking on the sidewalk disappear so fast into a church in my life."

Carol joked, looking down at the empty space in front of the Methodist doorway.

Cord just smiled; he'll collect his hundred bucks from God, he figured.

"I guess we'll settle up later; when I drop off that signed lease. Oh, that's right, there *is* no lease."

Cord said through a grin; Carol just smirked – she was being a good sport, she really was.

"You'd better be a gentleman with that chit, that's all I have to say."

"I'll be as much a gentleman as I would have expected you to be a lady with yours."

C volleyed back.

"Fair enough; since I wouldn't have even cashed it in, we'll call it even."

"Nice try, but I think I'll hold onto it for a bit, and see what rises to the surface."

C teased.

And with that Carol smiled at them both.

"Congratulations, Cord. And Earl, I'm *very* proud of you. Thank you for helping me with my bet. We'll get him next time!"

With that, she put her hand on Earl's broad shoulder and squeezed it. That was the first time she had ever touched Earl; his muscle was as hard as rock.

Earl beamed at her, but didn't say a word.

"I expect I will hear from you sometime soon, Mr. Brin; here's my email – that's the best way to get in touch with me. Be gentle."

Carol turned, lazily tossed her hair to the side and headed for the house.

"I wouldn't know how to be any other way."

Cord called out to her.

He looked down at the address:

ccrowe@actaeon-capinvest.com

It had the sound of a hedge fund or investment banking firm; a lowly brokerage wasn't paying *F430 Spider* dividends.

He took the folded piece of paper and slid it in his tee-shirt breast pocket. He smiled and wondered if she knew who *Actaeon* really was.

Cord did; he knew Greek history, knew it fairly well. *Actaeon* was a heroic warrior, a Thebe, the pride of Greece; but no one really remembers that part.

Actaeon was forever tagged as the sap who had the misfortune, while hunting stag with his pack of hounds, to stumble upon the Goddess *Artemis* bathing in the nude (some suggest it wasn't such a stumble, but rather a peeping Tom, caught in the act).

That little *aperitif*, that eye candy of godly virginal goods, proved costly; *Artemis* caught him gawking in the woods and forbade him to speak, lest she transform him into a stag, like the ones he was just-then hunting.

Apparently not one to heed simple instructions, upon hearing his pack of dogs approaching, *Actaeon* called out to his hunting party, whereby he immediately assumed the form of a stag, and was summarily ripped to shreds by his own hounds. It's hard to imagine snatch, even goddess snatch, was worth that fate.

Who would name their investment fund after that clown? And why would investors follow *that guy* with their hard-earned dollars – it didn't make much sense. But C wasn't wasting his chit on a silly question like that.

390

Cord asked Earl how long he had been lying on the grass.

"I don't know, maybe five minutes."

"What have we been doing?"

"Talking! You've been talking with Carol. Well, you were mostly breathing heavy and saying: *wait a sec wait a sec wait a sec* over and over. No matter what someone said to you, you kept saying *wait a sec;* Carol was the one doing all the real talking."

"The whole time?"

C asked.

"Yeah, the whole time!"

"What did she talk about again?"

C shook his head as he spoke, trying to remember any of this.

"Lots of stuff! She said she was proud of how fast I ran! And she really likes my bumblebee shorts! Don't you remember?"

"No, not really."

C said.

Earl was listening, but not really paying attention; he had so many *Carol things* to occupy his mind for the next month, his head was swimming. He just smiled and looked up at the sky; he was so happy, he didn't know what to do or say next.

"Hey Cord, can we stop on the way back home to see if Al's around? Can we?"

"Sure, but no more running; let's walk over, okay?"

Earl just looked ahead at the path in front of them and beamed. He had a great smile, Cord thought; it was a genuine shine, there was no onion to peel, no hidden agenda. With Earl, what you saw was what you got.

Cord couldn't help but stare at Earl and smile along with him; he and Earl had been on the same planet for roughly the same amount of time, but over those forty-odd years, what different paths they traveled.

Yet despite C's circuitous journey, and Earl's same-old-same-old, they somehow ended up side-by-side, walking in the Courthouse Park in the middle of Belvidere, New Jersey on Saturday, April 22, 2006.

And they were friends.

If Cord could simply push rewind, could replay his life and fix anything along the way for the better, and there was certainly a lot to fix, but such change for the better would mean his path would invariably veer to the right, or to the left, such that he would never meet Earl, their orbits wouldn't cross, he wouldn't be walking next to him right here, right now, well then, that was an easy proposition; Cord would pass on the rewind, without question.

He would remake all the bad decisions, the mistakes, the trouble, endure the pain and relive the mess that was his life, all of it, if he had to give up meeting Earl. Of that he was sure, more sure than of anything else.

Finding a true kindred spirit is a rare find indeed.

Most people shuffle through life surrounded by family, friends, wives, husbands, lovers, people they care for, some more than others, yet most will certainly live and die amongst them without ever meeting a true kindred soul. They may be out there, somewhere, but such paths seldom cross.

But rest assured, you'll know when you meet; it has a decidedly different feel.

That special present is tucked away, somewhere, in a far corner of your soul, a corner overlooked - a room with but one key. There it sits, patiently, waiting to be opened.

Oh, but if you find it, what a key, and what a room.

Kindred can't be described in words or captured in a picture, it simply has to be felt to be understood. Men would move mountains to protect it.

To truly know that feeling, to have it wrap around your being and slowly soak in, is a gift like no other; to never have felt it is a lonely hole in the soul.

Cord knew right then, right there, that he found his kindred spirit; he felt it when Earl uttered the first words to him as he dragged him along onto Carol's porch. But now, he just knew it.

Cord knew he befriended Earl for the rest of his life.

That certainly wasn't on the agenda when he boarded that faded bus.

Cord and Earl slowly walked through the Park, kicking stones along the path, making their way to the boat ramp. Earl was retelling once again how Carol smelled like some kind of flowers when she was standing next to them, and how white and straight her teeth were, with the ever-so-small gap between her two front teeth....her signature.

He asked Ay at least a half-dozen times if he saw that she squeezed him on the shoulder, and he kept asking

Cord why she did that. He just wanted to hear Cord's answer over and over, that she did it because she liked him. Earl couldn't get enough of that answer; he could have asked that question all day long.

Then Earl told Cord more about Ken, Sandy and *The Secret of Skeleton Island*, especially the scary pen and ink drawing on the inside jacket of the book, and the back jacket too; it was the same *exact* picture front and back! Earl was intrigued by that fact; it must mean something special, like a secret code or something. But he hadn't figured it out yet.

He would put the bed sheets over his head, turn on his little emergency flashlight and stare at that picture, with the book folded open in front of him. He could describe it exactly, the scene seared into his skull.

There was a little wood cabin sitting all alone, at night, on the wide-open prairie, flat and empty as far as you could see. He described the big, bright lightning bolt in the sky, heading for the cabin; it had eight branches, or fourteen branches, depending how you counted all the little twigs of light coming off the main bolt. It looked like a big upside down tree.

And it was scary, Earl whispered to C.

Then there was the little dirt road that ran up to the little house, the rickety porch, the two tiny black windows that looked like they had something, or someone, in them, looking out. Earl used a magnifying glass he borrowed from Marty to try and figure what was in those windows, but it was still a mystery.

They looked like bats; maybe they were bats. But why were bats looking out the window? It was all a big mystery.

Then there was that big dead tree alongside the cabin, ominously leaning toward the road, and the night clouds with the face of a spooky monster hidden in them; Earl was sure it was a monster. It had lips curled into a sinister smile – he would show Cord when they got back home; Lilly couldn't see it, and said he was dreaming, making stupid stuff up just trying to scare himself, but Lilly didn't know how to solve mysteries like Ken and Sandy could, so she couldn't see it. He knew Cord would see the spooky monster in the sky, just like he did.

Earl would picture himself laying down and hiding in the large tufts of grass and sage which were blowing in the night wind, staring at the cabin and wondering what ghosts were hiding in there. He would lie right alongside the dead tree trunk which had fallen into the grass; it was right at the bottom left part of the drawing. He couldn't wait to show Cord.

Other times Earl pretended he was *in* the cabin, all alone, looking out the black windows at the lightning bolt and the wind whipping through the scrub, wondering what monsters were lying in the grass, ready to get him if he ventured outside. Then, in that case he figured, when he was using Marty's magnifying glass, he was really looking at *himself* in the cabin window, looking out! That would always make Earl smile, trying to make out the shape of himself in one of those windows, hiding in the cabin.

He had so many stories conjured up, and that was just the inside jacket of the book!

Earl would scare himself thinking of all the spooky stories he and his mom used to tell each other. She always had the best stories; ones that made it hard for him to go to sleep at night. He remembered them all.

"Are we going to tell scary stories tonight, just like you said?"

Earl was rubbing his hands together frantic as he spoke, like he did whenever he got excited.

"You bet. After dinner, I can give you that surprise I have for you, and we can turn off the lights, put on some candles, and tell spooky stories."

"Oh boy, I can't wait! Lilly doesn't like to tell the spooky stories anymore, but I do! I'll get the book out and show you the cabin! I'll show you *me* standing in the window!"

Earl was getting too excited; Cord hoped he didn't start running.

They got to the ramp; lots of mallards, with a gaggle of mostly white geese across the way, but no Aloysius in sight. Earl hoped he was just sleeping in a tree and hadn't yet left, for good.

The ducks milled around the periphery, showing half-interest in the two of them standing at the shore, waiting for a sign they had bread to offer. When it was clear the boys were empty-handed, they drifted away in disinterest, some going downstream, the balance upstream, camping at the churn of water at the mouth of the Pequest.

"Why don't you remember talking to Carol on the grass?"

Earl asked.

"I don't know Earl, sometimes that happens when I get real excited, or scared, or mad, mostly mad, that's when it happens the most. And then I just kind of forget what's going on for a little bit. I don't know why or how, it just kinda happens, ever since I was a kid, ever since I was twelve. It usually gets me in some kind of trouble, except for today, I guess."

Earl sat on the base of the silty river bank and pulled his knees to his chest as he looked out over the Delaware; Cord stood nearby, also looking out over the water, flowing lazy right to left, at nothing in particular.

"Hey Earl, why did you talk to me that first time in the Park yesterday? I didn't think you talked to too many people, especially people you don't know."

"Because you're nice."

Cord figured it was Earl's way of thanking him for stopping the kids from picking on him.

"You mean because of what I did to those kids?"

"Nah, that didn't matter."

Earl said matter-of-fact, staring across the river.

Now Earl meant no harm or disrespect by saying that, it was simply the truth. And Cord knew that, he thought; but still, it was a bit of a blow to his ego, considering he thought he'd done a good deed and thought Earl recognized it as such. Cord wasn't looking for a pat on the back, but he didn't expect it would be summarily dismissed either. That was just human nature.

"Really? Then how do you know I'm nice?"

Earl shrugged his shoulders, indifferent.

"I just do."

"Earl, I would never do anything to hurt, or upset, you, but I want you to know that I'm usually not such a nice person, not usually in the beginning, and less so in the end. Even if it starts out good, something always happens to mess things up, it always does. When all is said and done, when the dust settles, I tend to hurt and disappoint people, or worse, usually worse.   It just happens, I'm good at it."

Earl heard him, but wasn't swayed in the least.

"She told me to talk to you because you're special, and nice, and she's never wrong about stuff like that….*never*."

Earl wagged his finger with the second *never*.

"Who? Who told you to talk to me? *Lilly*?"

Cord said in surprise; his voice rose a bit when he said *Lilly*, an embarrassing little yelp.

Earl just shook his head in the negative, slowly turned to Cord, cracked a small grin and whispered.

"No….my mom."

CHAPTER 33 – THEY BOTH HAD PAGE 3, FOREVER

It took Cord a few seconds to let what Earl had said settle in. He cocked his head and looked at Earl in disbelief.

"How would *your mom* know I'm nice, Earl?"

"She knows you, she met you in the Park!"

Earl said, matter-of-fact.

Now Cord was confused; there was no woman in the Park but Lilly, and he thought Carol was dead. Was he wrong about that? No, she was *real dead,* like twenty-five years dead, wasn't she? Wasn't he right about that?

"Earl, *where* was your mom in the Park? I didn't see her."

"On the bench; you were sitting on *our* bench. We sit there all the time together, since I was a kid. She was sitting right next to you!"

Cord just looked at him.

Okay, *now* he got it.   That was fine, Cord figured; he was sure that an imaginary mom helped Earl cope, and if it was helpful to Earl, so be it, who was he to judge. Cord figured he would continue their *discussion,* because it was clear Earl wasn't joking; Earl really believed his mom was on that bench.

"Earl, there wasn't room for a piece of paper between your ass and mine on that bench, how could your mom fit between us?"

Earl just turned to Cord and smiled in a way that one does when he understands something the other simply doesn't.

"There was plenty of room on the bench."

Was all Earl said.

Cord didn't say anything for a bit. He wasn't mocking Earl; to the contrary, he found himself entranced by Earl's calm, quiet demeanor. He wanted to ask more questions.

"How does she talk to you? I didn't hear you say anything?"

"Oh, she just holds my hand and smiles at me, and I hear everything she has to say. And she said lots of nice things about you. She knows you did some bad stuff, she didn't say what, but underneath you're a good person, and she knows that you're my friend, a real friend….a kindred spirit."

Cord turned, mouth open, and looked at Earl in disbelief; the back of his neck tingled and the hair on his arms rose to attention.

There was *no way* Earl thought up that phrase on his own. *Kindred spirit?* The same phrase Cord had just thought about himself walking through the Park when thinking about his friendship with Earl….**no way**.

Cord squinted as he spoke, carefully concentrating on his words.

"Did she say that, Earl? Did she use those exact words?"

Earl just nodded his head slowly in the affirmative, still looking out over the water, wholly indifferent to the question.

Cord couldn't believe he was having this conversation with Earl; he couldn't *really* believe what he just heard.

"Earl, what does *kindred* mean?"

Earl simply shrugged his shoulders in the negative, as he stared blankly across the water; the question didn't faze him in the least.

C's arm hair tingled a second time; he looked down as they all stood at attention. Then it happened.

"Hey! There's Aloysius! He didn't leave! Look, he's flying right at us!"

Aloysius appeared from a tangle of trees across the river and glided to a beautiful landing in the Delaware, bobbing on the slow-moving current, about twenty-five yards off shore, looking directly at the two of them. Earl called to him in a grunt, and Al answered once, before disappearing below the water's surface; time to fish. A smile a mile wide creased Earl's face, waiting patient for Al to come up for air.

"What else did she tell you about me?"

C whispered.

"Nothing really, she just told me you were different, and that you wouldn't believe in her at first, but not to worry, hopefully you would, eventually."

Earl paused a bit, then continued.

"She also said you would tell me what you want to tell me, *when you were ready*. She really believes in you; she thinks you were sent here special, for Lilly and me. She thinks you're kinda like an angel, kinda."

Cord just stood there, staring at the back of Earl's head. This conversation can't be happening. He felt the need to sit down; he wasn't thinking clearly upright.

"An angel? She said that word? And she said I would tell you something *When I was ready?*"

Earl nodded a simple yes to all the above.

When you were ready; there it was again. *Open When You Are Ready* – what was it about those words? First it was about Carol's note to Lilly, now Earl's mom said it to him, but she was dead and Cord wrote it to *himself* on his own box, years ago, for his own reasons, so he thought.

What the hell was going on? Cord thought to himself. Why does that phrase keep coming up? Is it all just a coincidence? Seems unlikely. Or is he simply making a big deal out of nothing? Probably.

And Earl's mom thinks Cord is an angel, presumably a good one? Him?   Earl said his mom used the word, *angel*, and it was the first time C heard it to describe himself, outside the same thought that bounced around his own head for years. It was one of the only explanations that made the mess that was his life, the predicaments he got into, and invariably out of, make any sense. But the angel in his head was never good, he never thought of it, of him, as being anything close to *good*. It was more like fallen, a lost soul, a backslider, heretical....an *ame damnee*. Take your pick – they all fit. And none were good. But he really didn't believe in good angels, or bad angels, or any angels at all for that matter – it was all stuff-and-nonsense....until he did, when nothing else made sense. And even then, with time, C would slide back into believing the whole notion was silly and the idea would shelve, until the next time.

And now he found himself in a *next time*.

Cord had so many questions queued for Earl, he didn't know where to start.

One thing C *did* know….he really *didn't* know why he was in this dead-end called Belvidere. He wondered if Jenny even knew. Maybe this was beyond Jenny; maybe the fourth dart was something very different indeed.

Maybe.

And as C squatted beside this over-sized man whom he just met, a kindred spirit for reasons he didn't know, he returned to the same thoughts that haunted him for years, the one he would never discuss with anyone, ever. The voices, the dreams, the rhymes, the routines, the compulsions, the ability to never lose, ever, not when it really counted, even when he wanted to….it never made any sense, and he long ago stopped trying to figure it all out, the never-ending conflicts in his head. And as stupid as it sounded, and as antithetical as it was to dead-doesn't-age, and dead-is-dead, which is what he believed, most of the time, maybe he *did* die on that fence in '75. How else does one explain Jenny, the pale horse or the puppet, the crickets and the flies….the whole *game*. Maybe lights out really wasn't lights out, maybe lights out was Belvidere; maybe this strange place was the end of a long, painful journey, the end of the line. Maybe this was where the puppet lived, along a lonely stretch of river in some forgotten out-wash town.

Over the years, he found himself in a myriad of journey's end, countless, breathless destinations spread to the far reaches of the map, more than he could remember, some by choice, but most by Jenny – she was the doer. And with all that, now he winds up in bum-fuck Belvidere, New Jersey, *New Jersey* for Christ-sake, and somehow it's suppose to be something orphic? He shook his head in denial; sorry, this place just wasn't that special. It can't be, not this God-forsaken patch of nothing at end of the road to nowhere.

Back to Earl.

"Who else does your mom talk to, besides you? Can she talk to me? Does she talk to Lilly too?"

"No, Lilly won't listen, she's still mad at mom; she's *so* mad *all* the time."

Earl just shook his head and looked down, dejected and slowly mouthed, in barely more than a whisper:

"Mad, just mad."

As his voice trailed off.

"Ever since my mom went away, Lilly's never been happy, for twenty-five years. But my mom didn't *really* go away, she's still here, but it's just different now. But Bibby just won't see it. My mom says Lilly's very sad, and hurt; she never understood why mom did what she did. My mom wants to talk to her, but Lilly won't listen; she says she wants to, but she really doesn't....she's just not ready, I guess."

"Why did she Earl? Why did your mom go away?"

Earl just shrugged and put his head down again, and shifted his shoes left and right in the silty sand along the river bank, making deep grooves in the dark tan and rippled gray soil.

"I don't know, it was kinda time, for her, I guess. She told me it was hard to explain, but it didn't mean she didn't love me and Bibby; she loves us more than anything, always has and always will.   It was just hard for her; she made some bad mistakes, and she had to go. She didn't want to, not really, but she kinda made this *really big* mistake, or something; I told her *everybody* makes mistakes; I make mistakes all the time – just ask Lilly! And if she made a big mistake, so what? Who cares?   I didn't care - it was okay with me, but she doesn't really like to talk about it; it makes her sad, and I don't like when she's sad. I don't really know about all this kind of stuff….I wish I was smarter."

Earl shrugged again. He looked like he was going to cry.

They both sat side-by-side, in shared silence.

Then Earl spoke.

"You know, my mom never told me what she wrote to Lilly on that note; she said Lilly would read it when she was ready and explain it to me….but Lilly's still not ready."

Cord was taken aback….again.

"You *know* about the note, Earl? I thought Lilly never told you about that note?"

"Lilly doesn't know I know, but I do – my mom told me to keep it to myself, and I *always* listen to my mom. Bibby thinks only Uncle Frank and Uncle Sam *[Earl sometimes called Sam 'Uncle', even though he really wasn't]* know about it. She keeps it in her purse; she's carried that note every day since my mom gave it to her, but she's never opened it. She just moves it from one new purse to the next. I wish she would just read it, then maybe she could talk to mom too. Mom misses her so much, and Lilly misses mom every day, *every single day*. They both miss each other, but Lilly's too stubborn, and scared….and sad."

Cord could see Earl's eyes were red. A single tear crested his left eyelid and slowly made a track along his cheek; the curve of his lips arching into a broken smile.

Cord couldn't stand to see Earl sad, so he changed direction.

"Hey, does your mom ever talk to Aloysius?"

Cord had picked up a rock to skip, but it was too round, so he just tossed it out into the river in a lazy overhand throw. The kerplunk sounded about ten yards offshore.

Earl looked over at Cord with a condescending look. Man, Earl was *good* at that look; he must have practiced it on Lilly over the years.

"Duh, Al's a bird; he can't talk *people* talk! He just grunts!"

Just then Al surfaced and flipped a tiny minnow down his gullet, there and gone.

Cord smiled, and then so did Earl. He grunted to Al, who answered once, then quickly dove again....gone fishing. Earl wiped the single tear off his cheek with his sleeve and gave a hearty sniff to clear his nose.

"Well, did you ever actually *ask* your mom if she *can* talk to Al? Maybe she can talk to him the way she talks to you and never told you, how about that? Maybe she and Al talk about *you* all the time, and *you* don't even know it. Maybe she asks Al to keep an *eye on you.*"

Cord smiled, raised his eyebrows and tilted his head toward Earl, planting the seed.

Earl frowned, then his face turned studious, like he stumbled upon a nascent thought, and now he was turning it around a bit, fingering it in his mind, thinking about it some more. Then he slowly smiled.

"Maybe you're right; I'm gonna ask her."

"When, now?"

There comes the look again. Jesus, Earl could sure make you feel dumb.

"She's not here *now*!"

As if it was obvious.

Then Earl lowered his voice.

"Hey, don't tell Lilly about any of this, okay? She gets super mad when I talk about talking to my mom. And she doesn't know I know about the note; that would get her *real* mad."

"Jesus, we don't want that; Lilly gets mad enough on her own without any help from us. No problem, Earl, I'll never mention it; done deal."

With that, Cord turned to Earl and stuck out his hand; Earl took it and gave it a hearty shake. Cord's hand was engulfed in Earl's big mitt; he felt like a little kid.

Earl stood and brushed the soil off his butt, stretching his arms overhead.

"Do you talk to *your* mom?"

Cord frowned to himself a bit, still seated and facing the Delaware. He answered in a reflective tone.

"Not everyone's as lucky as you, Earl."

"I'll ask about her, if you want; maybe my mom knows her."

Cord felt a well of emotion and his eyes moistened as he stood up.

"Maybe she does, thanks."

As he gently put his hand on Earl's back and patted it.

Earl called to Al, to say goodbye, but Al didn't answer this time. He just bobbed along lazy on the current watching as the two boys slowly ascended the ramp, away from the river's edge. The two remained silent for a couple blocks; Cord was still swimming in everything Earl told him.

How could he, he of all people, really believe what Earl said. But given it was Earl, and given some of what he said, how could he not?

It didn't take much debate; Cord didn't doubt Earl, he didn't doubt any of it. He just accepted it for now as something he didn't understand. But then, he could say the same thing about himself, his life, the game, all of it. In a strange way, it made him feel even closer to his new friend.

Earl broke the silence.

"So, what are you suppose to tell me? My mom said you were going to tell me something."

Earl asked Cord in an excited manner, hoping for a good story.

"I don't know what I'm suppose to tell you Earl, nothing comes to mind right yet, and your mom didn't drop me any hints. But I'll let you know when it does, or she does."

"Oh, well I got something to tell. Sometimes I help out at Marty's farm baling hay for his dad, or helping fix things out in the barn, I pet the cows when I'm out there too. I really, *really* like the smell of cow manure, most people don't, but I do. Sometimes I ride on the rakes and tractors doing stuff with Marty's dad. Sometimes I work down at the mill loading feed or bagging it – nobody can load as many bags on the trucks as I can! I help out at the maintenance shop sometimes, over at DSM, helping Marty's brother fix stuff and clean-up – I get to wear a hard hat and goggles – everyone else is always trying to take them off, saying they look goofy, but I like wearing them, I think I look smart! And I'm not that smart you know, so I like looking smart!

Sometimes I help Lilly at work, and I watch all the old jelly-belly ladies doing exercises, bouncing all around *[Earl snickered to himself thinking about their chunky boobs and butts, jiggling like the red Jello cubes he used to suck off the plastic picnic plates during the summer as a kid]*. Sometimes I help unload Monday's food trailer for Sam. I do lots of stuff. Sometimes I don't do anything at all....sometimes."

Earl stopped just as abrupt as he began, sucking in a big breath of air.

"That was a mouthful Earl; did you breathe somewhere in there? That was the most out-of-breath I've seen you yet."

Earl just smiled, his chest heaving, taking in oxygen. He always talked extra-fast when he was excited.

"Okay, I have a little story to tell, are you ready?"

Cord looked to Earl to see if he wanted to hear the tale.

Earl's eyes widened and he smiled in anticipation. That was a yes.

Cord stared straight ahead and kept walking as he started to slowly speak in monotone – it was rote.

"I got a 2nd Lieutenant Commission and was assigned to the Basic Training Center at Camp Lee, in Virginia. I was an instructor, and would drill new recruits in basic training – class room, drill field and field training – all at AP Hill, a large outdoor military tactic facility. We used to sleep in tents, and I would lead 20-mile forced marches, with backpacks. I had about 50 soldiers, which was one platoon, in each class, which lasted 6 weeks. There were four platoons per Company, each with a Captain, who was the Company Commander. I was at Camp Lee for about a year when I was discharged.

After discharge, I went home to Columbia, Missouri for a few weeks, then left for Detroit to look for work. I stayed with my Grandma Ayotte in the old section of Detroit, near the General Motors Headquarters building. I looked for work at the Henry Kaiser auto plant, but they were only hiring car stylers for new models. I went to a couple other plants as well, with no luck.

After a few days, I left for New York by train and arrived at Grand Central Station – Manhattan."

"You've been to New York!"

Earl yelped, excited about Skeleton Island; if C had been to New York, then he *must* know where Skeleton Island is, where it's hiding! He was right, and Lilly was wrong, it does exist! Then he realized he interrupted Cord's story, and was quickly quiet again, hoping Cord would continue, and maybe tell him about Skeleton Island too, maybe later.

Cord continued.

"I walked to the terminal and took a bus to Paterson, New Jersey to ask for a job at Wright Aeronautical Corporation. I was hired on the spot as a test engineer and worked in the test facility running in the new radial aircraft engines. I got a room at the local YMCA. I was hired for $50 a week.

After a few weeks at Wright, I saw a newsreel at a local movie house of a rocket engine being tested in New Jersey. I was interested, so I took a train to Dover, New Jersey, about 30 miles from Paterson, in late August and then took a cab to Rockaway, New Jersey, to the Reaction Motors Personnel Office. I got an interview with the Chief Engineer, some guy named Nesbitt, at Reaction Motors in Lake Denmark – about 5 miles from Rockaway. I was hired as a test data analyst for $65 a week, $15 more than Wrights...."

And that's where Cord stopped speaking, mid-sentence. He didn't break the monotone for the whole story, right till the end. Then he just kept walking in silence.

"And then what? What did you do next Cord? Did you get another raise? Oh boy, I bet you did! What's next?"

Cord just looked over at Earl and frowned.

"Earl, that's not me."

"What do you mean? You said it was you when you were telling it."

"Earl, there's no Camp Lee, not since 1950 anyway. Henry Kaiser Auto went out of business sixty years ago. Wright Aero, or Curtiss-Wright, hasn't been making *new* radial engines for over fifty years, at least I don't think so. Reaction Motors is long gone, absorbed into Thiokol Chemical in 1958, which became something else, which became something else again. Who knows what it is now. My guess is Nesbitt's dead, unless the guy is over a hundred. And if I got a *raise* to sixty-five dollars a week from fifty bucks, it would be $1.62 an hour; that's pretty low, even for an entry level grocery boy."

Earl just looked at Cord, confused, waiting for the rest of the explanation.

"That was my *dad*, Earl, in 1946, after World War II ended, sixty years ago. He was a mechanical engineer, a rocket engine designer. At least he was when he was in his twenties.

I found an old, yellowed paper with his life story on it, that snippet anyway, carefully scripted in pen, with later string thoughts written in the margins….he must have remembered them after the text was already written. It was all on a single page of undated, white-lined composition paper, like the kind you use in school. You could tell he took great care to write it down; it was his life, how it unfolded, and how it made him who he was. The quiddity of a movie theater newsreel prompting him to move, change jobs, and alter his life, forever.

I found it buried amongst twenty-year old electric and phone bills, when I was going through his estate papers after he died.   Someone just randomly dumped reams of disparate papers into a whole load of different cardboard boxes, all set in neat stacks in the foyer, to be sent to the document destruction firm.

But I wouldn't let them do it; I made them save every fucking box, so I could go through them first, page by page. It took me weeks.

I lost count of the boxes; one after another filled with utility bills, mixed with reams of medical reports and prescription instructions, mixed with tax returns, mixed with dishwasher instruction manuals, mixed with business financials, marketing materials and to-do lists, mixed with Board minutes, mixed with tiny bits of gold, like that yellowed paper.

It was the only document that really mattered.

It had a number *3* circled on the top of the page; Page 3 of the story of my father's life, written down by him for someone, anyone, to read.   For someone to care about….to at least remember.

My dad wasn't a big talker; he never shared stories of how he grew up, how he wound up where he did, why he was doing what he did.   What forks in the road he took, and why, if he even knew, and what regrets he had, if any. I'm sure he had regrets….we all have regrets.

No one on the planet but him knew those answers and could have written that story, or cared to; if he didn't write it, it would be lost to time, and no one would be the wiser.

To me, there isn't much that's sadder than that – an eighty-year old man's life reduced to a single yellowed piece of paper, capturing a slice, a snapshot of time in the 1940's – and even that was destined for the shredder.

I never found Pages 1 or 2. Page 3 ended at the bottom of the paper in mid-sentence, presumably continued on some lost Page 4, or maybe Page 4 never left my father's head, maybe *Wrights* was the last word of his story.

I don't even know when he wrote that down Earl; he would find an old pad of paper and just use it, he didn't throw much away; so the fact it was yellowed didn't mean anything. It might have been written the week before he died – it might have been ten, even twenty years prior. I just don't know. I'll never know.

In any event, it was sad; and I was determined to make his story live on; at least that snippet from sixty years ago. So I kept the paper, and I memorized his story.

It's been swimming in my head for the last five years, Earl, and now, hopefully, it'll swim in yours too, if you want it to."

Earl whispered, as he gently put his hand on Cord's back.

"I'll never forget Page 3, never. I just wish I had a Page 3 from my dad; I never even met my dad."

Cord, with his head down, cracked a laconic half-smile. He didn't deserve an Earl, he really didn't.

They passed through the street-side door adjacent to *Nonpareil*, which was hopping; through the plate glass they could hear the fifties music playing, and made their way up the steps. He followed behind Earl and his bumblebee shorts.

It was a little after 11 am on Saturday, and they were hungry, and they were home.

And they both had Page 3, forever.

414

CHAPTER 34 - A SHOWER, SOME FOOD AND SAFE SURROUNDINGS

Earl cracked the door and peaked inside, to the left, down the hall into the kitchen. There, wearing her black gym tights and a rib-hugging tank-top was Lilly, bent over the counter, working on something. Earl knew exactly what is was.

"Ravioli!"

Lilly turned slowly and looked toward Earl.

"Yeah, ravioli, a *lot* of fucking ravioli."

"Hi, Lilly."

Cord said, with no sarcasm or histrionic tone; just a simple, heartfelt hi; he really was glad to see her. And it came out of his mouth exactly the way he felt, exactly the way he wanted it to. When does that ever happen, he thought to himself.

"Hi Cord."

She said it exactly the same way, no sarcasm – it actually sounded as if she meant it. And then she did something entirely unexpected; Cord didn't know quite what to do….she cracked a faint smile at him. Yes, that was a smile, and it actually looked sincere.

It lasted long enough for Lilly to realize what she did. The smile vanished from her face, and the diatribe began.

"Earl, do you know how long I've been bent over this God-damn counter making these stupid ravioli for you and your boyfriend?"

"Well, it's 11 am now and I left at 9 am, but you were still in bed, so it must…."

"Never mind with your stupid math; you better both eat dinner before dinner, because you're having appetizer portions, I can tell you that."

"Lilly, don't make any for me, really, it's quite…"

"Shut up you; you're the one who started this whole thing."

"Me?! How's that? I wasn't even here when you talked about *ravioli* with Earl."

"Oh, trust me, you're to blame, and don't even try to deny it!"

Cord just looked at her, dumbfounded.

"See, you don't even have a response….**guilty!**"

With that, she turned around, hunched over, and continued the play as martyr.

Then came the question Earl was dreading.

"So, did anything happen during your run?"

Earl just looked at Cord, wide-eyed; he never knew Earl's eyes could get so big – they looked the size of cue-balls. It was a *trap!* It must be a trick question; how could she know about it so quick? She must have spies! Ken and Sandy would surely know how to slip out of this one! Earl knew he couldn't lie, and he knew if he told her about having fun with Carol, the rest of the day would be utterly miserable. But Earl straightened his backbone, stood up like a man, and answered brave.

"I have to go the bathroom, Cord will tell ya."

And with that, Earl was gone, in a flash, leaving Cord holding the bag in the hall, alone, with Lilly's back facing him. He gulped and realized his mouth was instantly dry and pasty. He needed water.

"Well?"

She said as she turned around, hands on her hips.

"I'm waiting; it can't be that interesting."

"Can I have a drink of water?"

"No, you can't."

"I can't? Why?"

"Because I said so."

Cord just looked at her, smacking pasty lips.

"Thanks."

"You're welcome. Now, again, for a second time, what happened? And why did my brother just run away like a little girl, and why do you look like you just saw a ghost?"

Oh, boy, we're not even going *anywhere* with that one, Cord thought; spilling the beans about the *living* Carol was bad enough, let alone the stories about Lilly's mother he just heard all afternoon.

Lilly stood in silence, hands still on her hips, tapping her foot, waiting for an answer. She was quickly getting annoyed, not that it took much.

"Did you get my brother in trouble? No wonder you were being so nice when you strolled in; *Hi Lilly* - what a bunch a shit!"

"Why does everything have to be a big mystery with you? Nothing happened; we went for a run, went to look for Al at the ramp, found him, and came back, all in all, pretty boring. Your brother's a pretty fast runner, by the way."

He threw that last comment in nonchalant, trying to casually deflect her curiosity.

She wasn't impressed, and she certainly wasn't buying it.

"Nice try. I'm gonna find out anyway – you might as well tell me and try to spin it, not that I would believe anything **you** say anyway. Then I'll make one phone call, *one* is all I need to make *[Lilly thrust an angry, upright pointer finger at him, for emphasis]* and I'll check the facts out myself. So here's your last chance to change your bullshit story. Okay, what happened?"

"I don't have to report to you; it's none of your God-damn business what happened….how about that! It's just between Earl and me and *Carol.*"

Oh, why did he say that? It only felt good for, what, about a half-second, but the pain was going to last and last and last.

"*What did you say*?"

She dragged that statement out much longer than she needed to, as she walked slowly toward him, down the hall. Lilly was still carrying the fork she was using to crimp the edges of the little ravioli she was making for Earl and him, and her hand was already speckled white and red, blotchy from her now vice-grip on the utensil. He could see her fork hand shaking, just a bit.

Fuck, this was big trouble; he wondered where she was going to try and stab him first.

"Whoa, whoa, whoa, take it easy, I was just kidding."

But Lilly wasn't smiling, and she kept coming, straight at him. There was no escape route, unless he tried to run her down.

Just then, from nowhere, Earl swooped up behind and landed a bear hug, pinning her arms to her side.

Lilly was startled, then instant-livid, all in a matter of seconds.

"Earl! Let me go!"

She screamed as she tried to wriggle free; nothing doing – Earl was a vice.

"Cord, hurry, tickle her, right on her side, or get her feet!"

"Tickle her?! Are you fucking insane?!"

"It's the only way she'll drop the fork, trust me! Tickle her! Do it! Now!"

"Earl!"

She directed her scream backward at him, then she turned to Cord and said in as serious and calm a tone as she could under the circumstances.

"You had better not listen to him; I **swear** you had better not tickle...."

She never got to finish the sentence before she was howling; Cord couldn't tell if it was a laugh or a horrid scream....or both. It would scare a banshee; it sure as hell scared the shit of out him.

But he kept on it, although it didn't take much; just a touch of his finger up and down her side and she went crazy. But she still hadn't dropped the fork; to the contrary, she clenched it in a death-grip, jabbing wild in short, herky-jerk strokes, trying to bury the fork in Cord anywhere the tines would bite. But it was futile; Earl had her pinned good and Cord stayed outside her short swings.

"The feet are better! Go for the feet!"

Earl yelled.

Cord couldn't believe she could be more ticklish there than on her sides, but to her feet he went. If he was lucky, she would go lightheaded from the lack of air and pass out, then he could make his getaway.

Unfortunately, Ay forgot that Earl's bear hug didn't control her dangling legs.

A fatal mistake.

He bent down toward her feet to tickle them; he remembered the last time he had bent over in her company he got Sam's front door in the face. Those legs were hanging there awful quiet he thought to himself.

In ended as quick as it began.

A lightning swing of her foot and a swift, direct shot – bullseye to the groin; C exhaled a low, extended moan, and down he went like a rock.

Now it was Lillian laughing, hysterically, right at Cord.

"HA! HA! HA!"

She bellowed, forcing the fake laughter at him, her face turning beet red in the process. Then she deliberately threw down the fork, the bear hug sprung open, and the tempest was over as quickly as it began. She stood over him, smiling.

"Sorry C, I forgot to warn you about the kicks – she's good at the kicks – kick-boxing and karate class. She's the kick-boxing teacher!"

Earl bent over C, hands on his knees, assessing the crime scene. Cord was fetal, with eyes clamped shut, moaning low, like a little kid.

"Fuck, thanks, Earl – a bit sooner with the info next time."

Lilly just smirked wider, still standing over him.

"Stop your belly-aching, I didn't even kick you that hard. Plus, it's better than getting stabbed. Count yourself lucky."

With that, she walked away, back into the kitchen. Her anger passed, like a freak storm, and it was calm once again. Vintage Lilly. Earl bent over and whispered to his fetal friend.

"She's right, she would have stabbed you, trust me."

Cord slowly sat up and grimaced.

"You really are fucking scary, you know that! *What's wrong with you?* Shouldn't you be in jail somewhere?"

"Maybe I should ask *you* that question; have *you* been in jail? Something tells me the answer is yes; just a gut feeling, and I'm usually right."

She wagged that pointer at him a second time. Cord didn't answer; he just sat there, recovering.

"Ask your boyfriend about his hand."

She said, pointing to Earl.

Earl held up his right hand in front of Cord's face, palm down – smack in the middle of the back of his hand was a faint, cream-colored, circular scar, the size of pencil eraser. Earl flipped his hand palm up; an even a fainter scar shadowed his palm, in the same spot.

Cord just looked at it, then he looked up at Earl.

"Knitting needle."

Earl said, shaking his head negative, as if he'd acknowledged doing something wrong.

"Knitting needle? She stabbed you through your hand with a fucking knitting needle?! Jesus, what for?"

"He put a blanket over me, laid on top of me and tickled me; he knows I'm claustrophobic, and ticklish, but Earl did it anyway.....*didn't you Earl?*"

Earl shook his head slowly in the affirmative – guilty as charged.

"Why in the world, knowing your nutty sister, would you do something like that Earl? And excuse me for being skeptical, but somehow I don't see **you** sitting in a fucking rocker, knitting a scarf!"

He yelled the second half at her, down the hall.

"She doesn't knit, my mom did. And I didn't know she was scared of blankets, I was only four."

"Four! You stabbed him when he was *four*? How old were you, five?!"

"Five and a half, and Earl knew better, don't let him kid you. He learned quick enough; you never put the blanket over my head and tickled me again, did you Earl?"

Earl shook his head vigorous in the negative.

"The needle stuck right in the wood coffee table! It didn't hurt *real* bad, just a little bad; I remember starting to cry, but Bibby told me to shut up - she said she had to think - and she couldn't think with me blubbering, so I stopped crying – just like that *[Earl snapped his fingers]* It wasn't that bad, really; the doctor said I was lucky - it missed most of the important stuff. Lilly didn't even get in trouble; she convinced my mom that I stabbed myself into the table; she's good at convincing and stuff like that."

Cord's mouth was agape; was there a hidden camera somewhere? No matter how he figured she couldn't amaze him more, she did.

"Stabbed yourself, at four? That's ridiculous! Why didn't you just tell your mom the truth, Earl? Rat her out!"

"No way!"

Was all he quickly said, implying that tact would have been much worse in the long run; and he was right.

"Earl did the right thing, didn't you Earl?"

Lilly smiled at the memory.

"Jesus Christ *[Cord shook his head in disbelief, speaking lowly to himself]*!"

Did you ever think about anger-management class?"

He said, not really loud enough for her to hear. But she did. When she wanted to, Lilly heard *everything*.

"What?"

"Never mind."

Cord quickly said.

"I thought so."

She said, then after pausing a moment, she continued.

"You know, all I try to be is nice, slaving over a stove, making hundreds of ravioli on a beautiful Saturday morning, while you two go off and play....and all you two give me is grief. I wonder why I even bother being such a good sister to you Earl."

Earl and Cord listened to the martyr routine and just looked at each other, and said nothing – nothing needed to be said.

Cord sufficiently recovered to stand somewhat erect; he leaned into Earl and studied his brow, looking for the evidence.

"She never got *me* with Uncle Sam's door – I knew about *that one.*"

Earl said, smiling with self-satisfaction.

Cord nodded in agreement.

"That makes one of us."

He shook his head, breathed in slow, then forced a blow of air from his nostrils before he spoke.

"Well, it's been a *real pleasure* talking with you; have a nice day Lilly."

Then he turned to Earl.

"Earl, I'll see you later for dinner; come on up around eight or so, that's not too late is it?"

As Earl was shaking his head no, she interrupted.

"Oh, nice, nice manners. My fucking back is sore from bending over making you both ravioli, and right in front of me, you make dinner plans and don't even invite me? Real nice."

To his mild surprise, Cord felt bad; that *was* pretty inconsiderate, not that she really deserved any better, since his balls were still throbbing.

"I didn't know you would even *want* to join us for dinner. Your right, that was rude, I'm sorry."

Cord stopped momentarily and then continued.

"Would you like to join us for dinner, Lilly?"

He actually sounded sincere. She didn't even turn around.

"Are you kidding me? Fat chance I would *ever* eat dinner with you, by choice! Nice try sister, but you're dreaming."

"And there you have it."

Cord said sarcastically aloud, mainly to himself. He slowly shook his head; how did he fall for it over and over?

He borrowed Earl's cellphone, walked out and headed upstairs for a shower, some food and safe surroundings.

CHAPTER 35 - DINOSAURS ON THE PROWL

After a quick shower, he went down to *Nonpareil* and parked in a rear booth, had a leisurely lunch and perused the phone book for some Belvidere ethnic fare. Linda was there and he was glad to see her; what a bright disposition and a truly happy girl - that was a welcome change.

She got herself another big tip, just because. He figured one or two more of those and her little panties would be around her ankles, if he asked nice enough. Such were the fantasies of a middle-aged man.

He flipped through the book, looking for either Japanese or Thai; nothing, just as he suspected in this bum-fuck backwater. The most ethnic food in Belvidere was the greasy Chinese take-away he passed on his way into Town that first day, and some goofball place specializing in Friday night all-you-can-eat barbecued, pulled-pork sandwiches and root beer floats, served from 5:00 to 6:15 pm.

6:15 pm? Why not 6:20 pm?

Loosen Your Belts Boys – Here Comes Another Rack!

A quarter-page double-entendre - a buxom cartoon waitress with a firm, round rumpus in a short skirt, she had the look of a Bavarian, carrying an overflowing tray of pig, dripping sauce over the sides. Good God, marketing genius.

He pictured the girl on payroll, prancing around in her short skirt, with a painted face and heaved cleavage, puckered and plump rosy lips, finished with platinum pigtails – in this place, he could believe it. She would have to be a Catholic though; a good Catholic girl, swinging around the saucy ribs.

Enough of that nonsense; back to the task at hand.

He found some decent-looking Japanese and Thai ads in Hackettstown, which was a twenty-five minute ride east on Route 46, according to the next door booth, when he leaned over to ask. A quick call to a taxi service confirmed they would swing by for cash, then pick up dinner and deliver.

Sounds like a plan.

Cord ordered a medley from both places; an eclectic mix for the novice Earl to sample. Earl told him he had never had anything but Chinese and *regular stuff*, whatever that was – Cord figured it consisted of hamburgers, pizza and pasta, along with a helping now and then of Friday's pulled-pork and all sorts of meat cuts from Sam's. He told Ay he had fish and seafood from Sam's sometimes, but not very often; Lilly didn't like to cook that stuff – *it smelled*, she said.

Cord made Earl promise to at least try the food he was going to have for dinner; to his pleasant surprise, Earl didn't put up a fuss at all – he was excited to try new stuff. Actually, Cord figured he was only really excited about the ghost stories and the *surprise* he had for him after supper, and if eating ethnic food was a necessary stop on that trip, so be it. Nevertheless, Earl seemed to be a sport about it, for which Ay was happy.

Cord heard the street-side door open at 7:45 pm; he had been in his apartment kitchen, sitting at the bar counter, waiting for the taxi to arrive.

The gaunt, older man with a greasy comb-over slowly ascended the steep stairs. He had a mid-sized paunch, covered by a wrinkled, ashen, once-white dress shirt that rode partially out of his pants; his trousers, pulled by gravity, creeped south of the flat ass-end older men sport. He figured that button-down shirt was tucked in neat for the first half-minute he stood in front of the mirror in the morning; it was crumpled and disheveled around the waistline the rest of the day, as he constantly pulled his pants up by one or both hips. He wore a thick, too-long, imitation leather belt that simply didn't do the job.

He had the haggard look that comes with a steady stream of booze and cigarettes - a lifer. Cord figured the man felt as good about himself as he was going to in that same thirty seconds looking in the morning mirror, when his shirt was tucked in and his pants were cinched tight around his belly – the rest of the day was simply a trudge, mixed with smokes and hooch. All he had to look forward to was drinking himself unconscious in the evening. All he dreaded was the morning, where he would wake and do it all over again.

The long flight of steps winded him; he struggled while carrying the two overflowing plastic totes of food; Cord went down the steps, half-way between his place and Earl's landing, to help.

Cord could smell the tangle of Thai and Japanese spice wafting through the hall; the closer he got to the satchels, the stink of stale butts and booze on the driver's labored breath infused and corrupted the Oriental aroma. Cord grabbed both bags; the old man followed him, and felt the need to talk, being a bit guilty walking the rest of the way empty-handed. But not too guilty.

He thanked him by way of complaint.

"I never saw so many God-damn stairs in one big row like that, they'll kill ya, for Christ's sake, thanks."

As he coughed hard, it rattled the phlegm clinging to his lungs. It was a deep, resonant hack; the snot was thick and Cord was sure there was a partial re-swallow somewhere in there.

"That's a first, for sure; never chauffeured a dinner before – sure smells good."

Actually, the old man thought the sundry mix of food smelled like shit, but he was trying to be polite, playing the conversationalist.

"What's your name?"

Cord asked.

"Smillie, Sheldon Smillie, Smillie's Taxi Service *[he pronounced it with a long I, as in the yellow icon – in fact, he had a large mustard magnetic face on each door of the cab, an avocado rust-bucket Country Squire station wagon, with simulated wood paneling. As he spoke, he pulled his worn wallet and handed Cord an obnoxious yellow business card, bent and scuffed, with dirt stains on the edges, sporting the same sap smile]."*

This was the first Sheldon he ever met, C thought, and a fine specimen at that.

"Here's the bill for the ride *[Sheldon stuck his grimy hand in one pocket to pull out a hand-written receipt]* and here's your change from the hundred you gave me *[he stuck his hand in the other pocket and pulled out a loose wad of crumpled bills and loose change, dropping it into Cord's palm]."*

"Here you go, Sheldon, be good."

With that, Cord paid the fifty dollar cab fare with a hundred note, and told Sheldon to keep the rest.

That tip had a weekend's worth of wine written all over it – bought rot-gut by the carboy; that was the first thought that entered Sheldon's mind. Shelly liked it best when he placed the bottle on the edge of the table and positioned himself on the floor, directly under his rubber siphon hose, for a direct-down-the-throat; a feat Sheldon had perfected, a skill for which he was mighty proud. Shelly smiled to himself, it was definitely gonna be a

Saturday night carboy party-for-one this evening. Life, right about now, was pretty fucking golden.

Sheldon looked up at Cord, grateful for the generous tip, not really sure what he did to deserve it. He shifted his feet and stood more erect, trying to feel a bit more worthy of the unexpected green.

"Thanks, thanks a lot."

Was all he came up with, followed by a hack of phlegm.

"No problem, just one thing *[Cord said it while holding the C-note firm, waiting till he finished his statement, before letting go]*. In the future, if you **ever** you see this number flash on your phone, whenever that may be, no matter the day or the time, ever mean ever, *you answer it*. And that call, at that time, takes precedence over whatever else you're doing, whatever, and another two hundred tip on top of the fare comes along for the ride. Agreed, Sheldon? "

"Yeah, yeah. Sure!"

Sheldon was half-listening, focusing on the carboy-to-come.

Cord poked him hard in the chest, to bring him back.

"Hey, this is fucking important, Sheldon, are you sure you understand what I'm saying, or do I need to find someone else to take my money?"

Cord said in a lowered voice, as he looked into the man's eyes, which made Shelly a bit uncomfortable.

"Yes, I understand, I really do."

He parroted.

"Good. Now be sure to put that number in memory in your cell phone under the name **Important**. When it rings, if that day ever comes, I'll be on the other end, and it *will* be important."

"It's Shelly, and thank you, thanks a lot; I promise I won't forget."

Shelly felt part of some fuzzy conspiracy he didn't quite understand, but was excited nonetheless, since it must be important. This was turning out to be a good God-damn day, a banner day.

And with a quick shove, the crisp bill disappeared into Shelly's pocket, and the little man was on his way down the steps. He took a sharp right outside the door and in less than five steps found himself inside the discount liquor store – score.

Cord programmed Sheldon's number on Earl's phone – under *Smillie*.

Although C doubted the old drunk would come through in a pinch, it was cheap *just-in-case* insurance; because you never know when you might need a *just-in-case*. Sometimes the outcasts, the loners on the periphery with no one and nothing to lose, they're the ones who more-often-than-not answer the phone when it rings off-hour and it's *that* call. You could never have too many of them in the wings; Cord had learned that a long time ago.

C shut the door and fished around in the cabinet for a set of dishes to serve the olla podrida. Then he made his way down to the second floor landing and rapped on the door.

He only got one rap out when the door swung open, like she was expecting him.

"Earl, your girlfriend's here."

He heard the big man trot down the hall from the front room, with a big smile on his face as he squeezed by Lilly, careful not to bump her, even though she was deliberately standing in the way.

"Now, mind the time, you know the curfew."

"I don't have a curfew!"

Earl yelped.

"Well you should, with him."

And that was the extent of the insult as she half-heartedly slammed the door on them; pretty mild actually, C thought.

"Oh, boy, I'm so excited!"

Earl was beside himself; he was already four steps ahead of Cord.

Into the apartment they went; and Earl was introduced to the aroma of the Far East.

"Okay, Earl, a little explanation is in order."

Cord began, as the medley of cuisine was laid out on the dining room table in the big front room. The table was set neatly, all the various food set in shallow bowls lined in an arrow-straight row, the Japanese separated from the Thai. The dinner plates and napkins were set just right, as were all the various chutneys that went with the myriad of different dishes. It had the look of a fancy holiday feast. There were four chairs around the table, two on each side.

Cord sat in the chair facing the hall, expecting Earl to sit across from him. However, Earl walked around the table and sat beside him; why, Cord didn't know, nor did he ask. He was sure there was a reason, there always was with Earl, and that alone was good enough for C.

"First, the Japanese. This here is sushi, raw fish on rice, mostly. We have this red one here, which is tuna – it's called *maguro*. Then we have…."

"Maguro! That's the name of one of Carol's cats, one of the one's that lay on the roof and watch us run!"

"That's right! That's why I got it. Do you remember the other one?"

"Yeah, Tobiko!"

"Right again; I knew you'd remember. *Tobiko* are flying fish eggs, little tiny red eggs; there it is, wrapped in seaweed."

Earl didn't look too excited about that one. He twisted his face in a contortion which spelled unpleasant.

"No, it's good, trust me. I used to eat it all the time.

"Used to? Hey!"

Earl said, suspect.

"I'm a vegetarian Earl, remember, but when I wasn't, *Tobiko* was one of my favorites."

"Why are you a vegetarian C?"

C sighed.

"It's a long story Earl, and it's sad. I'll tell you some day, promise, just not now; I'm in too good a mood and I have way too much other food explaining to do, or we'll never get to eat."

Earl let it drop.

"Hey C, why does Carol call her cats *tuna* and *fish eggs*? That's kind of funny, calling a cat a tuna, and a fish egg, isn't it? Why'd she do that?"

"I don't know, maybe you can ask her next time."

"No way! I'm not asking her; you ask her for me."

"You know, Earl, it's not gonna kill you to talk to Carol a bit more; she likes you, she really does."

"You think so, *really*?"

"Yeah, really. Do you ever ask your mom about her?"

"We don't really talk, I mean she mainly does the talking, and I listen. I don't ask a lot of questions. She hasn't said too much about Carol, but I think she likes her."

"I'm sure she does, since she knows how much *you* like her."

Earl began a blush.

"I don't talk about stuff like *that* with my mom."

Cord smirked, then continued the food lecture.

"Okay, here we have an order of *edamame*, which are salted, steamed soybeans, in the pod – they're like potato chips once you start eating them, Earl, real good and you can't stop. Then we have *kani*, which is called crab, but it isn't real crab, it's really some white fish meat, and it's cooked.

Then we have some rolls; this one is a *spicy tuna roll*, which is the *maguro* all chopped up and mixed with a hot sauce; then we have a *vegetable roll*, which is avocado and cucumber – that's for me; and lastly, just for you, we have a *New York roll.*"

Cord waited for the inevitable response, which came quick enough.

"*New York roll!* I want that one!"

"I figured you would; it's apple, avocado and *sake,* which is salmon."

"Do you think Ken and Sandy ate *New York rolls* on their way to Skeleton Island?"

"Doubt it, I don't think sushi was too popular in 1948, after the War. I don't think the Japanese were too popular at the time around here, even as late as '48."

"Oh."

Was all Earl lowly muttered, not really understanding anything Cord just said.

Cord knew Earl didn't get it, and he felt bad for saying it; but he felt worse for making Earl wait to eat.

"Forget the rest, Earl, let's eat! I'll tell you about the other stuff as we go."

Earl didn't need to be told twice; right for the *New York roll* he went, but there were no forks to be found.

"Here, use these."

Cord handed him a set of bamboo chopsticks, sporting the little plastic lever piece you slip on the end to make them work if you never used sticks before. Earl was more fascinated with that piece of petrol engineering than the food; he kept opening and shutting the chopsticks; they looked like toothpicks in his big hand.

But he worked them very gently. Cord was amazed he could be so delicate with such big, beefy mitts.

Cord showed him how to put some *wasabi*, hot green mustard – which wasn't really all that hot – and a paper-thin shave of ginger root on top of the roll, and then dip the tower in a small tray of soy sauce, which soaked into the rice exterior. Earl was fascinated with the whole process. This was way better than a fork chasing peas around the plate. It wasn't eating, it was more like art class, and he always liked art class.

"The black seaweed stuff looks like paper."

"I know, but it holds all the stuff inside together, like wrapping paper."

That wasn't such a good analogy; Earl didn't seem to like the idea of eating wrapping paper, or seaweed for that matter. He scrunched his face.

"Who eats seaweed *on purpose?*"

Earl said, doubting the whole notion.

"Lots of people! It's good Earl, trust me. Go ahead, don't bite it first, put the whole thing in your mouth, all in one piece, then chew it."

Cord showed by way of example; a vegetable roll roundel going down the hatch. Earl smiled and followed suit. He chewed it a bit, sporting a studious face, like an official taste test.

It passed; he smiled a big cheesy smile, with a black sliver of seaweed stuck to his front teeth.

"That is **good**!"

"I told ya; you are now officially Japanese."

"Woo-hoo!"

As he was hooting, Earl let out a combo - a mini burp, soy sauce-induced, followed by a near simultaneous high-pitched squeaker.

Now, no matter how old they are, burping and farting amongst male friends is funny, it always is - women simply don't understand this sort of thing. Male bonding.

And when the combo is accidental, like Earl's, it's even funnier. Unlike the horror of farting in front of a girl, the better looking the worse, air from any hole, ass or mouth by guys, amongst guys, is a-okay. And funny to boot.

When a six-foot eight inch man farts, you expect it to be baritone, yet this tiny chirp from Earl's ass sounded like a schoolgirl fart....dainty.

After a brief pause, while *what-just-happened* registered, the two gut-laughed, the kind where it's hard to catch your breath.

The seaweed stuck to Earl's two front teeth made it that much funnier. Cord was beet red, like he was having a coronary. He fell off the chair with a loud thud onto the wood floor; Earl thought it looked fun, so he slowly rolled off his chair and hit the floor too, in a thunderous thump. It shook the furniture.

They both kept laughing. Cord tried to squeeze one out, a companion fart to keep the joke going, but no luck. If he squeezed any harder, he might shit himself.

Grown men, having stupid fun; life doesn't get much better than that.

At first, neither one heard the loud knock at the door, the knock Cord knew was coming; he was surprised it took this long.

"It's open; come in Lilly!"

Cord yelled as he caught his breath, surprised she actually waited for the invitation. He expected the inevitable tirade about the noise, the plaster falling off the ceiling, take your pick.

What she said he didn't expect.

"Are you two okay? That sounded pretty bad; I guess you are."

As she asked the question, she could clearly see they were recovering from a laughing jag, and answered herself.

Cord noticed no edge to her remark; it actually sounded normal….sincere. What a nice surprise.

Truth be told, Lilly was feeling lonely.

She wasn't used to being the one home alone, while Earl was out having a good time – for pretty much her whole life, it had been just the opposite. And for the past three years, since Button had gone away, Earl and she had done most things together – and stayed home together. Cord was putting a crimp in that routine – if today was any indication of times to come, she wouldn't be seeing Earl all that much, and she was already melancholy. But rather than being mad at Cord, which she expected to be, and likely would be on numerous future occasions, at least for right now, she was just happy to join them.

Not that she was going supine just yet.

"What is that *awful* smell?"

"Dinner and farts!"

Earl yelled, which made them both chuckle some more.

"Lovely. Earl, you've got black stuff stuck to your teeth; wipe it off, for God's sake."

She said condescendingly. A swipe of his tongue and he colored it gone. He smiled wide to show her his teeth; she nodded a bit, acknowledging he indeed took care of the seaweed.

Cord chimed in.

"Don't knock it till you at least try it; pull up a chair."

She walked over to canvass the smorgasbord, and noticed the too-neat table.

"First, a couple of simple ground rules for you, young lady."

Cord continued. As he spoke, she casually moved around the table, shifting plates and such around, making them crooked and out of order, to annoy him, of course. While he spoke, he followed her around the table, moving them right back into place.

"No utensils, especially knives and forks; I don't trust your temper. What do you think Earl, do we let her use the chopsticks? They look an awful lot like knitting needles, or do we make her use her fingers?"

"I'm not eating with my hands! Give me some chopsticks!"

"What's the magic word?"

"*Asshole?*"

Cord smiled and nodded his head; he set himself up for that one. But he didn't give in, he just continued to stare at her, waiting for the proper answer.

She acquiesced without any more struggle. But she did continue to re-arrange the table as she spoke.

"Please, Mr. Brin, *pretty please,* can I have a set of chopsticks and join my brother in feasting on this fine fare, which smells just like...."

"Okay, okay, I'll take it at face value, don't need the punchline."

Cord grabbed a pair of sticks, broke them apart and started to put the child's plastic end cap on, like he did for Earl.

"*Please,* I'm not a rube!"

She announced, while grabbing the sticks from Cord, and tossing the plastic piece back at him, hitting him in the face with it; it glanced off the side of his nose."

"Nice."

Was all C said, as she smiled at her unplanned aim.

She took one of the chairs from the other side of the table, pulled it around and jimmied it between the two of them.

What a self-centered little girl, Cord thought to himself. But, he liked that she did that, and he didn't know why. Well, he actually did know why. He couldn't say it enough to himself, as much as he hated to repeat it over and again in his mind. She was the most beautiful woman he had ever seen, bar none. She was definitely the dictionary picture adjoining his *Criteria* list; and now she was sitting, somewhat civilly even, next to him....by choice, no less.

At this moment, life was pretty good.

Although she struggled with the chopsticks, she got them to work well enough, and didn't ask for help. He saw her purposely delay picking them up till she studied him, trying to be discrete about it. He was impressed, and happy that she actually looked to him for guidance, although she would never admit as much.

He went through his explanation of the various sushi and accompaniments again for her; but they ate as he spoke. . Earl tried everything, and to his utter amazement, so did Lilly, except for the *tobiko;* she couldn't get past the thought of eating thousands of little fish eggs in a big mouthful. She did eat the rolls with the *tobiko* on the outside though – Cord figured she hadn't really focused on them. He figured since Earl was eating it, she would eat it, just to keep up, so to speak.

She was competitive, even in food.

Earl liked everything; Lilly pretty much liked nothing, except the *edamame* – she was a convert on those. She also ate, and liked the *negamaki,* since it was cooked meat, with a mild sauce. The roulade of meat and asparagus was a last-minute choice, in case Earl didn't like the sushi; C was glad he thought to add it, for her sake.

They cleared the table of the Japanese order pretty quickly; most of the time they talked and joked about the food at hand, and not much else. They moved right into the Thai dishes; Cord provided introductory explanations as they pushed around the plates.

Throughout the whole ordeal, Earl was having a good time, and to his surprise, so was Lilly. She was actually smiling and joking along, sans sarcasm, for most of the meal, directing a majority of her comments toward Earl, asking him about the food. But Cord was not offended by that; to the contrary, he enjoyed spending time with her and not speaking – any time he spoke with her it was like walking a tightrope, hoping against hope not to say the wrong word or phrase and stirring a storm. Now he could enjoy her company and be protected….a third party observer.

Nothing came up about the Carol incident that morning; Cord wasn't sure if she grilled Earl about it when he left, or if she let it drop. If it was the latter, he couldn't imagine it was dropped for good. He hoped it would be at least for tonight – this was turning out to be a pleasant meal.

Cord had ordered some *perkedel* (Thai spicy corn fritters, with a garlic and basil dipping sauce), *indomie soup* (Indonesian curly egg noodle soup, complete with a floating poached egg and assorted exotic green vegetables), *rotie cania* (Malaysian extra thin wheat pancakes, with a creamed coconut, yellow chicken curry chutney) and vegetable dumplings (with a soy and ginger dipping sauce).

Other than the soup, the rest of the food from the Thai restaurant was easily eaten by hand, which they all did. Earl spent half the time sucking any remnant of the dipping sauces off his fingers. Lilly was issued a blunt spoon for the soup, and instructed by Cord on its use for eating, not weaponry. She took the barb and was good-natured about it. She had never eaten such a medley of foods at one sitting, and all of it was new to both Earl and Lilly.

Everyone had a good time, and everyone was full. There were no leftovers….not a one.

"Is it time yet? Is it? Is it?"

Earl urged; Cord knew the cue.

"Sure, I'll clear the dishes; do you guys have any candles?"

"Yeah, I'll go get some; how many?"

Earl asked.

"I don't know, enough to see, but still make it kind of scary."

"Hey, wait Earl, I'll go get them."

Too late; before she could convince him otherwise, Earl scooted out the door, leaving the two of them alone, sitting side-by-side, at the table.

And suddenly, everything that felt surprisingly comfortable and natural, quickly felt uncomfortable, and unnatural. It immediately felt to him like the two of them, by some fundamental force of nature, shouldn't be in the same room together, alone.

He could sense she felt the same way.

He pretty much knew why he felt that way, as much as he hated to admit it. He hoped he knew why she felt that way as well, but he doubted it.

Lilly didn't know how she felt about Cord; she certainly didn't find him attractive – well, maybe a little attractive, okay-looking at best. The kind of *she wouldn't be embarrassed being seen with him kind of okay-looking* she thought to herself.

He was not nearly as good-looking as Button, she thought, not even in the same league. Nobody could touch Button.   And that stomach had to go; she never was with anyone who wasn't fit – not that she was *with* him in any sense of the word, anyway.

She kind of chuckled to herself that she had been afraid of him earlier; what was there to be afraid of? But by the same token, she was still a bit wary of him; why was he here, in Belvidere, and what was he really up to? Not that she would give a rat's ass otherwise, but since he absconded Earl, she had to care by default. At least that's why she convinced herself she cared.

Regardless of what they were both thinking of, they at least had one thing in common – wishing Earl would hurry back, the quicker the better; he was the security blanket they were both looking for right about now.

"Um, if you want to have a seat, I'll clear the table."

Was all C could think of to say, as he quickly pushed away from the table, to put some physical distance between them. He wasn't sure she was staying for scary stories, he doubted she would – she would surely call it *gay* or some similar barb.

Cord didn't usually eat dessert, and he had figured he bought enough food for him and Earl, not the three of them, especially since Lilly was apparently a pretty good eater herself. So he did not get any take-out dessert.

"Okay."

Was the best response Lillian could muster.

At least she didn't say she was leaving. He figured if he stayed away from her and kept busy, she might stay put and wait for Earl to return. That is what he hoped, anyway. He liked having her here, and didn't want to see her go.

And before that thought left his head, he planted his foot squarely in his mouth.

"Why's your finger all pink?"

Was he a fucking moron? Did he have a split brain?

How could he be thinking about staying quiet and distant, while his mouth was in the process of spewing such a stupid, *stupid* question.

As he said it, he felt his face flush, and it was matching her face, shade for shade. He knew exactly what that pink was right after the words exited his mouth – he didn't even have to look at the aluminum foil wrapping in the closet. The next thought that came into his mind was the soup can – so he *hadn't* missed that it was askew after all – she must have played around with it, like she did around the dinner table, moving shit and fucking with him. He was actually happy about that small bit of good news, for his own sake.

But never mind that, now it was time for damage control. Whatever lame excuse she came up with for that pink finger, he would buy it without question and move on. He had to be convincing in his buy of her lie – they were both good liars, and a liar knows when a liar is lying – they can sniff it in an instant.

But she was uncharacteristically stumbling.

"Uh, uh…."

Was all Lilly could come up with.

Say anything for Christ's sake, and I'll buy it he mentally pleaded with her.

Then his mind started to wander: *When was she in his closet? And why? And how did he miss those pink fingers all through dinner?*

The front door slammed open, thank God, saved by Earl, with an odd pile of candles, all shapes and sizes, cradled in his arms.

He quickly walked away from her; she exhaled in relief, furious at herself for fumbling. That was not like her, she thought; as a last resort, she usually feigns coughing, not an exaggerated fit, just one or two hearty ones, like she's trying to clear her throat – that usually gives her enough time to think. Yet this time, she even forgot that trick. Maybe he'll forget the question – she vowed to keep that left hand out of sight until she sanded her fucking skin off, with a *Brillo* pad if necessary, when she got home.

Earl was walking fast and juggling about fifteen candles of all shapes and sizes, dropping them along the way, like bread crumbs. He lunged into the front room and threw the balance of the lot on the sofa.

"Every candle we got!"

Was all he said.

"Earl!"

"I want lots of light, in case I get scared."

Was his answer to the question she didn't ask.

"Well, I hope you're ready, Earl; *don't fear the reaper!*"

Cord growled in a low, ominous voice. Earl froze in his tracks like a cat that heard something and was debating whether it should stay and listen some more, or just run.

"What's that suppose to mean?"

 Earl sounded positively timid.

"You'll see."

Then Cord let out an exaggerated, maniacal laugh, kind of goofy actually. But the effect worked on Earl. He took off like a shot, right out the door.

"Earl!"

Cord called out.

"Nice, nice job."

"I didn't mean to really scare him, I was just kidding."

"Really?"

She said in mock astonishment, acknowledging the obvious. Then she followed herself.

"He's coming back up, he wouldn't miss *Storytime [Lilly emphasized the sarcasm on that particular word]* for anything in the world. Ten bucks he comes through the door with a box of *Animal Crackers* and the comforter off his bed, oh, and a flashlight. But, then again, that's just a wild guess."

Sure as shit, as Cord walked down the hall toward the door, he could hear the heavy bounding of the big man coming up the steps; the door opened and he appeared, with a big down comforter draped over his shoulder, dragging on the floor. In his right hand was an old-fashioned red metal flashlight. But no cookies were to be seen.

Ay looked back at her with a cocky smile, reveling in her mistake.

"Hey Earl, are you going to share the cookies?"

She asked, in a half-annoyed tone, the kind you use when you're highlighting the obvious stupidity of another.

"Sure! But I want the lions!"

He said as he pulled the box from under the comforter.

She returned the look, in spades. He should have known better.

"Earl, your favorite is not the lion, it's the elephant, or the giraffe, but not the lion. Anyway, I want all the lions."

Now obviously Lilly didn't want the lions, she didn't even eat the ridiculous cookies....it was just the point of stirring the pot, not for any particular reason, just to stir it.

"NO!"

Earl took the bait, like he always did.

She let it drop; she got the reaction she wanted and wasn't in the mood to continue the charade. Cord just shook his head.

"Hey Earl, I know why you like the lions....*good choice*."

Cord chimed in; Earl just smiled and blushed.

"I used to like the giraffe when I was a kid, because they're tall, like I was. But my mom said I had the memory of an elephant, so I wanted to be the elephant. Then Lilly would yell at me and say I had to pick one or the other, I couldn't be both. But mom said I *could* be both, there was no rule on the box about being just one *Animal Cracker,* and from then on I was both, an elephant *and* a giraffe!"

"Good for you Earl, now you can be all three."

Cord said.

"Really? Well, I just want to be the lion now."

"Oh, brother, how do I get sucked into these stupid conversations."

Lilly said in the middle of an annoyed exhale.

"YOU started the conversation!"

Cord said, incredulously.

"I never got to eat them anyway; Lilly would always steal the box out of the groceries and run away before I could even have *one*."

"You are pathetic."

Cord said, as he laughed and shook his head at Lilly.

"If she brought them back, it was only after she bit the heads off all the elephants and giraffes.....every single one."

"Stop fibbing Earl, I didn't do that."

"Did too! Then you just bit the heads off them all, even the lions! No animal was safe!"

"Christ, enough about the *Animal Crackers* already. Okay, let's hear your gay stories."

"You're staying for the stories? Who invited *you* to *Storytime*?"

Cord said.

Now Cord was happy she was going to actually stick around, but he didn't want to be too obvious about it.

"The only way you can stay is if you pony up a story of your own, you know that, right? Those are the rules in this house."

She didn't answer, but she didn't object; good enough for Cord.

"I want to go first!"

Earl exclaimed.

And with that, the two boys set about placing and lighting the candles and shutting off the incandescent, until the front room was aglow in flickering lumens, like the bank of prayer candles in church. Lilly didn't lift a hand to help; she just sat on the sofa and watched. She would never admit it to them, and even though she felt more than a bit juvenile about the whole storytelling charade, she was looking forward to it. She found herself searching her brain for a good story to tell; whatever it was, it had to be better than Cord's. To be better than Earl's was no problem; his were always so corny, at least they were the last time they told stories, which was, God....*years* ago.

Earl sat on the floor with his back against the couch; Lilly sat next to him on the floor. Earl put the comforter over his shoulders like a big shawl, and draped it over Lilly too; she scooted up next to him. Earl smiled warmly, remembering all the story-times they had as kids with their mom. She smiled back.

Two little kids.

Cord had gone into the kitchen, opened the bottle of Merlot from Woody and brought it out, along with three squatty, oversized juice glasses – it was all he had.

"Do you want some?"

"Earl doesn't drink wine."

Lillian answered deadpan for her brother.

Earl chimed in, talking over her.

"I'll try some!"

"Earl!"

Lillian objected, but it was in vain. Cord ignored her and poured himself and Earl the wine. Then he turned to her.

"Are you having any?"

She just looked at him, picked up the tumbler and thrust it toward him, wearing a frown; she was so easy.

He didn't say anything, he just filled the glass. But unlike his and Earl's, he kept filling it; he wasn't going to stop till she said so. She let it go past halfway, realized the game he was playing and pulled the glass away quickly, causing him spill the red wine on the carpet.

"Oops, the landlord's not going to be happy about that one."

She stated, straight-face.

"Yeah, you're right; Earl and I will have to go over and tell her about it tomorrow. How about it Earl?"

To his utter surprise, she immediately got up and went to the kitchen. He heard her fumbling around under the sink, throwing stuff here and there, and slamming the cabinet door. She came back with a medley of cleaners. She worked that spot hard and got that whole stain up, quickly too. As she did it, on all fours, she wagged her ass deliberately in front of his face. He didn't move an inch.

Then she stared at him with a mocking, *fuck-you* look, carelessly threw the cleaners to the side, hitting the wall with them for effect and threw the wet, now-pink white dishrag at his head, hitting him smack in the side of the face.

He didn't flinch; he simply stared at her as the rag briefly stuck to his face, then fell to the carpet beside him. He never uttered a word, he just smirked at her, then turned to Earl, who was carefully sipping his wine, like a connoisseur; his gut was experiencing a whole range of new sensations today, and he was savoring each one.

"You're up, Earl."

Before he started, Earl fingered the switch on the flashlight, over and over, just to be sure it worked, shining the light right in Lilly's face.

On-off, on-off, on-off, on-off....on-off. It was like the *Honeymooners*; Earl was Ed Norton, doing it long enough for Ralph Kramden to get annoyed and yell at him to knock it off.

Lilly was Ralph.

"Would you cut it out for Christ's sake, Earl, *it works!*"

Then he looked at Lilly, smiled mischievously, shifted toward her a bit and cuddled. Without warning or prompting, he kissed her on the cheek and whispered in her ear.

"I love you Lilly."

She hauled back and punched him hard in the arm, just because, then she answered sweet.

"I love you too, Earl."

And she followed the slug by kissing him gently on the cheek in return. Amidst the constant bickering, they said that to one another a lot. Then she fake-punched him in the chest for good measure, it was really more of a light pat than anything else, which made Earl smile.

Earl shifted his ass back and forth a few times on the carpet, like a big bear rubbing his rump on the trunk of a tree. He satisfied the itch, and settled in, cleared his throat and declared.

"Okay, I'm ready."

Then he licked his lips, looked at Cord, and froze; his eyes grew to cueballs and his throat closed.

Stage fright.

Lilly grabbed his hand and squeezed it gently, her loose thumb rubbed back and forth on the back of his hand in a soothing arc of motion.

"Sweetie, just close your eyes and breath. Think about telling mom your *favorite* story; she always liked your stories the best."

Now Lilly almost never talked about her mom with anyone, especially Earl; she even surprised herself. She didn't think about saying that, it just came out. But she knew what Earl's reaction would be, and she was glad she said it. Earl just smiled as he turned his head toward her; his eyes were already closed, just like she told him too, and he leaned over and kissed her softly on the top of her forehead. He was so much taller, to lean over further was always a chore.

Now he was really ready, and so he began.

Dinosaurs on the prowl.

Earl hunched his shoulders a bit as he began his story, scaring himself as he spoke. His head went turtle and the blanket covered his noggin like a babushka, till all you could see were the whites of his eyes.

"I was all curled up in a ball, hiding in the yellow flower bush; what's that called again Lilly?"

"You know it's a forsythia bush Earl, keep going."

"Yeah, that thing, when, I mean, I forgot what I was saying....oh yeah, the bush is right next to the road, it's a long bush, the length of a big yellow school bus, and you can crawl through it, like a secret tunnel, and be hidden. Anyway, I'm hiding in the bush, I'm all alone, Bibby's not with me, mom's not with me, it's just me, all alone. Looking through the twigs, I can see out, but you can't see in, you know, and I'm looking up the road, towards the *Big Hill.* Remember the *Big Hill* Lilly?"

"Yes, Earl, I remember....keep going.*"*

"Okay, anyway, the ground started shaking, and I start shaking, cause I'm scared, just looking at the very tippy-top of the *Big Hill*, but I don't see anything. I start to squint, it's getting dark out. It's not all dark yet, but getting dark, pretty dark, and I know something is coming up the hill from the other side, I can hear it, but I just can't see it. I squint some more. I know it's coming up the hill, coming up to the top, where I'm hiding, it's just out of sight, but it's getting closer, and closer, it's rumbling the ground, and getting even closer.

Just then I think maybe I'm not hidden enough, maybe it can see me in the bushes after all! And I start to get up to run out of the bush, I've got to find somewhere safer to hide. But I waited too long! Just as I start to, you know, stand up to run out of the bush, I see something move up there, over there *[Earl quickly pointed to his left with his hand still hidden under the comforter]*.

Right at the *Big Hill*, right at the *very top*, just barely peeking over the top, I see something move, like a big alligator popping his eyes out of the water. But it's not an alligator! It's a head! It's a big head of a Tyrannosaurus Rex! And he's just poking his head up past the tippy-tip of the *Big Hill*, spying like sneaky dinosaurs do!

It's looking for something to eat, anything that moves, even just a little, it's gonna eat. *Anything!*

It was only from here to across the street away *[Earl pointed behind himself at Water Street, then quickly put his hand back under the comforter for safety]*, and it was looking all around. I could hear it slowly breath through its nose, it made a gurgle sound like it's nose was stuffed up, like he had a cold, or something, spitting snots out as it breathed. And I was really scared, and its teeth were big, and white, and sharp! And there was stuff stuck to its teeth, parts of clothes and people it *already ate*!

It moved its head back and forth, back and forth, looking....looking.

I shut my eyes and held my breath, hoping it would go away. Maybe if I shut my eyes and held my breath, it wouldn't see me; that usually works for me, that's my trick, you know. Anyway, I held my breath as long as I could, and when I couldn't hold my breath any longer, I breathed.

But I breathed too loud!

I slowly opened my eyes, just a little, just a little squeak, enough to see if it was safe, if the big head with the big teeth had gone away.

And it did! It was gone! There was no monster head by the top of the *Big Hill*.   I was safe! And I yelled as I could.

"Yeah, I'm safe!"

Just then, I heard some leaves crunch and saw something move over there *[Earl pointed to his right, then scrunched his shoulders and buried his head in the blanket like a turtle]*.

And the big green Tyrannosaurus head peaked out from behind some trees and looked right at the bush I was in! The head was this big! Even bigger *[Earl whispered, as he tried to show how big it was, but he refused to take his hands out from under the blanket]*!

It squinted its yellow eyes and growled through its open mouth, which was dripping long strings of yucky drool on the ground. I saw someone's eyeball stuck between its teeth, with big gooey strings attached to it!

Then I figured out what had happened, and why it was drooling so much; it was still hungry, and….and….

IT SAW ME! RUN! RUN! RUN! AHH!!"

Earl lurched forward as he began to stand, spreading his arms under the comforter like the wings of a big bat and wailed a blood-curdling scream at the top of his lungs, leaning like a monster toward Cord, a dinosaur on the attack, causing both Cord and Lilly to jump out of their skins. Cord instinctively leaped back and fell into the wall. Lilly just went vertical and screeched. Glasses of wine tumbled over and candles flew through the air.

Pandemonium reigned.

Now Cord had no idea that outburst was coming, he could be forgiven for the sudden startle. But Lilly had heard this same dinosaur story roughly a thousand times since she was a kid, it's was Earl's go-to story, so she had no excuse. But jump she did, right along with Cord; her left foot landed on a candlestick, she lost her balance and fell in slow motion to her side, away from the action.

The two of them jumping around and yelling scared Earl even more than he had scared himself, which caused him to start screaming banshee from underneath the blanket, spinning in circles with his arms flailing in the air, like a little kid.

"WHAT? WHAT'S HAPPENING? WHERE'S THE DINOSAUR?!"

Earl was trying to figure who saw the dinosaur and what direction it was heading without actually coming up for air from beneath the safety of the comforter.

In all his spinning, Earl got dizzy, lost his balance and fell over the coffee table by the sofa, crashing onto the floor in a heap. The concussion of almost four hundred pounds of meat wrapped in a blanket shook the bones of the apartment and knocked a picture off the wall; it glanced off Earl's shoulder and landed on the carpet next to his head, still hidden under the blanket. Thinking dinosaur, Earl shuttered and freed a high-pitched girlie-yelp.

Cord gathered himself, propped against the wall, and assessed the carnage; *those wine stains definitely weren't coming out*, he thought to himself, looking at his new rose-red rug.

"Jesus, Earl!"

Was all Lilly could come up with. And as quickly as it started, it was over.

Earl was much too wound from the excitement and fright to continue his story, which, if he *had* continued, would have seen him run out of the bushes and into a nearby house, where he ran in circles, from room to room, hiding under tables and beds, all while the T-Rex slowly circled the house, drooled some more and sneaked peaks into windows, waiting for the right moment to snatch up and eat him.

The story would go on and on, endless circling of the house; the T-Rex would never actually go for the lunge and eat Earl – it was simply in a perpetual *stalk-and-growl* mode. The story would end when either Lilly or their mom got tired and would ask if that's how it ended, and Earl would always be glad to say yes, no matter where he was in the story, happy to stop thinking about the dinosaur and his role as an elusive appetizer.

"Whew, that was a close one."

Earl breathed a sincere sigh of relief, finally poking his head out from under the safety of the comforter.

"Wow, what a mess!"

Earl whispered aloud, as he assessed the scene. Cord made a half-hearted attempt to sop up the wine soaked into the Berber carpet, but it was futile, and he knew it.

"Why the hell were *you* jumping around? It's not like you haven't heard that one before!"

Cord scolded Lilly, as he gathered and righted the candles which fell victim to the melee, re-lighting them as he went along, and happy the place wasn't on fire.

Lilly ignored his comment and poured herself another drink, and proceeded, without offer or request, to fill both Cord's and Earl's now-empty tumblers. Right then, by the way she poured, a bit shaky, C knew if they could get their hands on another bottle or two of wine, they were all getting drunk. He could just feel it.

Lilly drunk could be fun, or dangerous, he wasn't sure which, but he had a feeling he was going to find out.

They all re-settled into their respective seats on the floor, sitting closer together this time around. They clinked glasses, all smiled at memories of the melee, and took hearty swigs of wine. Two trickles of red dripped down both sides of Earl's mouth; he wiped his face clean with his sleeve.

The next storyteller began.

Cord started to speak slowly, in a low, ominous tone.

"Now, there isn't much that's scarier than getting chased and eaten by dinosaurs, except, that is, if you find yourself alone, in the middle of the night, hiding under the covers in your bed, knowing you are slowly being stalked by a demon - a crazed, man-puppet. And he *will* get you."

That was all it took; Earl was already back under the blanket; he dragged Lilly under with him, not that she struggled much. As both their wine-infused faces peeked from beneath the safety of the blanket babushka, Cord began the weave of a tale of terror.

CHAPTER 37 – THE MANIACAL CRY OF THE DEAD

Cord stared with blank, lifeless eyes at Earl and slowly shook his head side to side, forewarning of what he was about to say.

In the candlelight, Cord's face was crossed with shadow, making it hard to detect inflection in his eyes, in his mouth.

Lilly and Earl, both feeling the effects of the alcohol, found themselves leaning toward C involuntarily, waiting for him to speak. Earl's heart was already pounding in his chest; he was sure everyone heard it. He squeezed Lilly's hand; she squeezed back, but didn't take her fogged eyes off Cord.

Cord started to speak in the slightest of whispers; the two were inches from his face, yet they could barely hear him.

"I was *in* the house, *upstairs,* in the same bedroom, the very last one at the end of the long narrow hall, with nowhere else to go, nowhere else to hide, and I *saw* it all happen. I can't explain how, but what I'm about to say is true *[Cord paused a bit, to let the statement settle].*

But to understand the story, you first need to understand the crickets, and you need to understand the flies *[As Cord finished his sentence, he suddenly ducked his head, dodging something that flew by].*

Did you see that? They always come when I tell this story. Always *[Earl tried to look around as best he could, without emerging from under the blanket. Lilly frowned at Cord's sideshow antics, unamused, but not entirely convinced that something didn't actually just fly by; Cord continued].*

In scattered areas around the globe, from Barbados in the Lesser Antilles, to China in the Far East, to Zambia in the Sub-Saharan Dark Continent, to find a lone cricket in your home is considered a harbinger of good luck: needed rain, financial windfall....*hope.*

But the visit isn't always an omen of good fortune; to the contrary, in some places, to find a cricket within your walls is feared, for the news they foretell is never pleasant....and never welcome.

In the remote, northeastern State of *Alagoas,* where poor Brazilian farmers live and die on vast sugar cane plantations, a place where endless acres of *Saccharum* grass swim in a sea of poverty, in that remote outpost, according to legend, the chirp of the cricket at your feet portends certain death.

Alagoas peasants hardly stand alone; crickets carry the ill wind of pestilence and *morte* elsewhere, places I have been, places I have seen, including a place you both know, all too well *[Cord pointed to the both of them under the blanket].* A place not far from where we now sit....*not very far at all [Cord looked down to the floor, right through the floor, to the apartment below. He paused again, took a long draw of wine, and continued his yarn].* And where there's the cricket, comes another. A parasitoid; a cunning little parasite, the tachinid fly....*Ormia Ochracea.*

It's just a small, yellow fly, hardly given to notice. But that tiny fly has awfully large orange eyes, the kind you can't help but notice *[Cord stared directly into Earl's eyes as he spoke the words].*

The *Ochracea* is a very scary little fly indeed.

On warm summer nights, when the crickets come out, a cacophony of chirps fill the night air, solitary males pining, longing, to find a mate.

He loved to listen to the crickets while he laid in bed on those warm summer nights.

But he wasn't the only one who loved the cricket's song; *Ochracea* loves to hear the crickets sing too.

It waits in the dark, patiently, silently, for the males to start chirping. The female fly can hear *exceptionally* well, more so when she's gravid, carrying a belly full of hungry maggots, waiting for the crickets to call.

She'll find them, she always does. She'll either light on their back or machine-gun a swarm as she flies by, coating the cricket with a black mass of squirming larvae.

It doesn't take long; the writhing maggots know just what to do. In an instant, they chew and burrow deep into their unsuspecting host.

Warm and safe inside, they immediately begin to gorge on live cricket flesh. And oh, are they *ravenous*.

The larvae turn and spin as they feast on the cricket's insides, growing ever larger as they slowly digest their host alive. For days, the hapless cricket still calls out for a mate, unsuspecting, all the while serving as an endless gorge for the voracious, squirming, maggots.

After a week, maybe less, the larvae, fat and ready to pop, shred the live cricket to pieces as they burst out of it's body.

That's what the orange-eyed flies do in *Alagoas,* just like they do in other places I've been, just like they do *right here [Cord stopped for a moment and stared at the two of them, both mesmerized, tucked deep in the blanket. He took another long, slow drink of wine, exhaling deep and slow].*

And so it began.

He didn't know the time, but it was after 2 am, of that he was reasonably sure. It was Indian summer, when you sleep with the windows open and the slightest of night breezes wafts over you....a sweet massage.

Sometimes on nights like that, he would awake in a start, for no particular reason. He never knew why. Once awake, he would lay quiet and listen to the cricket's raspy courtship stridulation, the rubbing of hind leg against forewing, till he drifted back to sleep. He loved to hear them sing, hiding out there, somewhere, unseen in the dark. It was a sweet tonic.

He awoke *that* night to the familiar night breeze and the chirping drone of thousands. But *that* particular night, it just felt different, *very* different.

That's when he heard, distinct from the blackness beyond his window screen, the lone cricket, hiding somewhere, unseen, in his bedroom.

It chirped quietly, irregularly, almost hesitantly, a genetic need to mate apparently tempered, conflicted, by caution. He found himself straining, arching his head off the pillow, to trace its origin, to try and separate it from the medley of calls in the wilds outside.

It was *so* close; it must be under the bed, he thought, maybe even *in* the bed, under the covers. It must be *very, very, close.*

And then it stopped. As if it knew what was to happen next, it abruptly stopped.

The long side of his bed lay directly against the outside wall, the top tucked just beneath the windowsill. The window was set beside his pillow. Prone, if he turned his head to the left, he would be looking out the second-story window, just above the height of the sill.

But in this case, the Venetian blinds were turned slightly downward, enough to let the summer air pass through the screen, but too far to afford a view, to heed happenings in the world beyond the sill.

He blinked his eyes hard, several times, trying to force out the sleep. He rubbed them with his thumb and forefinger, and blinked some more. Then he slowly grabbed the blind rod, turned it clockwise, and opened his ken to the quiet street below.

He scanned the scene; the crowned asphalt-tar road was recently chipped, just the week before. The new layer of white and gray quartz gravel hadn't yet been driven into the base tar by passing traffic, rather, it lay thick on the road in front of the house. He saw the simple black lamppost adjacent to the driveway and the curved concrete walk, which led to the three-stepped fieldstone and mortar front stoop, covered with a portico, sporting a weathered Dutch hex sign. The heavy, six-panel wood entry door was painted a dulled yellow; the brass knocker in the shape of a lion's head.

The lamppost was dimly lit with an amber bulb, which cast a soft yellow halo around its base, barely extending into the shoulder of the road, the driveway and the walk.

That light was never on, he thought; who turned on the lamplight tonight, and kept it on till this early hour?

Odd.

He turned his head slowly to the left, and gazed down the empty street, to the intersection with Lawrie Avenue, about eighty feet away. There wasn't a car on the road, there rarely was, and certainly not at this hour.

A lone streetlight illuminated the intersection; a large, thick pine, over a hundred feet tall, stood abreast the street post for Randolph Avenue, the road on which he lived. There were three houses across the street within his view – all cloaked in darkness, fast asleep.

The lamppost and streetlight lumens were the only glow to pierce the night, the crickets the only sound to tickle his ears. The warm, eventide air blew through the tiny holes in the screen; he felt it lightly kiss his cheek.

It was a serene setting, a perfect night.

Why was it that he awoke? He thought as he lay there, propped up on one elbow, gazing lazy out the window.

Whack!

[Cord yelled and slapped the back of his hand into his open palm in a hard clap, startling the two of them hiding beneath the blanket]

The first cricket hit the screen hard, a cannon-shot, and stuck in the mesh, instantly followed by two dozen more, a machine-gun clip, all chirping furiously. The wire mesh bowed in from the force of the impact.

Instinctively he jumped back from the screen; it took a second to realize what it was, and what had happened.

A shot of adrenaline raced through his veins; the hair on his arms stood at attention.

You don't *see* crickets chirp, he thought. You hear them chirp, or see them silent….never both.

The whole screen vibrated as they sang furious.

Was he awake? Was this real?

He cautiously approached the screen, leaning until his face was against the blind louvers, inches from the crickets. He focused his gaze on one, the closest, an oversized cricket chirping away, clinging hard to the metal screen.

It pined frenetic, but it seemed fine, it seemed happy.

And he started to smile.

But as he looked closer, the whole underbelly began to violently vibrate. Suddenly the cricket's head guillotined and shot into the darkness, as its body cracked, cleaving in two.

Two large, slimed maggots slowly squirmed from the head cavity and stuck to the screen, trying to pass through one of the rectangular openings, toward his face. They were too gorged to fit, but they strained against the wire, fighting to get into his bedroom.

Two dozen chirping crickets stuck to the screen instantly exploded in a mass of swollen maggots and digested innards, the larvae crawling on the mesh, some so swollen they simply fell to the ground, two stories below. He could hear them pelt the leaves of the mountain laurel below his window.

A shot of adrenaline jolted him as he withdrew from the screen in horror. He could feel the bile rise in his throat, ready to retch.

 It can't be real!

He called to his brother to wake; he could see the very top of his head, his jet-black hair, barely extending from beneath the covers, but he didn't stir. That was his hair, wasn't it? Was it hair? Or something else?

His mind raced, switching conclusions in rapid-fire.

Yes, that was black hair, it *must* be his brother's hair, right?

He stared intently at the sheets, squinting in the darkness, and watched the covers slowly rise and fall with his brother's breathing. He was alive; he must be alive.

He tried to yell over to him, but his voice was weak and low; no matter how hard he tried, it was muffled....useless. He tried to get up and fetch him, but found his legs wouldn't respond.

His brother lay still nearby, but he wouldn't wake, he wouldn't respond....he couldn't help.

He squeezed his eyes shut in a long, hard blink, wishing away the scene.

And just as sudden as it began, it was silent; there wasn't the sound of a single cricket, not a one.

Except the one in his room, the one that must be in his bed, right beside him. A single chirp.

Then silence.

He slowly opened his eyes; the screen was empty, clear of crickets, maggots and innards.

Were they really ever there? Was he really awake?

He ran his hand up and down his arm, he felt his own touch; it felt real, it felt conscious. Nightmares don't feel like this.

He turned and inched closer to the screen, raising the Venetian blinds slowly, as quietly as he could, so he could put his face right to the metal meshing.

Nothing; he saw nothing but the quiet street scene, just as before.

He kept his face quietly pressed against the mesh, breathing light, looking left to right, up and down, for any evidence of the carnage he witnessed.

Nothing.

He let out a long, low exhale, a sigh of relief. It was then he felt something lightly strike his right cheek. It was like a droplet of rain….a small bit of spittle.

A second one glanced the side of his nose, a third his lips and partially open mouth, landing soft on the tip of his tongue. He went to wipe it away, whatever it was, and found he couldn't move his hands; they were leaden - he couldn't make them work. He went to spit – to eject the foreign object, but found he couldn't, his face was frozen to the screen.

That's when he saw it.

The first set of large orange eyes, staring at him through the screen.

He blinked but once; now there were hundreds, thousands, of orange eyes and elfin yellow bodies stuck to the mesh, inches from his face. The amalgamate buzz of fly wings grated his eardrums, the high-pitch like fingernails on a chalkboard.

More shots of liquid peppered him through the mesh, in a viscous film of mucous.

He could feel his skin pinch; he felt a burn, like acid. He knew they were burrowing in, hundreds of voracious maggots into his face, his nose, his eyes, his mouth. And he couldn't stop them; he felt another wave of spittle spray his face, more black, squirming larvae shot onto him. An endless tidal assault.

Thousands of orange eyes focused on him, a live host for their ravenous offspring. He tried to scream, but no voice emerged.

Suddenly, somehow, his muscles worked; he pulled away from the window mesh, the drone of fly wings, the thousands of orange eyes.

But as he desperately clawed at his skin, nose and mouth, it was already too late; they had safely burrowed in, all of them. Black, empty wormholes were all that remained.

He ran his fingers quickly across his face and felt the larvae turning under the surface, moving…eating. He pinched his cheek and felt one squirm between his fingers; he clawed himself to dig it out – flesh ripped and blood poured down his cheek, down his neck, as he dug his nails deep.

But it was for naught; they were in too deep, and there were simply too many.

He had to simply wait, while the starved larvae slowly digested his insides, feeding until their engorged bodies would split him apart, decapitate him, crawling from the open hole that held his head.

He looked to his brother for comfort and help, but he offered neither, quietly sleeping, unaware, unharmed. He sat alone in his bed and waited, feeling thousands of maggots crawling through him, under his skin, eating him alive.

It was then that he first heard the call. The very first time.

A slight, ever so faint, whisper, in a slow, deep baritone. It was as if someone, something, had pressed their lips against his head, the moist hot breath tickled the tiny hairs inside his ear, the tongue lightly flicking his skin as each word was spoken. It was a simple phrase, uttered ominous.

"I'm going to get you."

Once again it was silent.

He heard himself quietly breathing. The thousand orange eyes were gone, the crawl under his skin had ceased and the wormholes vanished, the infestation disappeared as quick as it came. He was whole once again.

And it was quiet on Randolph Avenue.

Except for a second whisper in his ear. This, the high-pitched shrill of a maniacal child.

"I'm going to get you!"

He felt himself slowly pulled, involuntarily, back to the screen. He couldn't stop it, iron filings to a magnet. Again he canvassed the road below. But nothing was to be seen, just the glow of the lights and the tickle of the night breeze.

Nothing.

Except for a single cricket chirp, the one that must be right beside him in the bed....*it was very, very close.* But still out of sight.

A single chirp, then silence.

He peered out the window, straining his eyes, first to the right, up the street - nothing but ink. He looked to the left, down to the majestic pine by the street post, at the intersection.

And that's when he first saw it, beside the evergreen. It somehow went from hidden to exposed, but he never saw how it got there. It must have been hiding behind the pine.

It wasn't there, and then it was.

It was a neatly dressed little man, with a bow-tie, jacket and matching pants, but he looked too small to be an adult, and it wasn't a child. It didn't even look human.

It looked like an oversized doll, some sort of man-puppet.

He squeezed his eyes shut and open again.

It *was* a puppet.

It had exaggerated facial features, painted in once-bright colors, with a hinged lower jaw. It wore an overall dinge; dirty, unkempt, neglected….forgotten.

It stood motionless under the dim glow of the streetlight, slightly hunched, head bowed, as if a battery switch was toggled to the *off*.

It had the disturbing look of an old *Danny O'Day* ventriloquist doll. The creep-face was frozen in an expression that wasn't happy, nor was it forgiving, nor was it kind. It was somehow *off*; it somehow just didn't *look* right.

And this puppet stood upright, alone; there was no hand, no puppet-master, to guide it.

Then suddenly, as if it came to life consequent to his gaze, the puppet slowly raised its dirty, dimpled chin off its chest and looked up, with round eyes, yellowed and bloodshot. It swiveled its head and gazed right toward him, right into the second-story bedroom window, eighty feet away. Its mouth was closed, its eyes dead.

And then he heard the frightening whisper, the same whisper he heard twice before. Its high pitch cut through him.

Now he *knew* from where it came, and the words were so crisp, so close, it sounded as if the puppet was sitting right beside him.

"I'm going to get you!"

With that, its over-sized eyes opened extra wide and rolled back in its head.

It had real eyes!

It sprung open its jaw, like the ugly snap of a bear-trap, exposing a wide-open mouth, with a full set of brilliant white teeth. It slowly swiveled its head left to right and quickly snapped its mouth open and shut, over and over, its teeth making an awful gnashing sound, all while it laughed in a demonic, shrill howl.

The mannequin slowly started to walk up the street, toward the house, in a herky-jerk, stop-motion manner, like a marionette without strings. Every ten steps or so it would stop, slowly swivel its head and look up at the window, drop open his mouth and rapidly gnash its teeth together. He could hear the loose, road gravel crunch under foot as it ever-approached.

The doll left the dull orb of light at the far street corner; he could still hear it kick the gravel with each footstep, but it was hidden in the shadows of the night. Out of sight, but getting closer....and closer.

In the darkness, he would hear it stop and click its teeth, followed by a demonic, high-pitched laugh; he knew it had swiveled its head and was looking directly at him.

He just knew it.

He slammed shut the storm window, closed the blinds, rolled over and pulled the blankets over his head.

And waited.

It *must* all be just a dream, just a bad dream; he rolled the thought over and again in his head, trying to convince himself it simply can't be real.

Gulping the stale, hot air under the blanket, he noticed that everything had become quiet once again. He didn't hear the gravel kick, or the whisper in his ear, or the sickening laugh. He waited, frozen and prone, straining to hear something….anything.

But he heard nothing.

He poked his head slowly from beneath the blanket and turned to see his brother lightly stir and roll over; everything was okay, everything was safe.

He exhaled a long sigh and looked at the window. The blinds were again turned slightly downward and the window was open, just as it was when he first slipped between the sheets. The crickets were lightly chirping again, like they always did, and a warm night breeze licked his face.

He *did* dream the whole thing, thank God. He let out a long breath. And for a moment, he felt foolish. But the feeling soon turned to apprehension; he wondered if it would all happen again.

And with that, he lay frozen, breathing quietly, waiting for the cricket hidden in the room to announce itself, a single chirp, like it had done before, before the bad things began.

But nothing happened; no chirp….nothing.

He stared at the ceiling, blinked, and felt his heart beating normally. He smiled in relief, like one does when awakened to realize it had all been just a bad dream.

Just a bad dream.

But then his mind began to wander; why does it always have to wander? He tried to reason, to make sense of all that had happened, or hadn't happened, that night.

And the wandering led him to this; he just had to be sure.

He leaned over to the window, turned the wooden rod clockwise and slowly opened the blinds to see. His heart raced just a bit as the louvers rotated away and the leitmotif unfolded before him.

The street was quiet; he looked down to the left – down to the towering pine at the intersection, and the road was empty and safe. He smiled and an uplift of calm washed over him.

As he smiled, his gaze casually fell toward the amber glow of the lamppost, below his second floor window, to that light that was never on.

And that's when he saw it. It was in the front yard, adjacent the mountain laurel, just below his bedroom window.

Its oversized head slightly askew, looking skyward at him, stood the man-puppet, with yellow, bloodshot eyes. It was so close he could see the gray lint lay in the wrinkles of its soiled jacket and pants, along with a smudge of grime across the peel of its painted face. It was as if it had laid in wait, in a dirty, forgotten place, for this night to finally arrive.

When it knew he was looking, it deliberately swiveled its head in a quick-jerk and snapped open its mouth, showing him a full set of now-corrupt, malignant teeth.

And there seemed to be many more of them filling the widened gape of its mouth; they massed angular, sharper....dangerous. The once brilliant-white teeth had morphed to yellow and stained, with the earthen-brown tinge of rot *spider*ing the roots, coated opaque with a thick film of saliva.

He didn't hear the crickets anymore; all he heard was a low, deep whisper in his ear.

"No more silly games; now I'm going to get you."

Followed by the sickening click of its teeth, and the shrill laugh of a child possessed. Long stria of drool spilled from its mouth, dangling as they made their way to the ground, pooling at its feet.

His blood chilled and he again froze in fear; he couldn't move his arms or legs.

He watched helpless as the doll advanced in a jerk-motion up the concrete walk, mumbling and laughing quietly to itself as it climbed the three steps on the front porch. He heard it grab the doorknob and jiggle it; he could hear it out the window - at the same time, he heard the noise down the hall, from within the house.

The front door was locked; his father must have locked the door!

He heard the faint sound of whispering and a sickening snicker, like one who talks to himself in demented amusement, while assessing the task at hand.

He strained to put his head against the window screen, to see if it got in, to see where it went, what it was doing.

Then he heard faint scratching on the wood shingle siding, and he knew it must be crawling up the side of the house.

He jumped back and tried to shut the window, but as much as he leaned on it, it wouldn't budge. He didn't try to call to his brother for help; he knew that was useless.

The scratching on the wood shakes was getting closer; it must be just below his window, barely out of sight. The closer the puppet got, the more he felt himself pulled, helpless, toward the screen. He couldn't stop himself, his face pinned fast against the mesh, the metal pressing into his cheeks, checkering his skin.

The scratching was close now, it was *right* below the sill, inches from his face. His eyes were wedged wide open; he couldn't shut them. He heard the *click-click....click-click* of its teeth and a sickening light laugh, followed by its deliberate, slow, breathing, labored breathing, followed by a slight giggle and a mumble of incoherent words that made no sense:

Kitty Cow Go Moo

The puppet was *so close*, inches below the sill, but still out of view. He could smell its disease....a putrid mixture of mold, canker and rancid meat. In a moment, it would be only inches from his face, separated by the thickness of the wire mesh screen.

Why was it waiting?

He heard it chuckle, just once, right as he saw the slight curve of the top of its head, the oily mat of filthy brown hair, just below the sill.

He knew it was ready to come right through the screen, and he was helpless to stop it. His heart pounded, waiting for it to attack, to sink its razor teeth through the screen, into his face, and tear him apart.

He was still immobile, stuck to the screen, eyes glued open, staring straight ahead, waiting for the reaper to slowly raise its head above the sill, its dead eyes to meet his.

Then there was nothing.

The top of its head had disappeared; he heard not a single breath, nor trace of a chuckle....the smell of death had faded away.

There was simply nothing.

And it remained so for what seemed forever, but really was simply seconds. Because where he was, where he found himself, time worked like that, because it wasn't really time at all, it was something else. Something entirely different, which didn't have a name.

And then the nothingness ended.

Outside the window, he heard a distant click of teeth as the big wooden front door creaked open and slowly click shut.

The puppet was *in* the house!

His face peeled from the screen, like a magnet switched to *off*; he collapsed into the bed, and immediately craned his neck to listen. There was a swinging, knotty-pine door on the first floor, immediately off the entry foyer, which led to the second floor, where he quietly lay. To the wood was affixed an old spring, to keep it closed.

The door didn't stay closed for long.

He heard the large, coiled spring strain and stretch as the large pine door was carefully, slowly, swung open, followed by the same sequence as the spring relaxed into itself and the knotty planks quietly tapped shut, tempered by an unseen hand. A second of silence was soon followed by the dull thud of shoes on the stairway carpet runner, accompanied by the creak and moan of old, wooden treads, as the puppet began its ascent to the second floor.

One step, two steps, three, then stop. There were thirteen steps to the second floor landing; the doll stopped on step three.

The only route out of the house was to pass the puppet on that staircase, unless he leapt out the window. But he wasn't going anywhere; his legs had again turned leaden….useless.

It began moving again, climbing steps four, five and six, followed by a childish giggle and a triple-snap of its teeth.

Followed by nothing.

The cat, *his* cat, meowed – a single call. It was followed by a short giggle and a mumbled whisper. Another faint meow followed, cut short by snapping teeth, then silence. He never heard the cat again.

He peered into the darkness, down the short hall that led from his bedroom door. A small nightlight in a baseboard outlet provided thin illumination, nothing more than a dim orange haze, which barely washed the far corner of the hall, where it turned ninety degrees and extended to the stairwell the puppet climbed.

The manikin had seven steps to go; he looked for a weapon, something, but he had nothing, just a pillow and blankets.

He heard the distinct tap of its shoe on the hardwood landing; it somehow skipped the last seven steps, arriving at the top of the stairs. It was now less than ten feet to turn the hall corner and head directly at him, down the short path to the bedroom, with its open wide door.

His heart was pounding; there was nowhere to hide.

He heard it for the last time, spoken through a snicker, along with the clicking of its teeth.

"I'm going to get you!"

The puppet finished the words just as its left leg emerged from around the corner.

He closed his eyes hard and imagined dying.

Everything went black, and it was quiet once again on Randolph Avenue. No more footsteps.

He slowly opened his lids and spied the hallway; there was no laughing, no sickening click of its teeth....just silence.

No puppet.

His head turned to look at his brother, still fast asleep across the room. His head barely sticking from beneath the sheets. Was that his head? It didn't look quite right.

Then, from the corner of his eye, at the very bottom of his bed, to the left of his feet, he saw a small lump in the comforter; it might have just been a fold in the blanket.

That fold wasn't there before.

He stared at it, intently, mixing in the murk of the room. It seemed to rock a bit, back and forth, but he couldn't tell, since it was swaddled in the shadows. Did it really move?

He felt control of his legs, but he was afraid to sweep his limb toward it, or away from it; he just lay there frozen, for what seemed forever, not moving a muscle, waiting for something to happen. His legs started to tingle; they had fallen asleep.

He stared at the fold till his eyes saw double; staring....staring at the folds in the dark.

And then the fold in the comforter started to move; it was *clearly* moving. And it **wasn't** a fold; something was in his bed, hiding under the blanket. And it was slowly moving toward him.

It looked to be the size of a cat, a *large* cat.

Without warning, like the scurry of a roach, it tore right at him, scratching and clawing the sheets beneath the blanket as if it had talons. He squeezed his eyes shut, held his breath and tried to scream. Not a sound emerged from his lips.

And nothing happened.

His chest heaved in fear, but his bedroom, once again, was silent. He slowly cracked open his left eye, barely, peering through his eyelashes.

The lump under the blanket had grown in size, and was now *inches* from his face, separated only by the thickness of the fabric. He could hear it breathing; light, fast breathing, as the blanket moved in and out; a small wet circle of saliva emerged in the fabric, which slowly started to grow. The room filled rancid.....the smell of death.

Whatever hid below the blanket began to rise beside him, the blanket falling away, revealing utter blackness in the void.

A shape emerged, and he saw it, followed by the same four words, in the shrill of a tortured child:

Kitty Cow Go Moo

The hair on his neck rose and he screamed, but no sound emerged. The last thing he heard, before it went black, was a *click-click*; the last thing he saw was yellow, red and white....infinite white.

And then there was nothing.

His brother rolled over and pulled the blanket from his face, unsure of what had awakened him.

He looked over to see his younger brother, a lump tucked firm under the blanket. He called to him, but there was no response; he only seemed to stir, to sway a bit under the sheets, then stop.

It was Indian summer, when you sleep with the windows open and the slightest of night breezes wafts over you....a sweet massage.

On warm summer nights, when the crickets come out, a cacophony of chirps fill the night air, solitary males pining, longing, to find a mate. His brother loved to listen to the crickets while he laid in bed on those warm summer nights.

He loved to hear them sing, hiding out there, somewhere, unseen in the dark.

That's when he heard, distinct from the blackness beyond the bedroom window, the single chirp of a lone cricket, hiding in his room.

[Cord stopped his monologue, just for a moment, then softly whispered]

"I know what I say is true, because I was *in* the house, I was *upstairs,* in the bedroom, and I *saw* it happen....I **made** it happen."

[And with that, Cord rolled his eyes back in his head, clicked his teeth together, followed by the maniacal cry of the dead]

CHAPTER 38 - I'M DRUNK, LET'S DO IT! AND SO THEY DID

"Well, what did you think?"

Cord said casually, as he took another taste of wine.

Earl and Lilly had long since cinched the blanket shut, no part of them was showing, not even the whites of their eyes, at least as far back as when the puppet was standing under the bedroom window.

He saw the blanket slowly open. He didn't know Earl's eyes could get so big; Lilly lost her annoyed face too; she would never admit it, but she was truly creeped out.

"Where did you come up with that ridiculous story? Killer crickets, flies and dolls; please, how corny."

Lilly said, from under the comforter. Earl didn't buy it for a minute.

"You were scared Lilly, you were! You kept squeezing my hand like the puppet was going to get you, right under the blanket!"

"Did not Earl; stop lying!"

She bit back, trying to convince herself she wasn't really scared. But she wasn't very successful. Earl shook his head in secret to C, letting him know she *was* scared, and don't believe her, she was squeezing like crazy! But Earl didn't dare say it out loud, for fear of his sister's wrath from under the blanket.

C smirked at the exchange.

"They aren't killer crickets, by the way; the crickets are the ones who *get* killed. I had that dream a bunch of times as a kid, the first time was when I was twelve. It's been thirty-odd years, but I remember it, every detail, like it was yesterday. It was as vivid as I just told you, like it was scripted, just for me.   Scared the shit out of me.

You know, I dreamt the name of that little fly, said it in my head - *Ormia Ochracea*. I obviously had never heard of such a thing, certainly as a twelve-year-old, yet it was dead-on right; that fly not only exists, the name was right, the yellow body, the big orange eyes, eating crickets….all true. I could have never known all that, the Latin name even, especially as a little kid, yet I did. I knew it all, and I don't know how, or why. And that's the truth….that's the scariest part of all.

I've never even seen one, for real, the fly, that is, and I've never seen a cricket infested with them, but it happens….they really exist. It's all true.

Except for the puppet, that is. I assume that one's a bit of a stretch. I don't think he really exists; what do you think Earl?"

Now Earl's eyes were the size of saucers, his mouth partly open in awe. But he answered C with both force and conviction, a man with his mind made up.

"I'm sleeping up here tonight, that's what I think!"

"Earl! You're not sleeping up here, don't be a big baby."

Lilly squawked.

"Didn't you **listen** to the story? We live on the *second* floor! The ***second*** floor! And my room is closer to the windows! He's gonna eat me first!"

"Earl, didn't you hear him laugh at the end? ***He's*** the dummy!"

Lilly didn't plan the pun, but smiled nonetheless, amused at how brilliant she mistakenly was.

"I don't care, I'm sleeping up here; *you* go down there with the crickets and flies, *not me!*"

Lilly threw up her hands in exasperation.

"What do you care where he sleeps; perhaps it's that **you're** scared?

Cord offered, with Earl nodding in acknowledgment.

"Am not!"

My God, she sounded like a five-year old, defending herself, she thought.

"Fine, have your little *sleepover* up here with your gay friend; how old are you two anyway? For Christ sake, it's embarrassing."

They both looked at her and just smirked; neither said a word.

"How about *your* ghost story? Are you going to top mine, or are we done?"

Cord said, as he downed the last of the wine in his tumbler, picked up the bottle and chased the rest into his glass, but nothing came out - the bottle was dry.

"Shit, drained it."

C said, resigned.

"We got more!"

Earl said.

"Hey, Earl, that was a gift to me; you can't drink that….*no one's* drinking that."

"From Jerk-Face!"

"Jerk-Face? Who's Jerk-Face?"

"Don't call him that. And who *he* is, is none of *your* business."

Well, Cord figured he finally met the boyfriend he was sure she had, although hoping she didn't. At least Earl didn't like him. And where has he been all weekend? Questions to ponder over his next tumbler of wine, no doubt.

"I'm getting the wine!"

And with that, Earl mad-dashed down the hall.

"Hey! Hey!"

Lilly started after him, but Cord just caught her by the right wrist and held firm to give Earl the big lead; she tugged hard against his grip and glared back at him with red eyes, like a rhino ready to charge.

"Let go asshole!"

So he did.

But she was still leaning and pulling hard toward the door; down she went in a face-plant, a loud thump on the hardwood hallway floor.

Holy shit, he was in trouble.

He immediately assumed a fighter's stance, figuring she would come up swinging, or kicking. Or worse yet, head for the kitchen knife drawer.

But she did none of that.

She just got up, walked quietly past him, sat on the couch and crossed her arms in a pouting mode; she didn't say a word. He would never figure this girl out, of that he was sure.

"Sorry."

He knew saying sorry meant nothing when it came to Lilly; he wasn't sure why he even bothered, it just came out.

"It's okay; I shouldn't have fallen for that one."

She did it again, an unintentional pun, self-deprecating, no less. She half-smiled in spite of herself, and so did he. And just like that, the incident was over.

Yep, he was never going to figure her out….never.

The apartment door slammed open, with Earl holding two virgin bottles of wine; a red Cabernet, from *him*; and a white.

"Oh, I forgot about the white, Earl, where was that?"

"Way in the back of the pantry; it was from Uncle Sam, remember?"

"I've got work tomorrow."

Cord said in a half-attempt at restraint.

"So do I, and I get to jump around with a bunch of fat-asses, and one flamer."

Lilly sighed.

"Being drunk will help."

She said, while opening the white. Lilly couldn't bring herself to open the red; she was hoping they would stop at the white – she wasn't itching for a fight over the Cabernet, not in the condition she was in.

Lilly had been holding onto that bottle of red for three years – it was probably already skunked, but she kept it anyway, a combination security blanket, wish list and cudgel, depending on how she felt about Button at the particular time. At this point, it was in the *wish-list* category; it had been a long three years, and she missed him. Despite all the bad, she still missed him; he was her albatross, she could never seem to shake him.

She knew he would never change, but she hung on for the slim to none chance that he might. And even if he did change, *really* change, there was still the matter of Button and Earl; Earl made his mind up about Button years ago, and Earl rarely changed his mind about things like that. And, of course, Button had despised Earl from the day they met, day one, as kids.

Then she looked at Cord; now what was so special about this guy that Earl fawned all over him? She simply didn't get it.

Cord did seem somewhat interesting, in a strange sort of way. And he did look a bit like Button, just a bit….the bald head, quick temper….but he was not nearly as good-looking and had nothing like Button's hard, sinewy body and washboard stomach. But he seemed smarter than Button, maybe, and there was the mystery about him, it pissed her off, scared her a bit, and intrigued her at the same time. Wait, what the hell was she doing? This guy's an asshole, remember? Fucking alcohol; it's the drunk talking.

She wished Button would just knock on the door and she could be with him again – the past fully forgiven; she wished it was that easy. She didn't have a clue as to where he went, where he was, or if he was even alive.

But somehow, she knew he was out there, that he loved her, and would come back for her when he was ready….eventually. She had forgiven him completely for the disk incident; she rationalized and convinced herself it was all a conniving trap by the bitch on the Park - that was a convenient solution. Selective memory works that way.

So for now, she was still willing to wait, with her bottle of red wine to celebrate his return to her.

"Are you going to pour, or just stand there staring at the wall with the bottle in your hand?"

Cord broke her trance; she returned to the present, frowned a bit that it was him that interrupted her reminiscing about Button and proceeded to fill their glasses.

"I thought you weren't suppose to mix?"

She said nonchalantly.

"You're the one who opened the white."

C said, deadpan.

"Oh, yeah."

She mumbled.

"Are you okay? You look a bit lost."

Cord asked.

"Yeah, just thinking."

"I know what she's thinking about....Jerk-Face."

"Am not!"

Said the five-year old.

"Yes you are; whenever you get that face, that's what it's about. He's not coming back Lilly; I hope he doesn't ever come back....*ever!*"

"Who is this...."

Cord started to say, till she interrupted him.

"Enough! I don't want to talk about it anymore Earl, and I especially don't want to discuss it with *you*."

Thrusting her glass in C's direction.

With that, she put her glass down, empty, and started to bum-stumble her way to the door.

"Earl, it's getting late, are you coming or not?"

"I said no, I'm not going down there with the puppet and crickets and flies! He can climb up the building you know; you're *never* safe from the puppet!"

"Christ, now look what you started! I'm going to be hearing about this fucking zombie-doll for the rest of my life *[she barked, glaring at C, then she turned to her brother, indignant]*. Fine, you're supposed to help Marty's dad tomorrow on the farm – they're picking you up early, 6 am, so you better get downstairs in the morning; I'm not coming up here to get you!"

"Watch out for the flies."

Was all Earl said, and he wasn't being sarcastic.

The door slammed behind her and they were alone; so much for seeing her drunk. She forgot to grab her bottle of red.

That's the way it always happens in real life, he thought; the good-looking girl always gets up and leaves, and all the various scenarios you play in his head, all the different machinations which invariably end with you bedding her, her looking skyward, longingly, and thanking God that you are *so good* and marveling at how big your cock is....they all go out the pipe-dream window. And all you're left looking at is a roomful of guys in the same boat. Such is life.

Cord turned to Earl.

"Okay, who's the former boyfriend she's pining about?"

Cord was dying to know who the competition was; he had to admire the guy, since it sounded like he left *her* – took a powder and she was still sore about it.

"Button Pierce; her stupid boyfriend since she was about ten."

Earl said in exaggerated disgust, as he curled his lips.

[Button! There's actually a guy with the name Button! Cord thought to himself? That's what she was screaming when she was masturbating, yelling 'Pump me Button!' Nice....and he was laying on the bedroom floor jerking off to her masturbating about some boyfriend named Button. No wonder there was no 'Cord' in her sentence; there was no Cord, period. How pathetic; he truly felt pathetic. Enough with this stupid fantasy called Lilly; in his book, once and for all, he colored her done.]

"Oh."

Was all Cord said as that stream of conscious passed; then he moved on. Enough about Lillian; enough about her, forever.

"Hey Earl, remember we talked about the secret *List* we were going to come up with and not tell Lilly about? Well, now that Lilly is gone, do you want to work on it? Or is it too late? Or are you too drunk?"

"No way! Let's do it! It's not too late and *I can never be too drunk;* isn't that what you told me the number one rule is?   I don't want to think about scary flies anymore!"

And just like that, Earl forgot about the flies, the crickets and the scary puppet. Cord retrieved a pad and pen from the front of the fridge and looked hard and deep into his best friend's eyes.

"Earl, this is super-important, so you have to pay attention; these ten things, they will change your life, and once we start, there's no going back, ever; there are no take-backs – ever. Do you understand? I can't start unless you say so. Do you want to do it?"

Earl stood up and yelled, with arms overhead, while almost falling into the wall, well on a one-way to being sauced to the gills.

"I'm drunk, let's do it!"

And so they did.

CHAPTER 39 - A LITTLE STORY ABOUT THE PELICANS OF PANAMA

Cord and Earl stumbled over to the table, sitting across from each other this time.

"Okay, you start."

C said.

To which Earl answered quick.

"No, you start."

"Okay, you said it. And there's no going back *[C wagged a stern finger at his friend]*. Number 1, *the* most important item on the List, is a date with Carol; actually Number 1 is for you to have down-and-dirty sex with Carol, but the date comes first. No, better make that *dates;* you're not bedding the likes of her very quickly, trust me, she's no first-date-fuck kind of girl. But they go hand-in-hand, so let's just combine the two and call No. 1 *dates-then-dirty deed*, shall we?"

"What? What do you mean *you*? You mean *you and me* right?"

"No, this is a *just you* kind of deal, trust me."

Earl was quickly in a tizzy.

"No Way! I'm not going alone - you have to come too!"

"A threesome? We'll if you insist, Earl, I guess so, but that might be a tough sell with the lion girl."

Cord tilted his head and looked at Earl.

"*Earl,* this is *the* Wish List for both of us, the big stuff, important stuff - you can't shoot low. But it also doesn't mean we have to do all of it *together*. I'll help you, we'll get it set up, but when the time comes, you have to go solo, just the two of you, alone....those are the rules. But you gotta promise to make a grainy video of the second part for me; I hope she's got a nice, thick black bush, you know, 80's style, but trimmed, neat.   But that's wishful thinking; she probably has one of those useless, for-shit Brazilian micro-strips, or worse yet, shaved clean, like a pre-teen. What a shame that would be."

Earl looked positively mortified. This conversation was worse than worrying about the crickets and flies, *way* worse. He squeezed his hands together and wrung them while he stared at Cord. He didn't know what to say; he felt like he was preparing for a trip to the dentist.

C smiled at him.

"Earl, she likes you, she *really* does. She's nice, and I know she thinks the world of you; you'll be fine. Don't worry, I'll set it up, I'll do all the prep, okay?"

"Not now, not yet; I got to think about it more."

Earl's thumbs were circling each other frantically.

"Earl, you've been thinking about it non-stop for the past fourteen years, since she came into Town; how much longer do you need?"

"A little longer?"

He pleaded.

"Nope, time's up; we agreed we'd do this List, and were doing it. No. 1 is a date, and then some, with Ms. Crowe. Discussion over. Next."

Earl had a look that was half-troubled, half-excited and half-ready to wet his pants. But he agreed to move on; he would let Cord keep Carol as the top item on the list, but he would simply stop thinking about it. He learned that trick from Lilly.

He was already feeling better.

"Okay, No. 2. Wait, I almost forgot!"

And with that, Cord ran down to the kitchen and came back with a pack of matches and the miniature, *her* miniature. He stuck it in his mouth, trying not to gum it up too much, and toked while he lit the end. He took a long drag; the end glowed a dull red, and cracked a bit.

"What's that?"

"What's it look like?"

"A used cigar, that somebody chewed on?"

Earl said with a look of disgust.

"Well, there was some chewing, yes, but it was only a little cigar to begin with – a cigarillo; here, take a puff."

"That's not good for you; I don't want that. Jerk-head used to smoke and blow it right in my face when Lilly wasn't looking."

"You're right, it isn't good for you. It's a bad habit, and that guy's a dick. But just take one little puff; there's a reason I'm asking you Earl, please, just a little one....trust me."

And with that, he handed it to Earl, whose big fingers made it hard to hold the tiny roll of tobacco. He frowned at Cord, slowly brought the used stogie up to his nose and sniffed the end, pulling back in reaction to the smoke, the heat and the singe of his nostril hair.

"Yuck!"

"I told you to puff it, not sniff it! I know it stinks, but take a drag anyway; trust me, you'll want to when I tell you a big secret."

"A big secret? What big secret?"

Earl loved secrets, especially when they came from C. Those were the best secrets of all.

Cord just stared at him and motioned Earl to do the dirty deed.

Earl, in the slowest of slow-motion, put the wet end into his mouth and took a little puff, like his friend directed. He held it in his mouth and just held his breath, looking at Cord, hoping for additional guidance.

"Let it out!"

And he did; Earl blew the huff of smoke right into Cord's face, extending his oversized tongue in an exaggerated wag of disgust.

"That tastes like an *ashtray*!"

"Thanks buddy."

Cord said, as he opened his eyes after the puff of smoke dissipated.

"Why? Do you *like* smoke in your face? I don't like smoke in *my* face."

Cord looked at him with disbelief.

"Oh, sorry C."

"Never mind about that; congratulations are in order! Earl, you just jumped the first hurdle of your date, your first quasi-official kiss with Carol."

"What?"

"You heard me; that's *her* cigar! She smoked half of it, and wanted you to have the other half *[a bit of a stretch, but Cord took the liberty]*. Her soft red lips and tongue were *all over* that puppy!"

"Really?"

Earl's eyes lit up as he reached for the cigarillo stub.

"I thought you'd like it."

Earl took a second puff, longer and deeper this time, assuming the posture of a pro.

"You know, this tastes pretty darn good."

"Yeah, some ashtrays really do."

C said, deadpan.

And for the next fifteen minutes, all while Cord talked about No. 2, the next item on the List, Earl worked that miniature like an aficionado, savoring the smoke, swishing it around in his mouth, and blowing it out slowly. He was in seventh heaven, a cigar junkie. His eyes were closed most of the time. He was still drinking the white wine, coupled with deep inhales of tobacco; his head was already light, and now it was starting to slowly spin.

He felt relaxed and content, thinking how happy he was to have his very own, very best friend, Cord Brin.

Now Cord knew exactly what No. 2 was going to be even before he fetched the cigar, but he waited till Earl settled in with it, so he could explain it slowly, as Earl savored the smoke, drank his wine and enjoyed the essence of Carol.

"Okay, are you ready for No. 2?"

Earl nodded his head eagerly, like a little kid.

"You and me, we're going to Panama."

"What! Where's Panama? What's Panama?"

Earl sat up straight, ready for the important announcement he knew was coming. Ken and Sandy would certainly know where Panama was, but Earl hadn't solved that mystery yet.

"You heard me, now just sit back, relax, and let me tell you a little story about the pelicans of Panama."

CHAPTER 40 – A SLOW RIDE TO PARADISE

"I've never gone too far from home C; I've only been as far as Farmer Gill's farm, in Pohatcong, twenty-five minutes away, that's all. How far is Panama? Is it a lot farther than *Pohat*? I hope it's *real* far!"

Cord settled in his chair, smiled at Earl and began to slowly speak.

"Panama is a bit farther than Pohatcong; it's a long day's journey, actually two days, to get where we're going. But getting there's half the adventure, half the fun."

Earl smiled and rubbed his hands together furious, like he always did when he got super-excited. He was glad it was far away; it must be super-far, because he never even heard of it.

"First thing in the morning, we're each taking a bag, just one, small, 'cause where were going, you don't need much. We're gonna get in a car, just you and me, and drive to Philly….Philadelphia. Better yet, we'll take a big black limo, with lots of room, stocked with all sorts of food and booze."

"But I'm already drunk!"

Earl said, as he raised his hands over his head.

"Nothing says we can't drink more; there's always more drunk to get to."

C said, smiling.

"And what about maguro and tobiko, can we eat that in the car? Can you really eat sushi in a limo?"

"Of course, whatever you want."

"Can Carol come too?"

"Sure, why not; after a few dates, you might even be married by then."

Earl blushed. Then he whispered.

"How 'bout Lilly, can she come too, C?   Can she?"

"I don't think Lilly would want to come with us, Earl, certainly not with me along."

Earl put his head down.

"But if she wants to, Lilly can come, if she wants."

C said, which perked Earl, and made him smile.

Cord continued.

"Then we're gonna get on a really *big* plane; you can sit by your own window, in a big comfy seat, because we're going to fly first-class. And after we're way high in the sky, you can look down at all the cars go by; they look little matchboxes, fake.

[Earl sat mesmerized, smiling, listening to his friend, his mind trying to picture things he had never seen nor thought of before]

After a couple hours, when everyone in the back of the plane gets little shitty bags of peanuts and pretzels, and mini cups of coffee, you and I will be having a full spread of breakfast, with as much juice and coffee as we want, in real glasses and mugs. And alcohol too, as much as you want – they just keep it coming. Then we'll land in Miami, in Florida. But we won't stay in Miami long, only an hour or so, we won't even leave the airport, because we're gonna get on another big plane and fly straight across the Gulf of Mexico, over the jungles of Central America, all the way to the Pacific

Ocean, to a place about as far away from Farmer Gill's farm as you can get.

[Earl didn't know how to imagine what a Gulf of Mexico even looked like, or where Central America was, or the Pacific Ocean, but it didn't matter one bit – he smiled right on through, because he'd be with C, sitting right beside his best friend, the whole way]

We'll push our way through the crowded airport, surrounded by a bustle of English and Spanish, shouted all around us. We'll grab the first taxi we see and drive through the countryside, passed grassy fields and forests with strange trees, the likes you've never seen before, until the road kisses the ocean.

You should see it Earl, it's so cool; endless brown tidal flats stretch forever into the receding sea, stranding boats, buoys and fish, lots of fish - easy pickings for the birds, until the tide reverses, and the mud bubbles and submerges under the rushing froth.

The mud flats stretch like a brown carpet, right up to the shoreline in the distance, which is crammed with huge, shiny glass skyscrapers, one after another, sitting on a long curved shoreline….the Bay of Panama.

And you know what were gonna do when we get there?"

[Earl just looked at C, eyes wide in wonder, waiting for the answer]

"We're gonna take a long, slow walk toward the old quarter of Panama City, along the sea wall that curves endlessly along the edge of the bay.

[Cord closed his eyes as he told the rest of the tale]

And all around us, Earl, is a never-ending traffic jam, filled with blaring horns from a line of jalopies. We'll sidestep muddy puddles along the road from the late morning rain, past the countless creaky buses, old school buses, always crammed with too many riders, and painted wild colors, belching exhaust; the smell of burnt diesel hanging in the air. And we're going to pass people, loads of people, walking, running and sitting, all jammed along Balboa Avenue.

And in the middle of all that crazy Panamanian madness, we're gonna happen upon, almost by accident, a quiet little park I know, one you might just as easily walk by, without a second glance.

But we're not going to miss it Earl, no way…. *not us.*"

"No way, we're not gonna miss it! No way!"

Earl parroted Cord, rubbing his hands together in glee and shaking his head yes.

We're gonna sneak a left off the sidewalk, and duck under a couple of big old trees, some of the biggest, coolest-looking trees you've ever seen Earl, and sit on a little concrete bench, just like the one you and your mom sit on in Town. But you're not gonna be looking at Carol's Lion House, Earl, not this time. You're gonna be looking out over the Pacific Ocean, tranquil, blue and seemingly endless, with huge container ships and barges dotting the horizon, more than you can count, queued up in a long line. Ships so big you wonder how they can even float.

"Are they bigger than Marty's dad's boat on the river? His boat is *real* big!"

Earl couldn't believe boats could be much bigger than that.

"*Way* bigger, almost as big as Belvidere."

Cord said, then settled back into the story.

"And you know what else you'll see Earl? Right in front of you, just twenty feet past the Pacific seawall, bobbing out in the bay, without a care in the world?"

[Earl didn't answer, he just leaned in and looked at Cord in anticipation, knowing whatever it was, he was going to like it even better than the big boats]

"You're going to see birds, lots of big black birds, swimming and diving for fish. And your going to see Aloysius, and all his friends."

Earl jumped up like he was singing to Jesus.

"**What?** That's where Al goes when he leaves the boat ramp? He goes to Panama?! I want to go to Panama too!"

"Well, we'll have to ask Al if he's stopping there this year, but his friends surely fish in Panama Bay, loads of them, dozens and dozens of cormorants. They fly and float up and down the shoreline, catching all sorts of fish in the beautiful sunshine, all day long. It's the best Earl, the very best.

And when you're sitting on that bench in that tiny little park by the Bay, watching the cormorants fish, I'm gonna tell you to tilt your head back and lazily look up in those two big beautiful trees. And looking right back at you will be fat and happy pelicans, loads of them, twenty, thirty at a time, just sitting there wagging their tail feathers like ducks, stretching, preening, scratching, sleeping….until they decide to go fishing again with their best friends, the cormorants.

They're so quiet, if you didn't look up, you wouldn't even know they were there! Right over your head!

You and me buddy, were gonna sit our fat asses right there on that bench by the water, relax, close our eyes in the early afternoon sun and just waste time, watching the pelicans and the cormorants, waiting for Al to show up and join us. How does that sound?"

"That sounds like the best thing ever! I can't wait to see Al! And I never saw a real pelican!"

Earl whispered the last part, as he quietly sat back down, exhausted from all the excitement.

"Don't relax yet, that's not all we're doing, Earl, not by a long-shot.

The next day we're gonna wake up real early, take another taxi to a different airport, a tiny airstrip on the outskirts of the Old City. We're gonna jump on another plane, but this one's way different from that first jet; this one is an old prop plane, you know, with propellers, like an old troop transport from the 1940's, the kind that were around when Ken and Sandy were solving mysteries in New York."

"I want to solve a real mystery, like Ken and Sandy! And I want to go to Skeleton Island!"

"Okay, deal; those are Nos. 3 and 4 on the List."

Earl just smiled and waited for Cord to finish talking about Panama; he could listen to C all day long. To Earl, the Gill's chicken farm was the end of the world, beyond the distant wood line, beyond the old stone row that ran through the woods along the far end of the farmer's property, was unknown territory. All he knew was Panama, and Al, were waiting for him and C, somewhere....*further*. And he couldn't wait to get there.

Earl was going to see it, to finally see what was beyond that last row of rocks, with his best friend in the whole world, Cord Brin.

"Now be careful Earl, because that old plane flies low, a real puddle-jumper, skimming the jungle canopy. When you look out the window, the trees look just like broccoli tops, like you can reach down and eat 'em. The clouds look different there too; they're thick and dense, like hard, white ice, like you could shave them and put the shards in a glass of *Vernors*. You've never seen anything, Earl, till you've seen those broccoli trees and Panama clouds like ice out those little round windows."

Earl closed his eyes and tried to imagine what Cord was describing; he had never been on a plane, never seen clouds and trees from the top down, like Al did. It must be the best ever.

"We'll fly for an hour north, right over the Panama Canal, where you'll see all those big boats again, lined up in a queue, like they're buying popcorn. Then we'll fly over nothing, no people, no roads, nothing....just miles and miles of water and jungle, in never-ending shades of blue and green I can't even describe.

[Earl kept smiling, with his eyes closed]

"We'll dive down and land at an even smaller airport with just one short runway, a little backwater strip carved out of the jungle in a magical place by the name *Bocas Del Toro*, on the Caribbean, belly up to the southern border of Costa Rica.

We'll take another tinny taxi down a long dirt road, nothing more than a path in the mud really, full of potholes so big they can swallow a car; our driver will slowly slalom between them, and we'll rock back and forth along the curvy spine of the pike.

We're gonna ride right through the underbelly of the jungle village, where barefoot kids ride rusty clunker-bikes and groups of idle men sit and chat on plastic lawn chairs set in muddy front yards, strewn with abandoned cars, zigzagged by roaming chickens and roosters, who barely move out of the taxi's way, as if they own the place.

Imagine Earl, chickens and roosters wandering loose through the streets….that's *real* free range.

House after house is perched on cartoonish, skinny stilts, ready to topple at a breath; there are no windows, and the wood siding has just a blush of long-gone paint left here and there, the rest peeled to bare.

Yet, despite the poverty, all the locals you pass are happy, smiling, relaxed, lounging midday, with nothing in particular to do and in no hurry to do it.

Life just kind of happens there.

The mud path dead-ends at a long, rickety wooden dock, to which is tied a long, rickety wooden boat, which we'll climb in….just you and me."

"And Carol and Lilly too? We can't leave them in the mud with the chickens! Lilly will sock us for sure!"

"Yes, of course; although leaving the two of them in the mud with a bunch of roosters would be kind of funny, wouldn't it?"

Earl shook his head an emphatic yes, knowing they could always act tough when the girls weren't around to hear it….guys are good at that.

"And after that boat engine coughs and sputters to life and backs out of its slip, Earl, we are only twenty five minutes away from someplace *very* special, one of the most special places I have ever been.

Get ready for a slow ride to paradise."

CHAPTER 41 – THE LEAVING, THE WHAT FOR, AND THE WHY

Cord took a break from the story, sat back, looked at Earl, and smiled at him.

It was funny watching him try to make Carol's cigarillo stub last through the Panama tale, his big fingers could hardly hold it, the tips of his nails scorched when he took a drag. Made all the harder because he was drunk. Finally, begrudgingly, he had to acknowledge it was done.

"Can I keep it?"

"Of course you can, it's all yours."

Earl couldn't wipe the smile off his face, happy about Panama, and happy about the cigar; he didn't know which made him happier. He decided it was a tie.

"You know, you think that was good, wait till you kiss the real thing; I'm sure her lips taste better than that roll of stale tobacco."

"Do you think?"

"Yeah, I think….you'll see. Are you ready to hear the rest?"

Earl bobbed his head yes, his eyes glassed from the wine, his head light from the cigar.

Cord settled in his chair and continued.

"The boat will skim over shallow, turquoise water, which opens into a big bay, with an endless, green shoreline, full of coves and crags of mangroves; a thick, impenetrable fortress of roots and branches below the surface of the water. It looks like a dark, spooky forest of trees, thousands of knurled branches and stalks in water that's just a few feet deep. And right along the edge of the mangrove forest is where the stingrays sleep, the barracuda slowly swim and the lobsters hide."

"Lobsters! You mean lobsters live in Panama too? Do you think that's where Louie's from?"

Earl jumped up again, ready to kiss the sky, too excited to make a statement while seated. Just when he thought Panama couldn't possibly get any better, it did.

"Who's Louie, Earl?"

"Louie the Lobster! He's my friend up at the A&P; he lives in the lobster tank, along with all the other lobsters. He's my good friend; he's the one with the red rubber bands on his claws; I can tell it's him because he's the only lobster with the red bands, all the others have blue ones.

I've been friends with Louie for years!

I see him *every* week, when we go grocery shopping, Lilly and me.   I call him Louie because that's what mom was going to name Lilly if she was a boy, Louis, and she gets mad at me when I remind her of that, and that she's really a lobster, kind of.

She hates that name.

So I called the lobster Louie; everybody at the store knows Louie!

Lilly gets mad that I call him Louie; she keeps telling me she's going to eat him some day, but I told her no one is eating Lou - he and his friends are safe in that tank, no one bothers them in there - they just crawl on top of each other and watch the shoppers all day!"

Now Cord was pretty sure that *Louie* wasn't a permanent resident of the lobster tank; a whole series of Louies over the years had likely found their way head first into a pot of boiling water, with next week's victim wearing the red rubber bands. But nevertheless, to Earl, this week's Lou was the original Lou….the real deal. And that was all that mattered.

"I don't think Louie is from Panama, Earl; those lobsters in the tank are cousins from up north, cold water guys, my guess, anyway. But Louie's cousins certainly live in Panama, that's for sure. And you're gonna meet 'em, hiding in the mangroves. And they don't wear any bands on their claws, so you better watch out!"

Earl sat down and rubbed his hands together like a kid waiting to open a present; he couldn't wait to tell Louie he was going to Panama.

"After a while, quietly bumping along in that long, rickety boat, on the far right shoreline, at first just a speck in the distance, you'll see it come into focus…a little hut built out over the water, connected to the mainland by a long, elevated wooden walkway.

That's where we're going Earl.

There's no newspapers, no television, no radios, no phones, no clocks, only a couple solar-powered lights. And along the shore, far away, a single dim light glows here and there. Sometimes it's completely black at night - jet black. It's quiet, peaceful."

Cord shut his eyes and whispered.

"Every man should keep a special place to retreat, a secret-somewhere, to go and find himself, to heal….to be *better*. For me, it's *Bocas Del Toro*, at least it is sometimes."

"But it's not a secret anymore, you told me."

Earl sounded sad that Cord had mistakenly told him his secret.

"Earl, I've been going there for years, and I always go alone. You're the first person I've ever even told about it. And there's no one I would want to see that special place more than you. I've known you for all of what, a day and a half? And it feels like you and I have known each other all my life. Now, when I think of that place, I don't think of just me, I think of you and me, us, a team….best friends, forever.

I've never met anyone like you Earl….*never*.

I've had lots of people come and go in my life, just passengers on a train. I sit still and they come on, stay a bit, and move on, or they stay and I get off at the next station; either way, I could give a rat's ass about any of them. I don't really matter much to anyone, Earl, not really, not in a way that counts. And no one really matters much to me. That's just the way it is, always has been, as far back as I can remember, as far back as the game has been played.

And I'm okay with that.

But you, you're different….it *feels* different. Maybe I'm wrong about you, but I don't think so; you're a kindred spirit, Earl, a special soul. I certainly wasn't looking for you, just like I wasn't looking for this place, but it kind of just happened. And, so far, I'm glad it did."

Cord was talking to himself as much as he was to Earl, as he put his hand on Earl's massive shoulder and gave it a heart-felt squeeze.

Earl didn't grasp all that Cord was saying, but he understood the important part, the part his mom told him about...the kindred spirit part. Whatever that meant, it was super-important to his mom, so it was just as important to Earl. Maybe Panama was what his mom said Cord was going to tell him about, maybe it was about Louie, or Al, or the pelicans overhead....maybe it was *all* of it.

He just knew he liked spending time with C.

"You might not want to get hooked up with me, Earl; although you may be right for me, I doubt I'm right for you. I have a lot of practice being the wrong thing for people; things tend to go south around me."

Earl just smiled thinking about his mom; she was *always* right about things, and he knew she was right about Cord.

"You and me, we're going to Panama."

Was Earl's answer; he was sticking with his friend, and that was that.

"Tell me more, Cord, what else are we gonna do?"

Cord grinned, happy Earl wanted to hear more.

"Well, that little hut of mine has a wraparound deck, which opens up to a big wooden platform, facing the bay. There's a big old hammock set up there, which you can plop right down in and swing in the sunshine, and when you close your eyes, all you hear is the water gently lapping against the wood pilings below you, the loose ends of the roof fronds rustling in the breeze.

A bug will buzz by now and again; it'll sound like a plane cause it's so quiet, but you'll be too lazy to even open your eyes to see it Earl. Sometimes you'll hear the putt-putt of a tiny motor in the distance, a local fisherman in a small john-boat on his way back from a morning catch.

Spanish whispers and the clinking of plates and glasses in the distance; that's your lunch being delivered by the locals. And you'll feel the warm bake of the sun on your cheek, massaging you while you slowly swing back and forth, with your leg hanging over the edge of the hammock….siesta-style.

Once in awhile you'll hear a *swish, swish, swish*, right below you. It'll get louder each time you hear it, till it stirs you from your nap. Do you know what that is?"

Earl was mesmerized; he just shook his head slowly in the negative.

"That's your fat ass scraping against the wood decking; those cotton hammocks stretch in the sun, and soon your butt is rubbing on the floor boards, slowing down your swing. Such indignity, Earl, but you gotta take the bad with the good."

With that, Cord chuckled quietly at Earl, and Earl returned the gesture.

"Tell me more; I wanna hear more!"

"Okay."

Cord said, as he resettled and thought a bit.

"If you leave a bottle of water out, in no time you'll find little lizards will crawl inside, looking for a drink….lots of them. They come from nowhere, in all directions."

"Really?"

"Really. They look like little dinosaurs; hey, you want to see one?"

"Really? Now? Yeah!"

With that, Cord went into his bedroom, and in just a minute came out with a delicate, porcelain box, with a hinged top. He handed it to Earl, who just studied it.

"Go ahead, open it."

Earl carefully cracked the top ajar and let out a little gasp; before him was a perfectly preserved greenish-brown lizard, about two inches long, from snout to tip of tail.

"He unfortunately drowned in a bottle of champagne I left open one night, the first night I was ever there.

I found him in the morning with a friend floating in the bottle. His buddy survived, a bit wobbly, but this one didn't make it. I've been carrying him around with me for years, kind of like a lost companion. I felt bad about it, but the alcohol preserved him, I guess.

"What's his name?"

Come to think of it, I never gave him a name; you can, if you want to."

"Really? Okay, is it a boy or a girl?"

"I don't know, pick a name that doesn't matter."

Cord could see Earl squint as he was calculating, plodding, checking files in his noggin.

"Jonesy."

"Jonesy? Where'd that come from?"

"I don't know, it just popped in my head."

"Well, Jonesy it is. He goes back with me every time I go, so he can go home again. One of these days he's going to get confiscated at the airport; you really can't be taking lizards in and out of Panama, even dead ones. But so far, Jonesy and me have stuck together….partners in crime."

Earl was fascinated by the little guy; he gently put his pointer on its back; Cord was amazed Earl could touch so gently with such big hands, and ran it from the head to the tip of the tale. He was entranced.

"Do you want to take him home and keep him for a bit, Earl?   I'm sure Jonesy would like the change of scenery."

"Yeah! Do you think Lilly would mind?"

"Well, I'm sure she would, but it's up to you if you tell her. I wouldn't, but you would know better.   But you have to be careful with him, Jonesy is pretty fragile."

"I'm not telling her, I'll keep him by my bed, in my drawer, with the lid closed, but I'll open it up at night, so he can breathe and sleep next to me and not get scared. This is so cool. Keep telling me C, what else are we gonna do at the hut?"

"Well, there's lots of other neat stuff down there, Earl; when you shuffle slow along the wood walkway, over the water, and the mangroves brush by your face, if you look close, you can see little crabs clinging to the branches, trying to hide. Boy are they quick; you could hardly catch them if you tried! But I don't bother them, I just like to look at them, and they look right back at you.

And when you slip into the water, it's only about eight feet deep or so, and you can see everything - it's like glass. You see real starfish everywhere, all different kinds, they walk right along the bottom; you can actually watch them walk! And there's all sorts of fish of all different colors; some have beaks like parrots! And you can see shrimp that have long legs, like big spiders.

But the best one, the one I really want you to see, is a tiny blue fish, smaller than the size of my thumb, smaller even than Jonesy. He is bright metallic blue, with blue spots - blue on blue; he looks fake, like a fancy gumdrop.

I see him every time I go, Earl; he lives on a little coral outcrop right off the front corner of the hut, in just four feet of water. That bit of coral sits all by itself, it's a tiny piece actually, just about three-foot square, and this little fish just swims around and around that coral, circling it, hiding in it, never venturing away from it....never. I've watched him for hours on end.

He has this big, beautiful lagoon and bay to swim around and explore, but he never leaves his little coral island. I can watch him forever, Earl; I just hover above him with my snorkel on, watching him swim and dart and hide.

He's you, Earl, circling around Belvidere, with this big lagoon out there waiting for you to explore. It's decided; my little friend never had a name till now....I'm gonna call him Earl."

"Earl! You're gonna name him Earl! Really? I can go see Earl in Panama now?"

"Yep. And I know you'll love that little guy; I know I do.

And at night, when there's a constant southern breeze, we'll sleep side-by-side, on the two chaise lounges on the deck, under the stars.

And Earl, even with all that good stuff in Panama, there's something even better....the *very* best.

The night sky.

You have *never, ever*, seen anything like the stars in the Panamanian sky. The night is *so black*, and the area so remote, that the whole sky lights up with crisp dots of intense light, more stars than you ever thought existed - it looks like it can't even be real. And running right through the middle of it all, is a wide, curvy paintbrush stoke of light…the Milky Way.

[Cord closed his eyes and painted the sky in his mind]

I never saw the Milky Way, never understood what it really was, how it has fascinated and intrigued mankind for thousands of years, until I saw it down there. It humbles you, Earl, it really does. We really don't matter, in the big picture….we're really just a whole lot of nothing.

But once you see that sky, you'll never want to leave. The concept of heaven, whatever that may be, or whatever it may mean, it was certainly born in that Panama sky above the hut and hammock, hanging over the little blue fish, the coral and starfish, the lobsters, and stingrays and barracuda, above the lizards and the little tree crabs."

"My mom's in heaven; do you think she's in Panama?"

"Maybe Earl; maybe she's down there waiting for us to show up and swim with little-Earl. Maybe that's why we've got to go and see for ourselves."

Earl smiled wide and gave a big stretch, which prompted Cord to do the same. They had drained the bottle of white, but had yet to crack open the sacred bottle of Jerk-Face-red.

Cord ran his hand across his chin; he hadn't shaved since he got off the bus on Thursday, two days ago. That was the longest he had gone without shaving since he was a teenager. He didn't like to have any hair on his face; he never did. But now, he didn't particularly care. He would shave, eventually, he thought to himself, and smiled for even thinking such a thought was possible before he arrived in this strange little place.

"Hey Earl, the *List of Ten*, and more importantly, the whole trip to Panama, and all I told you about it, that's between you and me okay? Please don't tell Lilly or anyone else; that's just between the two of us, okay?"

"But what if I want them to come with us?"

"We'll, when we decide to go, we can tell them about it – deal?"

"But I thought we were going to Panama now? Why can't we go now? Can we go tomorrow?"

"I have to spend some time in Belvidere first, okay? It's just kind of something I have to do; some stupid rules to a game I can't explain right now, rules I can't really break.   But after that, we can go, I promise. And then we can tell Lilly and Carol, but not before, okay?"

Earl was disappointed; he was ready to pack tonight.

"I guess. But how long do we have to stay here? When is *some time* over? It sounds like a really stupid game, if you ask me; who even makes up rules that you can't break? Lilly breaks the rules of games we play *all* the time, that's how she always beats me."

C smiled. They were stupid fucking rules. And they should be broken.

"You're right Earl, they *are* stupid rules, but let's just give it a little time. I don't know how long, but not yet, soon maybe, but not yet. I know that's not as soon as you'd like, as soon as tomorrow, but I promise, when I know, you'll be the first to know....and we'll be on that fucking plane to Panama the next day."

Cord patted him on the back, smiled and changed the subject.

"Well, Earl, were you serious, are you staying up here tonight? Your welcome to, but the only bed I have is mine, and sorry buddy, I like you and all, but not that much. The other bed, the legs are broken and there are some *funky* stains on the mattress – don't suggest planting your ass there. You have to suck it up on the couch out here if you're staying."

"Oh I'm staying! I didn't forget about the puppet and the flies! I hope Lilly will be okay; she gets just as scared as me, but she won't admit it."

"Well if you're staying, let's down that last bottle of Jerk-Face Cabernet; what do you say?"

As Cord turned the bottle of white upside-down, confirming it was indeed dry.

"I don't know C, Lilly is gonna get *real, real* mad. He gave her that bottle three years ago, the day he left. If we really drink it, it's gonna be a problem…a *big* problem. I'm kinda drunk, and I still know that."

Now Earl was right, of course, and the prudent, adult thing to do would be to set the godly bottle aside and return it to Lilly in the morning, which is exactly what Cord planned to do.

"You're right Earl, we'll give it back to Lilly tomorrow….it'll just be empty."

And with that, they both laughed, knowing they could; the wrath known as Lilly would come soon enough tomorrow. But they were both drunk enough to feel tough enough to stand up to Lilly in absentia; it's always easier that way.

Thus the third bottle of slightly-skunky red was drained, quickly, in their state the taste mattered little. It was accompanied by more talk of Panama: the thin sliver of the moon in the night sky - like a smile, schools of jumping fish, pelicans, and of course, cormorants.

They decided to finally call it a night; by now it had to be sometime early Sunday morning. Earl tried his best to squeeze his enormous frame onto the couch, under the comforter he hid beneath earlier. Cord looked down at his best friend and smiled proud; in mere minutes, Earl was out cold, snoring loud - his first drunken stupor.

What a weekend C smirked, slowly shaking his head side-to-side, making his way in a punch-drunk tramp to his bedroom. C thought of the long ride to this forgotten place; my God, getting off the bus at *Luigis Rancho* seemed a lifetime ago, yet only sixty-something hours had ticked off the clock since the folding doors shut and the *Greyhound* pulled away, leaving him behind. Had all this really happened in the first three-plus days?

Cord wondered again why Jenny would send him *here*, to this bum-fuck no-one-gives-a-rats-ass-about, dead-end-of-the-road. And, more importantly, *what* would be the circumstances under which he would ultimately leave.

That's what scared him most of all; the leaving, the what for, and the why.

CHAPTER 42 – POLAR BEARS AND BABY MAGIC

Sunday, April 23rd; day four.

The first light rap at the door went unanswered; it echoed quiet in the kitchen and down the hall.

Succeeding knocks got progressively louder, till they roused him from a sound sleep.

He knew the voice.

"Cord, hey Cord, are you in there? It's Martin. You in here?"

Marty said as he slowly swung open the unlocked front door into the kitchen. He tentatively peered his head in to greet C, stumbling out of the bedroom in black boxer briefs, and nothing else. Ay pulled on his ball-sack, coughed rough, and answered in a gravelly voice, thick from the lingering effects of too much booze.

"Marty, what the hell are you doing?"

"I'm looking for Earl; figured he might be up here. There ain't no answer downstairs; I don't think either of them are home. I need to pick up Earl to...."

"I know, I know."

Cord cut him off as he yawned and stretched, his mouth dry and full of paste.

"Well, he was sleeping off three bottles of wine in the front room last I checked, assume he's...."

"Earl was *drinking*? Earl never drank in his life!"

"Never say never; we had a good ol' time last night."

Cord made his way down the hall, Martin in tow. First they saw Earl's tree trunk of a leg prone on the floor next to the couch; he must have rolled off in the night. When they turned the corner, it was attached to the rest of him, snoring on the floor, sans covers, simply clad in his underwear and tee-shirt; the comforter was still bunched in a ball on the couch.

They both chuckled at the big man sleeping off a drunk on the floor.

"Hey Earl, someone's looking for ya."

With that, he stirred and slowly opened one eye; they could tell it took a moment for him to focus on the two of them. A small pool of drool puddled on the floor where he slept, mouth open.

"Nice drool Earl; you're an official drunk."

Cord said, as he chuckled.

"Earl, come on, buddy, we're late; my dad's gonna have our heads if we don't get out to the barn!"

With that, Earl jumped up in a start and let out a little girly yelp, but Cord didn't see his lips move. Strange.

Earl, Cord and Marty looked around the room for Earl's pants; Cord saw them bunched up in the corner, over by the dinette. And that's when Cord first noticed the comforter move, just a bit, balled-up in a heap on the couch.

"Hey, did you see that? The blanket just moved."

Earl cautiously turned his head to look, feet still planted; the three just stood there and stared at the blanket, seeing if it moved again. And it did, just a bit.

"It's Danny!"

Earl screamed. And with that, the big man plowed between the two of them, sans pants, pushing Marty in front of him, like a snow plow, till he spun off to the side and fell into the hallway wall, yelling:

"What the hell's going on?!"

Earl never stopped to answer; he bulldozed down the hall in his underwear, out the door and down the steps, a stampede of one; he never looked back.

"What the hell was that all about? Who's Danny?!"

Martin straightened up, brushing himself off, looking down the empty hall where Earl had just been. They heard the apartment door downstairs open and slam shut. And that was the end of Earl.

"Never mind, long story. But I have a sneaking suspicion as to who's under this blanket, and I doubt its' name is Danny. This could be *very* interesting."

And with that, Cord slowly tugged on the closest corner of the blanket; it tugged back, like a fish on a line.

And with that C beamed; a shit-eating grin if ever there was one.

Lilly was mortified; how the hell did she sleep through the morning and not get out of that damn apartment before anyone was the wiser? And now what? With big-mouth Marty involved, this story would no doubt be around Town before noon, and she was sure it would morph into something much more than it was. Great, that was *all* she needed.

"Danny, do you want to come out and play?"

Martin was positively mesmerized, leaning toward the blanket, waiting for the mystery to be revealed.

Lilly knew she should have just turned all the lights on, the television on, and just sucked it up; but truth be told, that stupid puppet story creeped her out, and Earl's *second floor* and *fly* comments didn't help. She had never stayed in that apartment alone; Earl was always there....*always*. She was sure she'd be okay, until she woke up at 1 am and thought she heard Earl in the hall, but there was no Earl. And that was all it took to get her imagination racing, till finally she couldn't take it anymore and snuck upstairs, down the hall, to find Earl snug on the couch, snoring safe and sound under the comforter.

She proceeded to climb under the comforter with him, wedged herself behind him and the couch back, and proceeded to squirm and fuss like a little kid till she edged him off the couch and onto the floor. She kept the comforter too; she was a bit cold.

Thanks, Earl she whispered to him as he rolled off the edge of the couch in a thump. Vintage Lilly.

Poor Earl ended up on the floor without even a pillow. But he was two sheets to the wind in a virgin drunk, and never really knew what happened.

And for all that effort, she now found herself hiding under Earl's blanket, with the two men she least wanted to see her in this condition waiting less than a foot away, separated only by the thickness of the cotton twill.

"I'm naked; would you two please leave!"

Not true, but she thought for a moment that would make them scoot, out of decency. If she really thought about it, however, nothing she said would have made the two of them stick longer, like glue, until the end of time.

Now, Marty the detective started to solve the mystery.

"Lilly? Is that Lilly? That sounded like Lilly; why'd you call her Danny?"

C ignored him.

"I found Earl's pants here, do you want me to help you put them on?"

Cord offered.

"Funny, now please get lost."

"Hey Cord, I didn't know Lilly moved in; congratulations!"

Now Martin wasn't being sarcastic; he was just simple on certain fronts, most fronts, like this one."

"Yeah, we figured we'd give it a whirl. But you know, she gets a bit shy at times; she doesn't have the body of a twenty-year old anymore, right hon? She needs a little more toning around the tush and midsection; why don't you show Marty what I mean."

"You wish; not everyone has a gut like you.…*hon!*"

She turned her attention to Marty.

"Martin, I have **not** moved in, don't get the fucking story wrong. I was simply looking for Earl last night and found him up here; he was scared and asked me to stay and keep him company, so I did. Then he was nice enough to let me sleep on the couch, with the blanket. I told him to keep it, but he insisted I take it - he's such a good brother. I just overslept is all, nothing more than that. Nothing! End of story!"

"Uh huh, that must be it."

Is all Cord said.

Then there was silence; the two weren't budging and neither was she; a Mexican stand-off with the lump on the couch. The blanket looked like a big mashed potato.

"Martin, you want some coffee? I was going to sit here at the table and read the paper for awhile; want to join me?"

"Fine, you two juveniles have had your fun."

And with that, Lilly grabbed all the loose ends of the blanket and cinched them in, like a cocoon, and proceeded to stand up; all they saw were her bare feet and part of one ankle.

"Wow, naked feet, and an ankle! That is some good-looking ankle, what do you say Martin?"

Marty just nodded in acknowledgment; he really *did* like that ankle, but he couldn't get out of his mind what was hiding under that blanket just about two and a half feet north of Lilly's ankle. My God, Saturday and the *Officer's Ball* couldn't come quick enough.

Lilly fumbled with the blanket and positioned it so a tiny eye-hole emerged, so she could see where she was going, pushing her way past the two of them, down the hall.

"Hey Marty, I'm ready!"

Earl called from the hall; Marty went to join him, but was behind the slow-moving potato. He tried to squeeze by, but no luck.

"Take it easy, Marty, just step the fuck back and wait! And don't be touching the blanket, even by mistake!"

Martin stopped cold and put distance between himself and the potato; when Lilly barked, Marty listened, it was always safer that way.

She got to the door and made the turn into the hallway, with Martin trailing behind. He figured he would wait in the kitchen and give her a few step lead; the last thing he wanted to do was step on that blanket as she was going down the steps (well, that wouldn't be so bad in one respect, but *very* bad in every other).

He spotted the lonely Cabernet bottle on the counter.

"Hey Cord, cool wolf label – betcha that was one expensive bottle of wine; where's the recycling bin?"

Martin said as he grabbed the empty carafe by the neck.

Are you fucking kidding me Marty? You had to say that shit out loud? Cord thought to himself. *Fucking idiot.*

The lump of blanket stopped short on the steps, paused for a moment, then exploded.

"Empty? It's *empty*? Martin, bring that fucking bottle of wine down to my apartment, **now!**"

Was all it said, and Marty knew that blanket meant business.

Well, the payback for that one was going to be a bitch, Cord thought; he now had to worry about how, and when, Lillian was going to attack for drinking that sacred bottle of Cabernet. He couldn't stand this Button jerk-off already; what kind of queer goes around by the name Button, anyway?

Polar bears and *Baby Magic*!

Holy shit, it just popped into his head, just like that, from nowhere. He had a dream last night; he couldn't remember what it was, but it must have had something to do with polar bears and *Baby Magic* lotion, because he remembered both, vividly, just now.

He couldn't believe it; that was the first dream he remembered in years, decades, probably since he was a kid. If he *did* dream, if such a thing occurred, it never lingered, always forgotten long before his eyes opened. Except for now, right now. This dream, for some reason, he remembered. Well it wasn't actually remembering a dream, he just remembered two distinct snippets in what must have been some sort of dream.

What the hell could *that* mean?

The smell of *Baby Magic*, which he hadn't inhaled since he was a small child, *was* his mother; she slathered that stuff all over her face, either that or cocoa butter, every night before she went to bed. Those two smells were as much a part of his earliest years as anything he could remember.

He would smell the *Baby Magic* on her cheeks when she kissed and tucked him into bed; he loved that smell. The cocoa butter, on the other hand, was an entirely different matter; he could smell that nasty paste coming halfway down the hall. He used to tell his mom *never* to smear on the cocoa butter; he *hated* that white sticky cream!

It came in what looked like an oversized lipstick container; a milky-white, pasty, oily stick which she ran over her cheeks and forehead; that stuff just plain smelled bad. He would try to hide the container, but she would always find it, or replace it. She swore it worked wonders on wrinkles and would just smile and give him an extra snug kiss at night, just to be sure she smeared the white gook all over his cheek.

Cord smiled thinking about how he would immediately wipe it off in disgust, wondering how she always seem to forget he didn't want it slopped all over him - didn't she hear him? She would just smirk and whisper *Sleep tight,* waiting for him to finish the exchange....*don't let the bedbugs bite.* Cord mouthed the words silently to himself as he smiled, standing in the hallway, thinking of his mom.   Then they would both say *Goodnight* to each other at the same time, as she walked out of his bedroom.   They went through that little ritual every night for years; he wondered how old he was when he finally stopped - probably older than he would like to admit.

He closed his eyes and could see her standing beside his bed in her nightgown; at that moment, for a moment, he really missed his mom.   She was a good and kind woman, truly good.   He hadn't thought about that in years.

Where the hell did that dream, and those memories, come from? He thought to himself. Having a dream, a real dream, and remembering it after so many years – why here? Why now?

He figured the *Baby Magic* was from his talk with Earl yesterday; some subconscious reminder of his own mom. That wasn't so hard to figure.

But polar bears?   What was *that* all about? He would have to look that one up; it's got to mean something.

He smiled nonetheless. *He* had a dream! Not that he was ever trying to have one, but at least it was something other than a blank screen, the blackness that always preceded the first crack of his lids.

Maybe he would remember more of the dream later, but probably not, it usually doesn't work that way, but maybe. You never know.

Very cool….polar bears and *Baby Magic*.

CHAPTER 43 – HE DROPPED HIS ARM AND
KEPT HIS TEETH

Saturday, April 29th. Ten days in.

Marty stood in front of the mirror in his small bedroom, looking at his gut. Why hadn't he gone on a diet? He turned profile left, then right, to see which belly-shot looked better. Neither really. Maybe left. He would keep that in mind if the situation arose that evening, stay to her left, not the right; see left from the right....stay to her right.

Jesus, he's never gonna remember that.

His hands were sweaty; they had been sweaty since he woke up this morning. My God, the week had crawled by; he never thought Saturday would arrive. He was so nervous, so excited, he couldn't think straight.

He must have jerked off four times a day for the past week, two more than normal, just fantasizing about Lilly. For a second he thought about going for another pecker-squeeze, but no way, it was too close to the main event – no more choking tonight.

He had been waiting for this day his whole life. If only that shit-head Button was in Town to see it, then he could really gloat. But if Button was around, Lilly wouldn't be with Cord, and Button would never have let Lilly go, and Lilly never defied Button. *Never*.

Marty had mixed feelings about Cord; he wanted to thank C for letting him take Lilly out on a date, yet he hated that Lilly was once again *taken*. But he had to admit, he liked Cord; he certainly was the best of the lot she had ever been with. But if the situation arose, he would bang Lilly in a second, and deal with any fallout with Cord later. This was too important to let a newfound friendship with some stranger get in the way. He did think of Cord as his friend; he assumed Cord felt the same way. He was too clueless to realize Cord tagged him a harmless, bumbling bumpkin.

He found a reason to stop in Sam's every day that past week when Cord was working to buy something, and shoot the shit with him. Just to reconfirm, at nauseum, that the date was real and to ask questions about Lilly: how he should act, what she liked, the answers to which Cord made up on the fly, each one more outrageous than the prior. Yet Marty bought them all, filed away for future reference.

Cord figured if Marty even took a quarter of his advice, Lilly would strangle him before they got out of the car in the parking lot on the way to the party. Now Martin should have known better; he knew Lilly all his life, but he was consumed by the moment, and took any advice he received from Cord as gospel. After all, he must have made the right moves to land Lilly in the first place.

Martin took a full hour and a half to primp and dress after his shower, only to have to strip down and retake a shower after he realized he had to take a dump just as he was going out the door. He wasn't going to trust toilet paper to clean his ass good enough for such an important event - a re-shower was all that would do.

That put him from comfortably on time to running late, which got him sweating, which got him nervous about sweating, which caused him to sweat even more. The suit didn't help – a polyester blend; he could feel the trickles beneath his shirt, running down the bulge of his gut.

And with his sweaty palms and pits, along with an extra clean ass, Marty made his way out the door, to pick up the date of his life. The police cruiser was fully washed and detailed, courtesy of the taxpayers of Belvidere.

As he pulled up to the building, he could see Lilly looking out the window in anticipation, and he smiled a toothy grin, like a stud-muffin does, picking up his girl.

"Earl, do you think if you stabbed me in the heart right now with a pencil, I would have to go to the hospital right away? Please, dear God, stab me and put me out of my misery."

"Marty's nice! He's been talking about you all week!"

"If that guy lays a single finger on me, I'm breaking it, I'm telling you that right now. How I let *your girlfriend* talk me into this stupid thing is beyond me."

"You offered to go with Marty, Bibby; Cord just said yes. I was there."

"That's right! Why did he say yes? He had no right to say yes! It's his fault; he should be the one wearing this dress, not me. Although I have to admit, I look pretty hot in it, don't I?"

Lilly said as she admired herself in the mirror; Earl just rolled his eyes.

"Well, if I'm not back in thirty minutes, come rescue me at the Firehouse."

[Now Lilly knew the evening's litany of events spanned four God-awful hours, excluding the 'dancing till the last one's standing' part, according to the formal invitation Marty gave Lilly earlier in the week, which she promptly threw in the trash. However, her sarcasm was lost on Earl, which frustrated her even more]

I can't *believe* I'm going to an event at the *Firehouse* with Martin - how embarrassing; how did I *ever* agree to this, Earl?"

Lilly was getting herself all worked up.

"He's beeping the horn, Bibby, get going! Cord and I are watching movies tonight."

"Can I watch movies with you two?"

My God, she couldn't believe that could be a better alternative, but it was.

"No! Look, he's getting out of the car!"

Earl was up at the window, waving wild at Marty.

"Stop encouraging him, Earl! Maybe he'll leave."

Fat chance; Lilly realized the execution wasn't going to be stayed.

"Lilly go! Marty's waiting!"

"Oh, for Christ's sake, I'm going, I'm going! I never cease to amaze myself at how good a sister I am to you Earl. I'm doing this all for you, you know that, right?"

How that made sense even she didn't know; she was simply grasping at straws. Earl didn't answer; he shot back in front of the computer when he heard Joan Jett singing *I Love Rock-n-Roll* on his favorite retro-80's website.

"I love this song, it's my *favorite*!"

"*Really Earl?* I guess I kinda knew that from the *thousand other times* you've told me that! I *know* already for Christ's sake!"

"Stop being so grouchy, grouchy-pants."

"Earl, come on, aren't you going to help me? Tell Marty I'm sick, or I'm…."

"Nope."

Was all he said. And that was that.

Lilly sighed and resigned herself to her sentence; she walked slowly to the door and called out to Earl as she exited.

"Say a prayer for me."

And she left, head down, beaten before the fight began.

Marty was at the bottom of the steps, waiting, with a smile you could drive a truck through. He had been practicing his smile in the mirror all week; he wished he had a mirror to be sure this was the one he liked - he tried so many, he couldn't tell. Once she turned the corner at the top of the stairs, he took a deep breath and sucked in his gut. He was doing both now, smiling and sucking, and it wasn't easy.

Concentrate, concentrate.

Lilly frowned at Marty's suck and smile; boy *that* looked natural - what a God-damn dork. Maybe if he holds his gut in long enough, he'll pass out from lack of oxygen and the date will be over before it started. She could only hope.

Cord heard the horn, and made a dash to the door just as Lilly hit the bottom stair.

"Now you two scamps keep it clean tonight! Martin, remember *everything* I told you, buddy, and don't take no for an answer!"

He yelled from the top of the staircase. Lilly shot him an evil glare; he smiled a shit-eating grin in return.

Martin tried to gently escort Lillian by the arm; he almost got clocked in the jaw by a flying elbow as she jerked it away.

"Take it easy, Marty, don't get too comfy, or you'll lose
a fucking tooth."

Martin sighed; he dropped his arm and kept his teeth.

534

CHAPTER 44 – SHE TURNED LEFT….AND CHANGED HER LIFE

What a day, the kind you never forget, the kind that are just about perfect in every way….cherry red.

The warm summer air cascaded the windshield, rolling her black hair horizontal; she could feel it buffet in the wind as it danced to and fro, like the flicker of a flame, pulling gently on her scalp. It felt good; she felt good.

August 14, 1992.

She accelerated into the curves on the two-lane country road, gunning past dairy farms, separated by cornfields and stretches of virgin wood. She had passed just a single car in the first mile off the Interstate. The late afternoon summer sun speckled the oversized green hood, an abstract of shadows and glint. The bright scene was muted, cut through her filtered designer shades.

The new Aston Martin was a dream, fresh from the dealership yestreen, personally delivered to her digs in Carnegie Hill on the Upper East Side on a custom transport, accompanied by the manager himself. She could see the relief on his face when he handed her the keys, the baby delivered, healthy and unharmed.

A fresh, 1992 *Virage Volante 2+2* convertible, one of only two-hundred-twenty-four made, and one of only twenty shipped to the States.

She was the first female to get one Stateside, and the youngest, at thirty-one, her office made sure of it with both the dealership and the manufacturer. That was important to her; much more than the dry details regarding performance standards, engine size, gearbox configuration and displacement ratios, all of which meant nothing to her - boring statistics she forgot before the dealer even finished his sentence.

What she did care about was the look, and the cost, 145,000 British pounds, not including the *6.3 Conversion Package*; what the *6.3* meant was anyone's guess to her. All she knew was it added another 100,000 British pounds in cost to the bottom line and gave her some tony looks, including a wide body, bonnet refit, air dam and eighteen-inch split rim wheels. She would soon forget those features as well....boring.

The statistics she committed to memory, and kept at the ready, were few:

- 245,000 British pounds; or $490,000 US dollars at a conversion of $2 per pound (she rounded up from 1.83 – it made the math *so* much easier - doubling the 245,000 to a cool $490,000, for conversation purposes – not that she was bragging, of course) – paid in cash;
- one of only twenty sent to the United States;
- youngest and first woman to get one Stateside;
- fastest and most powerful convertible Aston Martin ever built; and
- $490,000, in cash - oh, she had that one down already.

That was about it.

The trip odometer, which started at a lovely *002* when she first turned the key and the baby came to life in the City, rolled over to *069* miles when she passed an immense sycamore in front of a white clapboard farmstead; she didn't know it was a sycamore at the time, she just knew it was one of the biggest, craggiest, and most beautiful trees she had ever seen, set right alongside the busy road, only a few feet from the white line.

The tree was enormous! It must have been over ten feet across at the base, ringed in a thick bed of lovely, burnt-orange tiger lilies, which tilted and waved at her as she sped by. The trunk rose through the mass of lilies and spread majestically into a huge mass of horizontal, tangled branches, covered in large green leaves, which waft in the breeze. The bark was tan and splotchy white at the base, with the trunk turning ghostly white as it climbed skyward.

It immediately reminded her of an oversized version of the angry apple trees in the *Wizard of Oz* – that was the first thought which came to mind. Without leaves, it must be the ultimate Halloween tree, she thought.

What a great tree, her secret tree.

She couldn't believe she entered the Lincoln Tunnel just sixty miles ago….Midtown!

She tired of hearing her friends rave about the country estates with gorgeous 19th century wood clapboard homesteads they were stealing from the yokels in Pennsylvania, just past the Water Gap.

They had streams with native trout, and ponds with fat catfish, as if any one of them knew the right side of a fishing pole. Deer and turkey roamed just beyond the window bay in the breakfast nook; there were the requisite stories of big black bears raiding the bird feeder and red fox scurrying across the country lanes they plied with their retro-two-seater bikes.

Real foxes!

There were the mandatory paddocks and ride-ins for the weekend horses. Lunch drivel spoke of early evening rides out past the far hay barns, to the fields of green and gold sung in songs.

Some sported old corn cribs, pump houses, long-house chicken coops, even grain silos, which the *uber-*architects and designers *du jour* would fix and primp as props to adore, or outbuildings to house English-forged stainless steel gardening tools, for the immigrant help, or perhaps a bathhouse, complete with oversized jet tubs and spa fit-outs for the occasional weekend guests; the owners rarely stepped foot in them.

Time was spent sitting on the lanai or lounging beneath the wisteria pergola with a dirty martini, waxing fond about how important it was to spend hard-earned money to preserve rural America for all to enjoy, at least those allowed to venture past the private entry gates.

It was the new *Upstate*, and so much closer.

It was all a bunch of nonsense, she thought, so of course she needed one of her own. But she would have to do them all one better; that was Carol.

So she christened the Aston to scout a country estate to call her own. The first stop inside the Pennsylvania border would be a quick drink with a friend, an investment banker and fellow charity foundation board member who bought his retreat several years ago, followed by a caravan tour of four estate-sized parcels set up by a local realtor, a doyenne who specialized in local *Price on Request*.

With directions in hand to the *prive* lane which hid the cloistered estate of her friend, she was still on the Jersey side of the Gap, on Route 80, about twenty minutes shy of her destination, when she noticed the amber glow of an idiot icon on the dash – right as she approached a large green sign along the side of the interstate:

Exit 12
Hope
Blairstown

Just beyond which was planted a small brown tourist-attraction sign, with an odd inscription:

538

What does that mean? she thought.

It was the same exit her friends would blow by at ninety miles per hour; the horde of New York plates on a Friday afternoon, a mix of luxury sedans and sport utilities, motoring in pack mode, ready to forage in fields further west. Never did one of them ever mention the Town of Blairstown to her, or the Town of Hope, let alone some orphic destination dubbed the *Land of Make Believe*. They were simply anonymous roadside markers that one passes, and ignores, on their way somewhere else.

She pulled off the ramp, hoping to find gas; there was no comforting blue highway sign stating one actually existed anywhere near this rural exit.

At the bottom of the ramp she could go left, and south – to Hope, or right, and north – to Blairstown.

It was one of those forks in the road which shapes the rest of your life, yet at the time, it disguised itself as a simple country lane, and a mere crapshoot, guessing which direction – empty road to the right or the left – would yield a closer top off of her tank; why the tank wasn't full at delivery was a question for the dealership she would bitch about later. But for now, it was just a decision on gas, nothing more or less.

How could you pick against a place called *Hope,* she thought to herself; and with no more logic than that, she turned left….and changed her life.

CHAPTER 45 – LIFE COULDN'T GET MUCH BETTER - THEN ALONG CAME LILLY

The southern selection proved providential; a tiny service station materialized on the right, just shy of a mile from the interstate. The other direction, had she so chosen, would have had her wandering lost along a lonely ribbon of northern rural road, with nothing but farms and forest for a good ten miles.

Actually, where she now found herself, there was no real town, not here anyway. It was simply a combined gas station and deli, with an adjacent bank branch set in a circa-50's converted residential ranch; across the street sat a non-descript four-bay white masonry firehouse, set beside two large white pines, still sporting remnants of last year's string of Christmas lights.

Yet once Carol fueled up, she pointed the Aston south, in the wrong direction, away from whence she came, further from Route 80 and deeper into the woods, toward a little sign stuck along the shoulder, which marked the way to the mystery down the road called *Hope*.

She wasn't sure why she didn't get back on the highway and continue on toward Pennsylvania to see her banker friend, but it was probably because her little set of directions said to do just that.

She came upon the Town proper in less than a half mile; a blinking red light marked the center of a too-quaint crossroads, which looked to extend a block or two in each direction, and not a building further.

The edifices were simply gorgeous; picture-perfect limestone block, circa-18th Century, each one neater than the next. But they were close to the road, and less than a mile from the Interstate, just a spit down the road from one of the few easy on/off gas stations on the ride out to Pennsylvania. Although none of her friends ever mentioned it, she was sure more than one must have gotten off to gas-up at this same exit at one time or another.

But regardless how beautiful the little hamlet of Hope seemed, no way she would buy real estate in a Town that her friends simply stopped at for fuel, a mere pit stop, on the way to their weekend *pied-a-terre* on the other side of the Delaware River.

'Oh, you bought there? That's nice. Hon, isn't that the exit where we stop for gas and a hot pretzel at that deli on our way out? The pretzels certainly aren't New York! And they're never very fresh....but I'm sure your place is real nice. Do you get your pretzels there?'

Forget that; she wasn't giving anyone that easy ammunition.

She passed through Hope and kept going, and a mile further down the county route is where she first eyed that enormous Halloween sycamore tree....that big, beautiful tree. *Her* tree; she took immediate ownership. And she felt it was some sort of sign, a friend urging her in, urging her onward, further into the breach.

It was as if she was entering a forbidden forest, down the fork of a road less traveled. She remembered feeling adventurous, curious, and just plain happy. Somehow, just seeing that knarled tree put her in a good mood; she forgot all about Pennsylvania, her friend and the doyenne caravan.

She maintained a southern course, to where she wasn't quite sure. But the day was splendid and she was in no rush to get wherever she was going, so she just drove on blind, letting the Aston guide her, listening to the radio blast, finding herself smiling.

After a ten minute jaunt, she ponied to a lonely traffic light at what appeared to be a major intersection in these parts; a green, iconic sign signaled the:

lay along the bridal path, straight ahead. Worth checking out, she thought.

So she followed the green markers for several miles, to a blinking red light, another country crossroad, this one occupied by an expansive dairy farm, complete with three dozen Holsteins lazily grazing along the fence line, followed by a corn field, with stalks that much have reached ten feet high. In a few years they would vanish, reincarnated as *Brookfield Estates*. The corn would be gone, with a crop of empty-nesters taking its place.

She hooked a right at the farm, following the *Court House* arrow, and cruised along the two-lane for another half-mile or so; more cows and corn.

Then the asphalt ribbon took a quick up and down dip, curving around a large bedrock outcrop, which seemed to emerge from nowhere. Just like that, on the other side of the rock, she was dropped in the middle of a quiet residential neighborhood of tiny, neat, one-story residential ranches.

She felt she somehow drove into the 1950's and *Leave It To Beaver*. She slowed the car and crawled past an expansive, two-story, dulled red-brick, Art-Deco gem to her right:

Belvidere High School

Two more blocks brought her past a timeworn cemetery, grayed and venerable, with large ornate headstones, intermixed with newer, smooth stone markers, all neat as a pin. For some odd reason, that made her smile.

The road ahead took a strange left-right jag, purposely realigned around a large white oak tree. A small brown historic marker was set alongside the shoulder; it read:

The
Shoe Tree

She pulled the car to the shoulder and idled while she read the tiny print:

Barefoot country folk sat
under this tree to put on
shoes before going to
worship across the
village green

Two tree moments in one day; she smiled to herself at the silly thought. She seemed to be smiling a lot on this conte. She put the car in gear and forged ahead, in search of the *village green*.

The sign was right; she took a left and traveled two quiet blocks from the *Shoe Tree*, passing a series of large, 19th century Victorians, with stately sycamores and maples lining the road....this must be the older, original part of Town.

At the end of that lazy stretch, she found herself facing that very Village Green, fronted by an imposing red-brick Courthouse, with huge, white ionic columns, three churches, and, immediately off her right shoulder, an

543

imposing, three-story, white Italianate Victorian, which bellied up to that beautiful country Park.

A bent, rusted sign speared the front yard, the lawn was sparse and unkempt, more weeds than grass. It looked as if that sign had been planted, and forgotten, a long while ago. It spoke two simple words:

For Sale

She hadn't taken in the view for more than five seconds; she really only saw two sides of the house, but that was all it took....she knew it straight-away.

She had stumbled upon her retreat, right in the middle of a New England-style village square; there was *no way* any of her friends had ever stumbled upon this gem, they would have mentioned it for sure....it was too unbelievable to be out here, sprouting in a patch of nowhere.

Eighteen minutes off the highway, and a century behind; she could just feel it.

She looped the Park twice clockwise, curbside crawl speed, checking out the environs, the churches, the Courthouse, not believing this place was dropped here....not convinced that it really existed.

Belvidere, New Jersey....she had never heard of it.

She drove two blocks to the realty office noted on the yard sign, and found Woody reading the paper and Moe, head cocked back, mouth agape, sound asleep at his desk. It was Friday afternoon; a bit of familial relaxation before heading down to the *Palace of Sweets* for a late afternoon ice cream sundae. The standard Friday routine for father and son.

She smiled; if she hadn't taken the day off, she would be working till at least 10 pm in front of a monitor, or with her ear glued to a phone; managing the portfolio and schmoozing clients in different time zones all over the world. She looked over at the old man napping - it looked pretty darn tempting; she had to figure a way to work *that* into her daily routine.

The creak of the door broke the siesta, and both father and son thought they had died and went to heaven; Carol was a presence, to be sure. As they eyed her up, her legs seemed to extend forever. This was not the typical residential fare stumbling into their office; this was a special find indeed.

The two spent the next three hours fawning over her, bringing her through the Beaumont house – all the way up to the fourth floor cupola overlooking the Park, parading her around Town, pointing out the sights. She got to see the *Shoe Tree* a second time, with the boys regaling in stories past and showing her off to anyone, everyone, in eyesight. The tour, which would normally take about a half-hour at best, stretched on; the tag-team wasn't about to let the eye candy loose any sooner than they had to.

Father and son were in their glory.

Neither had ever seen an Aston Martin, and she was the first hedge fund manager they'd met. Neither knew what a hedge fund really was, but they shook their heads in agreement and pretended well enough. They figured she had money, but the car wasn't the only hook - it was the dress, and the look. You didn't get that look in Belvidere; even Lilly didn't have that sophistication. It was hard to describe, but it clearly wasn't Belvidere; that variety simply wasn't local-grown.

As the afternoon wore on, their quips and corny jokes were getting a bit stale, but that was vintage Woody and Moe, more so because they were a bit nervous around her. But Carol just smiled and took it all in stride. Truth be told, she knew the two were harmless, and it was clear they were beside themselves. So Carol gladly played along and thoroughly enjoyed the royal treatment; she was their show-and-tell, and today's stories would be told and retold by Woody and Moe, embellished along the way, clear through the holidays.

Into Sam's they went; both Sam and Frank took one look and were smitten. Even Frank blushed....cranky, sulky Frank.

Woody introduced Carol as his friend, and big Sam came from behind the counter and gave her a gentle bear hug and greeting like he was the long-lost uncle he wished he was.

"Any friend of Woody's is a friend of mine, especially when they look like you!"

He bellowed, as he gave Carol a friendly wink.

The hug was a bit too long for a *I-don't-know-you* first hug, and Carol would have screamed in the City, but she surprised herself by not tensing or squirming; she even hugged back, as best she could - her arms didn't get very far around his enormous butcher's girth.

Carol was swept up in the hospitality; she knew she was good-looking, but in the City, good-looks come along a dime a dozen. And she knew she was wicked-smart, but in her business that was no great shakes either, if you were any good at what you did.

But here, at the corner of Water and Market Streets in a backwater county where the annual Farmer's Fair awarded ribbons for pit-spitting and cow-chip tossing, with the winners proudly published in the weekly rag, she was something new, something fresh.

She was royalty.

At least that's how she felt, and she couldn't stop smiling. What a genuinely nice place, what a gem, an absolute find, she thought. Life couldn't get much better.

Then along came Lilly.

CHAPTER 46 – A FIRST ENCOUNTER WAS AROUND THE CORNER

The next week was a whirlwind – due diligence, contract review and third-party discussions with old Doc Beaumont, who had long-since retired to Florida - Naples, with his wife. Carol took frequent trips to Belvidere from the City, racking miles on the Aston.

The buzz in Town was frenetic; the Beaumont place had sat empty forever. Woody's realty sign had parked on the lawn for several years, quietly gathering rust, marking time.

Earl's haunted house had waited all those years for Carol to finally find it. And she did.

And so, in the late summer of 1992, the empty Beaumont veterinarian estate would become her *L'antre du Lion*; she had found her retreat.

Serendipity.

She bought it for cash short of a week later; at $183,000, it was less than the upgrade package for the Aston.

As Carol met people in Town over the years, she found other transplants stumbled into Belvidere in a similar manner; it seemed a prerequisite of some sort - no one was ever really on their way to Belvidere, they just ended up there, and seemed to stay, just like the ones born there that had never left. A one-way door.

Strange.

With the sale, Carol-tales spread like wildfire through Town, growing by leaps and ripening with each iteration. It seemed half the male population in Belvidere was arranging their schedules to coincide with a Carol-siting; the other half was bragging about the minutia of their brief encounters; everyone wanted the chance to meet the City girl, the one with the James Bond car, model-body and oodles of cash.

Her mother was a Russian defector; she worked for some secret branch in the government; she did porn movies as a teenager; she was married to the mob and was in Belvidere to hide – witness protection; it was her ex-husband's money; she was a wunderkind who was locked in a basement as a kid and found by a psychic; she was….she did….she was.

Of course, none of it was true.

Every small town has its rumor mill, but Belvidere's was oversized on steroids, with a constant churn; it always took on a life of its own.

Not that Carol minded all that much. It was kind of fun to be an enigma, a very big fish in a very small pond. And she did little to quell the rumors, neither confirm nor deny. And her silence was an accelerant.

She didn't tell any of her City peers she bought in Belvidere; she never even told them about the Town; she just blew off buying a country estate for now. She would *focus on it later*, she would tell them, after the new firm settled down.

The new firm was Actaeon Capital Investments, *her firm*.

She named it Actaeon, but saw herself, her fund, as Artemis, the goddess that watched with detached, noble indifference, at the viscous slaying of a lesser male hunter who failed to heed her advice. She used the analogy to sell the fund, with the twist of naming it Actaeon, for the vanquished, as opposed to the goddess Artemis, who prompted his demise and carried on none the worse for wear.

It made for a good story.

Life was good; she found Belvidere, she seeded her fund with just under a half-billion in investments from two pension funds and a half dozen wealthy individuals, all carry-overs from her prior stint at *Brockman & Parden*. With a two-percent/twenty-percent fee arrangement, still *du jour* in the industry circa-2006, but certainly standard fare in 1992, she was looking at an annual revenue stream of approximately twenty-five million dollars, on a net return of eighteen percent. With a staff of just ten managing the load, there was plenty of room for Astons and Italianates, even with prime digs in Carnegie Hill.

Life was indeed good.

Carol had heard about Lillian from a slew of people in Town almost from day one, but for the first three months, she never met her – odd for such a small town – especially since she certainly seemed to have met just about everyone else. Sam did nothing but glow like a proud father when talking about Lilly, as did Frank. Sam was sure they would be the best of friends. As for the rest of the Lilly commentary, the jury was certainly hung.

She heard of Lillian's boyfriend too, some hard-ass former Marine, and supposedly a real looker, named Button. Odd name, she thought, kind of country-bumpkin; but she never met him either. Strange.

Carol hoped Sam was right, she hoped Lilly could become a friend without all the pretension of wealth and material trappings she had to contend with, and compete with, in the City. She fully understood she was a source as much as a product of that thinking, but it went with the territory, at least east of the Hudson. Out here, she could shelve it, and relax.

How nice it would be to have a real girlfriend out here to chill with, to talk about stupid stuff; maybe that girlfriend was Lilly. Sam certainly thought so, as did Frank.

Maybe that was a bit of wishful thinking.

A first encounter was around the corner.

Carol pushed open the door; the tinny bell signaled her presence. Sam looked up and a wide grin raced across his face, as it did each time Carol entered the shop.

She was a beam of light, so full of life and energy – just the sight of her passing into the market brightened his day. He found himself looking forward to Friday afternoons, hoping she would come in. If she was in Town, she always came to see him first; he was proud of that, and wasn't ashamed to tell anyone within earshot.

Sam was fifty-one, Carol was thirty-one; if he was fifteen years younger, heck, ten years, he would make a run for her, even though he knew it would likely be futile, his hat would nonetheless be in the ring.

But at fifty-one, and with the sad shape he was in, it all seemed just a bit silly, but it didn't stop him from thinking about it, about the possibility. He wondered how many times a day Carol got mind-fucked by the degenerates in Town. Funny, he didn't think of himself as a degenerate, just the others who shared his carnal thoughts. If Carol only knew.

Actually, she probably did; good-looking girls usually do.

It was a Friday in early November, 1992, a beautiful, late, Indian-summer day, almost three months since she first, accidentally arrived in Town. Carol had been in Belvidere just about every weekend since, and some days during the week, for furniture deliveries, decorator meetings and contractor issues. You never had to twist her arm too hard to make the trip; coming to Town was her new hobby, her new fun.

The purchase was still a somewhat loosely kept secret amongst her friends; by this time they knew she bought something in Jersey, they didn't know exactly what or where, and none were ever invited out. Belvidere was her hideaway, not to be shared; she knew they would overrun the place, buy it in toto, and change it to become some reflection of them, morphing it into what they thought a little gem like this should be, rather than simply enjoying what it already was. She was doing the same thing, actually, but she was still an island in a sea of unvarnished small-town. And that held great appeal to her.

And even though she had only become a small part of it so recently, she came to love Belvidere; and felt as if she truly belonged. People born in Belvidere considered themselves the only true Belvidereans, and even then you had to have generations of prior-borns behind you; transplants decades removed were still considered newcomers to the native set. But Carol was quickly accepted more than most, and felt special because of it.

So she would trudge solo out to northwest Jersey, greeting her favorite, craggy sycamore to and back each trip; she loved that tree, and would talk to it in her car at each passing, sharing thoughts and secrets, explaining her love life, or lack thereof, and the stresses of work. She wondered what her clients would think about her conversations with the Halloween tree, and the half-billion they trusted in her hands….the girl who talks to trees.

That thought would always make her smile.

Except this weekend she wasn't solo; her new boyfriend was in tow. He was a contemporary artist, a minimalist, in a Chelsea atelier she frequented to decorate her flat in the City - Deward Saunders. Only an artist or a trust-funder could get away with a name like Deward, and he certainly wasn't the latter.

Carol strolled casually back to the deli counter and walked around the back, where the patrons weren't allowed. She gave Sam a big smile and a bigger hug, not minding his bloody smock. He was like a big old teddy bear.

He lightly kissed her on top of her head; the kind of kiss a good friend gives.

"Hello young lady how was life this week in the big bad world outside Belvidere?"

Sam whispered as he hugged her.

"Hectic; I'm glad to be out here, like usual, always good to see your smiling face and to get away from the grind, to come out here and get a dose of reality….Belvidere-style."

As Sam hugged her, and continued to hug her, he looked over her head to see a tall, slender and sculpted dark-haired man standing in front of the counter; with a cropped black leather sports jacket, black leather boots and a pair of a-bit-too-tight black leather pants. His buttoned silk shirt was a midnight-blue, almost black. The top two buttons were undone, exposing the gentle waved curls of the dark hair on his chest; it almost seemed photo-shoot groomed....a bit too perfect. He had day-old stubble and a pair of matte-black, wire-framed shades, which he kept on inside the market.

In the five seconds it took to take in the man standing in front of him, Sam concluded he didn't like him….he didn't like him at all.

Carol sensed Sam met the man in black, at least by line of sight. She stepped away, half-turned, and presented her prize.

"Sam, this is my boyfriend Dew; Dew, this is Sam, my favorite butcher and adopted dad, the man I told you all about. You want meat - Sam's the guy. He's a pretty good hugger too!"

And with that, Carol stepped in and squeezed Sam hard around his ample mid-riff one last time before stepping back, halving the distance between the two men.

Sam blushed at the introduction. He loved Carol; she really felt like a daughter, at least how he thought having a daughter should feel. She was such a genuinely nice person, he thought. He felt about Carol how he felt about Lilly; well, no one could ever be a Lilly to Sam, but Carol was a very close second....as close as a second could come.

Sam extended his hand; Dew hesitated, then slowly reciprocated, as if he debated whether the physical effort was worth it. The two shook, but Sam's iron grip squeezed a dainty hand. Sam quickly let go, disgusted at the dead fish he just shook.

"Nice to meet you."

Sam said through a half-smile, although he clearly didn't mean it.

Dew barely half-nodded his head, and didn't say a word.

Well, *that* went well, Carol thought, as she frowned.

After the awkward exchange, Carol and Sam chatted about a variety of subjects, with Frank listening on the periphery, like a little girl. Dew wandered clumsily around the market, randomly picking up and putting down various fruits and vegetables he had no interest in, making pouty faces to himself in the process, bored and killing time – not really trying to show any interest in this place, or the process. He had been in this shit-burger Town about an hour, and it was an hour too long.

Carol couldn't help but notice - that was Dew's point; Carol decided she should probably end the embarrassing episode, for both her and Sam's sake.

But before she broke away from Sam, Dew had made his way out of the shop, and was standing in the sun on the sidewalk in front of the market, leaning against the plate glass. He seemed occupied with something; she figured if he could entertain himself for a bit, like a child, she could continue to talk with Sam.

Good boy.

Ten minutes passed; she turned and checked on him occasionally as she spoke to Sam, like one does a dog. He hadn't moved; he seemed to be talking to someone just beyond her ken. Good, he was occupied and not whining, for once; he bellyached the whole way out, not understanding why he had to see *this place* – he wouldn't even call it Belvidere, just *this place*; why couldn't they just go grab a drink and dinner in the City (on her dime, of course), and then hang out and discuss art with her rich friends (at his Chelsea gallery, of course). He was a big, spoiled kid, and using her as a meal ticket….no surprise there.

But he was Promethean in ceramics; at least, at times, she convinced herself as much. She considered him her personal artist-in-residence; others, Carol's friends that is, would say he was a leech, a stepped-in-shit-lucky adopted starving artist, or a gigolo, or both.

He got some decent press now and again, although largely due to favors from her press contacts. And he was simply gorgeous to look at, sweetmeat arm candy, no doubt about it. He wasn't a type-A who ran in her circle, also a definite plus. And when they first started dating a year ago, he actually was happy and upbeat, and working steady in the studio, most of the time anyway; that was apparently part of the hook. He had that part of the gig down, but good.

But once he set the hook, the charade didn't last. Now he was increasingly a drag, following her wallet wherever it went.

And to top it off, the sex was never really very good. He had a big, thick dick; she had never seen a cock with such girth. She decided thick was definitely better than long; although he was no slouch in that department either. But the best part was bragging about its size to her friends, or showing it off when he stuffed it in his leather nut-huggers, as they pranced from one headliner event to the next. But when he actually went to use that big prick, he was uninspiring, to say the least. What a waste of a huge cock, she used to think. And she could also never get used to the uncircumcised part; it just didn't seem right, kind of like a dog-dick, or some Euro-style look. For her, it was a real turn-off; that cock would be so much better looking trimmed. So she rarely blew him. And it was simply too big for her ass – he tried once or twice, but it was a no-go; it hurt like a mother. Instead she would just quickly bury it in her pussy; that's where it belonged.

He was lazy at sex, usually just laying there, admiring himself, and letting her do all the work. Not that she minded; when he tried to take control, he was clumsy, awkward and staccato, always starting, stopping and needlessly jockeying around - never getting into a smooth rhythm. So she preferred to simply mount, close her eyes, plant her hands on his washboard stomach and ride at her own pace, his prick being nothing more than an awesome personal dildo, which happened to be attached to a beautiful, brainless body.

She wondered why she kept him around - lethargy more than anything else; she simply got tired at the thought of trying to find someone better, who would just turn out to be some other mix of bad in the end.

As she looked out Sam's front shop window at him, she thought to herself just bringing him along was, maybe, not such a good idea after all. That was more prophetic than she could possibly know.

"Sam, I'll see you in a couple hours at the *Palace* for our usual Friday night date; I've been hankering for a chocolate shake all day."

"Do you have to bring Chew along?"

Sam whispered; he knew it was childish, but he couldn't help himself.

She tilted her head and gave him a wry smile.

"It's *Dew,* and yes I have to bring him along; sorry he was so….whatever, he's not usually like that - bad day, I guess." *[Sam knew that was a little white lie, he was probably always a mopey putz; in the three months that Sam had known Carol, she had only mentioned him in passing once or twice, so Sam knew he was probably no great shakes even before he showed up – one look confirmed his suspicion]*

"Okay, I'll save our booth. Woody will probably be there too, he was asking about you, wondering if you were coming to the *Palace.* I said of course, it's Friday night in Belvidere, where else in the world would a girl like Carol want to be."

Sam smiled at his own little joke, and so did Carol.

"Woody's a good egg."

And with that, she leaned into him and gave him a peck on the cheek. Her piece of art had slipped back into the market, wondering why he was still waiting for her. But he was smiling, which was a pleasant surprise, Carol thought. Maybe he found something to like about Belvidere after all.

She proceeded to escort him out the door; they hopped into her car, which was parked in front of the market, and sped off to the house. She drove; she wouldn't dare trust him behind the wheel of the Aston.

Neither Sam nor Carol noticed Lillian watching the whole scene, discretely, street-side, through the plate glass, when she wasn't flirting with Dew, that is. It was a half-effort, really, but enough to keep him more than interested and cull the information she was seeking. Deward could primp and prattle like a girl when he wanted to.

The wheels were spinning, they were always spinning with Lilly.

And Dew was hypnotized – barely making eye contact when they spoke. Her extra short skirt, with bare legs, and tight sweater sans bra made it that much better. She also was pantie-less, but he didn't know that. It just got her more juiced for the part, and she knew this was an important scene to play.

Deward gushed about wanting to sculpt her, never mind he didn't really have the talent to pull it off. His work was minimalist and abstract at best - vases, planters and large hodgepodge assemblages of various geometric shapes, fused together. Despite that, he suggested he would mirror her in clay, every *sinew* of her body (he knew that *sinew* word cold, and was intent on using it in a sentence to impress her).

For fun, as he spoke, she would, every now and then, slowly drop her gaze and focus on his leather-clad crotch, just for a moment or so, while at the same time discretely, slowly, licking or gently biting her lip, almost imperceptive, except she knew he picked up on it immediately, like all guys do.

She only had to work through two quick southern stares for his cock to react; in those tight leather pants, sans underwear – he never wore any, it became clear rather quickly how large it really was, and Lilly, in spite of herself, was impressed. Socks don't grow on demand; that prick was the real deal.

But rather than try to hide it in embarrassment, like most guys would, Deward gazed down at the swell in his pants and smiled with pride.

She smiled too, to herself; this was *way* too easy.

By the time Carol and Dew headed out the door, the spider had disappeared.

But not for long.

CHAPTER 48 – ALL WAS RIGHT WITH THE WORLD

Lilly casually strolled into the *Palace* and checked the time on the dainty watch dangling from her tiny wrist. It was 6:32 pm; a small inset dial marked seconds – the hand swept past twelve as the front door clicked shut.

Lillian rarely wore this watch; it was her mother's – Carol's *secret* birthday gift from Sam in 1964, when the two were *special* friends for a fiery, three-month spell. The definition of *special* depended upon whom you talked to at the time.   It was a subject Sam didn't discuss then, and never discussed later, especially with Lilly.

When Lilly wore that watch, Sam couldn't help but see Lilly's mom; the two could have been sisters.   It wrapped Sam happy and melancholy; he could wear both, in layers.

Carol was nineteen and Sam was twenty-three, home for the past six months after a four-year stint in the Navy.

That watch set Sam back a good half-month pay back then; it was beautiful – silver, with a gold wind stem, a mother-of-pearl face and a bejeweled setting.   It was stunning and petite - a piece of art to be admired, just like Carol.

At the time he discretely bought Carol the watch in '64, Sam was formally dating Elmire, or Elly, or El – she answered to all three.   She was a shy, kind-hearted girl who had a killer-crush on Sam since she first noticed boys.   She never pursued another, and had never been with any other. Sam was all she ever wanted.

El was good-looking, not model-quality, but certainly more than attractive, with a wholesome *girl-next-door* look.   She was tall, thin and somewhat gangly, with long, arrow-straight chestnut hair, forever cinched in a ponytail. She never wore makeup; her complexion clear and bright, with a faint hint of freckles. She had a slightly upturned nose and over-long legs, with bony knees.

She was a lithe tomboy; a born and raised farm girl from Harmony Township, just outside Town.

El had an attention-grabbing handshake – a firm grasp with long fingers. You always mark the smart ones as mousy, but not Elmire. She was wicked smart, but also a standout athlete – basketball – and was the only girl anyone knew who could palm the ball. As a teenager, she would walk about Town with that orange orb glued to her hand.

But El, when not by Sam's side, or shooting hoops, was most comfortable out in the family barn; quiet time with the animals was much preferred to the companionship of people.

Carol was the antithesis of Elmire. Although she too was kind-hearted, most of the time, Carol needed no one, and made that eminently clear to any man she happened to be with, including Sam in '64. She was a bonny free-spirit, and would frequently go off for bouts on her own to points unknown, only to return as if she never left, with nary a word of her absence.

No one ever asked for details, including Sam; not that Carol would have obliged – Carol did as she pleased, and answered to no one. Ever.

To be with Carol was to be draped in utter beauty, and to experience raw sexuality. And she was a head-turner like no other. Any man would kill to have her on his arm; but to be in that envious position was to be forever consumed and cursed with protecting that rite from the horde of men trying to take it away….a relentless, never-ending game of *king-of-the-raft*.

Add that Carol was a butterfly, giving one the feeling her decision to light on your arm, while a source of fierce pride and particular good fortune, was precarious and temporary at best. One had to lie still and breathe light, lest upsetting her stay, only left to watch, powerless, as she flitted away on the breeze, never looking back.

One finds himself forever on guard, anticipating when the wild ride will end, which it surely will, sooner than hoped, and certainly when it's expected least. It was a debilitating feeling for any man she was with, as it was for Sam. Catching a tiger by the tail….the stress of holding on was immense.

So in the end, Sam let go of the tail and married Elmire, and felt safe. But El never got a watch like that.

Elly surrendered herself to Sam, and devoted her life to making him happy; it was a simple goal, which she successfully fulfilled. Elmire bore him no children; she ultimately could not conceive. That was always a disappointment for the both of them, although neither spoke of it publicly.

Elmire stayed faithfully by his side, till she slowly succumbed to myeloma, a longstanding battle that consumed the last few years of her life. She died with Sam bedside, holding her hand, at the age of fifty, after twenty-four years of happy, safe, and traditional marriage.

Sam never second-guessed his decision to marry her; he loved Elmire. But he would be less than honest if he didn't at times, actually more times than he would admit, daydream with a tinge of regret the foregone days spent with Carol, lying naked by his side. That torrid time, albeit brief, was etched as if it was yesterday; he thought of it often over the years, like most men do when they're lucky enough to catch a tiger, even for just a spell.

That watch on Lillian's wrist would always flash-flood those memories, without fail.

Sam, Dew and Carol were already seated in the first booth on the right, past the ice cream counter. Sam faced the front door and sat alone on his side of the table; Carol and Deward shared the other side, with Carol on the inside, working the beginning of her favorite Friday treat - a large, thick chocolate milk shake, topped with a single maraschino cherry. The three occupied the booth Carol and Sam always sat in on Friday nights, which happened to be the same booth that Lilly and Sam *always* sat in. Sam was a creature of habit; in this case, that habit was just another straw on a whole pile of trouble quickly coming his way.

Lilly knew about the *booth issue* already, having heard about it endlessly over the past three months from various quidnuncs in Town, especially Jane, the fast-ass out on Oxford Street. She was the worst, flashing a treacly disposition while she slowly stirred the pot. But seeing Carol sitting in her booth in the flesh made her even more steamed; how could Sam, all happy, smiling and laughing, sit in that booth, *their* booth, with *her*. She could already feel her face starting to flush. She took a breath and tried to calm down; this was no time to get rattled.

Although Lilly has stolen glimpses of Carol several times over the past three months, this was her closest encounter. She quickly scoped her out, at least what she could surmise from the waist up in the first ten seconds. *Not nearly as pretty as I am* - Lilly convinced herself as she walked toward them.

The *Palace* was Friday-night busy; all the booths were full and the counter was buzzing with walk-ins buying ice cream and various goods-to-go. Retro-50's music filled the background.

Lilly wore the same outfit as earlier, on the sidewalk with Deward; it would do just fine for this second performance.

Here we go - game on she said to herself.

Sam caught a glimpse of Lilly and his eyes widened in anticipation.

"Hey, Lilly hey, come on over! Carol, this is great, you finally get a chance to meet Lilly!"

Now Sam had been bragging about Lilly to Carol since day one, and Carol was genuinely excited to meet her.

The needle pegged quickly, pretty much as soon as Lilly saddled up to the booth, still standing, looking down on the three of them.

Carol enthusiastically extended her hand toward Lilly.

"Lilly, so nice to finally meet you! I'm Carol.... "

To which Lilly emphatically replied.

"Dewie!"

She followed the exclamation with a large wet kiss on his stubbled left cheek, much closer to his mouth than was customary, and extended in duration a second or two beyond normal; just uncomfortably long enough to be noticed by all. As she withdrew, she left a large smear of cherry-red, lipstick lips on Deward's cheek, a tattoo that couldn't be missed. She ignored Carol completely, leaving her hand awkwardly extended in the air, waiting for an acknowledgment that would never come.

"*Dewie?* Where did that come from? You two **know** each other?"

Carol ogled Dew in disbelief, as she tried to discretely retract her offered hand in embarrassment, then anger. It had gotten frigid in less than fifteen seconds.

So far, so good, Lilly thought.

"Uh, uh…."

Was the best Dew could do under pressure, as he slumped a bit in the booth. He didn't look so GQ right about now.

"Oh, we don't know each other *that* well; Dewie was just talking about me modeling for him when we met out on the sidewalk in front of Sam's this afternoon. I guess you were busy inside talking to Sam, you know, my *dad*. He told you he's my father, right *[Lilly looked right at Sam as she spoke]*?

Anyway, Deward wants me to come into the City and sit for him, so he can sculpt me *poser dans le nu*, whatever that means. Did I say that right Dewie?

He said he likes my *sinews [Lilly said, as she looked at her sculpted arms]*. He said he had been looking a long time for just the right model; he could never find a girl with the right, what did you call it, *killer body*? And here I was, standing in front of him on the sidewalk - what luck! Thank God he came to Belvidere he said!"

Lilly rubbed Dew's shoulder affectionately as she waxed about their first meeting; it was pure poetry.

Dew sat frozen in fear; he didn't know what to say or do. He could feel his balls shrink as his meal ticket reared up next to him, ready to make a fatal strike.

"*Poser dans le nu?* We've been practicing our French have we? Funny, I didn't know you sculpted models, in the nude, to boot.....nice. When did that start, this afternoon? On the sidewalk?"

"Oh, I'm sorry, did I cause a fuss? I asked if you were his girlfriend, but Dewie said the two of you were just *friends,* and that you were just a client, or something boring like that."

The words actually sounded sincere, dripping from Lilly's lips.

"*What!*"

"I didn't say that....exactly."

Dewie stuttered the response; he would have done better with the prior 'Uh, uh' response, or better yet, a quick exit.

"Are you calling me a liar, Deward?"

Lilly's tone switched *instantly.* It was menacing, as if she was suddenly possessed; her gaze bore down on Dew as she took her hand off his shoulder in a histrionic fashion. If he knew her better, he would have hidden the silverware.

"No! No way, it's just that...."

Then his voice trailed off; he simply ran out of ideas - not a lot going on between those artsy ears.

"Dad? Did you say dad?"

Sam uttered in a low, robotic voice, emerging from his own fog, trying to digest the bomb Lilly just dropped on him. Then he saw the watch on her wrist, and a switch flipped in his head - standing next to him was Carol....my God, she looked *just* like Carol. He sat staring at her, mouth slightly agape, saying nothing more.

"What the hell's going on here? Sam, is she your *daughter*? You said you had no kids; you said that I was like an *adopted daughter* for Christ's sake! Why would you say something like that? Why wouldn't you just tell me she was your daughter? Are you *really* her father? What the fuck is happening here?!"

"Uh, uh...."

Was the best Sam could do under pressure, shifting uncomfortable in the booth; he and Deward had something in common after all.

Carol looked at him incredulous, eyes wide and mouth agape, searching for answers that simply weren't coming. After a few seconds of uncomfortable silence, she let out an exasperated huff, shaking her head in the negative.

"That's enough; let me out....now!"

Carol yelled to Dew, who understood the instruction clearly and figured he could do that safely; out of the booth he slid.

Carol stood face to face with Lilly, they were the same height, and were eye-to-eye, nose-to-nose, less than three inches apart. Carol didn't see, but both of Lillian's fists were clenched.

Neither backed down.

"I've heard a lot about you, and other than your *Dad* here, your fat, drunk uncle and the realty boys, most said to be *very* careful around you. I was hoping they were wrong, *but what an understatement, you're **much** worse than they described.* Your talents are being wasted here, honey; you can make a lot of money on stage with an act like that.

And for the record, he **was** my boyfriend, although mainly he was a leech. You can sculpt to your heart's content **Bibby**; he's yours; but be warned, he's expensive, not that I think you have the cash to shine his shoes, which, by the way, I own. Oh, and he sucks in the sack, even though he does have a big, thick head."

Lilly wasn't going to let that one lie; when she heard the word *Bibby*, she nearly went for Carol's throat. She was surprised she controlled herself, but she wasn't going to be upstaged this close to victory. She had waited three long months to shoot this bitch down and reestablish her turf; who did this asshole think she was? This was Lilly's Town, the *Palace* was her hangout, Sam belonged to her, as did any other guy in Town of her choosing, anywhere, at any time. And if Carol wasn't careful, any guy *she* had Lilly could, and would, take away, easily and quickly, like she did Deward. It was *that* easy.

So, after a brief three month period of instability, the interloper was on the ropes, and order would soon be restored in the strange little hamlet of Belvidere.

It was time for Lilly to thrust the final dagger.

"Oh, I know what you mean; I saw that big fat head; it got really big as we were standing on the sidewalk, especially when he talked about me modeling in the nude. He seemed to be pretty anxious to show me how proud he was of it, right out on the sidewalk. Maybe I'll get to meet *Joe* later; he said I should come up to your place tonight, you know, for drinks and….whatever, on the porch – there's all sorts of furniture to use. He said *Joe* could come out and play with me all night long, since you tend to go to bed early, since, you know, you're a bit *older* and get tired easy."

That last statement cemented it for Carol. The only thing Dew loved more than his face in the mirror was his thick prick; he named his cock *Joe* and talked to it, and about it, constantly….it was his best friend. And when he got a hard-on, he would always just watch it in utter amazement – like it was the first time he saw the spectacle. If he could suck his own dick, Dew would be in heaven. Deward was in love with Joe.

Carol turned her gaze to Dew and spoke plainly, in a low monotone.

"There will be a cab in front of the shop here in ten minutes; my suggestion is that you get in it. And I had better never see that face in front of mine, or any of my friends, ever again. You can hang with your new *model;* too bad she doesn't look more like an piece-of-shit dog dish, since that's all you can *sculpt* anyway. Well, maybe she does....the piece-of-shit part, anyway."

And with that Carol turned and walked out of the *Palace*, hopped in the Aston, and was gone in less than a minute. She never even looked in Sam's direction.

"I know a good realtor!"

Lilly yelled across the crowded cafe, as the front door lazily swung shut.

Deward just stood there gazing out the window like a lost pup, his meal ticket gone in a puff of exhaust. Then he slowly turned to his new best friend, Lilly, and began to crack his lips to speak.

Lilly beat him to the punch; she barked before the poor sap could utter a peep.

"Get lost asshole; you say a single word to me and half the men in this place will beat you to a pulp, while I watch and laugh."

Stunned, like a jacked deer, Dew was momentarily frozen, feet glued to the floor. What just happened? He slowly turned and shuffled out of the *Palace*, turned left, and was never seen nor heard from again.

Lilly tilted her watch; the time was 6:36 pm; the second hand had ticked to the quarter point.

Exactly four minutes and fifteen seconds had passed since she first walked through the *Palace* door....not too shabby.

She slid into the booth across from Sam, the big man was still in a daze, and picked the maraschino cherry from Carol's drink and, without looking, tossed it indignant across the floor of the restaurant. She removed Carol's straw and did the same; both lay in the middle of the wooden floor, quickly under foot of the patrons coming and going. Lillian reached over and stole the straw from Sam's vanilla shake and took a long, slow noisy sip of Carol's thick, chocolate smoothie, and cracked a tiny smile.

All was right with the world.

CHAPTER 49 – THE ULTIMATE MEMENTO

Perched in a diamond-tufted, burgundy leather desk chair, Carol stared blankly at the far wall of her office, regally attired in old-growth American wormy chestnut, a random pattern of nail holes, surface checking and knots, with an occasional, faint band saw swirl, peeking through the dark stain.

The room was paneled floor to ceiling in salvaged hardwood purchased from *Tresor, treasure* in French, an architectural salvage firm founded by a dear friend and long-time client. Carol liked to spend her money in a tight circle of clients and acquaintances, if and as possible; it was important to nurture those relationships – they were integral to her firms, and thus her own, success. The wormy chestnut paneling she purchased from *Tresor* traced its provenance to yet another dear client to whom she introduced the architectural salvage firm. This second client owned a gentleman's farm in New Hampshire, which he rarely visited – perhaps once or twice a year. The farmstead housed a historic, sixteen-stall wooden horse stable and caretaker's complex, which the client summarily razed to make way for a natatorium, built to host private swimming lessons for his twin girls, who were just shy of seven years old at the time.

Their swimming careers ended shortly after their eighth birthday, and the pool complex sat vacant, save for the occasional houseguest who donned a suit. Her client had never once dipped a toe in the water. The twin's interest had since swung to riding, which necessitated a new horse stable to replace the historic one razed less than two years prior. That original structure had been constructed using centuries-old, wide-width, American wormy chestnut, an all-but-extinct old-growth hardwood; when it was demolished, the ancient wood bones of the barn were carefully reclaimed and milled by *Tresor,* morphing into the paneling now gracefully lining Carol's office walls.

Of course, the *new* horse stable for the twins needed the proper accouterments. And thus it was accompanied by a palatial indoor riding ring and five acre fenced paddock, which sported a turn-out pasture, dressage arena and requisite jumping field, erected on the far southern end of the estate, connected by a series of winding, woodland trails to the main residential compound.

Carol hadn't seen that client in several years; it was her largest private account in '92, and the first client she brought with her to the new firm. She considered the client like family; she even had her own room in the guest wing for a spell.

But over the years, as her fund swelled and her client list grew, the personal touch invariably gave way to more frequent perfunctory email and written correspondence. She still managed a bulk of their personal and non-profit foundation funds, and they were always happy with the overall return she provided, but Carol hadn't been up to the New England retreat in years. The twins were in their twenties now and their riding interests, too, had long-since passed; she wondered what other monuments had been erected to their molten interests.

Carol refocused her gaze and looked down; her pen had been tracing an angry circle on a pad of paper, over and again, till the parchment was grooved and worn by the weight of her endless, counterclockwise scroll on the point of the scribe.

That was a Lilly circle.

After fourteen years, that first sucker-punch encounter at the *Palace* still boiled her blood, although she certainly got in her fair share of counter-shots. In fact, on any impartial scorecard, Carol had a commanding technical lead in the catfight; yet she was still unsatisfied. She won battles, but was nowhere near winning the war.

For the past decade-plus, it had been a textbook conflict, with the imperial outsider, flush with cash and fancy weapons, flummoxed by the skillful Guerrilla warfare of the local rabble. The result was a usually subtle, long-term campaign, waged with the end-goal to humiliate and grind the opponent into submission.

After that fateful first encounter at the *Palace*, Lilly took to work in earnest, turning the locals against Carol through a series of exaggerations and falsehoods, accompanied by good old-fashioned self-pity and sulking to the male set - a potent combination that Lilly had honed to perfection since childhood. When Lillian extended that lower lip ever-so-slightly and flashed the down-turned doe eyes, no man would question what she said, even when they knew it was a lie. To be in Lilly's good graces made a man walk a bit lighter, to feel just a bit better about himself; Carol was no match for that, and because of it, she became the sacrificial lamb.

And the first spoils of their war, and by far biggest trophy Lilly bagged, was Sam; he was the ultimate memento.

CHAPTER 50 – IT WAS JUST SOMETHING THEY DIDN'T DISCUSS

Carol and Deward were gone.

Sam and Lillian sat alone in the booth; it was dead silent. Sam simply stared into space over Lilly's head – he was somewhere else; Lilly was preoccupied with finishing Carol's milkshake, pushing the straw around the bottom of the fountain glass and noisily slurping chocolate from the around the edges. Not that she was hungry, she just worked it to accentuate the delicious discomfort she had created in the booth. And more importantly, to make a point to Sam, herself and anyone else who cared to know – she owned Carol – even down to her milk shake, although her stomach hurt because of it – bloated from downing the entire chocolate float.

Sam finally sighed deeply, then spoke in a hushed, hesitant tone; he was nervous - he always used her full name when he was nervous.

"Lillian Liddell, do you know something that you want to talk to me about?"

"No."

She said quickly, without emotion; her eyes never left the bottom of the milkshake glass.

More silence, until Sam again spoke in hushed tones.

"Then why did you say that?"

"Say what? I said lots of things."

"Stop playing games, you know exactly what I'm talking about. Why did you say it?"

She pushed the empty milkshake glass across the table toward him, dismissive.

"Because *you* never have. I'm twenty-eight years old, you've known me for what, about twenty-eight years *and nine months*, but we've never talked about it. You know we've both thought about it a million times, but still we *never* talk about it. My mom and I *never* talked about it, and you and I *never* talked about it; it was like it *never* happened. Yet everybody in Town knows you two were together, fooling around, even though you were with goody-goody **Elly**….and *don't* deny it.

And now you're getting all chummy with *her*, hugging her, kissing her on the forehead, smiling like, I don't know what, every time she struts her ass in, telling everyone in Town she's just like a *daughter* to you, the daughter you *never had!* I can't *believe* you would say such hurtful things, so I thought it was about time to talk about it. Sorry I hurt **her** feelings, too fucking bad. She's **not** your daughter!"

Before Sam could react, she lit into him again, pointing her finger angrily at his face, less than an inch from his nose.

"And then she calls me **Bibby! Bibby!** And she said it to mock me. She's lucky I didn't throttle her right then and there. How did she know that's what Earl calls me? That's supposed to be special, just between me and Earl; that's supposed to stay in the family, yet you told her anyway….*didn't you?!* "

Lilly's eyes were red and Sam could see a tear well in her right eye; please don't run down her cheek, was all he could think of, please stay in her eye. Sam looked around to see if they were the center of attention, but the *Palace* was loud and bustling, so thankfully, no one was the wiser.

"What, afraid someone will ***hear me***?"

Lillian raised her voice, and down the tear went. She just let it run its course, down her cheek, till it stopped on her jawline for a bit, and continued on. She refused to wipe it away.

Sam was sinking deeper in his seat. He began to speak in the lightest of whispers.

"Lilly, your mom and I, well we just thought…."

"You mean *Carol*? That was her name, you know, you can say her name, or would that be too confusing with your *new* best friend Carol. Who are we talking about? Which Carol? **Which one?!**"

Lilly was getting herself all wound up, her pitch rising with each word as she rose off the booth bench. She looked straight into Sam's eyes and it was clear she was close to breakdown; she was so angry, so vulnerable, so lonely, so unhappy. And she felt betrayed by the one man who was supposed to love her, to protect her, the most.

Sam extended his hands across the table and gently cradled her face, one warm, meaty hand blanketed each cheek. With his big thumbs, he gently caressed her eyes, which she closed; her eyelids were quivering and she was shaking all over.

His baritone gently whispered her way.

"Lillian, please listen. I loved your mother, more than you can ever know. Yes, we were *together* and yes, you might be my daughter. But there was a reason we weren't together in the end, and it wasn't El. I loved Elly, but your mother was something so special I can't even begin to describe it. But she didn't want me, she didn't want *anybody*, not for keeps. Your mother was a free spirit, and no one, including me, would be able to tie her down. She made no bones about that.

Now, I'll say this only once, and I'll never say it again; your mom was with another man when she was with me, she might have been with more than one, I really don't know, we never talked about it, and she was ferocious about keeping it quiet, just like she tried to keep her relationship with me quiet, but in Belvidere, in Town, it was harder, as you well know. I don't think she was ever *with* anyone else in Town, just me.

I don't know where your mom went or who she went to see when she *left Town*; no one does, not even Uncle Frank. Unless she told you, no one knows, and that's the way she wanted it.

When she got pregnant, with you, I offered to marry her on the spot, even though you might not be mine, I didn't care one lick, I knew I would love you more than anything, no matter what, and I was right. But she said no; she said Elmire was the right girl for me.

Lilly, I married Elly because your mom *told* me to. *[Sam own eyes had turned red; he slowly stroked Lilly's cheeks with his thumbs]*

No one knows that, just you and me, and your mom, and I know she watches over you, and me; I hope so anyway. Your mom was so proud of you and Earl; nothing meant more to her than the two of you….*nothing.*"

Lilly started crying harder, eyes still closed. She tried to cry silently, but she gulped air hard and held her breathe, staccato. Sam quickly slid out of the booth and jimmied up beside her, put his big arm around her and rocked her gently back and forth, while gently shushing her. He kissed her quietly on the side of her forehead, and kept his lips lightly touching her skin, rocking back and forth.

He whispered in her ear.

"At the time, El certainly suspected, but no one else really knew about your mom and me – they may have supposed, lots of people did suppose, but no one really knew, not even Frank.

It only lasted a couple months, but they were some of the happiest days of my life. I loved your mom more than anything….*anything*. When you came along, I was at the hospital right alongside Frank – just him and me. El didn't want me to go; we got into a big argument, one of the few we ever had, ever. *Why do you need to be there?! You know what people will say* she said. But I didn't care, I went anyway.

When Frank left the room, I was the only one there with Carol – just you, me and your mom. And I was the *first person* to hold you after your mom; I rubbed your little feet and I kissed you on the forehead, right in the same spot I just kissed you now *[Sam pushed his finger gently against the side of Lilly's head]*, and your eyes were closed then too. You were so beautiful, just like your mom."

The tears ran down both sides of Lilly's face. She missed her mom so much; it had been eleven long years, and it felt like she left yesterday, every day felt like yesterday, and yesterday lasted forever. It was exhausting; a non-stop, soul-crushing numb.

"You know what you did? The very first thing you did?

[Lilly shook her head negative]

You took your little hand, your left hand, with your eyes closed, and you wrapped your tiny fingers around my right finger and just held it, you had a good grip too, strong.....you have no idea how special that little squeeze made me feel. As I held you against my chest and rocked you, I could feel how warm you were; it felt so right just holding you. I knew right then how much I loved you, and I knew I was going to make sure nothing would *ever* hurt you *[Sam shut his eyes and smiled, reliving the scene in his mind; his eyes welled wet]*.

I asked your mom straight out if you were mine; I told her it didn't matter to me one lick either way, but I just wanted to know, but she wouldn't answer me....she just smiled that beautiful smile of hers, and she opened those beautiful eyes, and told me to always love you, and it wouldn't really matter either way.

[Sam shrugged his shoulders]

Your mom was exhausted, and she slowly closed her eyes and went to sleep. Both of you were sleeping.

I just stood there, rocking you gently back and forth in my arms, looking down at your mom. I remember it was so still in the room, the only sound was the faint ticking of a clock; I don't remember ever even seeing that clock, on the wall, or anywhere, I just remember hearing it. A light, gentle tick.

I was so happy; I wish I could have stopped time right then and there....the two women I have loved the most in my life were by my side. I was so happy Lilly, *so happy*.

I always thought how I felt right then, right there beside your mom, holding you, was how a family was supposed to feel. I never really felt that way ever again, not like how I felt that day; that was special....the real deal.

That was the very best day of my life; it's still the best day, the day you were born, in that hospital room, just the three of us, quiet, with the ticking of the clock. If I live another year, or another hundred, no day will *ever* be better than that one. I may not know much, but I know that."

Sam's eyes were puffy red; he closed them and pulled closer to Lilly.

"Lilly, I'm sorry about making you feel bad, you know, about Carol. You're right, what I did was hurtful; I'm the one who's supposed to protect you, not hurt you. I never meant to hurt you, *ever,* I was hoping you two could be friends. I guess that was kind of silly, huh? You matter more to me than anything in this world....*anything.* Don't ever forget that."

Lilly had quieted down by this time, the tracks of tears dried on her cheeks. She was breathing heavy, and slow.

"I love you three million times."

She said softly and flashed a faint smile at Sam, a good smile.

He whispered in her ear and smiled back.

"I love you three million....*plus one.*"

The two had exchanged that ritual a thousand times, back to when Lilly was a little kid – it was their own little secret saying - Earl didn't even know about that one. They hadn't said it to each other in years. And it felt good.

Sam gently tugged on her shoulder, so she was facing him. He looked earnestly into her eyes.

"Do you want to try and find out, for real, if I'm your dad? I think there are ways they can do it now, some kinda test; I can look into it, if you want."

"No, that's okay; it's kind of late now, don't you think?"

Lilly said, but she really didn't think it was too late.

"Yeah, I guess so."

Said Sam, and neither did he.

And that's where the discussion ended; neither ever mentioned it again.

Lilly didn't ask Sam to stop seeing Carol; she didn't have to, he knew what he had to do, and he did it.

It was just something they didn't discuss.

CHAPTER 51 – HE FINALLY REALIZED THAT TOMORROW WOULD NEVER COME

Friday, June 23, 2006; two days beyond the summer solstice, sixty-five days deep into the game. The clock was ticking.

Carol gazed at her laptop screen, at the email; memories of 1992 faded to white, as she returned to today. The email silently stared back; she reread it slowly for the third time. There was a lot to digest, mainly between the lines. She was angry and entertained and intrigued....mostly intrigued.

Who was this guy and what was he up to? And what was she going to do? What was *she* up to? She was as confused as the email.

It had been just over two months since that infamous race around the Park between *the boys*, that's what she called the two of them, both out loud, and in her mind. She liked calling them that. Summer in Belvidere had quietly rolled in, and this was the first time Cord had contacted her, even spoke to her, outside the presence of Earl. She had long-since found that he wasn't dating Lillian, never had, which made sense. But not much else about C did, especially as to where he was from, and why he was here.

Whenever she saw Cord, it was always face-to-face in front of her house or on the porch after their run; she never saw the two of them anywhere else in Town, not that she ventured far from the confines of the *L'antre du Lion*.

She drove into Town on Friday afternoons, directly to the house. She stayed indoors, usually relaxing in the cupola lounge, the billiard room, or the library; if the weather was pleasant she would invariably spend all her time reading or relaxing on the front porch, doing her toes, or soaking in the afternoon sun. The best were the short naps on the wicker sofa; they would always remind her of the first time she met Moe, napping at his desk. On occasion, she would venture across the street to sit or read in the Park, usually when it was empty. At the first sign of a bustle, she would quietly stroll back to the safety-net of the yard, the house. On Sunday evenings, she returned to New York.

She hated leaving Belvidere on Sunday evenings, until she got back to the City, and her other life began again, and took over.

She had bought a bike a couple years ago to flit around Town, the terrain was flat and easy riding, but she only mounted it once or twice, and again, never venturing more than a block or two beyond the safety of the Courthouse Park. A self-imposed exile on her tiny island at the corner of Hardwick and Third. That was her home base....safe.

And even though she owned the *Palace of Sweets* building next to Sam's, she hadn't physically seen it, or that part of Town, in well over a decade. It was a mere five blocks from her front porch, and half-a-world away.

She knew Lilly was always somewhere nearby, swimming endless in the sea surrounding her little island. Lillian never ventured beyond the Town limits, which was all of a mile and a half square – like the fox hiding in the scrub brush, just out of view, waiting to pounce.

Not that she was afraid of Lilly, hardly, but her rumors and innuendo had soaked into the fabric of Town for so long, she doubted anyone in Belvidere didn't believe it was all true, or mostly so, which made it uncomfortable to feel relaxed and accepted much beyond the sidewalk in front of her house. It was an albatross that hung heavy around her neck. She could see it happen right after the blow-up in 1992; the way people acted in her presence; the way they avoided talking or looking her way; it was subtle in the most obvious way.

Although she had, in that short three-month honeymoon in 1992, met most of the vendors in Town, she would not say she was particularly close with any of them, save Sam and the realty duo - polite conversation ruled. They were more interested in her, in the stories that first ran through Town like a brushfire. They were fantastic, and kind of fun. And of course, they liked Carol's money, and how she freely spent it in their shops, whether she actually needed what they were peddling or not....and it was usually not. On the other hand, the stories Lilly cooked were decidedly nasty, and most folk fell quickly under Lilly's spell, which came as little surprise. And with their increasing disdain, Carol's visible patronage and outsized generosity quickly ended, which simply fed Lilly's tall tales; *Carol really was a bitch* became the go-to opinion amongst the locals. It was a furious, viscous cycle, which quickly isolated Carol; she went from royalty to pariah in less than a flash.

Carol expected as much from most of the locals and vendors who only knew her peripherally, and worshiped Lilly from birth. But Sam was different. In Sam, Carol expected an ally, or, at a minimum, an impartial, or sympathetic, ear. But she got neither; that hurt most of all.

Carol ventured into the market on the Saturday morning following the Deward Friday night debacle; expecting to get an apology, or at least an explanation, and a well-deserved hug.

What she got instead....was Frank.

Frank, who had turned on a dime after Lilly *filled him in* on the details of Friday night at the *Palace.*

More often than not, Frank was an asshole, a sloppy, drunken asshole. And this Saturday morning was the *more often than not*.

Now Carol, to this day, wasn't sure if she saw Sam behind the counter when she first cracked open the front door to the market, she *thought* she saw him, she'd probably swear she did. But he certainly wasn't there by the time the door clicked shut behind her, and she made her way to the rear deli counter.

Frank announced that Sam was in back, busy, anticipating the question that never left Carol's lips. She simply ignored him.

When Carol started to turn the corner behind the counter, Frank stepped in to block her path and politely informed her, lips curled in a snide smile, that *patrons* weren't allowed past the glass. As she looked at him with indignity, he pushed his loose sack of a belly slightly into her, knocking Carol back a half-step, just to embarrass her.

She called out around Frank to Sam, but got no answer.

"Maybe he ran out to see Lilly."

Frank squeezed out the words, like wringing a dish towel, smiling at her the whole time; sheer delight.

Turns out Sam dealt with the Carol situation like he had always dealt with Lilly; let the storm blow over and avoid the subject, and hopefully, eventually, the clouds will go away. So Sam camped in the back store room, sitting at his desk in the dark, waiting for better weather.

But Carol was not Lilly; she wasn't going to yell, or cry, or create a scene; she just wanted to talk to her friend, her good friend Sam. But that wasn't to be.

Carol bowed her head a bit and walked out of the deli in silence. And she never went back; she never stepped foot in Sam's market again, not once in the last fourteen years.

Sam sent up a package of her favorite cheeses and meats the next day, Sunday, with a note saying it was on him and apologizing for not being there when she stopped by, even though they both knew it was a lie. He never mentioned the episode at the *Palace*.

And the better weather never came.

Carol crumpled and tossed the note in the garbage; she gave the produce to a shelter in the City – actually, her staff did.

She sent Sam a check for the full amount in an envelope from work on Monday – she attached a short, polite note telling him she donated the produce to charity and expressing her heartfelt disappointment in him, but understanding his predicament with Lillian, and asking him not to make any future deliveries; she would get along just fine. She wished him luck for the rest of his life and suggested they go their separate ways, it would be easier that way, no more unwanted conflicts or awkward moments requiring him to hide in the back room. She said this would be her final communication with him, and she thanked him in advance for his cooperation in that regard. It was clear to Sam that Carol's note was not meant to negotiate the point; she decided, and the matter was settled. The end.

That's when Sam truly realized he wasn't dealing with a Lilly. This wasn't a Friday night tantrum that would blow over by Monday; a flip of the hair and a change in mood, like the flicker of a candle. No, Sam realized he had made a grave mistake; he loved Carol like a daughter, even though he couldn't admit as much to anyone, and had hurt her….deeply.

No one ever saw the shame Sam felt for what he did, and he never discussed it with anyone. He vowed to himself to go see Carol, secretly of course, to make amends, but he couldn't stand the thought of Carol's rejection to his face, or the prospect of Lilly finding out.

Sam said to himself that he would plan on going tomorrow, or the next day for sure, then he'd try to make it right.

Tomorrow, or the next day for sure, turned into fourteen long years.   He couldn't remember when he finally realized that tomorrow would never come.

CHAPTER 52 – SHE CAUGHT THE HEADING AND HESITATED - *GROCERY BOY'S CHIT*

Sam never tolerated Lilly disparaging Carol in front of him, and Lilly didn't push it. She won, that was enough; she didn't need to rub salt in this particular wound. Lillian was always good at picking the right battles to fight.

Sam never cashed Carol's check; it had been push-pinned to the corkboard in his office for the past fourteen years, yellowed and curled at the edges, along with her note, just so he could look at it….his own personal penance. Lilly never once mentioned it, although she had walked by his desk a thousand times. She had read it just once, the first time she saw it, and never laid eyes on it or that corkboard again; she would always turn her eyes elsewhere when she passed his desk.

Out of sight out of mind; for Lilly, that always seemed to work just fine.

Carol, on the other hand, was never fine.

She was melancholy that whole weekend, sad over losing Sam. Carol's own father, while a good, decent man, was impersonal; the German flowing through his veins was cool, reserved, always distant. The first hug Sam gave her that first day was more heartfelt than any physical contact Carol ever received from her father. She tried to buy his affection with her acumen, with her tremendous financial success. But it had the opposite effect, making her father withdraw even more when he realized she was the rocket success he never quite became.

In Sam, Carol thought she discovered how a father's hug was supposed to feel, how a small kiss on the head or a light whisper of encouragement in your ear could make the rest of the day feel beyond special. In a way, she wished she never met Sam; a taste was worse than nothing at all.

All because of Lilly.

Carol rarely went out to dinner, preferring to cook for herself when she was in Town, one of her pleasures when out in the country. She would have the ingredients delivered from an organic grocery she frequented a few blocks from her digs in the City, haul them out to Belvidere, and experiment with new vegetarian dishes; she would go on veggie binges for a month or so every now and again, then return to meat. She ate out practically every night during the week in the City, with clients or friends or dates, occasionally alone - it was just part of the daily routine more than anything else.

So eating at home in Belvidere was a welcome respite….and the kitchen was one of her favorite rooms. She simply enjoyed looking out, and up, at the Methodist Church steeple through the elliptical window above the sink. She wasn't Methodist; she was raised Catholic, but wasn't a practicing *anything*, but looking at that unique, squatty steeple with copper ball finials and what looked like a modified widows-watch was comforting, even though she wasn't quite sure why.

She had paid for the top third of that Methodist steeple. The original was taken down in the 1930's - no one remembered the reason. In 2004, an old postcard and article about the church ran in the local paper, depicting the profile of the old steeple, circa-1910. Carol anonymously donated the funds to rebuild an exact replica of the top fifteen feet of the missing steeple, which local contractors erected, much to the delight of the parishioners and townsfolk in general.

The anonymous donation was never really so; everyone in Town knew the only person who could have, or would have, paid for such a thing was Carol. Most figured she was trying to buy salvation for all the evil she sowed, the fruit of Lilly's smear. Most scoffed at her trying to buy God's good graces, as they placed money in the collection plate, and took the tax deduction.

Truth was, Carol didn't give a shit about the Methodists, or God's good grace - she just wanted to stand in her kitchen, make dinner, and look at a pretty church steeple, the way it used to be a hundred years ago. It made her happy, it made her smile….it was as simple as that.

Her mind drifted back to the email staring at her on the laptop screen.

Carol almost hit the delete button before she even opened it; she was quickly purging unknown emails in rapid-fire succession, the ones that somehow always seem to skirt the spam filter. But out of the corner of her eye, right before she hit *delete*, she caught the heading and hesitated -

Grocery Boy's Chit

CHAPTER 53 – IT WILL ALL COME OUT IN THE WASH

She stopped and stared at the email, but didn't open it. Her heart raced a bit, realizing she almost unknowingly tossed it. She had been expecting information on that payback chit for quite awhile....too long.

She finished going through the rest of her emails, a good one hundred-fifty of them, most which required some sort of action....a reply, a forward, a phone call, distribution, or filing. By the time she cleared the lot of them, three hours had passed – Christ, she pissed away so much God-damn time on emails - what a waste of fucking time.

The trudge was worth it, however, because of that one unopened, bold-lettered teaser staring at her.

It sat patiently on her screen, like the Christmas present you don't open till the very last, because you just know that's the one you have been waiting for. It's the right shape and the right size, and with a gentle shake and you know, or at least hope you know, what it is. Those are the ones you save for last.

Just looking at it, unread and unopened, made her smile.

She didn't know why she was so excited, but she was. She had grown fond of both Cord and Earl, but she couldn't describe what fond really meant. She knew she looked forward to seeing them both, to the point that she thought about them during the week; she couldn't think of the last time that happened with *any* man, let alone *two* of them. She still dated, occasionally, but they were all in the business, in the City, and were all roughly alike; they were *her*, but with a cock....and she was with that twenty-four hours a day. She needed to get away from that typecast, to get away from dating herself. And she hadn't dated a *Deward*, a man more interested in her wallet than anything else, in years. She had at least learned to weed those parasites out.

She actually started to look forward to the weekends again, to taking the Friday drive west to Belvidere; she hadn't felt that way since those first three wonderful months back in 1992, when she thought she found *Valhalla*, only to realize her *Eden* was inhabited by a serpent, nee Lillian.

My God, fourteen years had passed; she couldn't believe it had been so long. She surprised herself that she stuck it out; Lilly's flippant comment about finding a realtor as she exited the *Palace* sealed her fate - no matter what happened, she would never sell her home in Belvidere….*L'antre du Lion*.

Never.

She even set up a non-profit to inherit the estate, under the same name, *L'antre du Lion*, after she died; to keep it as a house museum of sorts, with a Board of Trustees and the like - just so she would never, ever, truly sell the house. She didn't care if a single person ever toured the house, or even took a step through the front door; she was staying in Belvidere for eternity….just to spite that little fucking bitch.

She settled in her chair, got comfortable, took a swig of sparkling *Saratoga*; the water wasn't really anything special, she just liked the sapphire bottle, and read the email again, looking for more clues, trying to decipher the true intent of his note.

This part was fun.

CC:

I'm sure you will be delighted to know I've decided upon the chit.

However, it is best discussed in private, at L'antre du Lion, this Saturday, the 24th, after 10 pm. Can you stay up that late? I need to sneak away from my girlfriend, you know, your buddy Lillian. The sex is insatiable, but I can usually get away for a bit between go-rounds.

*My oh my, she just **loves** to talk about you; those stories **can't** all be true, can they? Let's just say 'thank God' I heard those stories before I gave up my golden ticket; it certainly expands the payback possibilities.*

Goodness, you sure are a naughty little girl.

But, alas, that's another story, for another time. And I'm sure you're not interested in all the sordid details, just like she isn't the least bit interested in what you have to say about her.

You're both mature adults, right? You wouldn't stoop to name calling and rumor-mongering; that would simply be uncivil.

Okay, back to the chit.

As a proper host, and a gracious loser, I would certainly expect you to accommodate the following 'petite demande':

Davidoff miniatures (my own would be nice, since you don't seem to be a good sharer) and a selection of hand-rolled Lancaster DeMuth's and some port wine, perhaps a Fonseca vintage-1963, a favorite year of mine. A bit pricey, but worth it, don't you think?

Artisanal Cheese and fennel crackers would be a nice accompaniment; perhaps a rustic Pitchounet, a lilly-white cheese derived from the sweet milk of the gentle ewe. Appropriate?

Augment the cheese with miniature sweet red Champagne grapes, served in sectioned stem lengths, although one can certainly dip and strip the stem directly, much like an artichoke leaf, I would prefer you feed them to me individually; they are tiny, but you seem to have small, delicate hands.

For our conversation over wine and hors d'oeuvre, I will take my respite on the front porch. You can recline casually on the loveseat in a submissive pose; I will occupy the master chair, facing the Square (you know, the one you usually sit in when you mock me running around the Park).

As for your attire, I will allow you some latitude in this regard; be tasteful, but the skirt should be short, very short. Undergarments are discouraged.

Okay, we'll stop there.

Hopefully you are still reading this and haven't forwarded me to the recycle bin via the delete button.

All joking aside, let me know if I can stop by on Saturday night, late, for a half hour or so, I do want to talk to you, and it is about the chit. Maybe just a drink of still water with ice would be nice; tap is fine. I'm easy. I have to talk to you about something important, in private.

You know, Earl can't stop talking about you; you make his day, his week, his life, whenever he sees you. He has become such a good friend, venture to say my best friend, and I want you to know he thinks the world of you; his face lights when the topic turns to you, not that you are the topic of all our discussions (we wouldn't want you to get too big a head, now would we?). Suffice to say if we talked about nothing but Carol Crowe, Earl would be a happy man indeed.

What did you do to deserve such attention? Probably the same thing I did....nothing. You and I have that in common; we are both lucky to have a friend like Earl.

Again, Earl doesn't know about my request to see you Saturday; please don't say anything to him. It's just between you and me; if he knew I came to see you without him, he would be disappointed, to say the least.

But this talk can't include him, not yet anyway, it would be inappropriate. Earl simply can't know about 'it'; it would be a significant problem if he found out about our little soiree.

I am sending you this from the library, down the street from your second home; I am deleting it upon hitting 'send'; so hopefully you don't spam it away, because I would never be able to remember all the witticisms again, or the innuendo; is there innuendo?

Hope to see you this Saturday morning (that is, tomorrow morning) Earl and I will be assuming our usual role circling the Park. If you got this message and it is okay to come by tomorrow, please yell to me the following code phrase:

"My goodness Cord, you are looking pretty sexy today; what happened to your belly? For heaven's sake, it's all gone!"

Okay, that's a bit over the top; I don't think you could even choke those words out without laughing. How about this:

"Hi Earl, how about you come up on the porch and have a cool drink when you're done running half-speed to go slow enough for your friend to keep up; oh, your friend can come along too, he looks like he needs to sit down."

No, you make that sarcastic remark, or some variation thereof, just about every week, nothing new. Okay how about this:

*"**Earl, how would you like to help Ji-Sue take care of my cats when I'm out of Town, I would really appreciate it.**"*

Yeah, that's the ticket. Use that as the code phrase.

And by the way, seriously, think about having Earl help Ji-Sue watch the cats; he would die and go to heaven if you let him. No man would be happier helping clean a litter box, of that I'm sure.

Now, right about now, this email has you a bit confused, right?

You are wondering what I want to talk to you about; the possibilities are many. I wonder if you should worry, or be excited, or be in a state of dread, or....or.

Forget about the email for now; go invest some money and make your rich clients richer. Oh, and make a little for yourself as well, because that Fonseca isn't cheap.

Well, that's enough flirty innuendo for now. Talk to you tomorrow, young lady; enjoy the rest of your day and don't think too hard. It will all come out in the wash.

Regards,

Grocery Boy

She smiled to herself, her eyes reliving the last line a second time, slow.

It will all come out in the wash.

CHAPTER 54 – AND WITH THAT, SHE FORGED AHEAD

Carol finished her reread, ripped off the top sheet on the pad, the one with the angry Lilly oval, and was ready to scribe fresh notes.

She had to make some important sign-off decisions by day's end on a package of currency derivatives, her particular forte, for one of her more aggressive, speculative funds.

She was also neck deep in research on creating her new *Brownfield Fund* to include an atypical, illiquid element to her hedge portfolio, real estate, contaminated realty. She had read a recent article about it in the *Wall Street Journal* and was intrigued.

She figured it wouldn't be an easy sell to her base, at least at first, but the returns could be more than attractive, if the right sites were acquired. At least that's what she gathered, based upon her research to date.

Problem was, she had to educate herself on the topic, which she knew next-to-nothing about. Carol never launched a new investment venture half-cocked, based upon the advice or heavy-lifting of others. She needed to understand it fully herself, before she would sell the concept to others; that was just her. *If you can't teach it, then you don't truly understand it* – years ago she had heard a portly, eight year old girl advise her father of that fact, as he struggled to answer a question about clouds the young girl had posed, eyes skyward. It was poolside at a chic, cliffside hotel Carol visited for a destination wedding many years ago, in Santorini, Greece. She couldn't remember the names of her long-since forgotten friends who got married, but Carol never forgot the shrewd little girl, admonishing her father as she splashed lazy around the pool....clever young lady. Maybe the father forgot his young daughter's advice, but Carol never did. And since her personal money was going into this fund as well – that's how strong she felt about its potential - she needed to know all she could about this *contaminated realty* subject matter.

She had to understand the nuances of soil and groundwater contamination - even what the term *groundwater* actually meant, exposure modeling, what an engineering and institutional control was - and why she should care, stigma issues, remediation options - both *in-situ* and *ex-situ*, and a host of arcane acronyms that were mind-numbing, including such teasers as BUST (Bureau of Underground Storage Tanks), and LUST (leaking underground storage tank), to name a few.

Erotic reading it was not. In fact, it was an unadulterated bore, but necessary nonetheless.

A lot of the redevelopment concepts seemed to be ground in simple common sense on a higher order, but she felt the need to understand the front-line science behind the ability to sell tainted real estate and have the end-user feel comfortable with the associated environmental risk.

She couldn't imagine spending a career on the minutia data-gathering end of this process; the engineers, geologists, environmental scientists and consultants - the ones actually taking the samples, assessing the data, and the like. It all seemed so utterly mundane....*shoot-me-in-head/put-me-out-of-my-misery* boring. But the idea of using this data to make financial decisions which ultimately resulted in fallow industrial or commercial sites, and their old empty buildings, being reborn in some new adaptive use - housing, entertainment, offices, high-tech, art studios, farmer's markets, parkland or whatever else made sense was invigorating, and potentially very lucrative. That was the exciting part that made this trudge of a science lesson worth it.

Even as a kid, she always loved looking at old, block-long brick factory buildings in the forgotten corners of her hometown, which hummed long before she was born, but now sat vacant, or largely so. The architecture, the bones, were so cool, and the garniture on the buildings, even the heavy industrial ones, marked a time when aesthetics meant something.

Placing a small satyr, a lion mask, cherubs at play, or a griffin *bas relief* on the frieze atop a six-story brick building that most people would never even notice mattered, at least for the few who did. Back in the day, she felt more people looked up, looked around than they did today. She hoped more would look again when they were reborn under her watch.

That was the plan.

Artisans to recreate the friezes, cornices, statuary and corbels adorning these relics were a rare breed anymore; yet these fantastic dinosaurs sat there, right in the midst of our day-to-day, patiently waiting to be noticed. She thought it was Promethean that someone like her, who was as far from scientific as you could get, could get involved in this, and make some serious money in the process.

If, that is, it was done right. And that was a big *if*. And she still wasn't sure she had a full handle on what *right* actually was. Hence the homework piled high on her desk.

She found the research slippery and multi-layered; she was constantly sidetracked on new ideas in this field, and the amount of information was significant. It was both exciting, and tiring, and when it got too technical, mind-numbing.

But the potential to scoop up wallflowers adjacent to existing, functioning city utilities and infrastructure, as well as financial centers, ports, and major transportation hubs, was simply incredible. Diamonds waiting to be plucked. And there seemed to be lots of diamonds out there, and that worried her. She didn't want to be the sucker to get taken; there were so many opportunities, so many viable properties, that lots of other smart people who rode around this arena for a living should have been there long before her, scooping them up.

Why weren't they?

She wouldn't be comfortable until she could confidently answer that question. But, so far, the field appeared to be wide open.

Now for the dilemma.

A gorilla of an investor she had worked with for years, on other unrelated funds, was hot to move into this *Brownfield Redevelopment* sector; a client with the deepest of deep pockets and a cadre of peers, with nearly equal access to similar liquid assets, and they typically followed his lead. He had spread some toe-in-the-water money into Carol's funds over the years, and was happy with the results, but the investment dollars he let her manage, although healthy on their own, were minuscule in comparison to his overall portfolio. He was a very big fish, who simply nibbled around the edges when it came to her firm, Actaeon.

It would be a major fucking win for Carol if he and his buddies planted their cash with her new contaminated property venture....*major*.

The introduction was purely accidental; she attended a second-tier charity cocktail she was going to ditch as a throw-away - it was the type of no-name social event she hated wasting her time attending. And it certainly wasn't of the caliber that he would attend; he is the last person she would expect to see at such a small-scale, junior affair. But for some reason he showed up, and the two got a chance to catch up, as the only A-listers at a decidedly B-list event. It was then that she inadvertently mentioned a move into this contaminated real estate market and learned, to her utter surprise, that her big fish was looking for such a fund in the near-term and was ready to invest in another hedge currently active in this field. It was for this reason alone - chance meetings and business opportunities that come at times when you least expect - that modest social events such as this one even made it onto her calendar.

Ability is of little account without opportunity

Napoleon Bonaparte

Carol loved that quote and replayed it often in her head. And it certainly applied to the situation at hand. And another actor was at play, one she would take any day of the week....serendipity.

But that said, closing this deal was by no means a slam-dunk.

However, this gentleman's respect for Carol, and the healthy investment returns she provided in the past on his modest forays into several of her more traditional funds, caused him to pause and consider, to see what she could bring to the table in this new arena. It didn't hurt the cause that he liked being around her too, Carol was bright and an undeniable looker, although he had much too big an ego to admit it. But it was obvious to Carol, and anyone else who bothered to pay attention.

Carol knew the other fund he was thinking of using; it was one which frequently fished in the same pond of investors as her. She briefly dated one of the second-tier founding partners years ago; what a pompous ass, the kind who wears no socks to the office in his designer duds, even in the winter. A real prick. They were City-based too, but twice her asset size, and looked upon

Actaeon, if they paid any attention at all, as a junior level affair, with no real seat at the table when it came to more complicated ventures and sophisticated top-tier clients. They considered themselves, and their clientele, the *real* players; Actaeon was a pretender, a wanna-be, especially because it was both woman owned and run, a real rarity in the field of portfolio managers. Of the close to seven thousand funds managing in excess of twelve *trillion* dollars of assets, about two percent were run by woman-only - firms like Acteaon were a rare breed indeed. The fund business was a boys-club, run by men who were largely overconfident, high-trading, herd followers, with a not-so-subtle sign posted prominent on the front door: *girls need not apply*. Carol bristled at the thought, and relished in throwing convention smack in their faces.

To that end, oh what a coup to steal this one, since the whale had all but told the other fund his money was theirs.

As Carol stood and casually talked to him while nursing a cognac, it was clear she was educated enough to toss the *contaminated real estate* lingo about, and he was educated enough to understand some of the spiel, and realize she knew the territory. Actually, they were both pretenders – neither really knew what they were talking about beyond a surface scratch, but she was a good month ahead of him in researching the topic, so she dazzled him with factoids that weren't entirely correct, that he was too ignorant to catch.

And Carol could always pull out her other tools to close a deal when she really wanted to, and they had nothing to do with her understanding of groundwater.

Countless times she would mock Lillian for brazenly using her body, her good looks, to her advantage; it was so obvious what she was dong - why did guys always falls for it?

But Carol did the exact same thing; not as often as Lilly, for sure, since she had more tools in her chest, but when she wanted something bad enough, she dealt the body card. She was cut from the same cloth.

She used her lingo from the research, the cumulative effect of his whiskey sours, her wry smile and a bit-too-short skirt to woo him. A small bite of her lip when she smiled at his banter, and the constant, oh-so-light, oh-so-subtle brushes of her shoulder, her hip, her breast against him to let him know it would be in his best interest to read the *pro forma* for her new Brownfield fund.

She had the drill down cold.

She would slowly, imperceptibly, lean in, keeping her body in light contact; she knew he felt it - he would never break the contact. After a half-minute or so, she would casually step away a bit, then do it again a few moments later. If it was up to him, she would have stayed attached at the hip all the way home.

Christ, men are so easy; in the end, he was easily persuaded.

He was sitting on up to two-hundred fifty million to start, his money alone, for this *new, little experiment* as he called it. He said there were more dollars to follow from him and his peers, if she could impress him.

Trouble was, Carol sold him the goods, but the goods weren't fully cooked.

That chance encounter was a full month ago, and she had clearly implied to him at the time that she was putting the finishing touches on a formal fund prospectus. That was her mistake; she was blinded by what she knew could easily blossom into a nine-figure virgin fund, an easy nine figures. And a chance to stick it good to her rivals across town was the fucking icing. So she fibbed, and alluded that she was much further along on finishing the document than she really was. And although she probably could have extracted herself from the not-so-little lie and fessed up early-on without materially damaging her chances with the whale, she didn't; now, too much time had passed to come clean. And properly vetted fund documents, with all the requisite legal and accounting input from both her on-staff attorney and accountant, as well as outside professionals, wasn't easy or quick to compile, not by a long stretch.

So now she found herself with time quickly running out, like studying last minute, unprepared, for tomorrow's final exams. And Mr. William *Bud* Wiseman, was not a patient man. His earmarked funds had been idle for over a month, unproductive, waiting on Carol and her unfinished prospectus.

This was a major fucking problem.

Carol couldn't explain it, but for some reason, she just couldn't seem to wrap this one up; she always felt she had to tweak the pro forma some more, amend the draft prospectus, do a bit more research; a never-ending term paper you can't seem to finish. To that end, she was uncharacteristically behind on this matter, and it was clearly the most important *to-do* on her plate; there wasn't even a close second. She was not a procrastinator per se, but she seemed to be on this one. This was too important to fuck up, and she was on the verge of fucking it up nonetheless.

So here she was, dreading the call from Bud that she knew was coming. She was supposed to have the draft documents over to him and his counsel two days prior – that was the latest promise. Why he hadn't made his infamous third call yet was both a mystery and a blessing.

Bud made all his follow-up calls between 7:00 and 8:00 am each Monday and Thursday morning; the list was usually comprised of twenty-odd calls, the last one always being to his long-time assistant, which entailed a list of additional second-tier calls she was to make, ones that didn't quite make Bud's biweekly morning list.

Bud had done this for years; that was the routine. Even with email, Bud liked to use the phone; he was old school in that way.

You got one morning call from him - that was it. After that first call, if you failed to respond, Bud would make a second call at an off-hour, based upon your schedule, which he invariably knew. If you worked late, Bud knew that, and would call you then; same if you worked early, or on the weekend. Or he would get you on your personal cell. If Bud Wiseman had some reason to know you existed, he knew how to get a hold of you.

By the second call, he was annoyed; he would always state in his message that this was his second call. Most who didn't answer or quickly return the second call never got a call from Bud again…ever.

You were done.

If he *really* needed you, or you were important enough to talk to, which meant you somehow were critical to making him money or keeping him out of trouble, you got a rare third call, the timing of which was completely random. And *no one* wanted to be in that third-call position with Bud Wiseman; that was an unpleasant place to be.

Carol was in third-call position.

Every hour that passed tempted fate; when the phone rang to her direct line, which he had, she cringed while screening the call, waiting on pins to first hear the voice as the message played, and pray it wasn't Bud's annoying nasal bleat. Bud was tall and graceful; a svelte, refined gentleman, with a neatly coiffed gray mane and an impeccable wardrobe; the tinny, grating voice simply didn't match the package. She always wondered why he didn't somehow fix it; it wasn't as if he couldn't afford a new one - can you buy a new voice box?

Having Bud displeased with you brought swift and certain dire financial consequences; he had a short temper, a long memory and a large Rolodex of fellow investors he could, and certainly would, bitch to.

But in this case, if the Brownfield documents weren't done the next time he inquired, he wouldn't just be mad – he'd be livid. Bud had never been incensed with Carol, and she wasn't looking to witness, to being the object of, that tirade. Expletives would fly, promised funding would be pulled, and she knew the first call made would be to the competing fund, bitching about her incompetence and bemoaning the fact that he was foolish enough to even invest a dime of his monies with her. He would likely pull some or all of his current funds with Carol, and take the huge, promised Brownfield dollars and dump them in her rivals lap; a disaster of epic proportions, on multiple fronts.

The other fund was run by Jewish partners, prominent Jews, who were both active and high profile. Carol didn't have a large stable of Jewish clients; most preferred to invest with Jewish money managers; it was just the way it was – keep the money in the *community*, so to speak. But of the Jewish clients she had, most were smaller investors, on the periphery both socially and in their commitment to the faith – quasi-Jews she called them. Although make no mistake, they still controlled ample wealth and were clearly on the upper end of high-maintenance.

Bud, on the other hand, was off the chart; he was a high profile, emotional and loyal Jew. And he was taking serious money out of the Jewish business community and letting Carol run with it. That was much more than a big deal to a guy like Bud, and he expected Carol to recognize and appreciate the gentile gesture.

Just one more reason not to be in this predicament.

Now, with that pressure weighing heavy on her, let alone the currency derivative work due by day's end, Carol glanced over to the carriage clock on her desk. It was 2:15 pm. Determined to make the obstacle her path, she dialed her assistant, seated outside her office.

"Hey Diane, hold my calls for an hour or so; I'm putting the phone on *Do Not Disturb*. I need to get some work done without interruption. And if Bud calls and tries to get me through your extension, I am *not* in, and you don't know what meeting I went to; tell him I may be back late, but you're not sure. But tell him the prospectus is definitely going to be delivered to his office by courier tomorrow, before noon; no, don't say noon, just say *tomorrow*."

"*Thank God!* It's about time; unlike you, I can't dodge calls. I'm the one who gets the earful, and Mr. Wiseman doesn't like me to begin with; he's *so* nasty!"

Carol clicked the intercom without answering and forged ahead. But it wasn't on the Brownfield prospectus. It *had* to be the prospectus; there was nothing more important than finishing that damn prospectus.

But it wasn't what she placed front and center before her.

She couldn't help herself; she felt like a schoolgirl with a stomach full of butterflies. She knew that was corny, but the feeling was there - that goofy, nervous feeling that makes you feel like a little kid all over again.

She would spend just a *little* bit of time on this other thing, then she would jump right on the real work – the too-important prospectus….she promised herself.

She repositioned herself in her chair, pulled the keyboard slightly toward her, and delved into the process of dissecting Cord's email, trying to make sense of the ramble.

She would goof off on this little nugget for just an hour, then back to serious work on closing out the derivative issue, which should take three-quarters of an hour at most, then finalize the prospectus - no more excuses. She already resigned herself to staying till early morning if necessary to get it done. The fact she made the decision to finish the Brownfield prospectus tonight, and would stick to it, justified the extra one hour delay - good enough for her.

And with that, she forged ahead.

CHAPTER 55 - HIGH-PITCHED NASAL BLEAT

Carol shifted her ass in the chair again, Cord's email stared back at her. She began her dissection, sniffing for juice between the lines.

'CC'

It opened with CC; he never called her that in person, Cord must have made it up for the email. In fact, no one had ever called her that, in person or in writing, ever. She liked it; it was like Earl calling Cord *C,* which he did more frequently each time she saw them. She liked CC; she felt part of their little fraternity.

Wait a minute, she liked it? Did that mean she was starting to like *him*? She wasn't sure yet, she thought she might, but she wasn't sure why.

He was good-looking; not the best-looking guy she had seen, but attractive enough. He was smart, much smarter than he alluded to, and he dealt with the subject deftly, which made his esprit all the more magnetic. The majority of guys she dated over the years were invariably smart and wealthy, and spent their time letting her know just how smart and wealthy they were. Boring.

Cord wasn't like that; his shtick was sarcastic, scattered self-deprecation. Such self-deprecation is usually confidence in disguise. And Cord didn't seem to have any money to brag about, yet didn't seem too worried that he didn't. But the grocery bit was just too, you know, it just didn't fit. She could see him doing a lot of different things, stocking shelves just wasn't one of them. Why was he really working there?

That tied to the mysterious bit, the *mysterious stranger* that women like, at least in fantasy. The guy who *can* be bad, *is* bad, but treats *you* special. That was erotic and alluring. She had tried to figure out his story, but he clamped whenever she pried; actually, he was too busy peppering *her* with questions all the time, like an interrogator. She even called him that once or twice, to which he smiled wryly, and would stop, but just for awhile. He was like the tide, always coming at her with questions.

But just as often he was annoying, more often than not, in fact. And he had a short temper, and was out of shape, and short, and bald.

What was it she liked again?

Plus, there *was* the added bonus of the *Lilly thing*; even though Carol had come to find that Cord wasn't really *dating* Lilly, it was clear he liked her, and she seemed to like him, admittedly begrudgingly, but that was how Lillian operated most of the time. Lilly didn't have a reputation for caution when diving into a relationship. If something hadn't happened between them yet, it would soon enough, at least in the absence of Button.

So she could go after him, like she did Button, to humiliate Lilly once again. But that would be premature, and she wasn't sure she wanted to do that anyway. She liked Cord, and she was getting a bit old for sex games, although no one could top what she did to Lilly with Button - no one. That was a classic.

Carol felt ashamed of that charade at times, and still marveled at its success other times, at how that encounter was all formulated in her little head. Very scary.

That was certainly the nail from which Lilly had yet to recover; it had been three years since her little operation succeeded, three years since Button skipped Town. Classic.

She smiled to herself and refocused on the screen; what's next?

'I need to sneak away from my girlfriend, you know, your buddy Lillian. The sex is insatiable, but I can usually get away for a bit between go-rounds.'

He was obviously kidding about the sex with Lilly, wasn't he? Yeah, he was.

Anyway, she hoped so. Somehow she would lose respect for Cord if he was banging Lilly, like he switched teams – a traitor. She felt like Cord was on *her* team, that his loyalty rested more with her than Lilly, if ever he had to choose between the two. She banked on that. All the more important since there were very few people on Carol's Belvidere team to begin with.

Carol and Cord dealt in playful banter and double entendre - a bit flirty, but harmless. And she did the same with Earl, she thought, as if to prove to herself it was nothing special with Cord.

Until Cord arrived in Town, Carol would travel west once a month, sometimes less, mainly to check on the place and, later on, to visit the cats. It seemed more like a chore than anything else. It was sad, really, but she couldn't regain the wonderful feeling she had such a short hold on so many years ago, and she wasn't selling - she would never give Lillian the satisfaction, so a sort of purgatory set in - a holding pattern; a long wait for something to move her off *Free Parking*.

Regardless, she always liked to see the cats, and she wouldn't take them from the house; they were born as strays under the front porch three years ago, at least the original set of five were. *L'antre du Lion* was named before the first stray even showed up, because Carol always liked lions. But now, even more so, the name of the house seemed fitting.

Ji Sue, her diminutive, attractive part-time Korean housekeeper and cat-sitter would come every day to feed and entertain all five, all black; she loved them all.

Carol pondered the pride.

Edamame - the mom. Eda was a skinny stray when Carol found her, but fat and content now. She barely tolerated her four kids, constantly growling when they got too close, which, in her mind, was always. Even after three years, they always just wanted to be near her. She, on the other hand, was an empty-nester wannabe from the moment she dropped them out.

Wasabi – the lone boy. And he was such a *good* boy, with a loud, low rumble of a purr; an engine the minute you touched him. But that purr belied his yellow belly; at the first sign of trouble, all you saw was his ass running for the door, leapfrogging his sisters to put distance from whatever he was running from. Half the time he didn't stick around long enough to figure it out. Carol smiled thinking about him – he was her unspoken favorite.

Tobiko – a lovable, curvaceous, fluffy, shy girl. She would fall on her back, lightly purr, and spread her legs for a belly rub if she liked you, letting you rub as long as you liked; the kind of cat most men would want as a wife.

Maguro – a skinny girl, with a beautiful face and a big, bushy tail, nearly as long as her entire body. A neurotic who starved to be the center of attention; without warning, she'd madly dash around the house, chasing nothing, then just as quickly butt-in if any of the others were getting too much attention – she *had* to be in the spotlight. Carol sometimes mocked Maguro by calling her Lilly: *Serves you right for running into the door, Lilly.* Yes, it was childish, but she did it anyway.

Ebi – a bitchy loner, and a little squirt to boot. What she lacked in size she made up in attitude, usually bad attitude. But when she wants to be affectionate, you would love her to death, until she turned like a switch to bite you. Most men wanted Tobiko; most men got Ebi.

For the last three years, the cats made the trip bearable, but the sight of Town meant the thought of Lilly, which made the trip wretched - an albatross, the thought of which made her tired, and cross.

But since Cord showed up, the trip felt decidedly different. Carol liked coming to Belvidere again; she felt she had friends, real friends, outside the influence of Lilly.

Actually, that statement didn't apply to Earl; he was certainly under Lilly's influence.

Yet despite Lilly's endless attempts to control him, on certain, select fronts, Earl stood his ground and did as he pleased, despite Lilly's objections and visible ire. He didn't defy her often, but sometimes Earl would dig in and stick to his guns.

And Carol was a big gun.

Earl knew Lilly hated that he came to see Carol, and worse yet, that he thought Carol was attractive, yet he came anyway, and endured her wrath. That made Carol feel special.

And what did she think of Earl?

He had been delivering the rent to her house for the past three years, but she never gave it much thought, other a general feeling that he was a nice, shy man, who was unfortunate enough to have Lilly as a sister.

She had never really befriended a black man before, although Earl was really a mulatto. And she had never been so close to a man so big, so muscular. Earl was a physical specimen you spy in professional sports spreads, six foot eight and close to four hundred pounds, yet his body fat had to be ten percent, maybe less. He was simply a monster of a man.

But his face was adorable; it was cut, with a square jaw, yet somehow it was so soft, so caring. It was Earl's eyes that did it. The light brown pools were the sweetest she'd seen. And he was always smiling, with a toothy, brilliant white grin. His flat top looked military; and his skin looked so soft, stretching endless over that big frame, with no tattoos, no piercings, no blemishes, nothing….and surprisingly little hair.

The more she thought, she figured he was actually good-looking enough to be a model; his eyes were a bit close together, but that was being picky.

Yet despite his good looks and tender personality, she never thought of Earl in *that way* till now. She was ashamed to admit to herself why, but she knew the reason.

Everyone had always said Earl was *slow*, but if she hadn't been told that, she wouldn't really ever guess it from how he acted around her, she would just call it shy. She actually didn't know what was wrong with, or special about, Earl; no one ever told her and she never asked, it was just one of those things people in Town knew: *Earl was a bit slow*; that was it, further details neither asked nor offered.

But when you're around someone stuck with that moniker, you find yourself waiting for the shoe to drop, for the person to do something outside the bounds of what is considered normal, something that will embarrass them and you in a public place - it could be an outburst, a tic, some physical act beyond societal norms, whatever, but it colors how you act. You are cautious, and afraid to be alone with them for fear of not knowing how to react, how to act.

Carol was ashamed to say she felt that way around Earl; she was happy Cord was there, she felt some safety in his presence, safety from an embarrassing encounter.

She hung her head, ashamed she was thinking that way about Earl; it felt deceitful. He was such a good person - she never met anyone kinder; she considered him a true friend, a friendship which had blossomed over the past two months. Honestly, she couldn't think of any friend who cared about her, without condition or reservation, as much as Earl did.

She was sure Earl would do anything she ever asked him to do, with no strings….none. How many people can truly say they have a friend like that? He didn't deserve to be thought of in the way Carol was feeling now. She promised herself she would change that. She really would.

If only she could coapt Earl and Cord - she would marry that guy tomorrow. Did such a guy even exist?

Carol leaned back in her chair, propped her legs on the desk and stared at the ceiling, slowly closing her eyes.

Could she see herself kissing Cord?

Yes.

Could she see herself kissing Earl?

Yeah, she could, on a step-ladder.

Sex with Cord?

Yeah, she thought so, although it would almost certainly be a battle over control - who's on top, who directs the tempo, who picks the sequence, the setting, the foreplay, the process. She couldn't see him taking direction, and she certainly wouldn't listen to *his* directives; oh brother, she could see it quickly degrading into a debate. Definitely more trouble than it was worth.

Sex with Earl?

My God, how big must he be? Black *and* six foot eight? His dick must be a foot long, and thick, *real* thick. A real horse-cock.

She would love to get a peak, then she immediately felt a bit of a blush thinking that way, because she was sure Earl would have run and hid at the thought of it, had he known she was thinking of his *unit*. Yeah, she had to think of Earl's rooster as a *unit*; it was somehow more respectful that way.

She learned from Cord that Earl had never had a girlfriend, never been on a real date, never even kissed a girl, a girl he liked anyway. He was so pure, so good; thinking about sex with Earl made her a bit uncomfortable.

But she wanted to think about it. She wondered how having sex with such a big guy would be like; that cock *had* to be the size of a pipe.

With that, she got a little jolt in her crotch.

She would love to be Earl's first, thinking about how it would unfold. She smiled, fantasizing about slowly undressing a thirty-something year old virgin, showing him what to do, taking him through the dance, step-by-step. Unbeknownst to Carol, Earl knew *exactly* what to do, even though he never did it. He had the *Kama Sutra* memorized from all those years of bathroom research; the woman lucky enough to be with Earl first was in for a big surprise, in more ways than one; Earl figured you had to do pretty much everything in that Indian how-to book each time you had sex, all sixty-four positions. Good God, Carol had better be in shape.

Cord once said Earl would pass out from embarrassment if Carol ever kissed him; on that metric, sex would surely kill him, but what a way to die.

Carol returned to the screen for another snippet.

'My oh my, she just loves to talk about you; those stories can't all be true, can they? Let's just say 'thank God' I heard them before I gave up my golden ticket; it certainly expands the payback possibilities.

Goodness, you sure are a naughty little girl.'

Naughty little girl? What stories did Lilly tell him?

Lillian only knew *one s*tory, and **no way** Lilly would ever admit that one; she was sure Lilly hadn't discussed that issue with a soul, except, of course, Button, right before he skipped Town.

On the other hand, she could only imagine the horrid sex stories Lilly made up about her. She hoped Cord was joking and didn't believe a stitch of it. She wondered what they could be, and how close they were to what she'd really done over the years, which was more than she would ever admit to most.

Okay, enough of those memories, before she digresses further, and the hour she allotted turns to two.

But what was the chit? What was the golden ticket? Was he really looking for sex, as he not-so-subtly implied? Can't be, he wouldn't be that brazen. But if the chit wasn't sex, did he really want it to be? Did Cord ever fantasize about sex with her? Or just Lilly, assuming he wasn't already having sex with her. The fact that Carol wasn't sleeping with Cord had absolutely nothing to do with the fact that she *expected* him to want to sleep with her. In fact, Cord had *better* fantasize about her, she had more to offer than Lilly….much more.

Carol was getting herself all worked up over fantasies and pretend-sex; she took a long breath, and a drink of water. Breathing deep, she continued down the rabbit hole.

'As a proper host, and a gracious loser, I would certainly expect you to accommodate the following 'petite demande':

Davidoff's miniatures (my own would be nice, since you don't seem to be a good sharer) and a selection of hand-rolled Lancaster DeMuth's….'

A *Davidoff* miniature; he remembered from that first night on the porch.

She smiled. My God, that was the first day she met him, when Earl delivered the rent, Cord in tow. She later found that Cord only met Earl about a half-hour prior to that initial meeting on her front porch, a half hour! For some reason, she thought that was kind of cool.

My God, that seemed a lifetime ago, not two months. But what a good two months it had been. She didn't know what to think of Cord at the time; she still really didn't know.

She never told Cord how she knew he worked at Sam's; that tidbit came courtesy of the insatiable gossip Jane, from Oxford Street, two blocks over. Even Carol, who rarely left her front porch, got the latest hearsay in record time from that fat-ass yenta; she must have gone on a six-mile *walk* around Town to tell anyone, and everyone, she encountered along the way the juicy news about the *mysterious new guy* at Sam's Market. The gossip is always better when you lead with *mysterious*.

It felt a bit strange to Carol being on the receiving end of such innuendo, considering her same quicksilver treatment when she *mysteriously* stumbled into Town so many years before.

According to the quidnunc, word was that Cord was (a) some sort of hothead convict, who did something bad, real bad, but no one quite knew what, and no one would ask; (b) was a former Marine, gay to boot, who got tossed - there was a whole subset of stories circulating on the specifics, of course Jane was a tad too couth, self-proclaimed of course, to pass them on, although she drank in every detail; (c) was an undercover cop, on some secret assignment (an undercover cop sent to Belvidere? *Please*); (d) got into some scuffle with Frank the butcher, and Frank put him down with a single shot - knocked him out cold (Frank planted that sidebar on his own, but it didn't get much traction).

All that from Cord's first weekend in Town. The mill was a well-oiled machine in Belvidere, for sure.

'....and some port wine, perhaps a Fonseca vintage-1963, a favorite year of mine.   A bit pricey, but worth it, don't you think?

Artisanal Cheese and fennel crackers would be a nice accompaniment; perhaps a rustic Pitchounet, a lilly-white cheese derived from the sweet milk of the gentle ewe. Appropriate?'

Augment the cheese with miniature sweet red Champagne grapes, served in sectioned stem lengths, although one can certainly dip and strip the stem directly, much like an artichoke leaf, I would prefer you feed them to me individually; they are tiny, but you seem to have small, delicate hands.

For our conversation over wine and hors'doeuvre, I will take my respite on the front porch. You can recline casually on the loveseat in a submissive pose; I will occupy the master chair, facing the Square (you know, the one you usually sit in when you mock me running around the Park).

As for your attire, I will allow you some latitude in this regard….be tasteful, but the skirt should be short, very short. Undergarments are discouraged.'

She liked that string of *petite demande;* that made her smile, especially the French, which she knew fluent. But why was *he* using French? Did he know she spoke fluently? How could he? No one in Town knew that, and she never spoke a lick of it in front of anyone out there. Was it because she named the house in French, and he just assumed she must speak it too, so he dropped some phrases here and there, to impress her. Or was there some hidden meaning, some hidden message? That was by no means an accident; there *had* to be a reason.

Regardless of the above, this was clearly a gauntlet. It was so over the top, he knew she wouldn't oblige, but was she confident enough in herself to surprise him, and do as he suggested, and play along? Would that show weakness, or strength?

Not doing it would be easy; doing it would be hard. But would doing it show he didn't intimidate her, her own form of self-deprecation? He was serving it up, but would she take the bait?

She had to admit, she wasn't quite conversant in particular ports and French cheese, especially ones that were *'lilly-white, derived from the sweet milk of the gentle ewe. ';* she didn't even want to guess why he felt it necessary to describe that one in quite that manner. And did he purposely spell *lily-white* incorrectly, with *lilly* having three ells instead of the correct two, like the bitch downtown spelled her name? She hardly could imagine that was an innocent faux pas.

And the comment about posing submissively, sans underwear. Even if she took the bait, she was sure she wouldn't do that, would she?

She couldn't remember the last time she went on a date, a first date to boot, without underwear. Wait, did she just think *date*?; this isn't a date, is it?

'I have to talk to you about something important, in private.

You know, Earl can't stop talking about you; all joking aside, you make his day, his week, his life, whenever he sees you. He has become such a good friend, venture to say my best friend, and I want you to know he thinks the world of you; his face lights when the topic turns to you, not that you are the topic of all our discussions (we wouldn't want you to get too big a head, now would we?). Suffice to say if we talked about nothing but Carol Crowe, Earl would be a happy man indeed.

What did you do to deserve such attention? Probably the same thing I did....nothing. You and I have that in common; we are both lucky to have a friend like Earl.

Again, Earl doesn't know about my request to see you Saturday; please don't say anything to him. It's just between you and me; if he knew I came to see you without him, he would be disappointed, to say the least.

But this talk can't include him, not yet anyway, it would be inappropriate. Earl simply can't know about 'it'; it would be a significant problem if he found out about our little soiree.'

Which brought her to the next issue - overstating the secrecy from Earl. Cord calls Earl his best friend, yet Earl is kept in the dark, and he knows if Earl realized Cord came to see her without him, he would be devastated. She doubted Earl would suspect Cord of *making a play* for her, she didn't think Earl's mind would even think of Cord in that way, but she was sure Cord's mind did.

All joking aside, as much as she might like it, she hoped Cord wasn't making a play for her, for real; Cord wouldn't do that to his best friend, would he? And if he did, would she do anything with Cord, knowing how it would devastate Earl? No, she wouldn't do that, no way....she wouldn't. That would be wrong, right?

She read on, getting to the part about his running around the Park.

'Hope to see you this Saturday morning (that is, tomorrow morning); Earl and I will be assuming our usual role circling the Park. If you got this message and it is okay to come by tomorrow, please yell to me the following code phrase:

"My goodness Cord, you are looking pretty sexy today; what happened to your belly? For heaven's sake, it's all gone!"

Okay, that's a bit over the top; I don't think you could even choke those words out without laughing. How about this:

"Hi Earl, how about you come up on the porch and have a cool drink when you're done running half-speed to go slow enough for your friend to keep up; oh, you can bring him along too, he looks like he needs to sit down."

No, you make that sarcastic remark, or some variation thereof, just about every week, nothing new. Okay how about this:

"Earl, how would you like to help Ji-Sue take care of my cats when I'm out of Town, I would really appreciate it."

623

Yeah, that's the ticket. Use that as the code phrase.'

She loved Cord's quips about her. He could be funny when he wanted to be; she liked a guy with a sense of humor.

Well, that's enough flirty innuendo for now. Talk to you tomorrow young lady; enjoy the rest of your day and don't think too hard. It will all come out in the wash.

Regards,

Grocery Boy

Flirty innuendo, that's what he called it.

Was it really? She thinks so; she hopes so.

Grocery Boy....more self-deprecation.

She went back up, to read about the cats…and Earl.

"Earl, how would you like to help Ji- Sue take care of my cats when I'm out of Town, I would really appreciate it."

Yeah, that's the ticket. Use that as the code phrase.

And by the way, seriously, think about having Earl help Ji-Sue watch the cats; he would die and go to heaven if you let him. No man would be happier helping clean a litter box, of that I'm sure.

She smiled; Earl watching the cats? What a great idea.

The thought of Earl, a happy Earl, walking around her house, made *her* happy, like his quiddity would somehow infuse into the woodwork, into the soul of *L'antre du Lion*. And she knew the cats would love Earl.

Carol went back to his comments about her monologue when they ran around the Park; she loved when they came to run, which turned into just about every Saturday and Sunday morning. She would rise early, perch on her favorite wicker chair and have a cup of coffee, feet propped on the ottoman, patiently waiting for them, like a dog at the door.

They would always come into the Park on the far corner, Earl waving like a little kid the minute he saw her from afar. She would watch them make their way toward her, pass, and loop again and again. Carol would read the newspaper, only to dip it down each time they passed.

Without fail, Earl would raise and wildly wave his right arm like a kid at the back of the class who was sure he had the right answer, flash that oversized grin and shout a simple *Hi!*; he said it every lap they did, without fail, nothing more, nothing less. And she loved it.

Carol would smile broadly, wave lady-like in return, and yell encouragement to him, or insults at Cord. She would mix it up for fun. Maguro and Tobiko, prone, would droop their paws over the edge of the porch roof and watch the two pass over and again, in lazy indifference.

Carol had a grand time, as did the boys.

When they were done, Cord and Earl would end in front of her house, cross the street and come onto the porch to talk with her. At first it was for five or ten minutes, but over the course of the two months, it stretched to over an hour, sometimes two. Sometimes longer.

Carol bought bagels, crumb-cakes, orange juice, V8, coffee....the works. Soon enough, the whole post-run affair took on the air of an al fresco grand buffet. Anything to get Cord and Earl to linger longer and chat;

Carol wished they would stay with her on the porch all day. It was her favorite part of the weekend.

On one of those weekend morning buffets, she couldn't remember which, Cord told her and Earl about eating egg-on-toast, cut into neat little squares, which him mom made special, just for him. It was one of his most-favorite memories as a kid, eating egg-on-toast with his mom, while he watched *Kimba The White Lion*.

Carol told him she watched *Kimba* too.

What!

Cord didn't believe her; *Kimba* was his, and his alone.

So she described *Kimba*, remembered the theme song, at least part of it, and recalling episodes, characters and details that Cord certainly didn't. He got a bit sulky, his precious memory stolen.

Earl never heard of *Kimba*, but loved the little white lion anyway, because Cord and Carol did.

After the *Kimba* story, egg-on-toast became the standard post-run fare on Carol's porch, for all three of them. They would all help in the kitchen, making the concoction; well, Cord would mostly pretend to supervise, while Carol and Earl did all the work. Earl's and Cord's eggs were always a bit runny, the yoke and whites soaking into the toast; Carol's had to be dry.

Earl was in charge of breaking the eggs, which he did ever-so-gently. He also got to toast the bread; Carol cooked the half-dozen eggs and flopped them on the toast, one per slice. Earl then cut all six pieces of toast, two for each of them, into sixteen little squares; Cord told him his mother was very precise in her cutting, each little square of toast had at least a part of the egg on it, and they all stayed in line, like a neat checkerboard. It was harder than you think to cut them neatly, but Earl got it down pat. Then he would top each one off with a thin line of ketchup, which he did slowly, the tip of his tongue sticking out, belying his concentration, like a master pastry chef.

They were a work of art.

Cord pretty much just watched the whole operation; he never lifted a finger to help.

Then onto the porch they marched, and ate, each eating the eggs and toast in their own manner.

Cord ate them like he did as a kid, deliberately, in a certain order. He wasn't reclaiming his childhood; that was still how he ate, to this day. Carol had no particular pattern; Earl mimicked her sometimes, other times he mimicked Cord. It was Earl's favorite part of the day.

Egg-on-toast, it would forever remind her of *Kimba,* and Cord….and Earl.

It had become their own little routine, every Saturday and Sunday Carol was in Town, which had become just about every Saturday and Sunday. She made no plans for weekends any longer, Carol simply headed west every Friday night, no exceptions.

She started thinking about the boys mid-week; the anticipation would grow as the week stretched on. Carol loved her job, and she liked returning to work on Monday, no doubt, but a part of her regretted when the weekend ended. Till recently, till Cord came to Belvidere, weekends had just been days six and seven of the never-ending work week.

The change was not lost on Lilly.

For both Cord and Earl, the porch parties were a mixed bag; delightful at the time, but increasingly distasteful when they had to endure the subsequent wrath of Lilly, which magnified by the week.

But Earl was never happier than on Saturday and Sunday mornings, and Cord would never do anything to dampen his enthusiasm, so they endured the wrath.

Lilly would never ask for details as to why they were gone so long, and they would never offer, it was just a general sense of elephant that colored the balance of the weekend.

Of course, Lilly knew they were camping on Carol's porch; she got the scoop from numerous people in Town who were more than eager to share the juice. She also knew Carol had taken to feeding them aplenty.

So Lilly responded by making them a big breakfast, like a good sister, every time they came back, and would sit and watch them eat it, every bit of it, till they were both ready to burst. The later they were, the bigger the meals she made.

In the end, Lilly actually spited herself; the boys would eat quick with Carol, and hang for several hours to digest, then sauntered home to eat Lilly's guilt meal, which by that time hit the spot. If Lilly only knew, she would certainly have stabbed them with a fork.

Although weekends for Lilly had become something of a nightmare, the general mood above *Nonpareil* improved on Mondays, when Carol returned to the City. By mid-week, Lilly was close to fine, till Friday rolled around and the cycle started anew.

On the porch, Cord and Carol would do most of the talking, with Earl standing by, smiling, gazing at Carol. She would sit in her favorite chair; the boys would lean against the porch rail, or sometimes one would sit on the loveseat adjacent to Carol's chair, usually Earl. Cord preferred to stand opposite Carol, to talk to her straight on; Earl liked being off to the side.

Carol and Cord would pull Earl into the conversation as much as they could, but he didn't really want to participate, and didn't really understand a lot of the stuff they talked about; just seeing them talk to each other, and being close to Carol, was more than enough for him. A couple times, when Carol would hand him a bagel, or a glass of juice, her hand would touch his; Carol could always tell, because Earl would jump just a bit, like he got a static shock.

Yeah, sex would definitely kill him, she thought.

After two months, Cord had increased his wind to a solid nine laps, sometimes a couple more. And his pace was pretty good; Earl still looked as if in slow motion running alongside him, but at least he took C's advice and stopped smiling and talking the whole time, which he used to do while Cord sucked wind. Nine laps was about three miles, not bad for a man who almost passed out after a couple laps that first day.

And despite the double-breakfasts, Cord's belly *was* smaller, and his face more oblong than round, his chin becoming flat, chiseled; his cheekbones revealed. But Carol wouldn't give him the pleasure of acknowledging any of it.

Carol leaned further back in her chair, stretched and then pivoted forward against the screen, scrolled up and reread C's various sarcastic comments; it made her smile and chuckle a bit out loud.

She didn't even register that her cell phone had rung; instinctively, she answered it just as she finished a snort of a laugh. Only after the snort was recorded by the receiver, after it was too late to take back, did she realize her predicament. She slowly registered the number on the deep-blue backlit display; she unfortunately knew that number.

And she recognized the high-pitched nasal bleat.

630

CHAPTER 56 - STARE BACK AT CAROL IN THE MIRROR

"What the hell is so fucking funny! Can it be the pro forma for the fund I'm **not** investing in? What the fuck kind of operation are you running over there!"

Now Carol was furious; mostly at herself for her dimwitted slip-up in answering her cell, but also for Bud's profanity, directed at *her*. She had seen him lash at others, but it never was hurled her way – and she somehow felt immune to his wrath, till now. And it got her immediately pissed, but good.

Her ire worked; rather than mumbling some excuse, or yammering a weak apology, which Bud would have eaten and spit back at her, she went on the offensive - a *blitzkrieg*.

"I'm finishing up the God-damn pro-forma right now! And that wasn't a laugh, it was a cough."

She hesitated for just a second, then launched a second assault.

"And don't you **ever** speak to me that way again! I had to make changes to the format and content to satisfy *another* investor; if you want to go elsewhere, it's your prerogative, but the document is being sent out tomorrow via courier. If you still want a copy, let me know."

Silence rang in her ear as she held the phone; her hand was trembling, a mixture of anger and being scared-shitless, mostly the latter. A quarter-billion rode on that off-the-cuff bomb she just hurled his way.

At least it wasn't a dial tone, not yet anyway. So far so good, as she balanced herself on very thin ice.

Another few seconds passed in silence; he was thinking. He pierced the dead air with an annoyed bark back, but restrained nonetheless.

"What other investor? What did they ask you to change? Why the hell have they seen a draft and I haven't? Who's investing? Is Stuart in on this deal? I shouldn't have told him about it, fucking Stuart, it's *got* to be him, meddling and mucking up the works. It's him, isn't it?"

"No one has seen the pro forma outside this office; questions have been asked which I didn't feel were fully addressed in the prospectus, so I modified it. You know how that goes, you make one change and it ripples through the report, requiring multiple modifications. It's a pain in the ass, but worth it. It was good input; this investor usually has good input, and I trust their judgment."

"What input? Who? Who do you trust? It can't be Stuart, he's a moron."

Silence.

"Well, who is it?!"

"Exactly."

"Exactly what? Stuart? Who? I can't hear you."

Carol was silent.

"So, what is this? You're not going to tell me!?"

"If they ask me who the other investors are, I'm certainly not going to tell them Bud Wiseman is in; I certainly wouldn't divulge that privileged information, unless, of course, you want me to tell them about you."

"NO! Don't tell anyone I'm in; just send the document over tomorrow and I'll take a look....see if I have any questions or suggested modifications. I want to wrap this up by the end of the month - is that doable Carol? Are you going to take my call next time?"

"I *took* your call this time, didn't I?"

She said with a waft of indignity, ignoring the fact it was by accident.

He chuckled a bit.

"You **were** a bit testy young lady, you know I like that, especially...."

She cut him off; whenever he called her *young lady* she knew two things: (1) she was in the clear; and (2) ever-more kittenish dialogue was on the way. Even though Bud was well-preserved, she had averted the train-wreck, and flirty was not a game she was particularly in the mood for now, even if the man was plunking down a shitload of money with a gentile. She already made the sale; she really needed to finish the prospectus.

"Goodbye, Bud, I gotta get this document done, and I want to go home before 2 am."

She heard a soft click, followed by a dial tone; no goodbye.   She let out a big breath and an extended sigh; that was fucking *close*.

For some reason, the fact that Cord often called her *young lady* too drifted into her mind; that had always been Bud's line. Strange. Could they know each other? No way; no possible way.

Enough of the junior-high play-pretend; she quickly filed and closed Cord's email and opened the currency derivative spreadsheet.

She leaned back in her chair and let out another much-relieved sigh. Thank God for that *other* astute investor who still had questions, who also happened to be the *only* other investor who had committed to the fund.

An astute investor alright, who also happened to stare back at Carol in the mirror.

634

CHAPTER 57 – AN UNDENIABLE VIOLATION IN THE CELL

It was still Friday, June 23rd; downtown Belvidere.

C reopened the pantry cabinet and scanned the shelves a third time, slowly running his eyes left to right. The rows of cans, the lines of boxes, all labels facing forward, all in symmetry….perfect.

Nothing awry. After two months, she was getting better.

The pantry was Lillian's favorite, especially the sweetener packs; but if it wasn't there, the next bet was surely the underwear drawer. She apparently had a thing for his boxer briefs.

He walked in a half-quickened pace back to the bedroom. He was going to be fucking late getting back to work, and was pissed at the thought, but he couldn't leave without finding it; he would obsess about it the rest of the day - and that simply wasn't worth it. And, of course, if he did obsess the rest of the day, without finding the disorder he knew was there, lurking in his apartment somewhere, hidden from view, she would win.

There was no way he was letting her win.

He opened the drawer fully and scanned the neatly folded rows of boxer briefs, all twelve of them, all black, all folded exactly the same way, facing the same way, in equal stacks of three.

Nothing.

Damn! He had gone through the whole fucking apartment, twice, and couldn't find it, but he knew it was there, somewhere.

The filiform of clear tape along the exterior hallway upper door jam was broken; like it was at least twice a week, sometimes more. Lillian had been there all right.

Where the fuck is it! I don't have time for this! he announced aloud to himself, pacing the apartment.

They never spoke of her little charade; it was a secret she didn't realize they shared. She figured her little diversions would be mistaken for carelessness in his own neatness, and he would eventually catch his own mistakes. She got a kick thinking he would scold himself for placing something slightly ajar.

But that's how a person who does not obsess thinks a person who obsesses might act.

Wrong. Lilly had no concept; none whatsoever.

A soup can turned a degree or two out of kilter with the others - a label letter off from the can stacked above it, a backward sweetener packet – one out of a hundred all facing the same direction, a single stack of underwear in a closed dresser drawer slightly ajar, would never be missed, never be allowed to remain askew….never.

If he tried to fold the towel sloppily, to leave a drawer slightly open, he wouldn't make it to the doorway without returning to fix it. Such was his obsession.

Yet to this point, it had always been a game Lilly played whereby she had plausible deniability; theoretically, he could have set ajar whatever it was she moved. Theoretically.

Wait, maybe she went in and didn't touch *anything*; was that the new trick? In that case, she would be acknowledging he was aware of the game, and she would have made a game of the game.

"Fuck! Fuck! Fuck!"

He yelled in frustration as he slapped the bedroom doorjamb. That was probably loud enough for her to hear downstairs. He didn't have time for this!

Then it hit him, the aluminum foil?   No, it can't be. She wouldn't dare go there a second time.

He never let on he knew she fingered one of the three stacks hidden behind the box on the upper shelf that first weekend, even though he saw her pink fingers, and mistakenly commented on them. They never spoke of it again, and it soon dropped; he assumed she figured she got away with it.

But he knew she had dragged the dining room chair over to the closet and eyed those stacks many times since. And unlike the other traps she set, she really didn't want him to see any change in the lay of the stacks, or in the footprint of the over-taped box which they hid behind.

But of course he knew, not that he really cared. Well, he cared about the box, it's contents, but she wouldn't dare open that, he didn't think. Would she? God, he hoped not; that would open a whole rash of problems he had no interest in dealing with at this time, especially with her.

But the aluminum foil wrappers, he knew it gnawed at her, wondering what was wrapped up, knowing she figured it must be cash.....*lots* of cash.

He never fixed her finger smear of the red ink on the one stack; that deviation didn't bother him, surprisingly enough, since it had to remain smeared to convince her he never saw it. In his mind, he could live with that imperfection, since its existence served a greater purpose. Conversely, if he had mistakenly smeared the ink, it would have to have been fixed immediately. He didn't know why his mind worked that way, it just did.

But he hadn't touched those stacks since he moved in; it wasn't part of the daily routine - underwear, kitchenware, and the like. Therefore, if she had purposely altered the stacks in some way, that would be new territory, an admission she saw the packets, with the inevitable questions that would follow. In all, a bit more daring than her forays to date.

He dashed down the hallway, grabbed a dining room chair, swung open the closet door and clicked the light, a bare bulb mounted to the wall, adjacent to the top shelf. He hopped atop the chair, and studied the box; it was exactly as he had left it. He slid the box down the shelf, to expose the three aluminum packs. He stared intently at the erasable red marker patterns, little amoebas, drawn by the hundreds over each surface of the foil. It took him countless hours to do.

He stared, and stared, looking for something awry. And sure enough, he spotted it. Hiding in plain sight, a couple inches in front of his nose.

"Son of a bitch."

He whispered allowed.

And that's when he smiled; a single one of his hundreds of little amoebas had been altered.

It was an undeniable violation in the cell.

CHAPTER 58 – RELAX, CLOSE YOUR EYES AND OPEN YOUR MOUTH

A single, small amoeba-like shape was devoid of small, red internal dots, unlike the hundreds of other amoebas sporting pointillist. It was no mistake in his artwork; he could see how she must have painstakingly used a small wipe, maybe the very tip of a cotton swab, to carefully dab them away, a trio of them, a hint of red smear was still visible.

C smiled at the discovery.

Lilly's little game stepped it up a big notch; now she clearly put the foil packs into play.

Lilly was getting better, much better; the dot efface would have easily been missed by most. But Cord wasn't most.

C let out a big sigh, happy he found the breach, his mind at ease. And now it was time to return the volley. He had planned his counterattack a full month and half ago, waiting for the right time.

Now was right.

He pushed the stacks back to their rightful place, slid the box to the right, shut the light and neatly repositioned the chair. He quickly made his way downstairs, to the sidewalk, and down to Sam's.

The tinny bell caught Earl's attention; he was stocking and straightening the glass jars of sun-dried tomatoes, packed in olive oil, along with boxes of organic pasta in a bevy of unpronounceable shapes and sizes:

- *ancini di pepe;*
- tiny ears of *orecchiette;*
- ribbons of *reginette;*
- *buctani* straws;

- ribbons of *vermicelli;*
- *roccheti* spools; and
- Earl's favorite, *gigli,* the little cone-shaped flowers, with the fluted edges.

Cord told him *gigli* meant *lilies,* since it looked like the flower. Earl was fascinated that his sister was a pasta; he made Lilly cook them for dinner at least once a week; thanks to Earl alone, *gigli* became a popular pasta sale at Sam's.

Earl would tell Lilly over and again at the dinner table:

'*You taste sooo good!*'

Or, his favorite:

'*I'm stabbing you with a fork! Gotcha! Gotcha again! Knitting needle! Gotcha!*'

As he speared and shoveled in the *gigli*; he cracked himself up every time he said it - to Earl, the joke never got old - while he coyly gazed across the table at Lilly, with mischievous eyes.

The more Lilly got annoyed at the stale joke, and the more she yelled at him to keep quiet about the whole thing, and how stupid it was, the more Earl would repeat it, snickering at her as his fork tines poked and scratched noisily back and forth across the plate, chasing the little buggers.

It usually ended when Lilly threw something at him; her favorite was the wooden salt shaker.

Then, when Earl discovered *spaghetti* actually meant 'a length of *cord*', he was positively ecstatic. Now his best friend was pasta too.

He would bring home box after box of *gigli* and *spaghetti*, making Lilly cook both at the same time, so he could mix them all together on his plate, Cord and Lilly all rolled up into one.

"Cord and Lilly; Lilly and Cord....Cord loves Lilly; Lilly loves Cord."

He would sing the jingle aloud *ad nauseam*, like a little kid, smiling at her as he scooped up the tangled pasta pieces, glued together with gobs of grated Parmesan cheese he smothered atop the plate.

That jingle was a trigger-switch, unleashing a torrent of profanities from Lilly, followed by a barrage of flying salt and pepper shakers, utensils and whatever else was within reach. Earl would laugh the whole time as she bounced tableware off his head, shoulders, whatever; he would cover-up, like a boxer pinned on the ropes, waiting for her to tire - arm fatigue.

"Sorry Lilly."

He would always say in a sad tone, when the respite finally arrived.

"No you're not."

Was her standard retort; and she was right, because he would start up singing all over again, till she got tired of the whole affair and shoved away from the table in disgust. Then Earl would smile to himself and get to eat the rest of her dinner too. Mission accomplished.

Earl could push buttons just as well as Lilly; he learned from the best.

Yet despite the bickering, and the inevitable annoying pasta-taunts from Earl, Lilly always made Earl the *gigli* and the *spaghetti* pasta when he asked; she never said no. Never.

It was midday on that June Friday afternoon when Cord returned from his lunch break sleuth. He eyed Earl stocking the epicurean ingredients where scores of cardboard boxes containing instant mashed potatoes and expired macaroni and cheese stood two months prior. Now, there was nary a box of the meatless cheese-wonder to be found, save a few lonely cartons, nestled in a small, reserved section of the top shelf in the last grocery aisle. Nearby, a fancy, old-fashioned wooden sign in the shape of a human hand hung from the ceiling on a black iron chain – its pointer finger extended in an exaggerated manner toward the macaroni box, with a single word stenciled across the bottom of the finger:

~ Antiquities ~

Prehistoric dry goods saved for the diehard patrons of old, who still stumbled in for Sam's dusty produce of yore. It was a memento to what had been Sam's. The macaroni and cheese premix survived the purge largely as an employee perk; Frank bought it for dinner at least once a week.

The ability to eat on a daily basis the choicest cuts of meat and seafood, free to boot, made no matter; Frank never partook of the bounty he dished all day. He preferred to eat from a premixed, powdered box. And it was his small way to rebel against Sam and his success; to idly spurn what Sam was most proud of, at least when it came to the store. And it was his *fuck-you* to Sam's decision to bring on Cord and to give C, some nobody newcomer, free reign to upend the steady-eddy world all around Frank. For these reasons, Frank simply ignored the store upgrades, as if they didn't exist. He wanted no part of, and would not contribute a penny to, its success. Sam knew this, and simply let the pathetic macaroni mix stay on the shelf, without comment.

Frank's favorite box of macaroni and cheese was saved for Friday nights; it had the stale pasta pieces shaped like Fred and Wilma Flintstone; Frank and the *Flintstones* were a regular Friday evening date. Frank ate all the Wilma's first.

He would carefully balance the micro-waved bowl of creamy goodness on his rounded belly as he slumped on the couch, swallowed by the blue glow of the tube, till he fell over sometime after midnight, the empty, cheese-crusted vessel falling beside him on the couch, along with a dozen or so empty bottles of rot-gut beer, whatever was tagged as the sale-of-the-week at the packaged goods liquorette, two doors down, the opposite bookend of *Nonpareil*.

Save the *Flintstones*, Sam's had undergone a metamorphosis; the store was filled with wicker baskets and misted-crispers exhibiting exotic organic fruits, vegetables and cheeses, to accompany the usual mix of top-shelf meats and seafood at the venerable deli counter.

Gone were the tired paper banners in the window; the plate glass was transformed into a welcome cornucopia of produce, tastefully displayed, with a minimum of verbiage. A new retractable awning hung over the shop, to complement the one at *Nonpareil*.

Al fresco tables extended along the entire front of the market, to service Sam's patrons, as well as overflow from the next-door restaurant. *Nonpareil* became one of Sam's largest accounts, modifying their lunch and dinner menus to reflect use of the organic and exotic cheeses, fruits and vegetables Sam's now stocked. *Nonpareil* and Sam's fed off each other; two civilized outposts at the fringe of frontier-land.

Cord, the self-appointed produce manager, smiled at Earl as he pushed into the shop.

"It's Friday afternoon Earl, you know what that means."

"Mae's on the way!"

Earl yelped.

"You got it."

The Brookfield convoy was surely en route, making Friday an extra busy day.

Cord never did toss that scrap of notes he jotted down on day one, to which he added as the work days accumulated, picking the brains of the various patrons. A fair bit of input originated in long talks with Mae - in the store, while he carried her groceries, leaning against her car, and in her car, where she always tried to coax him to join her for an innocent *spin around the block* in the little Cooper.

She loved that little car.

The single spins around the block with C soon became two or three loops about Town, which eventually extended to the *Brookfield Community Center* to meet new neighbors, under the guise of *marketing*. Mae loved marketing, since it was really just an opportunity to show off C to the other senior women, to advertise what she landed, and they didn't.

Invariably the adventure would include a stop by Mae's house for something or another, all a flimsy ruse, where she would never fail to find some reason to respite on the sofa, the patio loveseat – she hadn't contrived a plausible scenario to get him into the bedroom....yet.

Cord went along, letting Mae eat the attention. To date, he had been a perfect gentleman, much to his surprise and her disappointment.

But the innuendo was thick, and fun for both. Cord had never banged someone Mae's age, not even close; although if he did, he would imagine he wouldn't ever find a better specimen than Mae. For her part, Mae never failed to segue into their little marketing trips a recount of her liaisons with younger men, always invariably south of Cord's age.

Unlike in their younger years, the total head count a woman fucks diminishes in importance as one reaches a *mature* age. The age differential between the woman and her toy, the more years the better, takes significant precedence.   Bagging a markedly younger man is a trophy; bagging a twenty-something more so, and if he's happily married, has a brain, and is sober at the time, it's Olympic.

For Mae, the younger, within reason, the better. She didn't have much use for men her age, no libido and generally saggy in every sense. Yuck.

When they behaved, Cord and Mae would incessantly pick the brains of the Brookfield transplants on what produce they would like to see stocked at Sam's, ethnic or otherwise – the kinds of products they previously purchased in Manhattan and tonier New Jersey towns to the east, throughout Bergen and Essex counties, which was largely devoid in Belvidere and the surrounding boonies.

And because of it, soon Sam's aisle stock was turning over as quick as the deli goods; profit margins had close to doubled in the cheese, vegetable and fruit lines alone. The cash register was getting hard to close; Sam was in a perennial good mood.

After the first month of foot-dragging, soul-searching and general consternation in changing what had been a comfortable business, with comfortable cash flow, Sam basically gave up and let Cord do as he pleased in the shop; the greenbacks won him over, and a produce manager was born.

Since Cord negotiated a percentage cut of the increased revenue from the non-deli receipts, with an escalator as revenue hit certain benchmarks, he was seeing a bit more of a bulge in his pocket as well. He actually didn't negotiate anything; he told Sam what the cut would be, and Sam agreed. He didn't even negotiate a piece of the increased deli revenue, although it clearly rose with the increased market traffic driven by produce. That would be the next round of negotiations, which Sam suspected was coming soon.

The deli revenue numbers were getting scary, and word of the little niche market on Water Street was extending beyond the confines of Belvidere and Brookfield.

With the increased business, Sam gave all the staff raises; he gave Frank a new, blue-stitch label on his apron - *Master Butcher* and he gave Frank an extra day off each week, paying him for the time off to boot.

Everyone was happy, except Frank.

He simply hated the new look of the market, he hated the bullshit **Antiquities** sign Cord bought to poke fun of his macaroni and cheese, he hated the increased patrons, which only meant increased meat to hump into the display case, slice, dice and wrap. He hated waiting on more and more people, especially old, stupid people who mumbled and couldn't hear very well. He would just assume deal with none of it and go back to the way things were, when he was only mildly miserable.

But most of all, the thing he hated above all else, was Cord. He despised him.

When Cord came to work that first Monday in April, after the grape throwing incident, Sam brought the two together, stood beside them, waxed of

646

misunderstandings and misdeeds, and preached they should all just move on for the greater good, to be men about it. Sam was proud of himself for addressing the problem head-on, certainly not his forte and assumed his go-team speech cured the ill.

Such was not the case.

Cord nodded in silent agreement as Sam prattled on about teamwork, smiling the whole time. And as Sam walked away, Cord sealed the deal by extending his hand in friendship, to which Frank responded with an odd look and a tentatively extended hand of his own. Which Cord grabbed and heartily shook.

"No hard feelings Frank; for the greater good."

He said aloud, for Sam to hear. Sam didn't turn, but smiled to himself….conflict resolved.

As Cord continued to grip Frank's hand, he started to squeeze, and it was clear Cord's grip was much stronger than that of the *Master Butcher*. Then he gently whispered at Frank, while looking at him with an intense, vicious gaze.

"Now, listen carefully you fat fuck; stay out of my way, don't talk to me, don't even look at me, and don't ever do anything to fuck me, and you'll stay safe. The next time, it won't be a fucking grape; the next time, you'll go down and you won't get up."

Frank's hand was throbbing from the wicked pain, his fingers crushed together and hand folded in half; Cord threw Frank's hand away dismissively as he released his grip.

Frank's face was beet red; he wanted to rub his hand, to relieve the pain, but he didn't, he simply let in fall to his side and throb. He closed his eyes and tried to wish away the flame burning at the end of his arm.

Frank was seething inside; he wanted so badly to lash out, start wailing on Cord, to beat him to a pulp, to take his butcher's knife and slice his throat, and watch him bleed out on the floor like a stuck pig. He envisioned choking him, sticking his fingers deep into Cord's eye sockets, gouging them out. All method of abject retaliation and maim flashed through his mind; Frank couldn't decide how best to kill this fucking bastard who was standing in front of him, smiling with a shit-eating grin. No one talks to him like that and gets away with it….no one.

Yet, for all the bravado and mayhem ricocheting in his brain, Frank just stood there and said nothing, did nothing, like most frightened, middle-aged, out-of-shape white men would do. While he boiled on the inside, he was impotent on the outside, afraid of getting beat up by Cord – it was as simple as that.

He hung his head and walked back behind the deli counter; a man with low self-esteem now had even less.

And from that moment on, Frank never spoke to Cord unless he absolutely had to, and then it was only in bitter fragments. And he steered clear of him, and never once proffered a thought or suggestion on all the changes around him, except he asked Sam, in private, to please keep the macaroni and cheese.

Frank stood idly by while Cord systematically took over the market.

Even the extra day off Sam promised went unused, although Frank would have liked nothing more than to sit home, watch television, masturbate, and drink himself to unconsciousness. But he knew that day off would be spent with Cord behind the glass, wearing Frank's old apron, playing junior butcher. Not that Frank gave a shit about butchering, but he did give a shit about that shithead taking his job. No job means no money to buy booze and pay the cable bill.

So, he couldn't take off the day Sam gave him, because of that bastard Brin. How he wished it was March, before this asshole ever showed up. How he wished he had the guts to stick a knife in his belly, or watch someone else who did.

On cue, the Brookfield horde funneled in, Mae on point, with a new face in tow. She headed directly toward Ay, with a wide, familiar smile.

"Anne, this is the young muffin I told you about; isn't he just the cutest!"

Anne nodded eagerly in agreement; she actually didn't think Cord was so great after all, kind of a disappointment, in fact – but considering the endless promo she had heard for the past week, any less enthusiastic response would have been disrespectful to her friend Mae.

"Don't let her kid you, she says that to everyone, it's the politician in her, she can't seem to shake it. Except for Frank, of course, she never says that about him."

Cord said it loud enough for Frank to hear, which he did, and tried unsuccessfully to pretend he didn't. He started to cut the rib roast harder, driving the blade into the wooden block.

"Cord, tell Anne about the produce; he's so good at explaining it all. Most of the varieties he has came from suggestions from all of us at Brookfield, isn't that right Cord?"

"Right you are, young lady."

She loved when Cord called her *young lady*; Mae ate any compliment he sent her way.

And with that, Cord stepped Anne and Mae over to the wicker baskets. Mae took up her usual position adjacent to Cord, and indiscreetly slid her arm into his as he launched into his primer.

"Let's start with the fruit; those are my favorite."

Cord grabbed a small hand basket and led the women over to the produce.

"This is a *pepino* – it's a Peruvian mellow-fruit *[Cord picked it up and squeezed it while slowly turning it, like displaying a priceless jewel at auction]*; it has yellowy flesh, which tastes like a cross between a cucumber and a cantaloupe, if you can imagine that. Some people eat it with brown sugar; you can also eat the seeds."

Anne didn't know quite what to do with the papaya-sized orb, which was smooth and golden, with random, bright purple steaks, the color of eggplant. So she sniffed it, squeezed it, rubbed her finger along one of the violet tiger stripes and, with a small smile on her face, gently handed it back, like it was a show and tell family heirloom. Cord dropped it in the basket.

"Okay, here's a horned melon – a *kiwanos*. It comes from New Zealand. It's tastes like a combination of a banana and a cucumber, a bit tart and sweet at the same time. Actually, that's the second one that tastes kind of like a cucumber – maybe we should just go get a cucumber. Anyway, here….try it."

Cord took a knife in his pocket and cut open the bright yellow melon, studded with horns, exposing the pale, yellow-green innards. He cut out the flesh, which had the consistency of jelly, and handed it to an apprehensive Anne. She really didn't like other people touching her food, but she braved Cord's fingers for the sake of etiquette. She hoped his hands were clean; she thought more about that than the lump of *kiwanos* sitting in the palm of her hand.

A second piece went to Mae, but she didn't put out her hand, she simply opened her mouth, like she was receiving communion, or something else. He smiled and gently dropped the jelly blob onto her waiting tongue; she pulled it in and gently worked it around her mouth.

"Wow that *is* fantastic!"

Anne cooed, unprompted; Mae just chewed slowly, deliberately, smiling at Cord. C dropped the remainder of the cut fruit into the basket and moved down the line.

"What's next Cord, I want to try something else, something more interesting on my tongue."

Anne missed the double entendre completely, much to the delight of Mae; it made her feel younger, more hip, even though Anne was seven years her junior.

Cord didn't.

"Well, we have Colombian *pisang susa*, the *baby banana*; it's very small, but the sweetest banana around. How about that Mae, do you want to down a *susa*?"

"He's right Mae, I've had them before; the little ones are *so sweet*, they almost melt."

Anne proffered, the taste of *kiwanos* fading on her tongue.

"No thanks, I've had plenty of *pisang susa* in my day, I was hoping for something a little more tempting; I was hoping you had something bigger than a *baby banana* to offer, Cord."

"I don't' know Mae, sometimes the small ones are the best tasting, but let me see if I can accommodate your request. How about a *red banana*; red skin, with a light pink flesh, it's almost as tasty, but there's a lot more flesh to eat."

"Now *that's* what I want, volume! I've been a bit starved lately for good, hearty fruit. Can you peel one for me dear, please? I'd just assume eat it right here, right now."

Tying to fluster Anne with sex-charged talk was half the fun; but alas, Anne had moved on to the next fruit basket, oblivious to playtime between Cord and Mae.

"Sorry Mae, she seems to have moved on; do you still want to taste the banana?"

"Just keep your red banana in its basket for now; you can feed it to me when you deliver the groceries, personally."

And with that, Mae gently brushed her hand across Cord's crotch.

"Goodness, that feels more like a *pisang susa* than a red-hot!"

Mae laughed at her little joke; Cord smiled, acknowledging the esprit.

"When am I going to get a private fruit *primer* Mr. Brin; I certainly think I have earned one by now."

Mae gazed around the shop.

"Things sure seem to be looking up at the market, and I hear through the grapevine you negotiated a bit of a percentage deal for yourself, which is paying off nicely, thanks to my aggressive promotions with the Brookfield contingent. By the way, do they teach contract negotiations and escalator clauses in high school? Or was it grade school? Or was it butcher's school? Where *does* a shelf-stocker learn about such things?"

"The streets are a good teacher Mae; you'd be surprised what you can pick up if you just learn to listen."

"And what about my primer? Don't think you are getting off that easy; where were we - I think we were talking about red bananas."

With that, Cord stepped close to Mae, paper-close, and put his hands firmly on her shoulders, looking directly into her eyes.

"Okay, okay, enough. Are you *really* ready to play? Do you want to play a game Mae? "

"Do you think I'm pretending? A blunt crack to the back of the head would be more subtle. Yeah, of course I want to fucking play."

"I'm not kidding; if you're really ready, we'll start it right here, *right* now, with your new little friend wandering around in the next aisle. Are you sure you're ready? Remember, this is a one way street, and I'm not a good boy."

Mae felt a tingle shoot through her body, ending at her crotch. She shook her head slowly in the affirmative.

"I want to hear all about the bananas."

"Okay then, relax, close your eyes and open your mouth."

CHAPTER 59 – *ANOTHER STORY FOR ANOTHER DAY....*

Anne was wandering aimless around the store, filling her own little basket with new-found treats; Earl was still stocking, but constantly eyeing Cord in the next aisle, between spaces in the stacked produce, trying to see what C was up to. Frank and Sam were working the deli counter; the cod-fish was struggling to keep up with the small queue of shoppers at checkout.

And there was Cord and Mae, standing face to face in Aisle Four; not a word could be heard, but it was clear he was talking, and she was listening, intently, her eyes were closed.

"Now here's how we play the game; I'm going to ask you a series of questions, and you are going to give a simple yes or no answer, okay? And the minute you open your eyes, or you answer in the negative, the game ends. Do you understand the rules?"

Silence.

"Mae, are you still with me? Are you ready to play?"

The sexiest *yes* Cord had ever heard left her lips in the slightest whisper; wherever she thought he was going with this, it was clear she was already there.

"Now, you're going to tell your little friend that something sudden has come up, that she has to find another way home, aren't you?"

"Yes."

"And I'm going to take your little bag of groceries to your car, and you're going to follow me, glued to my side, slightly rubbing your body against mine every now and then, like you always do, is that right?"

"Yes.."

"You like when I let you get away with that, don't you?"

"Yes.."

"And you know that I do it right back to you, don't you?"

"Yes..."

"I'm going to open the passenger door, and you are going to slowly slide in, aren't you?"

"Yes."

"And when you do, are you going to let your little sea-foam linen skirt, the one you know is my favorite, the one you're wearing now, are you going to let it slide up your thighs just a little more than it has to, to show me some more of those pretty little legs you like to show off?"

"Yes..."

"I know you will."

Cord stopped for a moment, and slowly slid his left hand off her shoulder and let it run down her side, stopping on the curve of her hip, right at the top of that little green skirt.

"Do you want to be a good girl or a bad girl, Mae?"

He could see she was just about to answer, and caught herself. Like a kid picked by the teacher, who was trying to hide, she tensed, not knowing what to say.

Silence.

Cord smiled at his pupil.

"Good girl; now let me rephrase the question?"

"Do you want to be a good girl, Mae?"

Silence.

"Do you want to be a bad girl?"

"*Yes.*"

Came her answer, in a breathy whisper.

"Good. Now when I slide in next to you, right in the parking lot in the middle of downtown, I'm going to tell you to slowly spread open your legs and slide up that little skirt, but slow, ever so slow, while you slowly lick your lips. Show me how you're going to lick your lips, let me see it."

And right there, in the middle of Sam's, with her eyes closed, pushed up against the outside shelves of Aisle Four, Mae extended the tip of her tongue slightly past her upper lip, and slowly ran it from left to right, moistening her upper lip, then running it back, right to left, before she pulled it back in.

"Good girl; it looks like you've done that before. Now, the bottom of your skirt is getting close to your crotch, it's *so close*, but not quite there yet; just a bit more and you're going to show me your panties. You want to show me don't you?"

"Yes."

"And I want to see them….and there they are! I can see that tiny mound of pussy hair under the lace, can't I? Tell me your pussy has a nice, little neat mound of soft, brown hair, tell me right before you pull your panties off for me in the parking lot. Tell me."

Silence. But C saw that Mae had dropped her hand down by her crotch; she wanted badly to rub herself in the middle of Sam's Market, but she didn't. Not yet.

"Okay, now slowly lift your ass off the car seat, grab you panties, I hope they're black, I love black panties, and slide them down past your knees. Let them fall to your ankles, and spread your legs open wide, so I can see that little pussy, the one that you have been teasing me with for the last two months, the one you're going to let me do with whatever I want, isn't that right?"

"Yes...."

"And you're going to take your fingers and spread you lips open for me, just a bit, so I can see how wet I make you, aren't you?"

"Yes...."

"Okay, now slowly slide your hand toward my crotch, and tell me what I have in my pants just waiting for you, right now? Think about what I'm going to do, over and over, to that wet little pussy."

"Oh my God....."

Was all Mae said, as she slid her hand under Cord's apron and felt his cock straining against his pants.

But by then, she realized her fatal flaw.

Instinctively, she opened her eyes; and just like that, she broke *both* rules.

"Wait! Wait!"

Cord stepped back and smiled; too late.

"You know the rules, Mae; game over."

"Do Over!   You cheated!   Oh, come on, you tricked me!"

Cord just smiled.

"Anne's on her way over; take her home and if you want to play again, if you're a good girl, maybe we can finish it up at...."

Cord stopped abrupt, mid-sentence, as if struck by a heavy blow. He turned his head and watched a small, dented, faded red *Beetle* slowly scrabble by the front of the shop; it was the second time it passed; he only heard the distinctive staccato engine rumble the first time it crawled by. The first time he suspected, but this time he saw it, and he knew.

Mae looked at Cord, then looked toward the street, questioning his sudden interest in the goings-on outside the shop.

"What?"

Cord stepped away from Mae, heading for the door.

"I'll be just a minute."

And with that, he disappeared onto the street.

The Bug had pulled to the side of the road, two doors west of Sam's, idling. Cord walked slowly toward it, and the passenger side door swung open toward the curb.

Onto the sidewalk lightly stepped a thin dark black woman, with gently loose, faded jeans, frayed on the ends from the drag. A tight black tee-shirt exposed distinct muscular lines in her back and shoulders; she had short, somewhat unkempt, spiked hair. Her facial features were sharp, and she was attractive, or rather could be, but was decidedly less so, due to what appeared a general lack of sleep, combined with a large dose of worry.

She smiled faintly when she saw Cord, more in relief than anything else, stumbled toward him a bit and fell quietly into his chest, as if she finally crossed the finish line in a marathon. He gently put his arms around her, squeezed and whispered something into her ear. She was motionless. He kissed her gently on the side of her temple, followed by a long embrace, in silence.

Now Belvidere had always sported a black family or two, the highest tally in recent memory topped at three, scattered amongst the two thousand-seven hundred or so townsfolk. Of course, that didn't include Earl; no one in Town really considered Earl to be black.

The balance was pure white-bread Republican, a mix of third and fourth generation western Europeans – Italian, English, Dutch and German, mainly, with a smattering of French-Canadians.

Belvidereans neither celebrated nor despised the small contingent of blacks; they went largely unnoticed, weaved into the fabric of Town without comment, good or bad.

But seeing a new black face on the sidewalk outside Sam's, one that didn't call Belvidere home, now that was bound to be noticed. Not necessarily in a good way, or in a bad way….just noticed.

Mae moved slowly over to the storefront and eyed Cord and the girl from inside the plate glass, as did Earl; neither spoke as they watched the two stand statue on the sidewalk.

Earl never spoke to Mae; she was always loud and generally the center of attention; that made him uncomfortable, and she simply scared him. Even now, he felt a bit uncomfortable standing this close to her, without Cord nearby. Earl was never quite sure what Mae would do next, and the uncertainty made him nervous.

She lifted her head off his chest and began talking, at first through quiet tears, then calmly, him listening, then listening some more. Finally Ay spoke for a bit; she looked at him intensely as he did, soaking in his words; she leaned forward, so their temples lightly touched.

Cord kissed her long on the forehead, and pushed her gently away from him; she slowly rotated backwards, coming to rest against the side of the car. She smiled the faintest of smiles – what a beautiful face when not in despair. He returned the look, spun and quickly disappeared into the apartment hallway.

She dropped her head and stared at the sidewalk for a good half minute, then slowly lifted it, like hoisting a heavy weight, eyes closed. Pretending they were still shut tight, she cracked her lids ever so slightly, peering through the thinnest of slits, between her intertwined eyelashes, to see all the roving eyes, in the shadows, she was sure were watching.

And she was right.

An older woman and a big man were pressed against the glass of the deli, along with a young girl with pouty lips, off to the right. A whole contingent of people were staring not-so-subtly from the counter area of *Nonpareil*, including a thin blonde woman, who seemed a bit *too* curious.

She frowned and squeezed her lids tight.

Cord reappeared, blocking her from the voyeurs. He slid his hand in his pocket, trying to discretely remove a thick wad of folded bills.

She didn't smile, say thank you, or anything; a single tear tracked her right cheek.

She kissed him lightly on the neck, several times, in a tender, loving manner, while hugging him hard. She didn't want to let go.

She handed him a scrap of paper from her pocket and slowly slid back into the car. Cord leaned down, spoke something to the driver and quietly clicked the door shut. The Bug K-turned and drove away, east, down Water Street, the way from which it came.

Cord watched till the little red Volkswagen faded from sight on the long stretch of road, out the same wormhole he came in, down past *Wanda's*, past the old firehouse, past the peeling *Painted Ladies,* till it was out of sight, knowing it was passing the groundhogs, the herons, the distant popping of the water in the creek, out past *Luigi's Rancho,* to a world outside a strange outpost called Belvidere.

Gone, at least for now; surely to be part of a future chapter, yet unwritten.

He hung his head and closed his eyes, knowing he was now a solo act on stage. He ambled back toward Sam's and cracked the door. The bell sounded and he walked over to Mae, resuming as if no one had hit the pause button.

"So where were we Mae? Are you done shopping? Do you need me to bring something out to the car?

She looked at him incredulously.

"Are you kidding me? What was *that* all about?"

Earl leaned in, anxious to hear the answer.

"It's another story, for another day."

And with that, Cord walked to the back of the deli and grabbed a book of matches from the drawer. He pulled the slip from his pocket, studied it for a bit, then lit the end, dropping it into the dry sink.

He whispered sad to himself as he watched her scrap of paper slowly spin, curl and turn to ash.

"Another story for another day...."

CHAPTER 60 – SHE COMES WITH A NICE SHINE

Lilly quick-stepped it into Sam's, eager for information and hot to find that scrap of paper. She didn't think to note the license till it was too late; one bat of her eyes and Marty would have run that plate without question. She was pissed she missed that easy opportunity; she didn't catch the state, but it was one she definitely didn't recognize.

Must be far.

But that scrap of paper, that was gold.

It had been two months, and she still knew next to nothing about Cord; she tried to worm information from him, searched his pant pockets when she snuck into his apartment, went through his drawers, looking for anything to link him to a time prior to April 20th.

Nothing. Still no wallet, no phone, no mail, nothing to link him to….anything.

Except, that is, for a fleeting encounter with a stranger, a skinny, not-so-attractive black girl in a beat-up car; that was the only link to Cord's life outside Belvidere, the only known link to his existence outside what he had created within the confines of this little Town.

It was more than idle curiosity.

Over the past two months, save for the Carol weekend porch-party agita, and the general feeling that Earl didn't need her quite as much as he used to, she found herself increasingly enjoying Cord's company; although she would never admit as much. She liked him; she really did, for the most part, at least more than she had liked any other guy in the recent past.

Usually, for her, it, whatever *it* was with a guy, was quick and messy. But with Cord, it was a longer-term curiosity, that was becoming somewhat of an acquired taste.

But *she liked him* was all it was so far, nothing more, which was a big step up from hating him, the emotion *du jour* at the outset. What an asshole she used to think he was.

Truth be told, as much as she had grown used to him, the fact that he was so good to Earl, and that Earl was infatuated with everything Cord did, made her feel good. And she knew Cord's feelings were genuine; it had nothing to do with her, in him trying to get to her, or in her pants, through Earl, by using Earl.

Although, at times, she kind of wished it *was* all about her. But it clearly wasn't.

She didn't know what it was about Cord that Earl liked; why he ever even talked to him in the Park that first day. He certainly never talked to any other strangers, *ever*.

Earl avoided that question; he never told Lilly the real reason, the talk he had with their mom. Earl knew that bit of information wouldn't go over well with Lilly; she'd only yell at him for making up stories again.

Regardless of the reason, the friendship between the two ran deep.

And that was something she could never say about Button; he hated Earl, and Earl disliked him, greatly. She didn't think Earl really hated anything, but if he did, if he had to pick one thing, it would be Button. If Button could wish Earl out of existence, could put him on a one-way bus to anywhere but here, he would, in an instant. He had no use for Earl, and it was clear he hated the fact that Lilly loved Earl more than him, that Earl was so big and strong and that everyone loved Earl.

And that her mom loved Earl most of all….above everything else; Button hated *that* the most.

She suspected, no, she knew, well, she suspected, that Button called Earl a nigger; she never heard him say it, but she knew he did. And she knew he called Earl a retard, and picked on him when Lilly wasn't around. And she knew Earl would never say anything, nor do anything, to Button, even though they both knew Earl could easily break him in half. Earl didn't give two hoots about what Button did to him; but he cared about what Button did to Lilly. And if Lilly ever told Earl, ever admitted to what Earl suspected had happened at times, the physical and the emotional abuse Button inflicted, that she absorbed, Earl would have ended Button. And Lilly was convinced Earl was the only man who ever could.

How he treated Earl always made Lilly sad, and it had made her mom sadder still. Her mother had always treated Button like a son, like part of the family. Carol loved Button, but she loved Earl more. And Button knew it.

Lilly loved Earl more than anything in the world, and she knew that Cord loved Earl too, without conditions or exceptions. Those feeling wrapped around her when she saw Cord lately. Not that she didn't curse and taunt C on a regular basis, but that was just Lilly; it came with the package.

In a way, Cord gifted some of her life back. The free time she had when Earl was with Cord, which at times seemed to be most of his waking hours, she spent working out, prepping for her classes, practicing her dance, which she had let fall by the wayside, reading fiction and, of course, surfing the web for news articles, movie trailers and clothes shopping, with each adventure invariably ending in a marathon dose of video smut.

She was actually becoming pleasant more often than not, much to the surprise and delight of those around her. She also tended to tag along with the two of them more than she would like to admit, and despite complaining the whole time, usually had fun in the process.

And of course, she was loving the secret forays into Cord's apartment; loving that she was fucking with his things and he had no clue; he really wasn't as smart as she thought.

She figured she would keep screwing with him, till he found the aluminum foil erasures, then she would come clean on the months of moving things, thinking the whole process would be one big hoot. Then, of course, she would hit him up about the aluminum foil, on what was wrapped in that foil, or more to the point, what was he doing with all that money, since she was all but convinced that's *exactly* what it was.

Actually, she had to get back up to his apartment; that was as important as the scrap of paper he took from the girl. That wad of cash Cord gave to his secret friend came from somewhere, and her bet was there was now a somewhat smaller brick of aluminum foil in the closet; she needed to confirm her theory.

But first, the scrap of paper.

Lilly breezed down the aisle, accidentally bumping Mae in the shoulder as she passed, knocking her off balance, just a bit.

"Oh, sorry."

She said brusquely, never saying Mae's name nor turning to mouth the words, but simply continuing on her way. The accidental bump and apology were actually genuine, for once, but the delivery was more than a bit rude. Lilly couldn't really be bothered; she was on a mission.

Mae didn't say a word, but it was clear she wasn't happy.

"Hey C, who's the squeeze? How's she know you? Where's she from? How much did you give her? Where'd she go?"

As she rattled the questions, she joined him behind the deli case, pretending to grab a piece of cheese off the wood block behind him.

And just as he began his typical non-answer, she swung up behind him and quickly buried her tiny hands in both his front pockets, spreading her fingers out against his legs, digging like a mad squirrel for a nut, groping him blindly for the golden scrap of paper. She had never done anything like that before to him; the feel of her scurrying hands on his thighs was the best thing Cord felt since he arrived in Town.

Lilly had no idea how completely C had her number. He didn't say a word; he just stood motionless and enjoyed the grope.

"Where is it? Where?"

"It's there, it's there, in my right pocket. You win."

Her left hand stopped; the right moved more deliberately around, fingering his thigh shamelessly.

"Where? I don't feel it."

"It's there; here, let me see."

And with that, Cord stuck his hand in his right pocket, on top of hers, rooting around and blatantly fondling her hand.

"Funny, I put it in my pocket, there must be a hole. Ah, it's in my pants leg, I can feel it! Hey, come to think of it, get your hand out of my pocket! You can't look at that paper, it's private!"

And with that, Cord made a feeble attempt to pull her hand out of his pocket; she took the bait, believing his rebuff was legitimate, and resisted. She yanked her other hand free and started to frisk his leg, down by his knee.

He wanted her a bit north, so he grabbed his pant let just below his crotch and pinched his jeans.

"Ah…."

Signaled he had it between his fingers.

She took the chum and, with both hands, attacked his leg, leaning into him, knocking him to the floor. Cord pretended to resist. She was a hungry dog on a ham-bone.

"Hey, hey, your pushing it up! Hey, you don't want to go there, leave it be! Off base!"

That was actually home base to Cord, but Lilly was too caught up in the chase to catch on.

He finally stopped and let her work his upper thigh area, till she realized she was actually just about groping his sack. She was in a full-body squirm.

"I can't feel anything! Where the hell is it? Give it to me!"

He started to chuckle.

Then she stopped, looked at him, and realized she was practically dry-humping his leg, behind the deli counter, with Frank standing over them.

"Are you *okay* down there, Lilly?"

Frank offered.

She ignored him.

"Just give me the paper Cord; I'm not rooting around your crotch – I know that's what you're hoping."

He just smiled, enjoying her mount.

"Well?"

"Oh, that's right, I think I put it in the sink."

"**What?** In the…."

And with that, most girls would get up, flushed from embarrassment and brush themselves off, realizing they'd been had.

Not Lilly.

She took her right hand and jammed it straight up to Cord's crotch, found his ball-sack, and gripped it like a rosin bag.

"Ah!"

Came out first, followed by a desperate plea.

"Lilly, please, I was just joking, don't kid around about….**Ah!**"

"What's the matter? I thought that's what you were hoping for?"

She gave a harder squeeze, just a bit, along with a pirate smile, that's when he knew, for the first time, this dance was not meant to cripple or maim, this was the first volley of foreplay, Lilly-style.

What a beautiful thing; never had a man been so happy to be in pain from a scrotum-squeeze. He lay there, pretending it was worse than it really was; she knew it, and played along. He liked the feel of her warm leg against his; such stupid, little things are the ones that matter, the ones you remember.

"Uncle Frank, is there a scrap of paper in the sink?"

Frank, looking bored by the whole charade, shuffled over and spied the curl, which had disintegrated into a loose ball of ash.

"Was, not anymore."

As he stuck his pointer into the gray grit and held it up for Lilly to see. Lilly frowned and gave Cord's nuts a last, good squeeze, before she let go; this one wasn't so gentle.

"Mother-fuck…."

Cord groaned, as he went quasi-fetal.

"Well, who is she? And why would she ever come from wherever she was looking for *you*? She must be hard up."

Cord didn't favor her with an answer, or even a look. He slowly straightened, made his way to his feet like an old man, and looked down Aisle Four.

Empty. All that remained was Mae's basket on the floor.

Fuck.

"She left."

Earl offered, then he finished the knife thrust.

"And she didn't look very happy."

"You got women leaving you left and right, driving away, walking out. Looks like they got your number."

Lillian laughed and turned to talk to Frank and Sam.

Cord didn't return the retort; he didn't feel like getting into it with Lilly, and he felt bad about Mae. She was always so good to him, and he knew the Lilly leg hump escapade burned her up but good. He wondered if that Lilly act was for him, or Mae, or a little of both.

Mae was possessive when it came to Cord and her time with him, and she knew Cord was all about Lilly, and she really couldn't do anything about it. And she hated that, that lack of control, that she had a handle on pretty much her whole life. Till she got old.

Lilly aside, Cord was nervous about Mae. Her inferences were less veiled, more direct, by the day. She wanted him to throw her, and good. Not that Cord was adverse; he would actually like to fuck Mae - he thought it would probably be a good roll.

It was the *after* he was worried about; no play-out of that scenario bode well.

Somehow, he didn't think a solo fuck, roll-off and go back to work, was what she was looking for; and there was no stepping back from that Rubicon. A solo fuck, or even the occasional, casual bang, would invariably come with emotional strings, he was sure of it. Even if Mae denied it, he could simply point to the lonely basket sitting on the floor in Aisle Four, or her face pressed against the plate glass checking out the sidewalk scene earlier, as proof of her reaction.

And he knew once he banged her, she would want more. One thing Cord did well, was fuck. He always did. He wasn't so good in a lot of other relationship necessities, but the sex part was usually well received. At least in the beginning, until he got bored.

But it wasn't evitable; it was simply a matter of time. And when Mae turned it on, she did get him juiced, no doubt.

Jerking off for the last two months was getting a bit old. And although he usually jerked off to Lilly or Carol, or Lilly *and* Carol – that was his favorite – or some face from his past, he did throw Mae into the fantasy mix too, more than once.

He lifted the basket with the *pepino, kiwanos, pisang susa* and red bananas, and saw one of the *susa's* had been squeezed hard in the middle, the banana split, fresh flesh oozed from the crack in the peel.

Ow, he knew that *susa* had his name on it; that certainly wasn't a good omen. By reflex, Cord protectively cupped and squeezed his crotch.

He traveled down the balance of the produce aisle and filled the basket with an assortment of additional fruits; *cherimoyas,* some thick-skinned California oranges, *Calimyrna* figs, and Jamaican green papayas. He threw in some vegetables as well, *sunchokes, anise* bulbs, and a few *cardoon* stalks and *salsify* roots for a soup recipe he told Mae about.

"That should be enough to buy some forgiveness."

He whispered low, to himself.

Ay gave it to Sue to ring up.

"Put it on my account."

He grabbed the bag and headed into the back, past Frank and Lilly, to find Sam. She tried to step into his path, to be mildly obnoxious. He sidestepped her outstretched hip and gave her a smile.

Sam was in a good mood.

His too-big body was squeezed into a tiny chair in his back office, which was really just part of the hallway behind the deli. In front of him lay a desktop piled with loose papers and various business magazines, folded open to half-read articles on inventory management, accounting software, and a host of primers on the importance of understanding the finer points of accrued expenses, cash and cash equivalents, intangible assets, net unrealized gains, and a myriad of other financial terms which swam in lazy circles in his head, none of which really made any sense to him.

Truth be told, Sam was just plain giddy. Surrounded by pulp, and flush with the newfound success of the market, Sam had the feel of a business titan. To that end, he would endlessly jot down figures and formulas on scratch pads and run arcane calculations he would never understand the next morning – a businessman burying himself in the minutia of sales and inventory, figuring the key to even more glorious growth was somehow hidden inside those magical pages of business scripture.

So Sam sat there, punching the calculator in a deliberate, confident manner, watching the paper roll whiz figures that grew by the yard, till they curled onto the floor by the base of the desk. He never really looked at the printout, he just liked hearing the clicking sound of the printer on paper – it had the sound of important calculations.

All this stuff was important, he guessed, if he could just figure out how it helped sell more pork chops.

Cord turned the corner and stood before him.

"Hey Sam, where are the keys to the truck? I gotta run out to Brookfield and deliver this to Mae; she left it here."

Sam leaned lazily back in his chair and looked at Cord with a smile of self-satisfaction; marveling at his acumen for making the bold, executive decision to hire that fine young man.

"Mae didn't leave it here; she didn't want it, according to Frank. You were too busy behind the counter playing with Lillian; that's the story I hear. Actually couldn't help hearing it, myself. Are you two *official*? Surprised it took so long."

Sam said, peering scholarly over his glasses, which slid slightly down his large nose.

"Don't worry about Frank's stories, just give me the fucking keys."

"And Lilly?"

Sam hesitated, waiting for a response to the second statement.

"Listen, Mae has been good to *both* of us, *very good*. I think it's important to go out there and deliver her produce, personally; it would be a nice gesture."

"Why don't *I* go? Maybe it would mean more, you know, the gesture, coming from me."

Sam queried, thinking like a true titan.

"Thanks, buddy, but somehow I don't think it'll be quite the same; I think she wants me to go out there. Just a hunch."

"Come on Sam, grandma just wants to bang him, and C's looking for a little senior time, since the sidewalk girl gave him the brush, *after* he gave her a big wad of money. Where'd that money come from anyway? Looked like an *awful lot* of money; did you raise his pay scale?"

Lilly popped her head around the corner into the back room, injecting herself into someone else's conversation, like usual.

"Come on Lilly, I'm not in the mood."

Cord sighed.

"Apparently you are."

"Sam, the keys...."

"I'll drive him out Sam. You know, C can't drive the truck without a license. Or, better yet, why don't you show Sam your driver's license Cord, then I'm sure his insurance company will be okay with you driving the company vehicle. Your license is probably in your *wallet*, right? Just tell me where it is; I'll go get it for you."

Cord frowned....she never fucking quits.

"You *do* have a wallet, right?"

She stood with hands on hips.

"Maybe she's right Cord; why don't you let her drive you out, unless, of course, you *do* have a license?"

Sam said the last part in a hopeful tone; Cord looked at him like he was an idiot.

"Why does *Lilly* have a license? She doesn't have a car and doesn't leave Town."

"I can leave anytime I want."

"I didn't say *couldn't*."

C stared at Sam, waiting for the executive decision on the truck keys; Sam simply stared back blank. The room was silent.

Cord finally shook his head in disgust and sighed loud, as Sam sat paralyzed, unsure how to solve this problem.

"Christ."

With that, C left the back room, *kiwanos* in hand, and went to find Earl, who was outside sweeping the front walk.

"Hey Earl, mind if I borrow your bike?"

"No, go ahead; it's out back."

"Does it still have that gay basket on it?"

"Yeah. Hey, I *like* that basket."

Earl thought a bit more.

"Hey C, who was that pretty girl you talked to on the sidewalk? She seemed nice, and she had such a nice smile, when she wasn't so sad. You know, you can tell a lot about someone by their smile."

Cord looked at Earl and shook his head.

"You know Earl, you're one of the few around here that *gets* it, you really do. Did your mom tell you that? Did she tell you that girl was nice?"

"No, I figured it out on my own."

Cord put his hand on Earl's back and gave it a light pat, followed by a rub.

"Yeah, she's a real good girl, and just like you, she comes with a nice shine."

CHAPTER 61 – SHE CHANGED, JUST A BIT.
AND IT WAS GOOD

Cord frowned as he leaned the bike toward himself; the seat was close to shoulder height. He needed a ladder just to mount it, and then would certainly fall off, being about ten inches shy of completing a full pedal. He looked in the little blue basket, decorated with plastic daisies; sure as shit a wrench set waited.

"Son of a bitch."

He said as he smiled.

"That must be for the *Lilly seat adjust,* although she also had her own bike, which was an obnoxious hot-pink, as if it would be anything else.

He dropped the saddle and mounted the steed, finding it was still a bit of a stretch, even with the seat lowered to the crossbar. It sucked being short.

He wobbled down the alley, onto the sidewalk and started out to Brookfield. It was a mile at most, and the day was sunny and warm, so he took his time. He was surprised at the number of people who waved on the way; in two months, he had become a known entity around Town, accepted and acknowledged.

It was a rare feeling, and he kind of liked it.

As he pedaled along, his thoughts wandered, from times past, to the present, and back to the past. The sun kissed his right cheek; he felt it and welcomed the warmth. He lost himself in the sounds around him: the guttural rattle of scattered crows overhead, a distant lawnmower chewing grass, the sound of the bike chain climbing the wheel gears, all accompanied by the near-constant rustle of overstory leaves in the canopy of old-growth maples and oaks that lined Oxford Street, out past the Cemetery and the High School.

Why did he *really* end up in this little nowhere? Why did Jenny send him here? The thought ran through his head, as did the darts, all four. That dart story was fucked up, for sure; he had no answers, so he stopped thinking about it.

He heard a low, guttural rumble out of sight, up past the School, up the incline of Oxford Street that led out of Town, where Brookfield lay. Just as the low percussion registered, he saw the nose of a sleek candy apple red *Spider* creep down the hill toward him, its metallic skin sparkled in the June afternoon sun.

Carol's hair was dancing, like it always did with the top down; the scene could have been an ad, it, and she, looked that good.

She slowed when she saw the biker coming at her on the shoulder; she slowed even more when, to her delight, she saw who it was. What a nice smile, Cord thought; he couldn't wait to see her tomorrow evening; for a second, he forgot where he was going.

When she was practically on him, and crawling to a stop, her warm smile and anticipated greeting inexplicably turned to stone. She raised her hand in a forced, half-gesture hello, downed the accelerator, and blew past him, hitting him in the leg with a small twig and a cloud of stones and grit she kicked up on the shoulder.

What the hell! Cord said aloud to himself. He stopped and turned to watch her race away, and saw the hot-pink bike coming up behind him, about twenty yards away, and closing.

Lilly waved and threw a cheesy smile at Carol as she passed.

Cord swore he saw that *Spider* quiver, the millisecond that begins a swerve onto the shoulder that wipes out the pink bike. It was just a fraction of a split second, a 1/100th tic of the wheel to the right, then a correction. But C saw it; he *definitely* saw it; the spider almost pounced the pink fly.

A pay-per-view with those two locked in a room? A girl-fight gold mine.

The *F430* veered down Third Street and disappeared; Lilly pulled up alongside and stopped, wearing a shit-eating grin.

"Hey, wasn't that your little friend?"

Cord looked at her with an annoyed, sarcastic expression.

"And we're delivering a basket of goodies to your *other* wrinkly friend?"

Cord just looked at her; same annoyed face.

"Boy, you got *lots* of friends."

"You didn't include *you;* aren't you my friend too?"

"Me, nah….I'm just your boyfriend's sister."

"You know, next time she'll take you out; I wouldn't put it past her - right up on the curb - *pancake.*"

[Cord slapped the back of one hand into the open palm of his other for emphasis]

"I'm not afraid of her, she's harmless. Ten years of no talk, no action. Why she even still comes out here is beyond me."

"It's been fourteen years, but who's counting. And why don't you ask her?"

"Why would I care?"

Lilly said, with a shoulder shrug.

"Uh huh."

Was all Cord said, as he remounted his bike. She pedaled along, on the inside track.

"Lilly, what are you doing?"

"Going for a ride out to Brookfield?"

"And why's that?"

"I don't have to tell you why; I don't have to tell you anything. Maybe I have friends out there."

Three peddle rounds passed in silence.

"You know, people going by, they're gonna think you and I got something going on."

"Please, don't flatter yourself fat-boy."

Cord just smirked and didn't answer at first. She knew he lost a good fifteen to twenty pounds in the last two months, but she would never acknowledge it.

"Well, I'm glad you feel that way; it might have ruined my date tonight."

Lilly just looked at him in disbelief, lowered brow and pursed lips.

"*Please*, like who? Grandma can't stay up past six."

"What do you care?"

"I don't."

Lilly snipped.

"Good. She wouldn't want you to know anyway."

"Oh, so your date's a *she*?"

Cord let it slide. And the *date* wasn't tonight, it was tomorrow, but C was just fucking with Lilly anyway, so telling her the right day didn't really matter.

A couple more pedals in silence; Lilly was processing.

"Okay, I'll bite, who's the poor soul?"

"What?"

Cord said.

"Who is she?"

"Who's who?"

C said, innocent.

"Okay, I get it; no way, pal, I'm **not** playing your stupid fucking game, C, so forget it. I'm not getting sucked in again."

"What game?"

Lilly bit her lip hard, trying to avoid being sucked in, like she always was, into Cord's circuitous conversations, whose sole goal was to provide no information and simultaneously annoy the shit out of her.

But she couldn't help herself; she couldn't let the bait sit without a strike.

"I know you're going to see that little bitch on the Park, so don't bother even denying it; I know all about it."

Lilly could not even bring herself to say Carol's name aloud, such was her distaste. And of course, she knew nothing about a date with Carol, it was simply an educated, albeit blind, cast into the pool.

"I never said I was seeing Carol."

Lilly vowed not to respond, but she only lasted ten seconds.

"Are you seeing *her* or not?"

"I just saw her."

Cord pointed back down the road, where the *F430* disappeared.

"I mean *tonight!*"

"What about tonight?"

Lilly raised her voice.

"You mother-fucker! Stop playing your stupid games and answer one, simple God-damn question."

"What question, you've asked me about ten questions. Why are you cursing at me?"

Cord answered in a calm, even tone, to annoy her even more.

Lilly started to ride in a drunken line; she was so concentrating on her dialogue to corner him into a confession that she wasn't paying attention to the road. A car horn gave a short toot that startled her, almost knocking her off the bike.

"Hey, Lilly, be careful! You're gonna get hit!"

It was Greg, the State Trooper who lived in Town….good-looking guy.

"Sorry Greg."

She smiled and waved.

"See, you almost got me hit….by a State Trooper! Quit fucking around!"

"Me! You're the one who can't ride straight."

Lilly rode in silence for a bit, formulating a different assault.

"You know, she really doesn't like you; she's just using you to get back at me."

"What does Mae have against you?"

C said, innocent.

"Not Mae! Jesus Christ! Go have a fucking date with her, I don't care."

"With who?"

And with that, Lilly turned sharp to the left and rammed her bike into Cord, knocking them both down into the grass median alongside the Cemetery sidewalk.

Lilly laughed at Cord, who was trying to extract himself from under Earl's oversized bike, muttering expletives to himself.

"I'm telling Earl."

C said, like a kid ready to tattle; the hair on his leg smeared with grease from the bike chain. She laughed again, and this time, so did he.

Cord thought to himself how much he enjoyed just being next to her; it really didn't matter the circumstances. He was hoping she felt the same way; she must, right? Otherwise, why would she be here?

As they sat on the grass along the curb beside one another, Lilly looked at Cord and gave him the faintest of smiles; it looked like a smile that meant she was thinking what he was thinking.

But then Lilly suddenly realized where she landed, and her smile evaporated. She had a look of fright on her face, like a kid ready to be scolded. Carol was lying quiet just a few yards away, and didn't say a word.

Lilly righted her bike and quickly pedaled in silence down the street, putting distance between herself and the Cemetery.

Cord remounted and caught up with her, but rode beside her in silence. He never saw the headstone, but knew it was close, it had to be for Lilly to act the way she did. He felt bad for laughing and joking with Lilly, there of all places.

They rode side by side, quiet, for the rest of the way, till they got to the base of the hill leading out of Town, just past the High School. It was a simple hill, but Cord was a bit nervous he might get winded, and yet again be the butt of another Lilly fat-joke. Before he could think about pacing himself up the hill, Lilly stood up on her pedals and began a hard sprint up the incline, clearly egging him into a race.

"I'm not chasing you."

He said, till she got about fifteen yards ahead. Then he took the bait.

"Fuck!"

And he tried to sprint, as fast as he could on a bike where he still barely reached the pedals. His foot slipped twice, driving his balls into the crossbar. Not good.

By the time he reached the crest, panting, she had already dismounted, leaning off her bike, smirking.

"Fine, congratulations."

He said, trying to control his heavy breathing and not massage his sore nuts.

"Thank you."

Was all she said, the smugness thick as molasses.

Cord gazed down and saw an earthworm, stretched in a slow, desperate death-crawl on the hot asphalt, heading toward the white line. It was already starting to dry and die. He bent over and gently tried to lift it; it was thin, so he had a hard time grabbing it. He lightly licked his fingers, got on his knees and gently raised it off the pavement. He then dug a tiny hole with his two fingers and deposited the delicate worm carefully into the grass divot a couple feet away, and buried it, out of sight. Saved, or at least that was the plan, the hope.

He looked over and saw Lilly staring at him, awaiting an explanation.

He put his head down and sat on the grass next to where the worm now was. He let out a long, slow breath.

"Many years ago I was in Seattle, on an early morning run, beside the trolley line downtown, along Alaskan Way, by the bay, Elliot Bay, Puget Sound; the City is right on the bay.

It had rained heavy overnight and that morning there were earthworms all over the paved running path, some heading into puddles of water, others into the street. I found myself stopping every twenty feet or so for about a half-mile, saving worms.

Even though it was early, there were quite a few people out and about, walking dogs, jogging, sitting in their cars, whatever. And they were all eyeing me, wondering what I was doing, why this nut job was stopping every ten steps. What was on the ground that I was so interested in?

At first, I pretended I was tying my shoes, then I pretended I had a leg cramp, and would rub my calf as I bent over, trying to be inconspicuous.

But after awhile, every twenty feet, that looked a little ridiculous, so I figured the hell with it, just let them go, and I ran by some of the worms, knowing they would soon be dead – drowned in puddles, or crushed on the road by traffic.

[Cord paused for a bit, then he simply frowned, shrugged his shoulders and stared into Lilly's eyes, with a look of sadness….resignation]

I couldn't do it Lilly, I just couldn't.

So I turned around and went back and saved them, all of them. I *had* to Lilly, I couldn't help it….I couldn't help myself.

I felt utterly foolish; they're worms for Christ's sake. But I also felt really good at the same time. And you know what? The *really good* felt better than foolish. So I said fuck it, fuck all those people staring at me, and I saved as many worms as I could, regardless of what they thought. And I've been doing it ever since, everywhere I go. My own little attempt at redemption, I guess."

That's all Cord said, all the explanation he was willing to offer.

And Lilly smiled at Cord, a genuine smile.

And on that day, Friday, June 23rd, although Lillian didn't realize it, she changed, just a bit.

And it was good.

CHAPTER 62 – SHE PURRED THE WORDS - COME INSIDE, PLEASE

Lilly mounted her bike, pointing it back down the hill.

"Well, I guess I'll let you get on with your date; be gentle, don't kill her."

"The other way around, more likely; I thought you had a friend to go see?"

"I already did."

And she smiled.

That was one of the nicest things Lilly had ever said to him.

Then she looked at him sincerely, and asked gently.

"Hey C, when are you gonna talk to me, for real?"

He knew what she meant; she was looking for the story, the story as to why he was in Belvidere, and what came before. He smiled small back at her.

"Some day, soon maybe, some day."

That was probably a lie; he would probably never tell her. And there was more than one story to tell anyway, many more. Too many. And none of them ever ended well.

Never.

"Well, it's only a matter of time, your story's starting to unravel anyway. I know you have a skinny black girlfriend with bad hair, who's okay-looking at best by the way, who drives an old VW, God knows where she came from to find you out here, but I'll figure that out. And I know you were in Seattle, enough to know what the road names are anyway, and you have a curious fondness for worms….all little clues that I have to paste together to find out what kind of nut you really are. I should probably stay far away from you."

He smiled mischievously.

"I think you're onto me. Hey, thanks for riding with me; it was fun, I think. And thanks for letting me make the delivery solo; I'm going to get in enough trouble regarding you as it is….she's pretty possessive."

"See you later Seattle."

Lilly yelled as she made her way down the Oxford Street hill, back into Town.

He watched her descend the Oxford Street Hill, pass the High School, and slowly shrink and disappear into the horizon, till she was out of sight. He felt a little pang in his gut, the kind you get when you already start missing someone who just left.

Standing in the sunlight on the side of the road, he thought a bit more about Lilly, then he thought about Mae, then Carol. Not too shabby; three attractive women in his wheelhouse; one he could bang, two he would bang.

So much for blending into the background; so much for being incognito.

He turned the bike onto Kensington Circle and ambled along past rows of cookie-cutter pad ranches in alternating shades of cream, white and tan, with the occasional outlier sheathed in light gray. Each sported a white mailbox on the curb, a sentry of boxes lining the winding road, most straight, some leaning a bit, drunken forward or back. God knows how the over-55's kept track of where they lived; a couple of drinks and you'd be wandering the development aimlessly, trying to figure out which cream dream was yours.

He pedaled down Kensington, to a left on Brookfield Drive, to a left on Ascot Drive, to a left on Derby Lane.

Mae liked to say *stay left and you'll find me in the end,* a little joke she'd tell the old Republican cohorts who came to see her.

C stayed left and the trail ended at the dark gray house – the only one out of five hundred in the development that shade of gray, along with a glossy, regal eggplant front door; that was Mae, the only eggplant in the whole development.

She was in the kitchen; from that vantage, she could see the full run of Derby Lane, which ended in a cul-de-sac, and her place at the far end of the bulb. She had been watching for a while, figuring, hoping he would be by, yet pleasantly surprised when it actually happened. She smiled when her instinct proved right; she knew that little basket drop in the aisle would find her....Cord was no dummy.

She waited till he knocked on the door, basket in hand. She reached over and pressed the *play* button; Nancy Sinatra began to sing to Cord:

'You keep saying you've got something for me....'

Mae had been waiting a long time, for the right time, to say three simple words to Cord; she hoped to be saying them again, and again, very soon....like in about five minutes. She slowly cracked her back door as she purred the words -

"Come inside, please."

CHAPTER 63 – ON HER KNEES, BLINKING AT A BIG SURPRISE

Mae wasn't ready to give Cord a free ride just yet; she kept a somewhat stoic face, as much as she could, to drink in his apologies, which she knew were coming.

*'These boots are made for walking
and that's just what they'll do.'*

"Nice selection of tunes, Mae, don't suppose that's a coincidence."

"Oh Nancy? Nah, she just popped on. Why? Do you know this song? A bit before your time, I imagine."

'One of these days these boots are gonna walk all over you.'

"Something about not appreciating what you got, not stepping up to the plate, greener pastures, missed opportunities; something like that. Sound about right?"

'

Mae just grinned.

"Why is it that women feel the need to play music at me, to teach me some sort of lesson?"

"Oh, I'm not the only one?"

"Carol has done it too; more of a mockery, hers was."

"Is that the young black girl on the sidewalk you so *rudely* left me for? At a most inopportune time, I might add."

Cord mouthed *sorry*; Mae smiled at the acknowledgment.

"No, she lives in Town, up on the Park, the house with the big lions out front. She's another problem."

"Another problem? You seem to have all sorts of woman problems; am *I* one of your problems?"

There was only one right answer to that one, an abject lie.

"Of course not; am *I* a problem to you?"

"That remains to be seen."

Cord placed the basket on the counter and started to unload the bounty. The song ended, and the disk moved on to Sinatra songs he didn't know.

"I took the liberty of bringing some fruit and veggies I know you like....on me."

He was going to apologize for the Lilly affair on the deli floor, but by Mae's body language, and the lack of distance between her leg and his, it was clear that apology was no longer necessary; she had moved on. His visit was the apology she was looking for.

"Thanks, but I was expecting a conclusion to the story we were sharing, that is before you lost interest for points beyond the sidewalk, and then for points behind the *deli counter*."

Mae emphasized the latter. She wasn't wasting any time; she came home mad, mad at being denied what she wanted. For Mae, that didn't happen very often.

And the primary source of that denial being Lilly made the frustration and anger all the more palpable. In Lilly, Mae saw herself as a younger woman, turning heads and commanding the attention of every man in the room. Seeing her lying on Cord, practically humping his leg behind the deli counter, was the straw.

And when Mae got stressed, when she was frustrated, her release was masturbation. And given her stress level after the deli affair, she had finished herself three times since Aisle Four, reliving Cord's fantasy that he whispered in her ear. The second time was on the sofa in her living room, the third was lying on her belly in her bed; the first time she masturbated was in the *Mini Cooper*, on the ride home, barely two blocks from Sam's; that's when her panties first came off.

But, like C's story, she was nowhere near done.

And under that little sea-foam skirt she was still wearing, there was nothing; those little damp, black panties, the color Cord liked, the color he knew she wore whenever she came to Sam's, were left on the bed about an hour ago, in plain sight, for him to find when she navigated him to her bedroom. Which, in her mind, was about three minutes away from happening.

Cord turned to face her squarely, putting his hands on her shoulders.

"Now, after we're done unpacking the groceries...."

"We're *already* done unpacking."

Mae interrupted.

"As I said, when we're done unpacking, I want you to say out loud that *if* anything happens, *when* anything happens, it's just for fun, and it doesn't go any further than that....agreed?"

"Why, you have something better you're working on? Lillian? She's more than a handful, I hear; or this woman Carol on the Park? The girl on the sidewalk?"

"Nothing else is going on."

"You mean *not yet* don't you?"

Mae was good.

"Nothing else is going on, but even if it was, or did, it wouldn't matter to *us*, right? Because what we're doing is just for fun, *right*? Right Mae? Tell me I'm right."

Mae ran her hand slowly down his chest, looking at him in the eyes, without saying a word. She got to the top of his pants, to the button on his jeans, and stopped for a moment, before flattening her hand and running it down the closed flap of his zipper, feeling his cock, which wasn't hard yet, hiding beneath the denim.

"What does he think? Does he think it's just fun? Maybe I should ask him myself."

His cock didn't take long to react; she could feel it swell under her hand; she smiled at him, proud of the fast reaction.

Now what Cord should have done was put a stop to this, knowing that what he thought would happen, what he feared would be the repercussion of having sex with Mae, even once, was playing out just as he suspected. He should have stepped back, reasserted the rules and walked away if they were ignored.

But he was a guy, and his dick was hard.

And for the past two months, the only sex he had was in his mind, accompanied by his left hand; he was a leftie. So he just stood there, closed his eyes and did nothing. Big surprise, end of story.

Mae sunk to her knees in front of him, lightly pressed her lips against the denim, and blew a long, warm breath through his jeans; the moist air surrounded his shaft and he got harder than he already was. He didn't think that was possible.

She looked up at Cord to see his reaction; his head was tilted back a bit and his eyes were still closed.

She smiled; he was so easy, and she still had it to give. That alone made her day. But it wasn't ending there, not by a long shot.

She started to pull her lips off his jeans, to move on to the next act in the play, but he would have none of it. He put his hands on the back of her head and not-so-gently pushed her lips back onto his zipper flap.

"You're not going anywhere, not yet."

He whispered sharp; she didn't resist.

He slowly caressed her hair as she blew into his jeans….slow, deep, warm breaths.

She took her hands and slowly undid the button, grabbed the zipper and directed it south, a couple clips at a time. She saw the beginnings of his black boxer briefs, the ones she always saw teasing her from the bottom of his shorts; this was the first time she got to see the top half.

She gently, firmly pushed against the pressure of his hands and raised her head a bit, to position her mouth a bit higher, to kiss his stomach, just above the scripted *B*, for the *Brooks Brothers* on the white elastic; she felt the dark brown hair on her face; his skin was warm and soft.

If she touched herself, she would have come right there, she was that close.

She grabbed the elastic and gently pulled it away from his skin; she was about to peak into the Christmas present she left wrapped under the tree for the past two months. This was the last one, the one you wait to open; the anticipation was almost as fun as the prize.

Almost.

Cord was leaning against the counter, about four feet from the back door; she knew she owned him, for the afternoon, at least. For the night too, if she played her cards right.

Mae, on her knees on the kitchen throw rug, was eye level with the back doorknob.

Which made it all the more startling when it began to turn; the latch clicked and the door began to swing open. All she saw was the gray blur of a person moving into the space of the open door. She didn't even have time to react.

On her knees, blinking at a big surprise.

CHAPTER 64 – THE LITTLE BASTARD STOLE HER UNDERWEAR

Mae learned a little something that afternoon.

Even in your sixties, when caught in a compromised position, you can spring off your knees with reflexes you thought left with your cheerleading skirt.

She was impressed with herself, and pissed, beyond belief.

Darkening her doorway, with his little red toolbox in hand, was Joseph Fishel, her ubiquitous Derby Lane neighbor. He was all of five foot four; a seventy-two year old spry, widowed Jew, thinner than her, wiry and full of zest - seven decades of roaming the planet had no effect on the libido left in this man's tank.

And he had a wicked crush on Mae.

From the very first day the young, sweet violet moved in next door, he always considered it a divine blessing, granted to an old man as payment due for a lifetime lived clearly within the lines. He just couldn't seem to convince her it was providential.

Mae had no interest in the little Jew next door with the impressive mane of white hair, except to abuse his kindness as a de facto handyman. She knew it was cruel, but she did it anyway. She would give him a peck on the cheek or a dessert treat on occasion in return, usually in the afternoon, after a couple glasses of wine, as she was whisking him out the door. And for that occasional crumb alone, Joe kept coming back for more. He figured he would wear her down, eventually.

But now, Mr. Fishel had a problem.

It was this bike in the driveway, this grocery boy bike; it seemed to be parked a bit too long for your standard produce delivery and tip receipt; there was only so long Joe could stand in the living room peaking from between the sheers before he felt the need to spring to action.

Mae didn't quite remember how, but she must have jumped up, stepped back and grabbed a banana - all in the same motion. So now she found herself standing solo, with a goofy look on her face, holding a *pisang susa* in her right hand.

"Uh, hi Joe, want a banana?"

That was the best she came up with, fumbling her words, a bit out of breath.

Unlike Mae, Cord wasn't so quick, nor motivated to alter the scene; he was leaning against the counter in exactly the same position he was before the doorknob turned. His button and zipper were splayed open, his underwear peaking beneath his tee-shirt.

Mae took a half step to block Joe's view of Cord's crotch; Cord fixed his pants with a general sense of lassitude. Who was this annoying little gnat?

"No thanks, Mae, I had my fruit cup this morning. I uhh, was just checking, uhh, is everything okay? I saw a strange bicycle in your yard and this bald-headed guy I never saw before seemed to be in here for...."

Mae had recovered; and now her anger returned like the tide, shoving any fleeting sense of embarrassment or propriety. And she unleashed a torrent.

"**And what?** What were you thinking while you were peaking at my house through the curtains? Were you wondering if I was being molested in here by my friendly delivery boy? Wondering if he was ripping my clothes off and carrying me to the bedroom to perform unspeakable acts? That he was going to tie me up and keep me as a sex slave?

To spend the night and have his way with me *over and over*? **Huh?** Is that why you came running over here with your stupid little toolbox? Were you going to rescue me with a pair of pliers, or did you just want to watch?!"

Joe just stood there, stunned at the vitriol, and the graphic sex talk; he didn't say a word. He could not imagine such an eruption of vulgarity coming from his sweet neighbors' lips. He was actually a little scared.

"Hey Mae, looks like I should be going."

"You're not going *anywhere*; Joe here is the one who's leaving."

But that Jewish constitution set in; he wasn't giving up the girl that easy to this bald impostor.

"But what about the squirrel? You told me to come over and get the squirrel out of the attic crawlspace? That's why I got the toolbox *[Joe held up the little red box as evidence for all to see, clearly showing he was equipped to handle the task at hand].*"

"*The squirrel*? The one I have been telling you to get for the past week? And *now* you're coming to rescue me from the killer squirrel?"

"But he could be making a nest in the insulation *as we speak,* or chewing the air conditioning condensate lines *[Joe wasn't sure what a condensate line actually looked like, or where they were, or what they did, but he heard the term on television and was grasping at this point, trying to keep a toehold in the kitchen and an eye on the bald guy].* It could get awful hot and uncomfortable in here pretty quick."

Mae stared at him with lowered eyelids; she looked positively possessed. She spoke in a low, ominous monotone.

"It's *already* uncomfortable in here. And that's why Cord's here; since you weren't available, eating your fruit cup, I had to have him come over and take care of the squirrel; in fact, he was on his way up there now. Come on Cord, I'll show you the folding attic steps in the hallway ceiling. Cord doesn't need pliers to get the squirrel, he'll do it with his *bare hands*. Good-bye Joe."

And with that, Mae took Cord's hand and led him, like a child, out of the kitchen, and down the hall, right toward her bedroom; it killed her to walk by that bedroom doorway with Cord in tow, and not throw him on the bed.

They stopped just outside the guest room entryway, where the ceiling trap door waited.

Joe simply ignored her order to leave; he was right behind them, trying to wiggle his way past the two of them, to the front of the line, but the hallway was just too narrow, and they weren't cooperating.

He was also hampered by the allure of Mae's abode; he hesitated a bit to get a good look at her bed. He stumbled even further behind when he saw the pair of black panties laid out neatly on the end of the comforter.

Nirvana.

Mae was a bit too short to yank on the pull-string; Cord reached up and down the steps came, the large springs vibrating and creaking as they stretched into position. The stairs folded down and before Cord could even grab the railing, the little man made an end-around dash, pushed off the wall and ricocheted himself halfway up the rickety steps before Cord could react, toolbox in hand.

Mae frowned.

"Would you please go get him down."

She said to Cord, like he was retrieving a stray dog. C
shook his head in disbelief that he was involved in this
charade and took two steps up the ladder; the little man
was nearing the top.

"I got it Mae! No problem with squirrels anymore, not
after I…."

Now Joe was so proud of himself for the quick move,
and his first position on the ladder, that he really wasn't
paying attention to where he was going. Add to that fact
he was looking down the steps at Mae while he was
climbing, like a kid on a jungle gym, impressing his
parents with feats of dexterity.

Alas, as he turned to finish the final mount of steps and
emerge into the attic as victor, he didn't accommodate
for the lack of headroom, and smacked his forehead, full
frontal, on a low, splintered rafter.

The concussion knocked the little red toolbox from his
hand; it fell onto the stairs, popped open and cascaded
tinny tools down the steps in an avalanche, showering
Cord and Mae with detritus.

Joe saw flashes of white stars, his head became light and
clouded, and he proceeded to brown-out. He teetered on
his heels in a slow motion, and began to fall from the
attic.

Cord was in the path of the projectile; if he stepped
aside, Mae was a goner. So he did all he could to brace
himself, and caught the one hundred fourteen-pounder
across his chest, like cradling a baby.

The impact knocked Cord back on his heels; had the little man been just a pound heavier, he would have taken Cord with him for the ride, both of them landing on Mae's head. But at one hundred fourteen pounds, Cord could buffet the blow; he rocked on his heels in recoil, and stabilized.

Joe looked up at Ay, dazed and limp, with a trickle of blood down his brow.

"Whoa, take it easy there little fella."

Cord said as he backed down the steps and deposited Joseph on his wobbly legs in the hallway. He put his hand on Cord's arm for stability, till he got his bearings back.

"I need to sit down."

Was all he said.

"You need to *leave*."

Mae snapped back. She felt no pity; she turned to walk him to the kitchen table for a seat, a quick mop-up and a scoot out the door. But Joe had other plans.

He made it ten feet down the hall, to the entryway to Mae's bedroom.

"I'm feeling faint, I gotta sit down."

And he took a quick left into her bedroom and planted his ass on her bed, right beside the panties. He lowered his head and shook it a bit, for effect.

"Jesus Christ, get out of my bedroom! You better not get blood on the bedspread!"

Was all the comfort Mae could muster, as she passed into the bathroom to get a wet towel to wipe his face, and a glass of lukewarm water. She didn't let the water run long enough to get cold.

She thrust the rag and water at him, expecting him to self medicate.

"That was sure Christian of you, Mae."

Was all Cord said, smiling, leaning relaxed against her bedroom door jam.

"Well, I was brought up proper, that's all I can say."

Joe let out a sigh and gave a weak smile.

"I'm okay, I guess."

As if the two of them were awaiting his self-diagnosis.

"Glad to hear it; now let's head out to the kitchen."

Mae announced perfunctory, as she roughly grabbed Joe's arm. But he stiffened and gave resistance, his butt glued to her bed.

"Jeez, just a minute more! You know Mae, that was a pretty good sock I took there; you really should do something about that beam."

"How about staying out of my attic, how's that for a solution?"

She snipped.

"Come on Cord, let's go; I have something to talk to you about."

She grabbed Ay gently by the arm and led him into the kitchen. As she arrived, she started to talk in a hushed tone.

"Okay, Joe will be...."

But as she turned to talk to C, she spied Joe's little face, peaking from behind Ay's shoulder.

"What the hell are you doing *now*?"

She screeched.

"You said to go to the kitchen; here I am!"

"Listen Mae, I *really* have to get back; I'm still supposed to be working, and I'm not the fastest bike rider, especially on that bike. Call me later at the store; I'll come take care of your *squirrel problem* we were talking about a little later....promise."

"Are you kidding me?"

Mae said in defeat.

"I'm calling you later Cord, **and you better** answer; I'm not settling for fruit and vegetables again."

Mae was defiant.

"I can take care...."

"Shut up Joe, just shut up."

Cord grinned wicked and let himself out; Mae was left in the kitchen with Joe, sporting a fast-growing red nugget on his forehead and his normally neatly tucked-in shirt disheveled and twisted.

"I'll go pick up my tools in the...."

"No you won't; I'll pick them up and put them on the front lawn - you can get them later. I have to go take care of some things now; goodbye Joe."

Mae turned to walk down the hall; Joe just stood there and watched her.

"I don't hear the door."

She said as she walked away.

He put his head down and skulked out. But he was still happy the grocery boy was gone, and he was amazed at his turn of good fortune, at his swipe of the trophy.

He picked up his pace and scampered out the door, lest he get caught, the prize safely stowed in his front pocket. He stuck his hand in to be sure he still had it, to be sure it was real. Joe smiled, thinking of the ways he planned to use it.

After picking up the tools and closing the attic door on a step-stool, shaking her head in disgust the whole time, Mae went to the bedroom lavatory to wash her face and recover from the high and low of the last hour.

She sat on the edge of the bed and sighed; what a disappointment.

She looked to her side and saw the clean bedspread, pulled taught - the clean, *empty* bedspread.

Her black panties were gone; the little bastard stole her underwear.

Cord felt bad leaving Mae with the runt; he felt much worse for the wasted hard-on. For a minute there, he was all about Mae; he wondered what it would have been like to bang her when she was younger – she must have been a knockout. He probably wouldn't have had a shot back then.

He glided down the hill into Town, past the High School. He really should get back to the store; he had been gone way too long already. It must be getting close to 3 o'clock; the store would be closed in another couple hours. Truth be told, he really didn't have to rush back; by this time, he usually made his own hours, coming and going as he pleased.   Sam cut him tremendous slack; increased profits will do that to a man, much to the consternation of Frank, who always felt Cord got special treatment – which, in fact, he did.

The Cemetery was coming up on the right; the sidewalk was empty and the sun still shone bright in the afternoon sky.

He knew he had to stop.

He carefully leaned Earl's bike against the trunk of a towering pin oak, between the street and sidewalk, and entered the Cemetery at the east end gate, about ten yards from where he and Lilly had crashed their bikes. The perimeter fence was black wrought iron, with a bit of a wave in spots, where footings had long-since shifted; round finials topped the six-foot fence posts at fifteen-foot intervals.   It wasn't a terribly regal enclosure, but it was nice enough.

A tinge of butterflies circled his stomach; he was excited and nervous at the same time. He felt he knew Carol, and, according to Earl at least, she knew him. Up until that moment, he had never thought to go find her in the

Cemetery; at this moment, he couldn't believe he had been in Town two months and never went to look for her sooner. He felt a strange sense of *needing* to find her now; that feeling enveloped him as stepped foot into the quiet graveyard.

Oxford Street, the road fronting the Cemetery, was a somewhat busy thoroughfare, at times anyway, with a fairly steady mix of car traffic, bikers and walkers. Yet once he crossed the threshold of the Cemetery gate, no more than twenty-five feet off the street, it seemed extra quiet, like someone dialed it down. It was if he entered a different world, a different place entirely from the streetscape mere feet away. He liked the feeling; it somehow felt *right* for him to be here.

He looked back at the gate he just entered, flanking the graveyard drive; there were two six foot deep-red brick columns, each three foot square and sporting a gently curved, spiked wrought iron swing gate, black, pitted with bits of rust. The craggy tops of the spearheads, fourteen of them per gate, were painted a golden-cream; a weak attempt at a gilded look. He stared at those spears and was twelve again, back to the State Park, to that fateful night when he met the puppet, the crickets and the flies. The night he died, kind-of, maybe, possibly, likely….at least it was interesting to think it was so. And it helped explain a lot of what had happened in the thirty-one years since. Then he did what he usually did when he had those troubling thoughts; he simply stopped thinking about it, switching the station to a different channel.

Instinctively, he picked up his shirt and ran his fingers lightly across the four circular scars, arranged in a precise, straight line. For thirty-one long years, those scars traveled with him, along with the puppet, cricket and flies; they had all seen an awful lot of bad.

He dropped his shirt and looked about. A square, black sign with yellow print hung on the gate:

BELVIDERE
CEMETERY

MAIN GATE

Nov. – April 9:00 – 5:00
May – Oct. 9:00 – 8:00

The late afternoon sun felt good on the back of his neck; a mix of mid-summer leaves rustled just a bit in a neat row of mature pin oak, black birch, linden, hemlock and sugar maple, just inside the Cemetery fence, parallel to Oxford Street. He figured they were all here when Carol was laid to rest twenty-five years ago – these same seven trees before him saw her lowered below, and covered over, forever. Instinctively, he placed his hand on the bark of the nearest pin oak and just felt its bark against his palm; he wasn't sure why he did that. The sentry of seven trees stretched to his left and right, but other than this column of green, the Cemetery was largely free of hardwoods, a scatter here and there; the largest concentration was along the fence, right where he now stood.

By Lilly's reaction when she fell from her bike, he figured Carol must be close by; he set out on his search for the headstone bearing the family name:

Liddell

The grass was thick and spongy, a good week past a needed trim. He started to walk south, between the first set of stones, concentrating on the names, looking for the present with the right name on the tag.

709

Beck
Pursell
Pierson
Stuart
Hicks
Bell
Whitmore

All respectable, gray and rose-colored granite stones, with alternating rough or polished sides and gently curved tops. The whole look was uncluttered, neat, proper. *Whitmore* was hugging the perimeter fence; last in the line.

But no Liddell.

He traced back to *Beck* and started a second parallel walk.

Stopp
Bossard
McFadden-Handelong
Armstrong
Gardner
Beers
Thatcher
Buchman
Ivins

He again came to the south side end of the Cemetery; the *Ivins* stone set close to the fence line. The side fences along the graveyard were modern chain link; the old wrought iron solely fronted the Cemetery along Oxford Street.

But still no Liddell.

Well, he thought, it would have been just plain lucky to find her in the first few passes; the Cemetery was fairly large and he could spend hours upon hours, probably a full day, if he had to look at all the inscriptions. But the way Lilly acted when they fell, he felt Carol must have been close by…. *real close.*

But maybe not.

As he stood there, pondering, lost in the unfamiliar names surrounding him, he heard a shoe-shuffle along the sidewalk. He casually looked up to see the pear-shaped penguin he first spied in front of the Post Office the day he met Earl; the little yapper who Earl inadvertently pushed down trying to hear Lillian tell him Aloysius was back in Town.

The guy had the look of a lost bird, waddling down the sidewalk, rocking slight, left to right.

Cord knew the fucker saw him, but the passer-by didn't look in his direction; he just continued on his way, both hands buried deep in his front pockets as he walked. He was wearing the same blue pants, floods, he wore on that first day; maybe they were his only pants.

Cord just stopped and stared at him, knowing what would happen next. And he was right.

After the penguin passed and was a good twenty yards down the sidewalk, when he thought it was safe to look back and satisfy the curiosity that was gnawing at him, he spun to look at Cord, not figuring C would be waiting, staring straight at him. Busted, he quickly spun back around and waddled on his way, never chancing a second look-back.

Cord frowned; in this fucking Town, that little tidbit, the new guy skulking around the Cemetery, would get a quick play in the circle of gossips. He would give it less than twenty-four hours before someone would ask him what he was doing in the graveyard. Less than twenty-four hours before Lilly found out he was walking around looking for her mom. He just had a good exchange with Lilly, and things had been getting much better between them, and an incident like this, involving her mom, could set him back to day one.

Fuck.

He shook his head a bit; he felt violated. His looking for Carol, he knew it sounded foolish, felt personal; no one should be looking in on him. It was a public cemetery, but it didn't feel that way now; he was the only one inside the fence, it was *his* Cemetery….his alone.

He picked up his pace and started to wander further away from east gate and the sentries along the perimeter fence, toward the center of the graveyard. The space stretched for a ways back from the road, football-fields deep.

The graves up by the road seemed to be newer; set in the past twenty or thirty years or so. As he ventured back, the dates slipped further into the past. Older headstones were starting to mix with newer ones; the designs became more elaborate, the stones larger, the inscriptions largely worn smooth in speckled white marble.

He started a third parallel run, deeper in..

Jones
Sarson-Brown
Harting
Miller
Levi
Lightcap
Levay
Laclair
Van Horan

To the fence for a third time; again nothing....no Liddell.

A row of pines stood sentry along the southern chain link fence and Pequest Road, the side roadway abutting the graveyard. He had by now wandered about a hundred yards off Oxford Street, deeper into the Cemetery, toward its center. He stopped, put his hands on his hips, closed his eyes, and quietly listened.

He heard the percussion of a riding mower, working the High School athletic fields across the street to the south; even though it was still afternoon, a steady din of crickets sang in conjunction with the mower, scattered unseen throughout the graveyard.

He opened his eyes to see two bikers stopped along the chain link fence along Pequest Road, fingers gripping the metal links, looking in to see what *he* was doing in the graveyard. They were a good hundred yards away; he couldn't see their faces, or even their sex.

He turned away, annoyed at being watched yet again; an experiment in a petri dish. He kept searching. Another two parallel rows, another twenty family names....none was a Liddell.

He gave up the organized hunt and began to wander aimless. He gravitated toward the larger, more elaborate headstones; they looked older, and he really didn't expect them to say her name, but he sought them out just the same. If one actually did, he thought, that would be cool, a real pleasant find.

But these markers were all unique in some fashion; over-tall, or fancy centuries-old carved marble, or overtly religious, or all of the above. Artisans didn't cut stone like this anymore; and they didn't cut stone like that in 1981 either. But he looked anyway, just in case.

The first was a twelve-foot white marble obelisk, impressive, with a large urn finial and wreaths set midway up the column face; Cord circled it to find the name.

Theodore Paul
December 7, 1798
September 30, 1887

There was a *Paul Street* in Town, a couple blocks behind *Nonpareil*; must be named for this guy.

A massive, rough-hewn light gray, speckled granite block caught his eye, thirty yards away. A large life-size angel, eyes cast downward and arm gently resting on the rough edge of the marker stood sentinel over the grave – it was beautiful.

Laninger/Seidel

That was the name written in large raised letters, on slant. Beneath, the names of three family members were scribed, death dates ranging from 1878 to 1922.

He noticed the air had thickened since his arrival; a lone dog barked at a partially obscured house, beyond the trees at the far end of the graveyard, close to two hundred yards away. The grass was still thick and spongy beneath his feet.

He crossed a gravel drive that wove amongst the headstones and walked along it a bit, further afield.

He passed a large stone arch just off the edge of the gravel, bearing three life-size marble cornucopia baskets atop the structure. The names *Huldah Luse* and *William Luse* ran along the curve; she died on January 3, 1910, at

714

seventy-six years; he died in 1877 at thirty-nine years, three months and two days. Cord read it as he passed by; he didn't bother to stop.

He saw the first grave for the *Mackey* family, one of dozens he would see as he wandered amongst the headstones. He knew there were still *Mackeys* in the area; several had accounts at the store. A farm in White Township still bore the name, selling fruits, vegetables, ice cream and seasonal items to the locals and day-trippers. Some of their family stones dated back two-hundred years. Maybe *they* were the original Belvidereans.

A gargantuan, white marble temple, over twenty feet high, topped by a simple cross next caught his eye, off to the left.

He started to walk toward the temple and was stopped dead in his tracks. The hair on his arms and shins stood at attention, a hot tingle ran down his spine and the tips of his fingers numbed. His hearing suddenly seemed to sharpen, as if on its own accord.

He swore he heard a whisper, a woman's whisper, indecipherable, off to his left, but close. *Very close.* She was whispering to someone else, too far beyond his earshot to understand what was said, but close enough to clearly hear the sound slipping from pursed lips.

It was two words, maybe three, and that was it….nothing more. He had no idea what was said, but it was something. He was sure it was something. He looked around and saw that he was alone; not a sole in sight, in or beyond the Cemetery. The bikers were long gone, the mower had ceased; the dog wasn't barking.

It was just him….all alone.

But he still heard the crickets, just the crickets – nothing else. And he thought about his own dream, his own crickets.

Crickets.

And that was it; he didn't hear anything more.

He stood motionless for a minute or two, the feeling of adrenaline passed, the hair dropped on his arms, and he began to doubt that he really heard anything in the first place; the whispers a figment of an active imagination. But that's not how it felt. It was still quiet, save the crickets, when a lick of summer breeze kicked up from nowhere and kissed his cheek, urging him on.

He walked slowly over to the massive marble shrine; good God, this can't be it, he thought to himself. But why the whisper? If there even *was* a whisper.

He walked gingerly, like he was approaching sacred ground; the name came into focus, the overwrought, scripted letters were hard to read, but appeared to spell a name not known to him.

Carhart

Theodore, Rachel, Mary and various other family members were recorded on ten separate marble tablets, some in the form of open tomes, around the perimeter of the massive marker; the dates ranged from 1819 to 1905.

What did that have to do with Liddell? Why was he drawn to that one grave?

He stood there for a moment, looking around at the neighboring headstones, walking around the Carhart memorial, searching for clues.

716

Nothing; no Liddell, no Carols….no clues.

He looked back toward Oxford Street and realized he had wandered quite far from the main gate; he doubted Carol was back here; these burials were mostly a hundred years old, some much older; no newer headstones were mixed in.

He frowned, turned and slowly made his way back, disappointed. Somehow he thought he would just walk in and find her; he wasn't sure why he thought that, he just did.

He stepped a jagged path back, weaving between non-descript, modest gravestones along the way; most he didn't even read. The ones he did stirred no particular interest. Up ahead, an eighteen-foot dark gray granite obelisk, with an impressive base that stepped-in as it rose, stood in his path. He glanced at the name as he passed.

Amsey White

He only caught the birth date: 1839; the rest of the details passed by before he had a chance to read them. No matter, because it meant nothing to him.

There was but a single private mausoleum in the whole Cemetery, and Cord altered his path a bit to inspect it.

It was a diminutive, gray-granite, square structure, with white marble columns flanking the entrance, supporting a pediment face. A modest, rectangular stained glass window, bearing an overlapping cross and crown, was set in the rear wall, opposite the entry doors. In his ken, he could see right into the building through the front door pane of glass, about twenty yards away. The interior of the crypt was awash in vibrant colors, blue, indigo, amber and yellow, glowing in the afternoon sun, refracted through the stained glass panels.

It was beautiful.

The surname stretched above the doorway and was also etched on a granite walkway leading to the bronze double-entry doors, sporting a century-old green patina. The doors were chained together, secured with an aged padlock, covered in a thick film of rust. There didn't appear to be any visitors of recent, with the operative term *recent* stretching back decades.

Cord looked down at the inscription along the carved granite mausoleum walkway.

Hoff
1853-1882

The crickets continued their soft, steady background din; otherwise, the Cemetery remained silent.

He inched closer to the doorway, and crouched just a bit to briefly peer inside. Through the bronze door panes, there were two stacked marble caskets on either side of the center aisle, with several family names and dates inscribed that Ay couldn't really read from the angle where he stood. He inched closer to the door, squinting, trying to decipher the wording on the plaques, till his nose just about pressed against the glass. He was startled by an entangle of stringy cobwebs that first found, then clung tight, to his nose and cheekbone, which caused him to instinctively pull back and wipe excitedly at his face, like a little girl.

As he stumbled back several paces from the bronze doors, he still felt a stray web glued to his skin that he couldn't seem to wipe free. His backward march ran him in a drunken line; his shoe caught, and then slipped off, the edge of something hard, buried in the grass, and he stumbled a few more paces, till he regained his balance.

He walked back to find the obstruction, and saw nothing. He was in the middle of a thick, open lawn area, with no headstones nearby.

He felt around with his shoe tip in the area he slipped, pushing the bushy grass and brown thatch aside. It was then he saw the square edge of what appeared to be a diminutive, dulled, bronze plaque, flush with grade – wholly hidden from view. He bent down on one knee and gently brushed aside the overgrown blades of green and tan thatch to reveal a non-descript, three by six-inch marker, proclaiming a fateful name.

Marcella Sparks
1912-1985

He smiled briefly, but it quickly faded to frown, because he knew he found what he was looking for. The hunt was over.

Marcella Sparks